R0700432461   01/2023

**PALM BEACH COUNTY
LIBRARY SYSTEM
3650 Summit Boulevard
West Palm Beach, FL   33406-4198**

NIGHTWATCH OVER WINDSCAR

Also by K. Eason

The Weep

NIGHTWATCH ON THE HINTERLANDS
NIGHTWATCH OVER WINDSCAR

The Thorne Chronicles

HOW RORY THORNE DESTROYED THE MULTIVERSE
HOW THE MULTIVERSE GOT ITS REVENGE

NIGHTWATCH OVER WINDSCAR

WINDSCAR

K. EASON

DAW BOOKS
New York

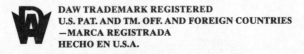

CHAPTER ONE

"I hear," said Gaer, from the doorway, "that Corso's found some suspicious caves."

Iari looked up from the much-wrinkled map on her table. Windscar's Aedis had a mix of old-style hinged doors and automated, depending on where you were in the compound. The Brood hadn't gotten to officers' quarters, last surge; Iari's door was still the original wood-and-metal arrangement. Gaer was a smear of shadow in the corridor, except for the gleam off his optic and the mesh on his jaw. "There's a briefing at the end of the day, Gaer, in the conference room. *Not* now and in my quarters."

"Yesss. But I'm here now. I assume that's why you left the door open."

It was, in fact, exactly why. Iari shrugged. "Because a closed door would stop you? Ha. But since you're here, come in. And shut the door."

Truth, she had bet on two things: that Corso would tell Gaer about the caves as soon as he'd cleared the debrief with Knight-Marshal Keawe, and that Gaer would sit with that knowledge for no more than a quarter-hour before he decided to come find her. Which—Iari glanced at the chrono on her terminal—seemed about right.

Gaer stepped into her quarters. He flicked a look at a few of the Windscar cats on her bed, and the propped-open window, and blew an amused breath through his jaw-plates. "It's warmer in the corridor."

"Now you know why the door was open. Come here." The table on which she'd spread the maps of Windscar took up most of the working floorspace. She moved over, making room for Gaer. Vakari ran hotter than everyone else. It was a little like standing next to an open oven door (welcome in Windscar, *especially* in winter, especially since she wasn't going to shut the window anyway).

Gaer canted forward, tilting his tall vakar frame from the hips. His spine, ridged with, well, *spines*, wasn't inclined to hunch. The effect made him look like the kind of menacing sculpture one expected to find on the facades of old alwar buildings.

"Is this a *paper* map? With *hand-drawn* notations? Dear dark lords. Do we not have holodisplays in the great wastes of Windscar? No tablets?"

"It is, twice, and we do, twice, but this isn't one of them." The Aedis AVs and their onboard systems were hexed against Weep interference, but even so, "Corso was regular army. You go prepared for equipment failure."

"You were regular army once, and I do not notice you handdrawing maps. Which I appreciate." Gaer reached out and hovertraced a fingertip over the fissure-line. "Corso thinks they're k'bal ruins. The ones we're looking for. The ones Jich'e'enfe's altar referenced. Do you concur?"

"No. I think they're the *other* ruins we just found by happy accident."

"Sss. Sarcasm does not suit you, Captain."

"Don't *setatir* call me that."

She mangled the accent a little (on purpose), and his chromatophores rippled amusement across his cheeks.

Ungentle Ptah have mercy, that she'd been around Gaer long enough to understand which colors meant what. Ungentle Ptah twice over, that Gaer was relaxed enough around *her* to let her see them. Most of the world got his professional (ambassador, SPERE operative, battle-trained arithmancer) neutrality in shades of charcoal vakar-hide.

"Guess your face is feeling better," she said, not entirely kindly. "You're talking enough."

Gaer snapped her a look, one of those sharp vakari motions, half raptor, half reptile. His jaw-plate flared out on one side, amused. The other side only opened half as far, stopped by a web of scar tissue and fine metal filaments holding the hinge in place. That mesh bumped up on the edge of the definition of invasive implants. Medical or not, necessary or not, it had taken special permission from the vakari Five Tribes Senate for Gaer to have it.

"Then you tell *me* a story, Captain." He cocked his raptor-stare at the map. The light caught his optic, washing it briefly and luminously opaque. "How did the Aedis miss finding these caves? Because they seem rather large and conspicuous."

"Yeah. They do." Iari straightened up, scowling as much at the map as the twinge in her back. "I went through the cartography archives. After the last surge, we ran patrols all *over* the steppes." Looking for Brood stragglers, but, "Patrols should've found them."

"Troubling that they didn't."

"Meaning?"

Her tone earned another side-eye. Less raptor this time, more surprise. "I'm not suggesting carelessness or dereliction of duty or whatever you're imagining. I *mean*—what kind of hexes were, or are, on this cave that concealed it from Aedis drones and templars, but not Corso Risar?"

Oh. Voidspit. "Right. Sorry. Um. Something aimed at Aedis hexwork specifically?"

Gaer's mouth had been open to answer his own question. He left it that way a moment, considering. "I had not thought of that. But yes, the hexes *could* be Aedis-specific. Corso has no implants or arithmantic training, and everyone on an Aedis patrol would have one or the other or both."

"Huh. So if you weren't thinking hexes specific to the Aedis, what *were* you thinking?"

"I was going to say hex-rot. It's hard to tell from this"—he jabbed at the paper map—"but it looks like the entrance is at least partly under this hillside. That would make sense. If this is where the k'bal went to hide, they would have picked something not readily observable from above. They wouldn't need much arithmancy to fool a drone mecha's scan, especially back then. But ground forces—and whether or not the steppes were crawling with angry natives and Confederation troops at the time, the Protectorate would have come looking for k'bal survivors anyway, you know this—would've been a problem. *They* should've found this cave."

He paused, waiting for her to ask *why, what problem?* She raised an eyebrow instead. Bared one of her tusks.

His chromatophores rippled again. "The k'bal would've needed hexes that make people look away, hexes that *actively* discourage investigation"—he flicked his fingers—"whether through provoking discomfort subconsciously, or by tricking the eye. The vakari had those sorts of hexes. The k'bal certainly did. But enough time, enough weather, maybe enough fissure emanations, and surfaces erode. Should an equation on that eroding surface smear, the concealment hexes fail." He folded his fingers into a fist, paused for effect. Sighed, when she only stared at him. "That's the most *likely* reason Corso could see the cave. How did he know where to look?"

"Finding things is his job. Probably the result of a lot of interviews."

"That a nice way of saying *bought a lot of locals a lot of beer*?"

"Yeah. And listened to a lot of grannytales."

"Oh. Well. *There* we go. Drunk tenju superstition has undone years of concealing hexwork."

She hesitated. Elements bless, she could guess what Gaer would say to this next bit. "Corso said those particular caves have a reputation. Haunted. Or, or cursed. That no one talks about them, or goes near them. He tell you that?"

She'd been expecting a hiss, laughter, mockery. Gaer surprised her by doing none of those things. This was working Gaer, arithmancer Gaer, all closed plates and muted chromatophores and his full attention.

"Well, that would make sense, if they're hexed for concealment. Even as the hexes failed, they'd still have an effect. People could see the caves. They just wouldn't want to linger."

"So the hexes could be rotting, and *that's* why no one goes there and no one's found them, or there are new hexes meant to hide them from Aedis scans specifically."

"Or both. Or Corso has the imagination of old bricks, and the hexes just didn't work on him." Gaer tried to sound snappy and dismissive, and ended up sounding like he had a mouthful of rotten meat. "No, that's not fair. I'd like to say it's just hex-rot, but honestly, I don't know without looking. Which I assume is why you wanted to talk to me before the general meeting. Wait. That's *not* all, is it?"

"You reading my aura?" She meant it to sound accusatory. Sometimes you didn't want a nosy arithmancer reading your emotional state in electromagnetic waves.

Gaer was immune to shame. "No need. Your face is loud."

Iari drum-tapped a pair of fingers on the table's edge. "Corso told me he saw something moving in the cave. He *says*. He also says, could've been a trick of the light, that time of day, his imagination. He mention that to you?"

"No." Gaer stared hard at the nothing half a meter over the table. "I'd lament his lack of confidence in me, but I am assuming he did not put this tidbit in the official report, either."

"He did not."

"He thinks the Knight-Marshals would doubt his credibility?"

"Not Keawe or Tobin. Probably the ones in Seawall, though. *Definitely* the Synod. He's not Aedis." She let her loud face tell Gaer what she thought about that.

Gaer clicked sympathetically. "He probably thinks *I* would report it, too."

Gaer's ethical balancing act, between being a SPERE operative for the vakari Five Tribes as well as an Aedis asset commandeered under treaty, was a delicate thing. She'd seen Gaer's Seawall superior, Karaesh't, no formal introduction, just passing in the B-town Aedis hallways. Smallish, as vakari went, even more inscrutable features than Gaer's. According to Gaer, she was a formidable arithmancer. Iari supposed there were ciphered reports going south from Gaer to the embassy in Seawall. Maybe orders coming north, too, first to B-town and now, with their reassignment, to Windscar.

So she had to ask. "Will you report it? The caves, yeah, I expect that. I mean, the thing Corso thinks he saw?"

"I won't, in case there is nothing," Gaer said. "If it turns out there *is* something, or someone, in residence. Like Brood. Or wichu insurgents. Or mundanely unpleasant raiders. Or a pack of *setatir* wolves—that, those, I will have to mention."

"Corso saw raiders heading north past those caves. And there are no wolves this close to the fissure."

"Wolves are wise. Brood *eat* wolves."

"I'm less worried about Brood than about wichu." Because Iari knew what to do with Brood—swarm, boneless, slicers, tunnelers, the big nasty one-off Brood you got in a surge. Wichu hexwork was something else. "If it *is* wichu insurgents, and they've got hexes against *us*, how will *we* see the caves?"

"I am not Aedis," said Gaer. "But if you're asking, *what do we do, Gaer, if the wichu insurgents have created hexes specifically to defend themselves against the Aedis?* Then I would remind you that wichu hexes are generally scribed onto a surface—*artificed*, if you will—and are as a result *more* vulnerable to hex-rot. Which means I tell you what bit of wall to blow up, or which bit for Char and Winter Bite to smash, and then, sss, no more hexes. And if there is a live arithmancer or artificer in those caves to repair the hexes . . ." He peeled lips back from his teeth, blue-etched and dyed: the marks of his house, his tribe, his mothers carved onto sharp, sharp teeth. No one who ever saw that expression could ever mistake it for friendly: among the vakari, bared teeth were both introduction and the first cousin to an oath, a boast, a promise. "Then, well. We have *you*."

Iari returned his smile, lips curling back, baring more of the ever-visible tusks in her lower jaw. One of them was capped, dull metal, a souvenir of a shattered faceshield in her army days. She wouldn't have gotten that wound if she'd been in a templar battle-rig. If something had the kind of force to shatter Aedis hexes—and some of the big Brood did—they took the whole face and the head.

Damn near had happened with Gaer, last summer, in that B-town warehouse cellar. Because Jich'e'enfe had managed a *tesser-hex* in close quarters, and Gaer's rig wasn't rated for void. Iari supposed her rig would've done the same thing, if she'd been caught in the same radius Gaer had. Instead she'd been buried by Brood. Instead, something *else* had happened. She'd become some kind of channel to the Elements (Ptah and Hrok, plasma and vapor). Or something alchemical, arithmantic, *magic* beyond her understanding.

Her stomach clenched like a nervous fist. Her smile hardened into a grimace.

Gaer was watching her, probably reading her aura (no sense of boundaries, what *did* you expect from a spy?). His pigments rippled. "I meant we would have your axe," he said, guilty-voiced. "But, ah. I do recall the other matter. How many people know about it?"

She wanted to stare at the map, to shrug. To act the way she felt. Instead she lifted her chin and focused on his optic. "You. Corso."

His pigments rippled again, a different spectrum this time. "Not Knight-Marshal Tobin?"

"Did I *say* Tobin? I did not. Swear to Ptah, you run through a list of everyone we know, ask me about everyone—" She stopped. Let her breath out. "You and Corso. Like I said. That's it."

Gaer sat with that a moment. "I thought you intended to tell Tobin, at least, before we came north."

"I did." As her commander, Tobin had a right to know. She had an obligation to tell him. And as *Tobin*—void and dust. Until now, she'd never lied to him, not by omission, not directly, in all the years he'd commanded her, from Templar-Initiate Iari to Captain, through the surge and things that stripped rank away from the way she thought about him, even if he was always Knight-Marshal of B-town when they spoke.

But whatever had happened to her—to her nanomecha—in that cellar . . . that was the sort of thing that got people taken off active duty. Subjected to tests, arithmantic, alchemical, medical, *whatever.* Iari wasn't especially bothered by needles, but she was fond of neither the chief chirurgeon in B-town, nor losing her field command. Especially that.

Gaer watched her, for once silent, likely enjoying her aura's pyrotechnics. She scowled up at him. "Who'd be in command up here if I'm locked in a lab somewhere? It'd be one of the Windscarrans."

"Luki."

"Is a sergeant. Char and Winter Bite are newly promoted privates. They need an officer."

"They probably have more field experience than any of us. But to your point, I don't relish the idea of that lieutenant . . . what's his name? The arrogant neefa Keawe's stuck us with?"

"Everyone calls him Notch." Because Keawe, Knight-Marshal in Windscar, wanted a fireteam of her people involved in this mission, not just Tobin's B-town detachment that included two riev. B-town and Windscar were the two northernmost Aedis compounds, its Knight-Marshal commanders allied by geography and proximity to the Weep fissure.

Gaer grimaced. "Yes, him. Notch. I don't relish the idea of him in command. The good Knight-Marshal has made her, ah, distrust of me rather clear, and I suspect he shares it."

"Not just you. Char and Winter Bite, too." The two riev wore templar badges painted onto their armor, so they were templars, and in public, at least, no different than a tenju or an alw or a human recruit. In private, however. Well.

Typically, Tobin and Keawe presented a united and sensible front against Seawall's southern command. But the riev were proving to be Keawe's sticking point. Riev had been the wichu contribution to the war against the vakari Protectorate: galvanic and artificed and controlled by a central Oversight. The end of the last surge had led to their decommissioning—no more weapons, no more Oversight. No legal personhood, because no one thought they had any. Then Char and Winter Bite petitioned to join the Aedis, and Tobin allowed it, and now—well.

Gaer blew a breath out through his plates. Half hiss, half sigh. "And it's the vakari with a reputation for xenophobia."

"I don't think Keawe's sure riev are entirely people."

"That's worse, Iari. You know that."

"Yeah. I know." Keawe was also remembering Jich'e'enfe in B-town, and how she'd attempted to recommission the riev as terrorist weapons. That had failed, sure, but Keawe was skittish. How much of Keawe's suspicion trickled down to her templars, to the four assigned to round out Iari's squad—Iari didn't know. Wasn't a good way to come out and ask that, was there? Over mess one night, just blurt out a *hey, so: how do you feel about riev? Think they're people?*

"All reasons why I didn't tell Tobin and get myself stripped of command."

"I'm not criticizing. Just surprised, is all." Gaer flicked his fingers—three on a vakari hand, not four, all of them with an extra joint—like he was banishing a pernicious insect, instead of dismissing her guilt. He had to be seeing it in her aura. She could taste it, bile-bitter on the back of her tongue. "But seriously—whatever happened to your nanomecha, whatever *evolution* occurred—and do not scowl at me, templar, because that is what happened. Your nanomecha responded to a threat from hostile arithmancy and rewrote their own code. That could happen again, to other templars. Or, *sss*, to priests. Your Aedian nanomecha all come from the same heretical source. Jich'e'enfe was a talented arithmancer, but I do not believe for a moment she is the only person who has the knowledge to breach Aedis code and mutate it."

"Neither do I." Iari looked at the map again, at the crudely drawn caves. "We're probably walking right into more of those people."

"Yes. And *when* we get a faceful of hostile arithmancy—and that will happen, and there will be hexes I can't counter—then we shall see if anyone else's nanomecha evolve, too."

"It's only happened the once, Gaer. It might not ever happen again."

"Sss. It will." He cocked his head and peered at her through the optic. "I don't need a hex to tell me the probabilities of *that*."

CHAPTER TWO ≡≡≡≡≡

T he cave was exactly as Corso had described it: a rocky hole where there didn't look like there should be one, stuffed in the side of one of the endless, gently rolling hills. That was the problem with Tanis, Gaer reckoned. You thought you had one thing—a hinterlands planet where nothing politically interesting happened, with a minor Weep fissure slicing through part of the northern continent . . . and *then* you got a faceful of wichu insurgency and found a lost k'bal cave under what turned out to be a remarkably *large* hill for the middle of what were advertised as steppes and the occasional clump of shrubbery.

Having done his bit—his optic didn't detect anything malevolent around the entrance, just the raggedy traces of eroding artificing and deeper, aetheric hexwork—Gaer withdrew into the last of the long shadows thrown by the hopper. It was at least five degrees cooler in the hopper's shade. Most of Gaer was tucked into a battle-rig, though, and *it* didn't care. And besides, it was easier to see what the templars were doing from this vantage.

So Gaer squatted, glad of his rig's flexibility and its insulation, and watched Lieutenant Notch and the rest of Keawe's fireteam combing over the loose stone in front of the cave. Iari stood a little bit back, faceplate up, supervising and wearing a look Gaer had privately dubbed *how the* setat *did Notch make officer.* Luki stood beside her, eyes narrow, lips flat, disapproval as sharp as her cheekbones, and her aura in every shade of exasperation. Now Iffy—who was still the both the smallest alw Gaer had ever seen, and the priest acting as field medic on this little adventure—was all business, her aura filled with serious blues shot through with yellowy tendrils of worry. (Which was normal for Iffy. She'd been Gaer's nurse while his face healed. She worried about everything.)

The riev looked—well, like riev. Winter Bite's stylized features suggested he had originally been human under that armor, though how much of that body remained was impossible to guess. Riev replacement parts were, Gaer knew (to his discomfort and unquiet dreams), a matter of what was available, close to the size of the exoframe. His aura was a tolerant violet. Char, however—Char was annoyed, their aura bright (-er than most riev's, including Winter Bite's) and spangled with shades of dried blood and fire. And Corso—

A shadow, distorted by season and latitude, edged into his field of view. Battle-rig angles, limbs stretched by the shadow to skeletal gauntness, scuffing through the grass. Rattling, too, bones and hooks and whatever *else* so-called traditional Tanisian tenju filled their braids with.

There he was.

Corso crouched beside him. "Thought you said the cave was clear."

"I did. They really want to find a monster, I think. Or at least proof of my incompetence. Or my wicked vakari mendacity."

"You're probably not wrong." Corso hesitated. Dear dark lords, he looked embarrassed. "Up here, you know . . ."

"The provincial opinion of vakari is dim. Yes. And Notch is, I believe, a native Windscarran."

So was Corso, who had the grace (or shame) to leave that fact unvoiced. "So's the little tenju. The corporal."

Little. Homer was *little* only by tenju metrics. He still towered over Iffy and Private Llian, both alwar, and his fellow corporal, Dodri, tenju-with-a-hint-of-human. Or he would, if he wasn't prone to a stiff-necked skulk, round shouldered as his rig would permit, like he didn't want anyone to notice him.

Gaer shifted his weight onto his toes. *Setatir* boots. So confining. One missed unfortunate earth between one's talons. "To be fair, I *could* have erred. Only an egoist resents others checking his work."

"Ha. You're right, though. And besides, monsters don't come out in daylight. Whatever's in there is waiting somewhere in the dark."

"Is that what the grannytales said?"

Corso side-eyed him. "The grannytales said this whole place was haunted. Don't come here ever. Bad things happen. Nothing specific about haunted by what, or where the haunting happened."

"That's good. Haunted by flesh-eating skeletons just ten meters past the front entrance would be a level of specificity I'd find disturbing, and also somewhat dubious."

"Hah. I'm less worried about skeletons than Brood. And I'm *more* worried about." Corso bit his lip. He'd lost part of a tusk in the same cellar skirmish in which Gaer had lost part of his face (bad day for faces, that). His cap was brighter than Iari's, and it winked in the watery northern sun.

"About . . . ?" Gaer followed his gaze. Ah. Char and Winter Bite. Not them specifically—Corso might have the social skills of a rabid badger, but he wasn't a bigot—but what could happen *to* them. In B-town, Jich'e'enfe had corrupted two riev with renegade hexwork Gaer still was not sure he could counter. "I imagine they're worrying about the same thing."

Corso chewed on that a moment. "You think that could happen?"

"To them specifically? No. Jich'e'enfe relied on the old Oversight network. None of the riev in the Aedis have those systems anymore. But I'm sure it haunts them. There is a horror and a shame in having a riev turn traitor, since they were designed and artificed to be proof against treason."

"Huh." Corso looked toward the riev again, and his expression morphed from thoughtful to ferociously blank. "Looks like the templars are done over there."

Gaer followed his gaze. Ah. So they were. Lieutenant Notch had straightened up, was turning to Iari. Notch was a very *large* tenju. Broader than Corso. Taller than Iari, and younger by a few years. That put him too young for the last surge, while *she* had survived Saichi. The young lieutenant was anxious to earn her good opinion, Gaer didn't need an aura to see that: read it instead in the cant of his shoulders, the thrust of his jaw as he spoke to her. The way he peered sidelong, checking her reaction.

She wasn't impressed so far. Gaer didn't need an aura to see that, either.

Gaer stood up, started walking down there. Arrived at the last, to hear Notch's crisp, "There's signs *something's* been in here, Lieutenant, but nothing in the last couple of days. Nothing that left muddy tracks, anyway, or anything visible to scans."

Iari didn't blink. Didn't smile. Impassive as Char, except Gaer could see the sparks of her aura, like heat lightning in a night storm. "Thank you, Lieutenant. That matches the report we got from Corso *and* the ambassador."

Oh, *the ambassador* now, was he? Gaer composed his features—more difficult than one might imagine, with one plate meshed into immobility—and planted himself near Iari, trying to look ambassadorish. He felt Char's gaze on his back. Notch's glare on his face. Reserved his own attention for the gaping maw of a tunnel, which was really neither gaping nor a maw, but filled Gaer with the same dread as if it were slime-slick and studded with fangs.

Color splotched Notch's cheekbones and darkened the tips of his ears. "Yes sir."

Iari cocked her head and gazed at Notch for a long, speculative moment, until the silence creaked with the weight of what she didn't say. Then, finally, "Everyone, get your gear. We're moving out."

For all its ominous demeanor, it was a very *civilized* cave once you got inside. First, there were lights a few meters down. Not teslas, nothing so mechanical. No. These were motion-sensing hexwork that threaded the ceiling and the walls from about halfway up, gentle and pervasive, incapable of shadows or glare. They lit up as bodies moved into the corridors and stayed lit. On the cave walls themselves, there were no marks. Just a gentle glow. The hexes were visible to Gaer's optic, when he looked for them. To everyone else it would just look like magic light coming out of the walls.

The tunnel was larger, too, than he'd expected. Four meters by three, taller than wide, big enough for two battle-rigs abreast, or one rig and a riev. The precision and neatness, the hexed light sources, didn't look like bandit excavation or the by-product of Brood. Or wichu separatists, for that matter. They would not have bothered with a ceiling high enough for a vakar or—Gaer cranked his head around to look at Char where they walked with Notch at the rear—an arrangement that pleased neither of them—or a very large riev.

"No hexes, except the teslas," Gaer murmured, because Iari was looking at him. She had set them behind the point team of Llian and Winter Bite. He jerked his chin at the riev. "He's more likely to pick something up than I am, with all his hardware. Presumably that's why you have him on point."

"It is, though I wasn't going to ask about hexes." Iari gestured at the walls. "Unmarked stone, no decoration. No signage. Is it k'bal?"

Dark lords defend, as if he were an expert. While Corso had been looking for caves and Gaer's face had been healing, and despite Iffy fussing over him like a malfunctioning med-mecha, he'd managed a great deal of reading about k'bal. They were, had been, a strange species, even by xeno standards. Not mammalian, not avian, not—*anything* anyone recognized. A partitioned brain divided among multiple crania on a single organism, two arms, two legs, no tail, fluid sexes and genders; a culture steeped in philosophy and arithmancy and elaborate social codes. And then the Protectorate, intent on its war of Expansion, afraid of their skill with arithmancy, had made their extinction a priority. Iari knew all that, same as he did.

"If you're asking, can I tell if this place was k'bal-built, no, I cannot. Can I tell if Jich'e'enfe came through here? Again with *no*. But if this is a k'bal shelter, it would have been built during the Expansion, and there wouldn't have been much need for culturally identifiable embellishments."

Iari side-eyed him. Remarkable eyes, tea-green and glass-clear and, right now, narrow with worry.

"Something feels off," she said, so softly he almost did not hear.

"Something *here.*" She raised her hand partway, in a gesture that could mean anything. Then rolled her eyes back, and cocked her head. So Gaer guessed that *here* meant the needle-socket in the base of her skull, where her templar nanomecha interfaced with the battle-rig's systems via an actual, *setatir* needle.

"Off *how*? Should you tell—?" Gaer did his own head tilt.

"No. It's not pain."

Gaer strangled a sigh and an admonition. Iari didn't ask for help. She might not know the word. He deployed a very tiny hex, one of the pre-loaded arsenal in his optic, to mute conversation. Ahead, Winter Bite slowed down, head turning partway. *Setatir riev.* Of course he'd sense vakari arithmancy. Winter Bite wasn't likely to announce it; he knew Gaer. (Didn't trust him, probably; Winter Bite was *riev*, and he was a vakar, and despite their individual association and alliance, the one had been created to kill the other.)

"I just hexed us a little privacy," he said. And then, feeling a little stupid, "Tell me about this feeling? Like a premonition?"

"Huh." Iari's aura streaked yellow and orange. "Thanks. And no. More like psychic skin-prickles. Do you even get those?"

"I am familiar with the idiom. And *yes*, vakari do get skin prickles." Under an open sky, in an Aedis corridor, he would tease her for being speciesist. But here, now, "Having some as we speak, in fact, listening to you."

"Hah. Had 'em since we got off the hopper in front of the cave. They're getting stronger, deeper we go. Can't tell if they're real or I'm just." A spacer-shrug she'd learned from Tobin, fingers splayed briefly stiff. "Nervous." She said the word like an obscenity.

"Nervousness is forgivable. I prefer that to overconfidence. Or carelessness." He cast another look over his shoulder, past Iffy and Corso, and the Windscarran corporals Dodri and Homer. Past

Luki, who caught him looking and half-cocked a smile before she realized he was looking past her at Notch. "Or whatever the lieutenant's problem is."

"Youth. Inexperience."

"Me."

"Because of the first two." Another side-eye. "That's why I'm not closing my visor and comming your private channel. We don't need to feed that insecurity. He already hates you're not back with Corso. He wanted the civs kept together."

"He should be glad of it. If you hated us both, you'd put him on *me* duty. *Guard the ambassador, Lieutenant. See to his every whim.*"

"Ptah's left eye. Don't tempt me." Iari's eyes crinkled at the corners. Smile, maybe, or serious contemplation. Or impatience, because Notch was not her concern, and skin prickles were. Gaer flared his jaw-plates in a *Notch dismissed* gesture before he realized the plate on Iari's side didn't, couldn't, move.

"To your worry: I don't sense anything. I've scanned on every layer of aether I know. But I *also* know Jich'e'enfe was"—bitter to say, *sss*—"a better arithmancer than I am. Or is, if she survived. And even if she didn't, her allies might be similarly skilled. And, truth—whatever happened to you in that cellar might've, ah, conferred some new sensitivity to your nanomecha."

"So I should listen to this feeling."

"You should." Although, now that he ran the scans again, through his optic first (easy, fast) and then manually, dividing his attention and sifting through layers of aether—there was something. A hint. A breath. *Something* fluttering around at the edges of his senses, deep in the aether. "Either you're making me nervous or you're right. I can't pin it, but . . . sss. Skin prickles."

"I hope—" Iari said, but Gaer didn't find out what she hoped.

Because at that moment Winter Bite's armor flared lambent green and Llian stopped like she'd slammed into a wall.

Gaer's optic lit up.

"Iari." Just that from Gaer, her name with no particular stress or emphasis. But at the exact moment Winter Bite's hexwork flared, he might as well have shouted. She didn't seal her visor—the suit wasn't reacting, no alarms or flashing teslas—but the sense of wrong under her skin turned from prickling unease to gut-punch certainty.

The syn shot white heat down her spine, all those nanomecha fused to blood and bone and nerve activating in concert. Those nanomecha set templars apart from regular Confederation troops: it made Aedis troops faster, stronger, all those little machines working together, linking templar biology to battle-rig tech through the needle-socket, making them faster and stronger still. Triggering the syn *had* been a voluntary process, once, her choice to activate it.

Then last year, in a B-town basement, a corrupted riev named Sawtooth had infected her and taken her nanomecha offline. When they resurrected themselves, the syn was a matter of instinct, not judgment. *Their,* the nanomecha's, instinct. Maybe hers. Maybe there was no difference.

She hadn't told Gaer that yet. Or Corso. Or anyone.

Iari rode the syn forward, gliding between Winter Bite and Llian before the latter had managed a syllable.

"Report," she said, mostly to the riev.

But it was Llian who said, "Ah, Captain, the tunnel ends about a meter ahead. Opens into a much bigger space," while looking wide-eyed at Winter Bite's glowing armor.

Llian wasn't entirely inexperienced with riev, Iari knew; she'd been part of the unit Knight-Marshal Keawe brought south from Windscar to B-town to help with the Brood outbreak. Llian had been there when the wichu separatist Jich'e'enfe had tried to reestablish Oversight and recommission the riev in service to *her* war. Llian had seen riev hexwork light up, and knew it meant nothing good. But the specific *what*, she didn't, couldn't know.

So, "Report, Private," Iari said again, looking at Winter Bite.

The riev did not turn to look at her. All his attention trained forward. And then, gentle Mishka, *the hell was that*—his chest opened, armor plates retracting over what would've been the heart on a human, just a little left of center. Not bone under there, no, but a scaffold of metal filaments, like a cage. And out of that cage came—cables *should* have been the right word. But they were tentacles. Clearly. Reminiscent of some of the appendages you saw on the rarer Brood, without the slime or the affront to physics. Winter Bite had three of them, unfolding and reaching a meter out of his chest. Iari felt the cold coming off them, saw the serrations near the tip, presumably to help with gripping (or stripping flesh from bone). The tentacle-tips themselves unfolded into three equidistant prongs that looked more like teeth, or talons, or hostile vakari fingers. In the apex between those digits, what one could charitably call a *palm*, a small aperture opened. Iari tried hard not to think about mouths.

"Hrok's *left tit*," Llian spat, which—all right, that told Iari a couple more things about the limits of Llian's orthodoxy, and jerked a smile out of her, besides.

"There is a large space." Winter Bite's tentacles shifted—organic movement, sinuous and beautiful like the Brood were, sometimes, and just as upsetting. An am-I-imagining-that sound scratched her awareness, oscillating between squeak and howl. "It is fifteen-point-two-three meters wide, fifty-point-two meters long. The ceiling varies according to natural formation. The walls are regular and consistent with the architecture of the tunnels. It is *not* empty, though nothing moves. There is considerable debris, some of which is organic."

Iari's mouth was dry. She sucked her teeth for spit. "And hexes?"

"Data is not definitive." Winter Bite sounded irked.

"Same." Gaer sounded irked, too. "Assume there are, and whoever laid them is better than we are."

"Right." Iari strained forward, eyes and ears and everything. Held up a hand for the rest of them: wait, hold. They would. Notch and especially Char would hate it, there in the rear, but they'd do it.

"Gaer, with me," she said, and took point. "Winter Bite. Llian. Hold position. Visors down," she added, thrown over her shoulder at everyone. That seemed wise, and also necessary to say, with Llian's current mental state mirrored in Homer's and Dodri's uncovered faces. Luki's visor, Iari noted, had already dropped. So had Notch's. Huh and noted.

Then Iari's faceplate sealed and the HUD peripherals lit up: targeting, squad biometrics, and a full 360 view in tiny panels across the top. The last one didn't do much good. The room was dark as a cellar under B-town. Dark as the void in a fissure.

Iari's heart banged into the back of her breastbone, tried to crawl up her throat. There were no Brood up ahead. The battle-rig was certain. Winter Bite was, or he'd have said. But whatever k'bal arithmancy had lit the place so far just stopped. A curtain of darkness, same dimensions as the corridor itself. Not a door.

"Gaer."

He slid between her and Llian, that teardrop-smooth visor gleaming opaque and black and ominous. Her own reflection, distorted, moved over its length. Probably protocol about ambassadors moving in front of templars, but hell with that. If there was a fight, she wanted him with her.

"I don't sense Brood or anything with an aura. Nothing's throwing hexes at *us*. That's all, Iari. I don't have a *setatir* map of this place."

"Right." The syn wanted her to run forward into that black. Iari held it back and took careful steps instead. She put her hand on the axe haft. Didn't draw it, not yet. She lifted her left arm and deployed the shield in the gauntlet. Whitefire unfolded itself, scaffolding first the outline, then filling it in with the Aedis crest, muted versions of Aedis red and gold and the individual Elements' sigils. No glow, except oh so faint on the edges, because it was hexed for stealth. That wasn't enough to illuminate the black. She had the headlamp on her helmet for that. It punched a hole in the dark, lonely until Gaer's joined hers. The lamps cast a hard-edged brightness, but illumination bled off the edges. The corridor walls fell away in that dimness. Vanished into a much larger space that Iari could feel in a way that defied sense, even before the battle-rig's telemetry started to mark out a border, its senses in line with Winter Bite's.

But this room wasn't empty, oh no. Winter Bite was right about that. Iari saw a chair first. Assume it'd been a chair, anyway— a bucket that might've held someone's posterior perched on a column that might've once led to wheels or feet if it hadn't been snapped off instead. Its edges gleamed jaggedly. The bucket-seat itself was cracked, all its length.

It was only the first one of many. Her headlamp plucked others, one by one, out of the dark. There were many seats (because yes, that's what they were). There were tables, too, in similar broken condition, and brackets in the floor where the tables had been mounted and fixed. The floor had been smooth, the native stone covered with tiles. Now it was cracked at irregular intervals, as if someone very large had gone after it with a hammer. She tried looking up, but her headlamp couldn't make sense of the ceiling. Too many jagged shadows, like broken teeth. This had been, what, a cafeteria? A classroom? A temple?

"A garden," said Gaer, in one of those moments that made her wonder if she'd spoken aloud, or if she and Gaer just thought that much alike. "Look, *there*. That's a garden-tank."

He pointed and did something arithmantic; the beam from his headlamp spilled along the floor more like water than light, swirling around a squarish object Iari had taken for a tipped-over table. It wasn't a table, though, you could see that, as Gaer's beam flowed up the sides. It was a box, maybe two handspans deep, with a deep crack on one side, and part of one corner broken away. There was, yeah, okay, if she squinted and imagined, there could've been plants in there, once. Shallow-rooted. Maybe hydroponics? She didn't see any visible water-delivery system, but first, these were k'bal, and who knew how they'd done things, and two, no reason to think any system they'd used would be intact enough to be recognized.

"This space must've been mixed use. A garden, but also a mess hall. That would make sense. Food production and food consumption close together, when space is at a premium. And the k'bal, though omnivorous, were culturally disposed to agriculture. Less violent than animal husbandry, more efficient use of resources. This, of course, is a *tank*, so . . . cloning, probably. They did not consider that taboo." Gaer slid a step toward said tank. His headlamp, having been redirected, left a great deal of dark around him. He was careful to stay within *her* headlamp's range, stretched up as tall as his frame would allow. "There is something in there, which I suspect must be some sort of growth medium. I can't see if there are vegetative remains, however. Winter Bite, can you—?"

"Yes, Ambassador. There are faint organic remains," said Winter Bite. His tentacles hovered, flexing. "But not flora."

Iari didn't even look at Gaer. She just started for the tank, trusting that he'd come along, that he'd stay close. They were almost there before Llian managed to ask, "Then what are they?"

Iari and Gaer were peering over the side when Winter Bite said, "They are bones."

Bones in much the same condition as the furniture. Smashed, snapped—oh Ptah's glowing *eye*, maybe gnawed upon. Iari prodded one, turned it over. There was something powdery in the box, which might've been soil or loam or just ash. It clung greyly to the bone fragment, gathering in the furrows that led to one jagged end.

"Gaer."

Fortunate that Gaer knew what she wanted, all in that single syllable. "Not Brood work. There *is* scoring on the bone, however," he said, as without inflection as if he'd been describing the color taupe. He did what she hadn't, and picked it up, pinned in the whiteness of both their headlamps. "Something sharp, regular, and even. See? There are no variations in the depths of the grooves. That suggests something manufactured is responsible."

No, she did *not* see. That degree of magnification wasn't part of a battle-rig's capabilities. It was, however, for his optic. She grunted assent anyway, because Gaer's explanation wasn't just for her, not when they were on general comms instead of a private channel. "So what, a weapon did that?"

"Ah. I believe so." She couldn't see through Gaer's visor, but the cant of his helmet aimed past her shoulder. He set the bone down gently. "I am no biologist, and it has been many years since I studied the subject, but I think that's part of a vakar's femur."

Which didn't answer her question, exactly, but it left a few suggestions. K'bal defenses, which might or not might not still be active. Which might or might not react to another vakar with similar violence.

"Captain?" That was Luki on the comm.

"Move up, all of you. Carefully. *Slowly.* There might be some old defenses still active." That last, for Notch's benefit. And because she wanted another particular set of eyes, "Char, I need you with me. Luki—fall back with Notch."

Iari saw the big riev reflected in Gaer's visor before her HUD even registered incoming movement: the faint sullen glow of hexwork crawling over their limbs. Char was built on a tenju frame, broad and solid, meant to haul heavy weapons (or house them; riev had been armed, once). They had lost an arm at Saichi during the surge; the Aedis replacement was a match for size and design, but the polysteel still had newness to it, which caught the gleam of the hexwork and made the arm look molten. Char was looking around, up, down, around, in a way that riev didn't usually, when they had a purpose.

Char was different, though. Char was . . . curious. And proactive. And *old.*

And careful where they stepped. "Char. You know what k'bal bones look like?"

"Yes, Captain."

"See if you can find any—check the floor, tables, anywhere. The rest of you—where's the rest of *this* vakar? And did they have friends?"

There were, as it turned out, *many* bones, most of such small dimensions that they looked like bits of broken plastic or tile at first. There were other garden-tanks, too, seven in all, though two had been smashed to fragments, and three more broken badly enough they defied identification, except as scrap. What gave them away was location: the tanks were evenly spaced, so that even when the tank itself had been powdered and broken, there were deep marks in the tile where it'd been bolted down. And, maybe oddest of all—the room had seven walls, with irregular angles and different widths.

Winter Bite and Llian found the first exit out of the place: one distressingly narrow door halfway up the left side of the room in the smallest of the seven walls. Its access was partly blocked by detritus, and the whole area especially ashy.

Iari found the second almost directly across from where they'd come in. A wall panel, k'bal height, shaped like what she assumed was a k'bal hand, beside what *had* been a sealed door. Now it was a crumpled wreck of metal and nanoforged parts, spilling partway into the corridor beyond. It had been made of segments that would've unfolded into a flat surface when closed. Not as strong as a flat polysteel panel, but a lot easier to install in a hurry, and adjustable to the width of the aperture. Iari panned her headlamp over the doorway fixture. It was a raised groove of polysteel, a few centimeters on the bottom and top, thicker and bigger on one side. The door segments had deployed laterally, rather than up and down. On this side, the fittings were flush with the stone.

The breaching party had not tried to pry it open. They'd just broken through.

"That's disturbing." Gaer crouched beside her, probing at the debris with a single finger. "There are no scorch marks. No signs of whitefire. Whatever did this just pushed really, really hard to get the door open."

She stared down at the back of Gaer's helmet. Weighed the wisdom of shifting to private comms to ask, *do you think it was riev*, because damn sure he'd had that thought, same as she had.

She took a deep breath instead, and said, "Char's coming over. They might've found something."

"More dead vakari, I imagine." Gaer bit the words off. "Did you find more dead vakari, Char?"

Char waited to answer until they had achieved polite conversational distance. "Captain. Ambassador. There are many dead vakari here, but I found no k'bal bones. There is a stain by the smaller door that I believe to be k'bal viscera, but it is difficult to determine. It is very old, and very contaminated."

"Your sensory hexwork is truly a marvel. I must commend the wichu artificers who made you." Gaer bit the words off.

Char turned their head. Cold ice-blue teslas, in stylized, perfectly anonymous tenju features. "I do not see why the wichu should get credit, Ambassador. Whatever did this, of whatever origin, left no trace of itself."

"Gaer," Iari said, before he could retort. (And he would. He always did.) Needling Char was his second-favorite pastime. There was history there, sure—but it was history before *Gaer's* time, though not Char's, before the Schism and the Accords, when the sole purpose of riev had been killing vakari. Char surely had done so. But there had been a time when Aedis templars and vakari killed each other too, and—"Char. *Guess.* Could it've been a mecha that did this? Or do you think riev?"

That was the biggest difference among the riev in Iari's acquaintance. They could all conceive of a self, they could all choose personal pronouns (and six months ago, no one would've thought that was possible). But only Char *speculated.*

"Mecha," Char said, after a pause. "The destruction is too thorough for riev."

"Even riev murdering vakari?"

"Yes, Ambassador," said Char, sharp as breaking bone. "We

would not remove all trace of ourselves. That would conceal our presence, when we wanted the Protectorate to know what we could do. We made—make—vakari nervous. Fear is a useful tool."

Times like this, Iari thought, you could miss standing nightwatch in B-town.

Iari keyed her comms. Everyone else would've heard that exchange. "Anyone *else* find any mecha bits? Or any organic remains *not* vakari?"

"No, sir," said Luki, promptly, quickly echoed by Notch. No and no trickled in from Homer with Dodri, then from Llian and Winter Bite.

And finally, "No," from Iffy, who sounded caught between horror and frustration.

"So whatever did this is still out there." Corso sounded bored by the revelation. Iari knew better. Corso been issued an Aedis battle-rig, and therefore was linked into her HUD. She could see the elevated everything in his biometrics. "Might've been what I saw when I found the place."

In daylight an hour ago, it would've been easy to dismiss the idea of rogue mecha prowling the tunnels. Here, in a mass grave of vakari troopers, amid so many broken things, no one said anything.

Except Gaer. Always, Gaer. "Two things to consider. First, it is probably not *one* responsible mecha, but several or many. Second, several or many might respond to specific stimuli: vakari specifically, which would leave the rest of you relatively safe, or intruders generally, in which case . . . well. Or—all right, *three* things to consider: there could be arithmancy affecting our hexes. Though arithmancy that can evade the Aedis, Char and Winter Bite, *and* me seems unlikely."

Silence on comms, broken by one very quiet, "Shit."

Homer, Iari thought, and wished she could look at him, offer something like reassurance. Tobin would've known what to say. All she had for comfort was, "Stay alert," which seemed both unnecessary and vital at once.

And, "Gaer. Did the Protectorate use mecha for warfare during the Expansion?"

She heard an asymmetrical click over comms, the sound of one jaw-plate flaring. "Toward the end, yes. But this carnage was directed *at* vakari, not *by* them."

"Maybe the defenders commandeered the attackers' mecha. Could k'bal do that? Hex through vakari command codes?"

"Possible. *Jich'e'enfe* almost certainly could."

"With all due respect, sir." That was Notch, stiff-voiced with poorly concealed impatience. "Whatever did this is long dead."

"Mecha don't die," said Gaer, at the same time Char said, "With respect, Lieutenant, that statement cannot be verified."

"Well, it isn't here *now*," Iari said. She knew very well what Notch meant. And he was probably right; lingering in a room of thoroughly dismembered vakari troopers would only inspire imagination, and in green troops, that was the worst. She considered the wisdom of sending him on point with Char, and—

Her HUD flickered. Not an alert flicker, not a tesla pulse. A *flicker*, as if the rig's power core had shorted.

"Sss. Did you just see that?" Gaer might've been asking anyone, but it was Notch who answered.

"A-firm." He sounded less impatient, suddenly.

"Hate to be that guy, but see what?" Corso asked from across the room.

"Sorry, Captain, but I didn't see anything." Luki sounded a little bit grim.

"No, Captain," from Dodri and Llian, promptly, and, "See what, sir?" from Homer.

"A flicker on the HUD," said Notch. The impatience was back. "If you didn't see it, Homer, then you didn't see it."

"I detected nothing." Winter Bite sounded a little bit disappointed, even offended.

"Me either," said Iffy. "I can come over there—"

Which meant she was already moving, knowing Iffy. Iari made a face at her uncaring HUD. "Stay where you are. All of you."

Then Iari realized that Char hadn't answered, which wasn't like Char. Iari looked. The big riev was standing where they had been. Not moving. A fine mesh of cyan and plasma blue crawled over their limbs, dimming the furious glow of their hexwork.

Iari's tongue turned to sand and ash. "Gaer. Look at Char."

"What—oh *setat*. Riev trap," in the next breath. "On it. The *setat* did that come from—"

At the same time, Notch said, "Movement incoming from the corridor, the *fuck*—"

And Iari's HUD, evidently remembering its duties, flashed an alert: incoming from the corridor on the other side of that broken door. Right. Notch had *just* said.

She snapped the shield up. The corridor had been a morass of shadows, stubborn and sticky beyond headlamp limits. Now that darkness seemed to be getting closer, actively chewing at the light, dimming, devouring. And *in* that darkness:

Clicking, metallic, sharp and sequenced. And accelerating.

"Contact," Iari said, and unclipped her axe. Deployed the blade in a shimmer of whitefire. And saw, as the darkness ate another length of the corridor, a shape: wide and metallic, which meant not Brood and for once that was no comfort. It seemed to be floating, until Iari realized it was holding itself off the floor with even *more* limbs (Hrok's breath, how many did that thing have?), tips jabbed into the wounded walls. It had no discernible head, only bulges distorting its silhouette, some of which might've been glowing faintly (or not; the HUD wasn't doing well, trying to lock onto it). But the larger appendages were obvious enough, thicker and shorter than the legs, with less bulge and more sinister angles, edges, *points*.

"Gaer." It was prayer and warning and plea.

"Fast as I can . . ."

The mecha seemed to hesitate. Paused, anyway, and raised two of those ghastly forelimbs. Iari saw the faint arc of whitefire across what looked like a trident of prongs.

Then Corso barked, "Contact!" and his biometrics spiked and that was *behind* her, void and fucking *dust*, that was the other side of the room, by that narrow little closed door—

And then Iari put that thought away, saved it for later, as her mecha charged.

CHAPTER THREE ▬▬▬▬

S ometimes, Corso thought, you didn't want to be right. Warn Iari that there was a maybe-monster in the cave, be gratified she believed him, hope to any power listening for empty tunnels—just a walk through stone corridors, everyone annoyed with him—that would've been *fine*. Shit, if he'd been smart, he'd have made his report and then stayed back at Windscar while templars did their jobs. His contract didn't *say* he had to be down here.

That was his own fool insistence, because he had to know if it was Jich'e'enfe (let her be *dead*) or one of her wichu insurgent Broodfucking friends in the cave, and if it was, well, he owed them a faceful. And if it was what the grannytales said—ghosts or old mecha or whatever—he needed to see that, too. Or so he'd told himself, back in daylight.

In the dark now, standing in the tepid glow of his headlamp and all the fancy little teslas on his borrowed battle-rig, hearing Gaer say that yeah, there was something out there, some veek-destroying mecha in the dark, *several or many*, fuckssake—Corso was glad only that *he* wasn't over on that side of this big creepy room, if there was something making the battle-rigs flicker.

He unclipped his longcaster—*his*, from his army days, white-fire and illegal as hell for a civ, but Iari'd gotten him an Aedis permit—and checked his HUD while its target-turing came on-line. Closest templars to him were Homer and Dodri, in the rough middle of the room. Then Winter Bite and Llian, who'd pulled back from the big door when Iari and Gaer and Notch had all muscled in there. Iffy was closest, right beside him, prowling around by that narrow, closed door, probably taking samples of what Char had said looked like k'bal gut-stain on the tile. Weird thing to care about, but Iffy was a healer-priest. She understood blood.

His longcaster finished syncing up with the battle-rig. A red-dish scope overlaid itself on his HUD, pushing everything else to the periphery. Only Iffy remained visible, crouched and peering at the tile, with a hard-sided Element-proof tablet in one hand, tak-ing notes. He started for her, because even if *several or many* ar-rived, they had to get through Iari and Gaer and big scary—

"Gaer," said Iari, over comms. "Look at Char."

"What—oh *setat*. Riev trap. On it. The *setat* did that come from—"

—Char was, oh shit, out of action, *not* good, hostile arith-mancy, *not* good, he had to be ready to—

"Movement, incoming, the fuck—"

That was Notch, who was over there with Iari.

Corso shifted the 'caster to one hand and reached back for Iffy with the other. Battle-rigs didn't come with handles, weren't meant to be grabbed, but you could slap a hand on a shoulder, trust the HUD to complain about the impact, get the attention of the per-son inside.

He did so. Iffy started inside the rig—he saw her head jerk, anyway, imagined the squawking alarm in her helmet. Her head turned, and he started to spit out an explanation.

His helmet went dark. HUD gone. *Everything* dead, for a second, and then—

Flash, flare, reboot. His HUD began trying to reconnect with his 'caster.

Now he saw something moving by that nearer, narrow door. The one that looked like it belonged to, oh, some kind of closet, and which *had* been closed. It wasn't now. Just a half meter ajar, near the top, and stuck that way, and widening.

Something spilled out of it and onto the wall, maybe half a meter across. It was descending, moving for the floor and the cover of all that debris.

"Contact!" Corso spat, before his mouth dried up.

He propelled himself forward, past Iffy, shoved between her and whatever was crawling out of the door. He raked his headlamp over the wall, swearing at his rig to get its slagging shit connection back to his 'caster, piece of neefa-shit worse than the goddamned army rigs had been—

Fuck it. He snapped the longcaster up, didn't wait for the target lock. Fired.

Whitefire chewed into the wall, spattering bits of molten stone that hardened into very hot solid projectiles as they fled the point of impact. He felt them ping off his rig. Supposed Iffy did, too. But the fucking target was still scrabbling along the wall—up, though, instead of down, so at least he'd diverted it.

It moved like a mecha—too smooth, too straight, too precise when it changed direction. But there was something about the silhouette of it, something about the way his headlamp bounced off the surface (carapace, his brain said unhelpfully). It *did* look a little bit like a beetle, or a scorpion—lots of limbs, symmetrically arranged; bulging body, except where the fuck was the head?

He checked Iffy's location—still crouched down, though all

her attention had shifted to the thing on the wall. She wasn't re-treating, he noticed. Wasn't pulling the whitefire sword pommel, either, that was clipped to her hip.

She raised a hand, splayed the fingers, thrust the palm out. Corso saw, for a split second, a corona flare around her gauntlet.

And the wall melted. Without heat, without any warning on his HUD—just liquefied, the stone turning molten (but cold? the fuck?) and running like wax. The mecha-ish thing slid with it, limbs sinking into the surface as it flailed and attempted to outrun the effect. Then the wall went solid again, trapping the *something* with three of—what, eight?—limbs stuck to varying depths in the now-solid stone.

That was Aedian priest-alchemy, that made one thing into an-other, that the grannytales *still* called witchery. Corso wanted to cheer.

The mecha-thing was less happy. Now that it wasn't moving, Corso could see its skin wasn't metal. It was made of something more granular, duller. More brittle; because as it tried to jerk loose, it snapped off a limb with a crack he heard through the ex-comms.

It screamed. Or something like a scream. A high-pitched wail of machine alarm.

Then Corso's HUD finally collected its shit and advised him of Luki's proximity, as the sergeant shot past with a synning tem-plar's speed and pinned the not-quite-a-mecha to the wall with her whitefire sword.

The carapace shattered on impact, spraying small familiar chunks that joined the litter already on the floor. Corso got an idea, suddenly, where all those fragments of vakari bone must've come from. Why they were broken in small pieces that looked ex-actly like the mecha Luki had just smashed. The floor wasn't just covered with dead vakari; it was covered with dead mecha *made* from dead vakari.

Whatever witchery was happening *here* wasn't Aedis. Wasn't veek. Wasn't Brood. Wasn't *any* fucking thing Corso had a name for.

Luki jerked her sword out of both wall and remains just as Homer skidded up, jagging past Corso, around Iffy, stopping only when he got to that partly open door. He poked his head around the edge, all templar bravado. Behind him, Dodri followed with sensible caution, shield up.

For a moment, quiet. Then came a gasp, from Homer, and a staccato, "Contact, *incoming*, lots of them."

Corso got his 'caster up just in time, as they came through the door.

Whoever, whatever had created this trap, they were good. Gaer knew battle-hexes, knew every way the vakari used to restrain riev in combat. Freeze their joints. Short their galvanics. Pummel them until something broke. Shred their hexes until they discorporated (all right, that one he'd seen in a drama, but he'd always wanted to try).

This hex was just holding Char still, and it was doing so conventionally by locking up all their joints, but Char's hexes didn't seem to be doing much to counter it. He spliced off enough attention to run an aura check. Was Char alive? Yes, and furious red and terrified yellow in near equal measure. He'd never seen Char scared before. Guess, then, that this hex was a new experience for them, and Char was old. They'd've seen a lot of hexes.

Novelty in battle-hexes was fine, but not directed against *his* riev. Gaer got back to trying to rip this *setatir* hex apart. His task was complicated because Notch was yelling from the doorway and Iari had gone barreling off down the corridor past the ruined door, shield up and axe out, to do what she always did.

"Get after her, Lieutenant," he snapped, because Notch wasn't *helping*, staying out here, and because whatever was down there tore vakari apart and he didn't want that happening to Iari.

He half expected an argument, or at least, Notch to stay where he was. But—miracle! Perhaps the Elements were real after all!—Notch took his suggestion. Probably didn't want to miss out on the action, *fine*, whatever it took.

Gaer just hoped it was Notch the incoming contact hit, not Iari.

This awful hex *could* be Jich'e'enfe's work. It was clever enough. But it was alien, too. So *many* equations, overlapping and interwoven *and* there was a variable he couldn't isolate. Gaer guessed, *bet*, this was at least partly k'bal hexwork, just because of that novelty. They'd been pacifists. No aggressive battle-hexes at all. And no reason to hex against *riev*, of all things, because riev were wichu creations. This hex was a *setatir* mystery, but it was one he needed to destroy, not investigate.

(A dull boom washed from the corridor, and a splash of dangerous heat. That was templars versus unidentified monster. Normal sounds of mayhem. Iari and Notch were *fine*. And they would be more fine if he got Char loose to go help them.)

Gaer picked an equation apart, solved it, went back, and unraveled another. If this wasn't a riev-specific hex, maybe it was *mecha* specific, because the vakari Protectorate had used battle-mecha as shock troops. K'bal would've needed defenses. And riev were not mecha. A vakari riev-trap exploited the organic element—targeted it, the theory being that without its organics, a riev was just a machine shell. But this trap was ignoring Char's galvanic animation entirely.

So great, yes, he'd figured that out.

(Notch came sailing past him. *Sailing.* As in feet not on the ground, flung back with great force. He crash-landed outside of Gaer's peripheral vision, in a startled squawk that turned violently profane. Without his weapon? Maybe. Gaer didn't spare attention to check.)

"Gaer!" in his comms, Iari's voice. Urgent, demanding, not screaming in last-breath agony.

(There was also comm-chatter in Corso's gravelly tones, and Homer's less impressive tenor, that Gaer ignored.)

At least Iari was still alive. Calling his name. Needing him to do his *setatir* job.

If these equations ignored riev organics, then . . . then perhaps the trick to dismantling it lay in making the trap think it'd caught a live person by mistake. Which would mean taking all Char's mecha systems offline. And the way to do *that* was—

Well. To kill them.

Iari realized, from the first trading of blows (she hit with the axe, the slagging mecha countered with one of those forelimbs and damn near took the weapon out of her hand), that she was in trouble. It wasn't the force of the blow—though that rivaled what she'd gotten from corrupted, mad Sawtooth, or the Brood tunneler—but the *angle.* The mecha had come at her from waist height, stretched across the corridor's width with legs on both walls. Now it was climbing up, trying to strike over her shield with its remaining forelimbs, which held a web of whitefire skeined between them. It jabbed down and she blocked with the shield, the syn singing through her nerves. The shield ate the impact. She felt the hex-surge, watched the rim flare up as it bled off the excess energy. The mecha was still a little above her. She couldn't shield-swat it aside. It'd take more of a lift-and-heave, which meant more effort expended, fine: the rig compensated. But it also meant more movement needed, which left her exposed. One of the mecha's alternate forelimbs licked back. The spear-tip point of it slammed into her chestplate and stuck there, for two HUD-marked seconds, before the rig's hexes engaged and ejected it and the forelimb skidded down her ribs and away.

Even Brood couldn't do *that*, stick a rig. And that forelimb was longer than she'd thought it should be. Telescoping feature, maybe? Flexible, fast, whipping back for another strike. She stifled a blink-and-duck urge, rode the syn and turned into the mecha's second strike. The whitefire rim of her shield sheared into the mecha's forelimb. Should've sheared *through*, that's what whitefire did—but it caught instead, like metal in bone, and Iari had to rip it loose. She put her back against the wall, raised the shield and the axe again. The mecha had advantage, still up by the ceiling. The twin plasma forelimbs hovered, twisting thoughtfully. The single spear-point limb drew back, still mobile, but maybe slower.

Hurt you, she thought. And, *Not enough.*

Her HUD told her the wounding was mutual. The rig's damage report scrolled along the bottom edge. Minor. She and it could take a lot more from this voidspit thing.

"Captain! Look out!"

The HUD showed her Notch inbound, to match up with his shout. On her lips to tell him hold, get back, *don't* crowd her space; but then her HUD flashed warning of a second mecha, this one on the ground and low, scuttling toward her with unholy speed from the corridor's dark guts.

The syn burned, wanting to meet this new challenge. She

retreated instead, half a step, to give more room for Notch. To force *her* mecha to come a little bit closer to her.

"Watch the forelimbs," she said. "They're fast."

Notch never had a chance to answer. The ground-level mecha propelled itself the remaining distance and met his charge head on, flexed a pair of forelimbs with whitefire strung between. Whitefire struck whitefire, full force.

The blast made her stagger. Her visor dimmed fast enough to alarm her, the hexes doing their job on her faceplate, protecting her vision, so she only saw Notch fly backward as a blur. His telemetry spiked—syn, exertion, and shock rolled together—and then he was gone again.

She looked where *her* mecha had retreated, up near the apex of ceiling and wall—

Where it wasn't now. The blast had dislodged it, made two of its limbs slip their grip on the ceiling. So it was sagging, scrape-sliding down the wall and flailing for purchase and *not* paying attention to her.

Iari adjusted her axe. Spared a split second to mark the location of Mecha Two, which had lost a little bit of its own forward progress. She'd get one hit in before it got to her, then two-on-one, then . . . then trouble.

"Gaer!" She needed *something*. She remembered the Brood-filled basement, that desperate moment when she'd gotten ready to die. When every one of her nanomecha had filled with what she could only describe as plasma and lightning, Ptah, Element That Burns. She'd felt herself change, in that moment, and turn into the Element's conduit. And she'd *ended* that fucking Brood.

She needed that now. Again. She reached for the syn, already online, and drew on that power. Called for that burst.

Ptah, hear me, help me.
Nothing happened.

Corso didn't try to count the mecha. He'd seen rats, once, coming out of a flooded drain. These mecha were *that*: a sea of bone-shard carapaces and wispy metal legs that looked (and were) fragile, but were also very good at finding the cracks and seams in armor.

Oh, yes, and good at jumping. Three of them came through the gap in the door, around head height, and flung themselves at Homer. They didn't have wings that Corso could see, or any means of gliding, but they crossed the rapidly spreading gap (Homer having backed the *fuck* up, right quick) and latched onto his rig. Homer began yelling like he was on fire, and Iffy lunged toward him, which left just Corso and Dodri and Luki in front of the door when another multitude came rattling out.

Corso could *hear* them, through external comms. Clicking, thwocking, not at all like Brood and that was what saved him. Because when they hit Homer, Corso flashed to last autumn: the cellar lit by the throbbing horror of Jich'e'enfe's altar, and the slick swirl of boneless coming out of the fissure she'd opened in the aether. His throat sealed up, too tight for screaming, and he forgot about the longcaster and firing and just flailed. Which was how he smacked one of the next wave of bone-crabs with the business end of that 'caster, and how he'd heard the *crunch* that was nothing like boneless (or any Brood he'd ever faced) and everything like the sound shells made when you walked on them.

That sound snapped Corso out of his panic, dropped him back into an adrenaline-soaked suit of muscle and a battle-rig more responsive than any he'd ever worn. These were *killable* things, or at least *breakable*, and breaking, yeah, he could do that. He flipped the 'caster and butt-smashed the one he'd hit first. By the time he went for the second, a third had latched onto his leg, but by then Luki had waded in beside him. Her sword wasn't as good as Iari's axe for smashing, but it worked well enough. Bone cracked and sizzled where the whitefire blade hit.

Homer stopped yelling. Corso couldn't tell why. Dead? Iffy had gotten to him? Couldn't look, because there were *more* of the slagging things coming, more and more again, *where* were they coming from, a fucking nest back there?

He must've blurted some of that out loud, or maybe Luki was asking the same set of questions, because she said, clear and furious, in his comms, "How are they still coming? I've killed a dozen!"

"Same," said Dodri, who sounded gritted-teeth grim and so *very* young.

And Iffy said, breathless, "They put themselves back together, you have to unmake them—!"

Corso spared a look Iffy-ward. She was standing up now, beside a still-living Homer. Llian and Winter Bite had joined Dodri and Homer, which surprised him—when had that happened?—and relieved him in equal parts. Two of the bone-crabs lay at Iffy's feet. Or what Corso assumed had been bone-crabs. Now they looked a lot like the rest of the bone-shard debris in the room.

Then, as if timed for demonstration, Luki stabbed and flipped a bone-crab off her blade so that it splatted onto the remnants of its friends. It *looked* dead, damn near riven in two, down three legs and motionless. (And here Corso paused to whack another one off his knee, where it had latched on, where his rig was reporting damage, *alert, alert*). But when he looked back, Luki's dead mecha was moving, its breach sealed, and two of those three missing legs were *growing*, only not like anything living would. It looked like the legs were assembling themselves whole out of blank aether, becoming visible only when attached to the limb.

It was—fuck if he knew what. *Witchery* was a good word.

As he watched, Iffy pointed and the bone-crab stopped repairing itself, and then, *ffft*, crumbled into a pile of fragments.

Fucking Aedian priests. Fucking Aedian alchemy. Thank all the old gods for *that*.

"How do *we* do that?" Luki speared another bone-crab (one they'd killed already, maybe).

Iffy said, "You can't, I can, just keep breaking them."

Which templars were good at. Which *Corso* was good at, too, except the door through which the resurrecting bone-crabs had come was still open, and seemed to him it might be a good thing to get it closed. So when Luki and Dodri started forking temporarily dead mecha toward Iffy, he went the other way, straight at the door. Ignored Luki's "Corso!" because he didn't take orders and she should be able to figure out what he intended.

"Winter Bite! Help Corso!" Yep. Luki was smart.

So Corso had a riev backing him up, which was better than one sweat-soaked tenju veteran running out of breath because he wasn't in combat trim anymore, not for years. Winter Bite had no bone-crabs dangling off him, which Corso at first took for superior crafting. Little mecha fuckers couldn't get a grip on that plating. But then he saw one of them charging at Winter Bite, and, when it got within half a meter, stop and redirect and come at *him*, instead. Like it'd decided on an easier target. Or like something about Winter Bite repelled it.

Hold that thought, Gaer'll want to know it.

Which made him worry for Gaer, for Iari, and that almost killed him. His battle-rig shrilled a warning, *breach breach* and the schematic showed *helmet* as the breach site. He blinked and then blinked again and nope, he wasn't seeing slag or shit, because there was a fucking bone-crab latched onto his visor, prying at the seams.

He reached up, one-handed, not having thought far enough to drop the 'caster. And then the bone-crab was gone, trailing sparks from the scoring on his faceplate. Winter Bite had it, suspended between two hands. The riev pivoted, snapping the bone-crab's body like a cracker, before flinging it back in Iffy's direction.

Corso splayed his gauntleted hands on the door and tried forcing it closed. It was composed of overlapping segments, should be easy to unfold, but it was fucking *jammed*. Or he just wasn't strong enough, one man alone.

But then Winter Bite came and helped, and together they hauled the door shut. And then the riev smashed the hell out of the frame and some of the segments, warping the metal so that it couldn't open again.

Unless something repaired it. Or something came *through* it. Which made Corso think about Gaer again, and that other mangled door. Iffy could stop these little bony mecha, sure, but Gaer would figure them out.

And then Corso realized he hadn't heard noise from the Gaer-Iari-Char side of the room in a small forever. A whole different flavor of panic stuttered in his chest.

Iari might've gotten busy. Or Iari might've gotten dead.

Corso pointed himself at the other door and the other fight, and ran toward it.

There was no particular trick to killing a riev. It was bringing them back, after—*not* frying the delicate galvanics, *not* reducing the organic components to slag. If you interrupted the artificing, decay could (did) set in, and depending on the age of whatever was underneath all that plating, it could happen very quickly. Artificing suspended time, somehow, and Gaer had to figure how to suspend the suspension, and then put it back again, before Char rotted to slurry.

This *setatir* trap-hex had been thrown from somewhere rather than triggered like most riev-traps were. More like a net. A projectile net. A, a *homing* net. The analogy broke there, but that was fine. Gaer knew where to look now, among the equations, for seeker code. And yes, there it was—well, *setat*, it was a Protectorate hex grafted in there. Old Protectorate, pre-Schism. A hundred-year-old vakari hex, nested here among equations profoundly not vakari, stripped and repurposed to look for some combination of animate mechanical wrapped around organic tissue, to kill the mechanical and leave the organic alive and intact. That meant battle-rigged soldiers or, quite by accident—riev.

Gaer solved that relic, nullified it, plucked it loose from the other tendrils to which it was grafted. He chased those connections, trying to find the points in this *setatir* web where the hexes were that held Char immobile.

A vibration shivered through the floor, rattling out of the corridor. Something hard hitting something harder, either heavy or thrown with great force. He winced.

The beauty of a vakari Five Tribes battle-rig was that it could display many layers of aether on *this* layer, organizing it all neatly on a HUD (never mind what his optic could do. So *many* layers needed for arithmancy). So he could *see* those *setatir* equations and Char's incandescent aural distress *and* the—oh dark lords, those were sparks coming out of the tunnel, sparks and tendrils of smoke.

Turn into plasma, Gaer wished at Iari. *Who cares Notch is watching, just do it, kill the mecha, save yourself.*

Or he could do his job, and free Char. Or kill them.

"I'm sorry," he said, suspecting Char could hear him. "This could kill you."

Char sounded like powdered glass and a sackful of stones. "Do. It."

Which, yes, made him look with his eyes on the material aetheric layer, through the visor and at the riev who shouldn't've been able to talk and was, anyway.

So the trap wasn't perfect. Or Char wasn't, because Char wasn't entirely riev, Char had an Aedis prosthetic arm to replace one they'd lost at Saichi during the surge.

That was his way in.

Gaer refocused and tunneled into those equations into Char's prosthetic, winding past the numbers, the variables. This was Aedis arithmancy, Aedis alchemy, and his understanding was imperfect. But he'd helped repair this very arm rather recently, and he knew just enough to pick his way through the seams on the mecha-graft where the new armor mated up with the old. Where the metal frame of the limb fused onto the bone of some long-dead tenju, whoever Char *had* been (oh *setat*, don't think closely on that, not now).

His visor's aetheric perspective warped, then refocused, but not on a new layer of aether, exactly—more like a new neighborhood in the old layer. Char's guts, in an arithmantic sense. So *many* hexes in here, most etched onto bone, onto filaments too small to see without better optics, that threaded through muscle and skin and anchored to the underside of the armor. Vessels moving liquid other than blood. Gaer followed that network over the border of the new graft and into Char proper. Nerves shuttled electricity, bordering on normal life—except where that same electricity powered the battle-hexed armor. It was the electricity

Gaer wanted to stop, just long enough for the trap to register *dead* on the armor plate and let go. In a living body, he would've gone for the heart. Easy to stop. Easy-ish to restart. But a riev didn't have a heart (a joke for an optimistic later), a riev had a whole *setatir* network of dispersed power cells and arithmantic redundancies. Riev were meant to take the worst a vakar trooper (or, later, Brood) could throw, and keep coming. Fry the system wholesale, yes, he could do that, but restart all of it again?

He could. He had to. The mecha arm had its own power core, independent of all that riev artificing. That would do. (Or it wouldn't, and he'd kill Char.)

Gaer sketched out a brace of equations, one to carry the message, the other the message itself, and sent them zapping along Char's network. Waited a forever beat (on this layer of aether; on Iari's layer, this was the time between heartbeats) for that message to travel.

Suspend operations.

And, as Char's systems began a cascading failure, he wove another hex and wound it all through Char's arm and set it on remote trigger.

Then he got himself out, fast, back the way he'd come, until he floated on the aetheric layer nearest material reality. It was like being submerged and looking up through the water, everything blurred into edgeless color.

But color was all he needed.

On the material layer, visible in his optic, Char's aura went blank and awful.

On *this* layer, where things were clear, the riev trap went blank and glorious.

Gaer triggered his new hex.

Restart.

He held his breath and watched as Char's arm lit up from the fingertips, hexes flaring red and alive as the arm's power core came online, sequencing, building charge. He watched as that hex-wave hit the graft point.

And waited for the next stage of, oh, call it ignition.

And waited.

More chaos from across the room now, yelling, the sizzle of whitefire. The discoloration on his optics' periphery that said some-one was throwing hexes, but not at him, and so he could ignore it.

Setat, come *on.* He didn't know how long the reignition would take. *If* it would take. But it had to come soon—

Char's aura went suddenly nova. Gaer let himself cheer, in his helmet's confines, one little airless whoop.

Then he got the *setat* out of the way, because turns out a riev coming back from the dead didn't come preloaded with balance, and Char landing on him might be an irony that broke bones.

He hadn't heard Iari demanding a miracle from him in at least a minute, and in a battle, a minute was forever. That the hostile mecha had not emerged from the tunnel yet was potentially good, unless its corpse and Iari's were in there together. Gaer shoved himself upright and propelled himself into the corridor with one hand on the ruined door, the other clawing the wall.

—And saw Iari reaching down with her shield arm for Notch, who took it carefully, who had a hand free to take it because *his* axe was stuck in the spark-bleeding back (front? top?) of the mecha.

Gaer arrested his forward progress and hung there, braced be-tween the walls.

"Gaer! *Gaer!*"

That was Corso, raggedy-breathless on comms, his rig still a meter behind and coming fast.

"Captain's fine," Gaer said, because he needed to hear it himself. Maybe everyone did. At least one other person on comms let their breath out hard, with what sounded a lot like relief. And then he added, because he wasn't *entirely* an ass, "The lieutenant's fine, too.—Iari. Where's the second mecha?"

Her visor flashed silver in his headlamp as she turned, a molten trick of reflection. Then it retracted and it was just her face looking back, beads of sweat and that twisted-up grin she got whenever she fought. Gaer didn't think she knew she did that. But her eyes weren't smiling. They weren't even furious, or accusatory (because he had taken his sweet *setatir* time with Char, who was grating around out there, in some stage of recovery). Those remarkable green eyes were . . . a little afraid, and that scared Gaer more than anything else so far had.

Iari's voice, though, was steady. "There was a second one. Ran away when Notch killed this one."

"When *we* killed it, Captain." Notch was standing under his own power now, one hand on the wall like he didn't trust his balance. His chestplate smoked from multiple scorch marks.

Iari prodded the mecha with her foot. It slid farther than Gaer thought it should. Lighter than it looked, then.

"Captain." Char sounded like they had been vomited out of all five hells. "Lieutenant. Ambassador—thank you."

Iari's gaze sharpened. Gaer glanced back, a little guiltily. Char *looked* fine, if you didn't know that their hexes should be uniformly lit up, not greyed out in patches.

"I'm sorry," he said. "That took too long."

Char leveled those cold blue teslas at him. "The trap is gone. The goal is achieved." Their aura sank toward the cerulean. No hard feelings, at least.

"There were little ones," Corso blurted.

He looked like another hell-vomit, Gaer noticed then. Actual gouges on his battle-rig, where something had gone for the joints.

"Little . . . Brood?" Because that was the only thing Gaer could think of that could damage Aedis armor like that.

"Little crab-mecha." Corso waved at the bigger corpse. "Like that, except made out of bone. Veek—sorry, Gaer, *vakari* bone, I think. Bone, anyway. They came out of that other door and swarmed us. They could put themselves back together, and they did until Iffy took 'em apart. They ran *away* from Winter Bite."

"Huh." Iari side-eyed Notch, who had just wrenched his axe loose and stopped to rest again. "Maybe that's why the second one ran. Didn't like the new odds, with Char loose."

"Wait. You saying there was *another* big one over here?" Corso sounded indignant.

"At *least* one more." Iari looked at Gaer. "Your *several or many* . . ."

"Is an accurate prediction. Yes."

"Shit," muttered Corso. "Definitely sucks to be right."

CHAPTER FOUR

"I t's not arithmancy. Not entirely," Gaer was saying. He squatted beside Iffy, both of them hovering over the big mecha's corpse. They had set up a makeshift lab on a clearish patch of floor near the tunnel mouth. ("Because that's where we have to go eventually," Iari had said, for everyone's confirmation. No one had looked surprised.)

"Not entirely alchemy, either." Iffy had her visor up and her nose closer than Iari liked to the carapace, staring at . . . something. Elements knew what. Alchemy, arithmancy—Iari knew the difference on the most basic level. Alchemy concerned itself with physical states and state-changes, sometimes substances; it was the underpinning of Aedis orthodoxy. Arithmancy was the parent discipline (Gaer said *superior*, but Gaer was a snob), numbers and mathematics and manipulating reality itself.

Not that Iari could spare much attention to whatever Iffy and Gaer had discovered, just now, except peripherally. She had cleared out her own space a few meters away, and was running a triage on the battle-rigs. Most of the damage was superficial. Corso had taken the worst of it, looked like, though she hadn't gotten a good look at Notch's rig yet. He was insisting on going last, that he was fine; Iari reckoned he just wanted to hover over Gaer and Iffy and be suspicious of everything. Char was the worst off, but Iari couldn't do anything with their hexes. Gaer could, maybe. Char said they would self-repair. Iari hoped the riev's protestations of *fine* were more honest than hers would have been.

"The bone-mecha things," Iffy was saying. "They had something like alchemy on them, too, but it wasn't quite. Betting that if it's not the same hexwork as this bigger metal thing, it's close."

"Except that *you* stopped the bone constructs." Gaer raised his head and squinted at Iffy. "Corso said you, what, unmade them? If Aedian priest-hexes—which are bastard alchemy—work, then that suggests whatever animated the bone mecha *must* be some kind of *setatir* alchemy too."

"You're telling me about alchemy, now, Gaer? Really?"

"He's asking for it." Corso pitched his voice low, for Iari's ears only. "She's going to unmake *him*."

"If alchemy was all it took to kill a vakar, we wouldn't've needed riev to win the war." Iari squeezed a few drops of emergency sealant into a minuscule breach on Corso's backplate and pushed the edges together. The power core hummed against her fingertips. You didn't notice that vibration, all gauntleted up, or inside the armor. It took bare skin to detect.

Corso craned his head around. His faceplate was open, and the teslas rimming his helmet stripped his face colorless. "You really think we won that war?"

Iari grunted. On her lips to say *no*, or at least make a face that got the point across, but then Notch whipped around, evidently tired of looming over Gaer, and interjected:

"You think we *didn't*?"

Corso did not grace him with a look. "You seen the Weep? Yeah? You and I have a different idea of what winning looks like, Lieutenant."

Ungentle Ptah. Notch had an *effect* on Corso. Iari slapped the back of Corso's rig under the auspices of checking the patch-seal, and he choked back whatever retort he'd intended.

"We did not win, Lieutenant." Char had positioned themself to stare sentry down the tunnel. Now they turned to Notch. The reflection from their optics blued the edge of his helmet and his tusks (unbroken, uncapped), as he opened his mouth to argue.

"How do you figure that, Private?"

"I was there." Char waited a beat, and added, "Sir."

"In the *Expansion*, you were there? Before the Aedis, before the Accords? That was, what, one hundred years—?"

Char tilted their head. "Yes, sir."

Notch gaped.

Iari patted Corso's rig. "You're done. Lieutenant? You said you had an alert on the HUD."

"It's—"

"Gone? No? Then come here."

Her tone didn't say *request*; Notch got it. He came over and submitted somewhat sullenly to Iari's examination. Quietly, too, though he divided whitefire scowls between Corso and Char. Iari pretended to examine his backplate. It was dented to all of Gaer's five hells, but the power cell seemed fine. No cracks. But there was a piece over the rib cage she wasn't sure about. She pushed his elbow up and leaned in to look.

And said, "That was well done back there, killing that mecha. You got up fast." *Thanks* stuck in her throat. His job, wasn't it? And hers, both of them, to win fights and keep people from dying.

Red crept up the rims of his ears. He found a new place to stare at. "Ah. Yeah. The syn, it really *moves*, you know?"

"Not used to it?" Softly, *softly*, because Corso didn't need to hear the exact shade of green that Notch was, lest he have more ammunition for later squabbles. (Char probably could hear, at their range; but Char didn't squabble. Or rather, Char didn't *start* squabbles.)

Notch dropped his gaze, his volume—deflated a little, shrinking into the rig's hard confines. "Not . . . like that. Not in the field."

"Mm." She couldn't tell him it would get easier. Or that he'd get used to it. Or, what was really chewing her insides, what she desperately *needed* to tell Gaer—at least his syn was working. Hers hadn't. Well. The regular one had, the little flood of nanomecha-driven adrenaline. But not . . . the other kind. The plasma. The whatever had happened first in the basement in B-town, when Jich'e'enfe made a tiny Weep fissure and dropped Brood on everyone's head. "Well done anyway."

He peered at her from under his raised elbow. "You were army first, weren't you? Before the Aedis."

"Mm." Most used word of the day. There was a tiny split in the panel, smaller than Corso's. She sealed it the same way and then checked her HUD's diagnostics. It reported everyone's battle-rig status. Notch's was definitely still yellow. She opened a panel in her gauntlet and plucked out a tiny cable. Pain in the ass, this part.

Notch was still watching, looking expectant. She made a face he couldn't see behind the visor. "So was Corso. Served together, he and I."

"But he quit. You"—

(—*found religion? Or you just have a death wish?*—)

—"joined the Aedis."

"Doesn't make him a coward."

"I didn't say that."

"Didn't have to." She had said it, back then; she knew the expression on Notch's face from the inside. Truth was, she'd *had* religion, had the Elements, even before she joined the Aedis. Corso hadn't. Didn't now, unless he actually believed in the old tenju traditions, and she was pretty sure he didn't.

"You weren't there," she said quietly. "In the surge. Corso was."

"No. But I *have* fought Brood. They come out of the fissure up here, sometimes."

"There's fighting a boneless or three, or even a whole pack of them, and then there's what *we* did. Confederation military isn't Aedis, all right? You might've quit, too, if you fought with the kit that we had. Try a reboot, see if that clears the alert off your HUD."

Notch's face said he would *not* have quit, but his mouth stayed mercifully shut. Her feed from his rig went blank as he rebooted.

"Corso's here now. So're we. On the same side, all of us." She laid a little more weight and edge on the *all*. Iari reckoned Notch was smart (whatever Gaer's opinion). He'd get it.

He blew out a breath. "Understood." He looked at her, but pitched his voice for Corso. "I got lucky. That fucker wasn't trying to peel me open."

Corso glanced over. Iari watched him make calculations, conclusions. Then he coughed up a laugh. "I don't know about lucky."

"I was. We only had two over here. You had—a lot more than that. And we could smash ours to death. Yours grew back."

"Huh." Corso pretended great interest in his own gauntlet. "That's true."

And that fast, Notch and Corso were, if not friends, at least not fighting, either.

Iari checked her HUD. The reboot had *not* cleared the querulous yellow advisement off Notch's rig. It wasn't even a specific alert. Just . . . something. Might be attitude from the battle-rig's onboard turing. Might be something worse. The rig's rudimentary med-scan said Notch had bruises, which the nano would repair in short order. No reason for that yellow alert she could see.

"I don't know what's the matter with your rig," she told Notch. "No option to deal with it now; might be nothing. But you keep an eye on it, Notch, tell me if something's wrong in there. Or if something feels off." She paused on the edge of the longer speech—*your condition affects us all, you play tough young officer and your rig fails, one of us might die*—and waited.

Notch looked unhappy. Probably like he'd rather eat that dead mecha than admit any weakness, ever, to anyone. She saw the sense of her directive strike home, spread out like ripples in a pond of tenju stubborn. "Yes, Captain."

"Go collect everyone. We're leaving in two."

Notch nodded. Iari watched him take a deep breath, watched him put that templar lieutenant armor back on, attitude, not hardware. That just-on-the-edge-of-swaggering confidence that he projected like a headlamp. She watched Homer and Dodri turn toward it, watched them straighten up a little more. Llian didn't react, but Llian was busy with Winter Bite in the far corner, poking through debris.

And Luki—huh. *That* was a look aimed at Notch, and not one bit admiring. Iari had a guess why. Notch was swinging his rank around without regard for Luki's experience, or despite it, or just (Iari's suspicion) not really thinking about how he came off. Windscar wasn't B-town. Knight-Marshal Keawe didn't put much weight on diplomacy. Didn't have to. And clearly didn't teach Windscar troops any either.

Iari added *unpleasant conversation* to her growing list of duties and stood up, winding her cable back into her gauntlet, and took herself over to Char. Their attention *appeared* to be entirely pointed into the corridor; Iari knew them well enough to know better. Iari joined them, staring into the dark. Her eyes couldn't see much beyond the dim bleed from everyone's headlamps.

Smudges. Shadows. Couldn't hear anything, except Gaer and Iffy, who had decided that the hexwork on the hostile mecha was both alchemical *and* arithmantic, though unfamiliar.

Iari side-eyed Char. "Do you recognize the hexes? Are they k'bal?"

"I do not know. I am old, but I was never an arithmancer." Char paused. "Or an alchemist."

Iari wanted to know why Char sounded so sure of it; her understanding—which came from Gaer, who admittedly had some issues with the process—was that riev didn't remember who they'd been *because they're* dead, *Iari, sss, that's the horror of them*

before whatever it was wichu artificing did. Had done. Confederation treaty forbade the artificing of new riev, in this era of mutual alliance against the Weep and whatever came out of it. That was concession to Five Tribe sensibilities. If it'd been just the Protectorate's protest, Iari bet the Confederation would still be making them. It had been the Protectorate's Expansion that'd made riev necessary in the first place; it had been *their* rebel clients, the wichu, who'd figured out galvanics and created the riev. But then the Five Tribes schismed off from the Protectorate, and allied with the Confederation—helped turn the war around, in a way even the riev hadn't. And since the Five Tribes had objected to riev, too, on religious grounds—that was the end of the riev-kilns. The Confederation didn't shit on its allies. Or at least, the first parliament hadn't.

Iari wondered if the wichu had objected to the parliament's decision back then. If riev had been their revenge on the vakari (all vakari, Five Tribe allies and Protectorate alike) as much as their gift to the Confederation. If they'd always planned—hoped—they'd get to finish the extermination, someday. Or, ugly thought, turn their old overlords into riev themselves.

That was a question for some time when monsters weren't hiding in a dark they all had to go into. A more pertinent question, the one a captain should be asking her templar, was: "How are you?"

She could see well enough. Char's hexwork crawled (mostly) blue, brightest on the prosthetic arm, intermittently grey on the body, the legs.

And Char, being Char and not an anxious young templar trying to impress her, didn't try to deny it. "I am functioning adequately, but imperfectly. And you, Captain?"

Char deserved more than a half-truth. Iari might be their captain, but Char worked better with more information, not less. "Same."

Char's stylized tenju features didn't move. Riev hadn't been built for expressions. (Hadn't been built for sentience, either, or personal pronouns, and certainly not for becoming Aedian templars, and yet here they were.) "And the lieutenant?"

"Something's wrong with his rig. Not sure what. I can't find anything mechanical." Her gut knotted around the admission. She didn't know what the problem was, she couldn't *fix* it. If she couldn't fix it—ungentle Ptah. Then she couldn't fix it. She ran the relevant lines of Jareth's *Meditations* through her mind like well-worn prayer beads (what they were, honestly): *Determine what is within your power to effect, and what is beyond your power. Spend your effort on the former, and put the latter out of your mind.*

Right. Jareth hadn't written *Meditations* on his first field command, either. The problem with Notch's rig could signal some new breach of Aedian hexes, something with his nanomecha. No one—not Sister Diran, not Iffy, not even Gaer—were certain how the poor, contaminated riev Sawtooth had passed their infection to Iari's nanomecha in the first place. *Could* have been through a hole in her rig. She'd had a few. Notch had had a breach, too, and there were all sorts of stray unknown hexes around here.

Char's voice dipped to whispers. "You are going to ask the ambassador about the lieutenant's battle-rig."

"I'm *going* to ask Iffy about everything. The ambassador will overhear and offer his opinion." And then it wouldn't look like she was consulting the Five Tribes ambassador-turned-special-attaché-to-the-Aedis for advice on proprietary Aedian hexes, only like he'd proven helpful when offered the opportunity. Keawe (because that's whom Notch would report to) would not like Gaer's involvement, but she wouldn't object to results. Hopefully.

"Ask me what?" Iffy materialized at Iari's elbow. Alwar skin came in a spectrum ranging from blue-black to an opaque, milky pale. Iffy was one of the light ones. Her nose and cheeks were red, fading back to pallid, probably because she'd been bent over the mecha and forgotten to breathe.

Iari looked back toward the mecha. "Your opinion on the Fifth Canticle of Mishka. Is the reference to sea foam literal, or allegorical?"

Iffy snorted. "Allegorical. Obviously. But seriously—ah." Iffy followed Iari's gaze. "You need Gaer."

"I *need* you both. But I don't need Windscar to know that. I came over here to talk to Char."

Iffy made a noise. "Mishka's sweet *sake*. Templar politics."

Gaer, who'd no doubt heard the whole exchange—they were well within vakari earshot, even if Iari had no idea where those ears really were on his bony head—chose that moment to glide over. His battle-rig was lighter than templar standard, lighter even than Iffy's priest-armor, and made of some amalgam that looked like oil on water, pink and green and slick, where the light broke against it.

"I think I heard my name, and the dreaded phrase, *templar politics*. Should I take myself elsewhere?"

Iari stared at him. "No. Wanted to ask you about the hexes on that mecha, and what happened to Char. What are we looking at?"

"What got Char was a fragment from an Expansion-era riev-hex, left over and apparently overlooked when the large mecha was repurposed into whatever purpose it serves now. Its hexes are not like Jich'e'enfe's innovations, in that they do not invite Brood into the systems they breach. But the theory is related, and the approach I saw here is consistent with some of the k'bal theory I've read, which would track if *they* were the ones to repurpose the vakari code—"

"Gaer."

"Sss. Fine. I don't think the hexes knew what they were looking at. They weren't aimed at riev. In any case—it was part of the attacking mecha's battle-hex array, and not scribed onto the floor itself. It threw the hex like a net."

"Fantastic. And the reanimated bone mecha? Are they also k'bal creations?"

Gaer looked at Iffy, who flapped her hands. "I don't know. I don't think so. It's mostly alchemy, anyway, holding them together. Those hexes were *related* to the healing properties of Aedian hexes—reassembling broken living things, right? Except those bones are not living, they're dead, but they're still animated. In that way it's more like the wichu artificing used on the riev, in that—"

"Iffy. I'm a templar."

Iffy made a face, delicate alwar features drawing together in irritation, wide blue eyes trying to look fiercely narrow and failing at fierce. "I don't find that impedes comprehension, generally. But fine. The *point*, Captain"—(oh ho, *now* Iari knew she was in trouble: her name traded for her rank)—"is that the bone mecha hexes look a little more like galvanism, which *is* what the wichu used to animate riev, because riev are made out of dead—" She side-eyed Gaer, amended, "—out of formerly living organic material. Except not *quite*. But related. And newer than the hexes that hit Char." She side-eyed Gaer again.

Who said, "We don't know that *for certain*. There are some equations on that big mecha no one's used since Kin'jatt-i—oh, never mind. Since *before* the Weep. They're Expansion-era. Maybe pre. Perhaps the bone mecha were the product of collusion between wichu and k'bal during the Expansion, when they were both trying to avoid the Protectorate troops. We *did* theorize that possibility. Or perhaps it's a parallel innovation by Jich'e'enfe's little collection of separatists. It doesn't matter, except academically, for our purposes here."

Iari blinked at him. "Did you just say some arithmantic minutiae *doesn't matter*?"

"Sss. I do not know *how* one reanimates bones, nor how one convinces them to organize themselves to look like mecha. But as long as Iffy can unmake them, for now, *no*. It does not matter whether they are old hexes or some new horror the wichu separatists thought up."

"Any sign of hexes targeting the Aedis in specific?"

And oh, Gaer's head snapped around. "Why do you ask?"

Iari told them about Notch's yellow alert. "Could be a turing thing with his rig, but . . ."

"But," said Gaer, "you don't think so. You think it's the rig or his nanomecha affected?"

"If it's the rig, I can't find the problem. I'm going to say nanomecha."

"Oh, Mishka's tears." Iffy looked horrified. "If his nano go down like yours did—"

"He is going to feel awful and his syn won't work. Keep an eye on him, Iffy."

"Yes. Right." Iffy blew out a breath, then shoved to her feet.

Iari waited until she was out of earshot. "Nothing happened. I tried to—you know. It didn't work."

Gaer's head tilted so that he was mostly looking at her through his optic. Reading her aura, probably, gauging how worried she really was. "You think *you* were hacked?"

"No. Maybe. Maybe I just can't control the effect yet. Maybe it only works when we're dealing with Brood." Void and dust, ungentle Ptah, she should've told Tobin before. Sooner. "If this thing with Notch is serious—if we have battle-hexes attacking our systems now, Aedis systems specifically, what do we do?"

Gaer's chromatophores shifted from neutral to faint orange distress. "We can't *do* anything. Your nanomecha repaired themselves, given time. If that is why they did not—flare up . . . if there was another hack, they will probably evolve again. I can try to offer defenses if, or when, there's another attack."

"So, soon then," said Iari. "Because you know they're up there—"

Then Char's voice filled the entire chamber, level and deep and galvanic-cool. Only the volume revealed the alarm. "Contact. The mecha return."

CHAPTER FIVE ═══════

Gaer had time to parse the subject-verb agreement, to realize Char meant *plural* mecha, before the templars leapt into motion. The hiss of whitefire shields and weapons coming online, that rattle and *bang* as battle-rigs crossed the debris, some more gracefully than others.

Iari, being Iari, simply stepped in front of him. "Fall back," she said, as her visor sealed. And then, thin and echoing, in Gaer's unsealed helmet: "Void and dust, Gaer. Close your visor."

Right, because he had forgotten the *last* time he and Iari had fought together, battling Brood and a wichu arithmancer in a B-town cellar, when he'd also taken a faceful of hostile arithmancy, along with shards of his visor, and spent almost a month in the Aedis hospice.

There was no time for that retort. He sealed his visor and cycled his optic to standby; it would work inside his rig, but there wasn't as much for it to *do*. A vakari battle-rig came preloaded with battle-hexes; it wasn't designed for spontaneous arithmancy. The optic was. And he had a feeling he'd need them both when he faced whatever came out of that corridor.

Iffy had retreated behind an entirely inadequately small barrier of broken chairs and crouched, compounding her smallness.

She gestured at Gaer, as if he'd fit back there with her. Or as if he had any intention of doing what he'd been told.

Gaer waved at her and yes, did move out of direct alignment with the open corridor. He couldn't sense anything up there—Char's range was better than his, always. But the sooner he *saw* what it was, either arithmantically or with his actual eyes, the sooner he could work up some kind of defense.

Though that might be complicated, because—

"The mecha are retreating again," Char said.

Someone—Homer, Gaer thought—let out a tiny, under-the-breath cheer. Someone else—definitely Notch—swore on one of Hrok's body parts.

"They know they're outnumbered," said Luki, with a firmness Gaer only partly believed. But he wasn't Luki's audience, either. Llian, Dodri, Homer—Notch, too, though he'd hate it—they were.

"Maybe." Iari hesitated. Then, as if the words tasted bad, "Or they're doing recon to set up an ambush further in. Luki, with me. The rest of you, wait here."

Then Iari actually *started walking* up the corridor with Luki, not Notch, and where—? Gaer looked. The lieutenant was at the rear of the assembling templars, probably because Iari was throwing orders around on a templar-only comm channel. It wouldn't be because he'd developed a sense of caution (or sense at all, since an unreliable rig shouldn't take point). Winter Bite, too, held in the rear—not happily, if Gaer read his body language correctly. The appendage in Winter Bite's chest flexed and flared, and, yes, when Gaer looked, the riev's aura was threaded with impatience and annoyance.

Winter Bite's aura was also brighter than it had been months ago, Gaer noted, though it was not yet as bright as Char's. Hm.

Char, at least, was holding position, as was everyone else. Gaer crept forward until he could just make out the tiny teslas on the back of the Luki and Iari's battle-rigs. They were moving carefully up the corridor; Gaer could see, in the glow from their headlamps, a whole lot of nothing.

"I can't do a *setatir* thing from back here. She knows that, doesn't she?" Low-voiced, but on the external comms.

"She knows." Corso materialized at Gaer's side. His visor was still open, which was so unsafe—oh, *setat*, so very Corso.

"Sss. She set you aside, too?"

"What? No. Yes. Years ago." Corso shook his head hard. "Listen. The bone-crabs *avoided* Winter Bite. I wanted to tell you. They ran at me, at Homer, at Iffy—everyone but Winter Bite."

"That's odd." Gaer said it absently, placeholder speech. He was thinking about Notch and Aedis-seeking hexes. About holes in defenses.

(Up the corridor, Iari was saying something about "hold position" and please dark lords, she followed her own orders. There was some connection he hadn't figured out yet. He didn't want her charging into another fight until he had.)

Corso smacked his rig, not gently, and Gaer's HUD flashed warning. "That's it? Odd?"

"Sss," Gaer whipped his head around, thrusting his visor somewhat close to Corso's naked face. Snark coiled up in his throat—*of course they avoided the riev, Corso, look at you, the far softer target*—but then Gaer really did look. Corso stood beside him, cradling that ancient longcaster that Gaer wouldn't've used as a walking stick. He was shorter than Gaer (everyone was, except Char), his broad tenju frame made bigger in the battle-rig. Huh. An Aedis, templar battle-rig, and Corso was one of the two people who'd needed actual patching.

"Corso. Your rig is all right? No alerts?"

Corso frowned. "It is now. I *had* one, when the little bone fucker cracked my power-cell casing, but it cleared when Iari patched me. Why?"

Gaer shook his head slightly. Realized Corso couldn't see the gesture and flicked his fingers instead. "Notch's rig has a persistent alert."

Corso absorbed that bit of intelligence with a grimace (he didn't like Notch, Gaer knew) that faded to thoughtful. "So that's why she sent him to the back. I don't get why Winter Bite, though, and not Char."

"Because if those mecha throw any more of those hexes, they could kill him. Char's different. Except. Sss." Gaer took a moment, a breath—as Iari started calling up templars, Char first, because she probably needed riev senses—and *thought*.

The bone mecha had physically avoided Winter Bite, who had no Aedis hexwork. The metal mecha had gone straight for Char, arithmantically and not physically, confident in the efficiency of their battle-hexes. And *maybe* bone and metal mecha shared nothing except this location, *maybe* their programming and origins were as different as their material construction, *maybe* the bone mecha just remembered being vakari and terrified of riev, but that seemed unnecessarily complicated. The k'bal had valued efficiency in their arithmancy. The metal mecha had hit Char because they'd seen a vulnerability in their armor, that border between Aedis and wichu hexes. Winter Bite didn't *have* that.

Gaer looked at Notch. Oh, five kinds of stupid, this. He was literally going behind Iari's back with her second-in-command. But he wasn't going to private-channel her in the middle of what might be the last moments before a mecha ambush, and he wasn't going to plead with her to trust him in front of everyone. She'd listen, she trusted him, he knew that, but that knowledge wouldn't comfort everyone *else*.

He keyed a private link. "Lieutenant. You need to send Winter Bite forward. Right now. The bone mecha avoided him. There's a chance the metal ones will, too; I think they target obvious breaches and vulnerabilities—any breaks they detect in a pattern. Char's armor has that, because of their arm. Winter Bite doesn't. I don't want to distract Iari, so—please."

Notch did not answer.

Oh, for the love of—"Winter Bite," Gaer said, on external comms. "Did you hear my conversation with Corso?"

Winter Bite turned to look at Gaer. The riev's armored exof-rame was a frosted pewter, which should've reflected the light and drank it up instead, etched all over with hexes a shade darker than the metal itself. One of his tentacles in his chest bobbed in Gaer's direction, flicking (*licking*, oh dark lords why had he thought that) the aether. "I did, Ambassador."

"Then go now." *Please*, Winter Bite showed a sliver of Char's initiative.

Winter Bite slid into motion with unnatural grace for some-thing made out of artificed armor and galvanic heresy. Maybe his original self had been a dancer. Dark lords, *perish* that thought.

"Lieutenant," said Iari, "You bring up the rear."

Still no response. Gaer looked over at Notch, who was trying to move—a step that did not go very well, as if the rig was mired in gelatin. Gaer arrested his own forward progress and diverted.

"Lieutenant?" Gaer kept himself on private comms. "Are you all right?"

And *still* no answer.

Corso circled back in a clomping of battle-rig. He'd closed his faceplate, finally, and his comm signal blinked on a private channel until Gaer opened the link.

"The hell you waiting for?"

"Notch." Gaer started for Notch with long strides. He shifted his perception sideways into the aether, into the layer where code lived, and fired a simple exploratory hex at Notch. The battle-rig—had it been healthy, whole, undamaged—should have snatched his code out of the aether, crumpled it up, and thrown it back at him as a warning. Instead his equation slid past the rig's defenses.

Well.

There were people in SPERE who'd like very much to see Aedian code from the inside, the guts and bones of it. Even guts and bones this compromised. Gaer's hex tangled in a knot of new code, something both elegant and invasive, very *much* like the hex that had infected Iari in B-town, except with the efficiency that Gaer had come to associate with k'bal arithmancy. The k'bal had been pacifists, however, and *this* code was not benign. Gaer could see where the variables could be adjusted *just so*, and the hex would slide neatly, and unnoticed, through the Aedis code. But this invader wasn't trying to sneak. It was drilling precision holes in the codes, gracefully slicing off variables, delicately overwriting whole equations to breach the defenses.

He could also see that this batch of code was running into an unholy mashup of alchemy and arithmancy that *had* to be Aedis nanomecha. *Templar* nanomecha, since Gaer knew from Iffy that priests got a different set. Templar rigs connected with templar bodies through the needle-socket in the back of templar skulls, which was—sss, horrible, appalling, *revolting* (fascinating). Presumably the nanomecha ran both ways, machine to meat, at will. Presumably—big presumption, check with Iffy later—Notch's nano would respond to this attack on his rig as personally as if it had been against his body. Which meant any contamination it was carrying would travel fast.

"Gaer." Iari's voice cracked through his helmet, private channel. "Notch's comms are out. What's going on?"

Should I send someone back, she meant, and *where the* setat *are you.*

"The lieutenant's rig is attempting self-repair." Which wasn't a lie. Technically. Gaer flipped that channel closed, and opened the private to Corso.

"Something's wrong with Notch's rig. I think he'll recover, but if he doesn't—"

"I need you up *here*, Gaer," said Iari, and Gaer's guts clenched.

"I'll stay with him," Corso said, private-channel. "You go."

So Gaer went.

The mecha were fucking with them. Iari knew they were up there. She could hear them sometimes through the helmet's audio feed. Clashing of steel on stone, one of those legs (maybe more than one). That was on purpose, *bet* it was. Both mecha had come out of the corridor fast and silent when they'd intended to kill her and Notch.

"You hear that?" Luki sounded hesitant, maybe scared, maybe embarrassed. She was asking on external comms, anyway, which argued she didn't want anyone but Iari to hear the question.

"The mecha stomping around up there? Yeah. They want us to hear. They're trying to get us to chase them."

"I—" Luki stopped and thought that over. "Can they do that?"

"Mecha are as smart as their programmers. You've seen the ones in the hospice. And these are probably k'bal-made, with special hexing by wichu separatists."

"Right," Luki breathed. "Kind of surprised we haven't run into them yet. The wichu, I mean."

"Me too." And two templars walking into an ambush alone was just bad decision-making.

Iari held up a fist, *stop*, and led by example. The battle-rig could do limited topographical scans, something about bouncing a hex off hard surfaces. Gaer would know what it was called. Iari just knew it worked, mostly, and that right now her HUD was reporting an empty passage that curved along to the right, following what she guessed was the shape of the hill above. She could *just* see a cross-corridor up ahead, where the tunnel split left and continued.

She could also see a pair of doors on either side of the corridor before that cross-corridor. Or what she assumed were doors: tall and narrow, and sealed with some kind of segmented panel. They reminded Iari of window shades. Probably sturdier. Maybe. And there could be a dozen mecha behind any of them.

And more disturbing—it was getting darker in the hallway. Or more intently dark, thick like mist coming off the Rust River some mornings. Except mist and fog were grey when teslas hit them, and this—if it was a *this*, and not her imagination—was just black. Luki hadn't commented on it, but Luki was also on her flank and might not notice the effect, between both rigs' headlamps. Or Luki might be waiting for *her* to deal with it.

Iari sidled forward and over to the nearest door, on her left. Had to shift the shield to lay her gauntlet on it. The rig didn't detect any vibrations. No heat. No cold. Just synthetics and metal. No Brood or anything else that set off the battle-rig.

Her gut said there was nothing inside, and every slagging second they delayed to clear the rooms would mean *that* much longer that Elements-be-damned mecha had to either get away or set up an ambush.

And on the other hand—doors like *these* had already coughed up bone mecha, so they probably rated investigation, and by more than just her and Luki.

She got on the open comms and issued orders, and waited while the rig markers on her HUD sorted themselves into motion. Char first, because—well, Char was closest, Char's sensory hexes were far superior to the battle-rig's, and truth, they were *Char*.

And even though he wouldn't like it: "Lieutenant, you bring up the rear," because Notch's rig was yellow—

Oh. No. It was orange, now, and when had *that* happened? That was bad, a captain not noticing one of her templar's rigs had gone bad to worse. But his vitals were fine, and that readout was easier to see; and truth, she'd been too busy trying to see through the dark up ahead and listening. So yeah, maybe she had some good reasons not to've noticed Notch's orangey-ness, but it didn't make her feel better.

Char arrived, then, and Iari cast a critical eye across their hexwork. The sporadic grey flickers were still there, but they seemed less frequent. And Char's cold blue teslas were steady. And, the real reason Iari was staring—the glow coming off all those parts of Char wasn't getting far, either, in the murk.

"Three problems," Iari said, quietly and on external comms, for Char and Luki only. "First, these doors. We need to clear the rooms. Second, we've heard the mecha moving around. That seems deliberate. Third, this darkness is getting . . . opaque. Some kind of hex?"

Her HUD wasn't showing any Brood warnings (thank the Elements). Wasn't showing any battle-hex alerts either, but she was given to understand—from Gaer, at some length and detail—that Aedian rigs mostly shook off battle-hexes.

"The ambassador is better suited to answer that last query,"

Char said. "I cannot sense anything specifically. It might be a visual effect, or some sort of defense."

"Monsters hiding in the dark, pretty effective defense." Luki kept her voice low. Homer, Dodri, and Llian were getting close, clomping up the corridor like templars who hadn't learned how to sneak in a battle-rig. Iari made a mental note to rectify that when they got back to Windscar.

"Not monsters," Iari said firmly. "Just mecha. Char. Open the doors, please. Start on the left. Homer, Dodri, cover Char."

The door had a keypad, dead and powerless. Char tapped it thoughtfully, and when it ignored them, calmly wedged their fingertips between a pair of unlucky segments of the door. The k'bal had been good engineers; the door did not want to yield. Char forced a crack anyway, then a gap, and then, with a shriek of abused metal, a hole.

Darkness spilled out, which was—absurd, but it happened, pooling around Char like aetheric oil before oozing upward. Slowly, like it was too heavy for normal aether, and too thick.

"What the." Homer caught himself and shut up.

"Some kind of gas?" Dodri sounded more curious than alarmed.

"Not according to my HUD," said Luki. "Some kind of hex?"

Gaer would know that. Gaer should be on his way—except his indicator, and Notch's, and Corso's, were still back in the big room.

"Lieutenant," she tried, private-channel. "What's the delay?"

Notch said nothing. His rig was still solidly orange. His vitals were showing signs of stress. His comms were—oh, ungentle Ptah. Offline. Something else she'd failed to notice.

"Affirm," said Char, and it took Iari a beat to track what Char was affirming. Right. A hex. "I cannot see into that space with any of my senses."

"I'm also getting nothing." Llian had moved up to flank Char.

Her headlamp died half a meter from her helmet. Just stopped in the darkness, which continued to spill out of the room and down the corridor. "My rig doesn't even *see* it. It's got to be arithmancy."

Ahead (far but not far enough) came the scrape of metal on stone.

Llian's headlamp whipped that way.

Iari tried again. "Lieutenant." Opened a second private channel. "Gaer. Notch's comms are out. What's going on?"

Gaer answered right away, like he'd been waiting for the question. "The lieutenant's rig is attempting self-repair."

Ptah's unblinking *eye*. The darkness encroached, wisping over everyone's feet now, getting more and more difficult to see through. It was like that fight in B-town, on the way to the cellar and the Weep fissure, when no one had been able to *see* Brood. And while Iari was fairly certain there weren't Brood down here, there was something this hex was meant to conceal.

"I need you up *here*, now," she told Gaer.

"Iari! Up the passage!" Luki was angled that way, headlamp dying before it even got to the edge of her raised shield. How the living Elements she could even see—

"What's up there?" Iari kept her voice level.

"Movement. I see—"

"I see it, too. Something." Llian paused for an audible swallow. "My HUD says there's nothing, but I *see* it."

"Hold position," Iari snapped. She looked back, saw Winter Bite's unmistakable silhouette (those *tentacles*, gentle Mishka), saw neither Corso nor Notch—

Then Iffy was there, a smaller figure among the templars, damn near wichu in size, in the sleek Aedian priest battle-rig that traded a shield for a hex-array on the gauntlet, a whole panoply of teslas and glowing sigils that were particularly, furiously blue at the moment. Not Mishka's comforting indigo. Hrok-blue, verging on white.

"Let me," said Iffy. She stepped around Char and thrust her open and empty left hand into the black coming out of the door. It looked like her hand disappeared (like the darkness had eaten it).

Iari heard at least one gasp on the comms (Homer) and shot a look at Luki (still holding position) with Dodri beside her now, braced like they expected a phalanx of mecha to come rushing at them. Iari bounced her attention back to her HUD, to everyone's vitals (Notch's were still going up) and positions (Corso was back there with him, Gaer moving up), and then back to Iffy, whose rig-marker had just turned a color Iari interpreted as *priest hexes are happening.*

She could see Iffy's hand now. Light seemed to be coming out of it, from a ring of what looked like whitefire on her palm. Except, when Iari blinked, it wasn't light. Not exactly. Or rather, it wasn't coming *from* Iffy. Iffy was *making* it, changing the darkness around the gauntlet. Transforming it, somehow, along a palette of ever-lightening greys. It was like dropping white paint into a bucket of black, but instead of evening out, the swirling white got brighter, at first opaque and then clearing, so that Iari could see into the room on the other side of the door.

She saw the barricade first—jagged and irregular and desperate. Furniture. Broken things. What might be ancient cloth, or some sort of fiber, jammed into the gaps. The remnants of the darkness curled out of the gaps like amorphous appendages that shriveled away from whatever Iffy was doing. The aether in here was old, stale, full of dust and impurities marching along the edge of her HUD.

And something was moving. Many somethings.

"Contact!" she snapped, and brought her shield around. Iffy

was too close to the barricade, to the movement, to *everything*, but Iari wasn't going to shove her aside. The darkness meant *no one* could see, and they were going to need to see—

"Is it bone mecha?" Gaer was *there*, suddenly, his tall, angular rig slicing into her periphery, skidding a little.

"Maybe, can't see yet." The somethings were still moving in the back of the chamber, but they weren't advancing. Seething behind the barrier, on the walls, on the ceiling—*waiting*, obviously, for someone to go in there.

"Send Winter Bite in." Gaer sounded a little breathless, like he did when he'd solved a problem.

Iari snapped her gaze that way, old habit, expecting the plates and spikes of vakari features and finding that teardrop-sleek visor instead. Finding her own headlamp blazing back at her, the comforting angles of an Aedian faceplate. Words backed up in her throat, pressed against the back of her teeth.

Riev aren't expendable, Gaer, he's *not expendable, did you see what happened to Char?*

"Sss, *trust me*—"

She did. She *did*.

"Winter Bite," she said, on external comm, loud enough everyone could hear it: "Clear that barrier."

"Yes, Captain." Winter Bite slid around Gaer like oil, avoided Iari's shield and Iffy's gauntlet as his tentacles coiled back into his chest cavity. The instant it sealed, he thrust both hands into the barricade. Artificed hexes crawled up his forearms, white and blue, as he tore the barricade apart. Then, yes, the small crablike mecha burst from behind it, bursting onto the HUDs in a cascade of *alert, contact.* They slewed around Winter Bite like water around stone, clattering over themselves to avoid him.

Iari slammed her shield into the first wave, and her syn jolted the length of her spine.

Gaer watched the first wave of bone mecha slam into Iari's shield, try to leap off (sizzling in the whitefire), and collide with the incoming second wave. Bone mecha bounced into each other, into templars' shields and battle-rigs.

Iari gave ground, shifting to clear her axe, twisted to fling the mecha off her shield and *not* into Iffy, who had not done the smart thing and stepped back. Gaer reconsidered his opinion of Iffy's sense—and his own—and jerked one of his monofils out of its sheath. There was an old SPERE joke about bringing monofils to a jacta fight. No jacta here, no 'casters, except (absent) Corso's. Just whitefire melee weapons, and his very *non* whitefire, very fragile blade that would still cut through anything. Even, *especially*—bone.

He dropped, folding both sets of knee joints, and cut low, beneath Iffy's expanding hex. The monofil sliced neatly through a pair of mecha limbs the circumference of his own fingers (oh, *there* was an awful comparison). So that confirmed to him that the mecha *were* bone again, and very likely animated by the same hexes as the last set. Which meant Iffy was going to take them apart—

Except she had one on her forearm, then another, pulling her hand out of position. *Gaer* didn't need hands to throw hexes, but Iffy wasn't a vakar, who knew—

Both bone mecha exploded into powder and sparks.

Iffy didn't need her hands, either. Gaer blinked behind his visor, then grinned, as Winter Bite reached over and ripped another off Iffy, crushing it before casting it to the floor. Gaer watched as it began reassembling. Fragments of limbs and broken carapaces slithered across the stone, drawing themselves into shape, repairing, returning to battle.

Gaer left Iffy's care to Winter Bite and took himself sideways, out of range of stray slashes and shields. He slid his attention into the aether, one-two-three-*there*, until he could see Iffy's Aedian heresy working, a swirl of equations as much alchemy as arithmancy. Gaer had done the requisite studies in pre-voidflight alwar alchemy, back in training. He knew *what* he was looking at, more or less, if not how it worked. Arithmancy worked with description—how the multiverse worked on all its levels, sketched out in variables and constants and functions. Some arithmancers— k'bal, vakari—had figured out how to change the language to describe *new* things, and thus create new effects, but even so, an arithmantic constant was, well, *constant*. The old pre-Confederate alwar alchemy (linked to some religious business, long relegated to myth) worked through correspondence between opposites, and controlling the proportions of each. Iffy *had* been driving the darkness back not undoing it, but by changing it, dark to light. What she did now was more sophisticated, *true* alchemy—transmuting that which was one thing into another unrelated thing, through Elemental correspondence when possible and rewriting reality when it wasn't.

Gaer set aside his horrified fascination and just *watched* as Iffy undid the bone mecha from their equational roots, turning *that* constant variable, aether to solid, solid to liquid. None of Ptah's plasma, Gaer noted; there was already whitefire on every templar shield and weapon, and the best they could manage was temporary dissolution. Gaer didn't understand it, what Iffy did. Or rather, *how* she thought about it. It was all numbers, but the shape of the equations, the logic behind them—sss. He thought he might be able to replicate the effects, like a child copying sounds and gestures. He didn't want to try. Turn the whole hallway to stone, maybe. Or undo those Elemental bonds between living tissues, instead of mecha reanimations.

But that was the horror, Gaer realized. The bone mecha were *alive* for some value of that concept. Maybe as alive as the riev, if not as aware. It wasn't galvanism, exactly, but it was related. The bone mecha had their own defenses, which could meet the arithmancy in Iffy's hexes, and sometimes match it, but they had no idea what to do with the (heretical) hybrid alchemy. That meant these things predated the Aedis (no surprise).

But then Gaer saw another horror, a worse one: flickering code, like faint misty threads, skeining between the mecha.

A network. The bone mecha were networked. Threads came *off* that network, too, anchoring deeper into the aether. Gaer wanted to chase that connection through the layers; but the part of his awareness still firmly anchored to body and brain (and battle) heard someone yelling, not in pain or in anger but in *fear*.

That was Luki's voice, his slow physical self told him. And Luki was not inclined to screaming.

Gaer pulled back through the layers (too quickly; he tasted blood in the back of his throat) and came back to himself in the dark between blinks. Forced his eyes open and looked for Luki. She was furthest into the tunnel from the battle in front of the door. She was also wreathed in that same inky mist (where was it coming from? *Setat*), which had coiled up her legs like vines. She was thrashing, whitefire sword scything at—something. Gaer couldn't see what. The blackness seemed unimpressed by her struggles.

Gaer engaged his optic. His battle-rig was vakari-made, had the preloaded battle-hexes and more range on its scans, but that

optic was meant for diagnostics, encountering new things and figuring out how they worked so that Gaer could take them apart
(and-or recreate them). He slipped his awareness sideways and
was pleasantly surprised to see that, no, this blackness was not
alchemy, just arithmancy—

Oh. Oh, not *just*.

These hexes were rooted like fungal filaments through layers
of aether. Not quite like nothing Gaer had ever seen, because he
was SPERE, trained for battle, trained on principles developed *because* of equations like this. These were k'bal metahexes, which
even vakari brains could not replicate (k'bal had *several* brains, so
it wasn't a fair competition). He just had never seen them *active*
before. These particular hexes had infiltrated Luki's rig through
gaps on aetheric levels. Not breached it, exactly; just sneaked in
through the cracks between numbers, on a scale so fine it was
absurd and amazing and awful.

Then Homer shouted, too, and began flailing about with his
axe, which was fortunately smaller than Iari's or he would have hit
Luki, first swing. What he was swinging at, though, Gaer could
not see. Nothing up in that blackness, not to his scans, or his eyes,
or his optic.

He remembered a lecture, years ago, by one of the vakari Expansion veterans, one who had come with the Five Tribes when
they defected from the Protectorate. *The k'bal*, she'd said, *could
make you see things.*

Right. *Right.* The vakari had worked around *that* trick fairly
quickly, but they weren't mammals. They weren't templars who
shot themselves full of little machines whose primary task was
manipulating their autonomic systems. Oh *setat.*

Gaer knew templar nanomecha had robust resistance, that
they'd adapt and evolve, but Homer and Luki only needed to hit

someone once to do serious damage. And with Iffy busy, that darkness was thickening and creeping closer. If it got to the other templars, then—well. Best not to let it.

Attack the darkness, neutralize it, trust templar nanomecha to right themselves.

This was (k'bal, mostly) arithmancy, and he was an arithmancer (vakar *and* SPERE) and that contest had been settled a long time ago. K'bal had used elaborate, intricate defenses, had been adept at turning their opponents' force (and wits) back on them, but once you saw how to break those defenses—

Sometimes you just needed a hammer. The vakari had figured that out.

The prism-hex was one of the simplest: Brood hated light, and so everyone who might fight Brood learned how to make it. Unlike Iffy, Gaer needed an actual source to make this particular hex work, but he had that: the glow of so many teslas, Winter Bite's hexes, all that whitefire on the templar weapons. He siphoned off bits from everyone, like taking a single facet from each of a handful of diamonds, and honed it, and hurled it past Luki and Homer. It pierced the black, disappeared into it, and Gaer had a moment of doubt.

But then he saw a web of lighter black under the dark. Wide at first, head-sized gaps in the weave. The strands thickened and multiplied, turning grey and then blue and then white. Tightening from net to fine cloth, squeezing and slicing the darkness to actual nothing.

Gaer didn't realize he had bone mecha stuck to his rig until he saw Iari's axe arcing down at him. *Then* he noticed the rig's shrieking alarm, and his HUD lit as bright as his battle-hex. He managed not to flinch.

It wasn't until he saw the bone mecha sheared in two, and

Iffy's prompt discorporation of it, that he even *thought* that she could've been compromised by that darkness, that some stray hex might've gotten to her.

"Ptah's own *sake*, Gaer!" Iari's voice was a little bit breathless. "What was that? What did you do?"

To the darkness, she meant. The distinct lack of yelling suggested whatever had been affecting Luki and Homer was over (or they'd collapsed and died, but Gaer doubted it. Iari was talking to him).

"It's an old hex. The prism. It's." He waved a hand. "I used a version in B-town." He glanced back. Homer was, no, not collapsed, and neither was Luki. They had helmets together in what Gaer supposed was a private comm conversation. The corridor was otherwise empty. The room was. No one here except templars and riev and him.

"You know what it was?" Iari sounded more like her ice-for-blood self. "That fog?"

"I have some ideas," Gaer started to say.

And then came Corso's voice, dry and drawling, "Well shit. What'd we miss?"

CHAPTER SIX ═══════════

They cleared the second room the same way, except this time Gaer handled the darkness first. Iari thought there might not've been as many bone mecha this time. She wasn't sure how she felt about that. Maybe this place was running out of monsters (ha). Maybe there just hadn't been enough bones in here to make the mecha. These two rooms, adjacent and identical, had obviously been quarters of some kind.

The shape of both rooms was wrong, though—too narrow, too tall, with angles that were not quite square. There were spherical alcoves in the walls, stacked three high. They were maybe a meter in circumference. Iari's back and shoulders ached at the idea of getting in there. Iffy would've fit easily, and Llian. Luki and Dodri, less comfortably—Luki was built human-average, and Dodri was slight, for a tenju—and Homer and Iari, only with misery. Notch wouldn't fit at all. Neither would Corso. Don't even think about Gaer.

Iari was, in fact, thinking about all three of them, clustered out in the corridor together, visors up, conversing in low, uncommed voices. There was some kind of unholy alliance at work. Corso and Notch had been marginally civil when she'd left them in the cafeteria, and Notch had mostly been ignoring Gaer. Now they were out there muttering together like recruits complaining about the drill sergeant.

Her sergeant was squatting against the wall beside Homer, with Iffy's full attention. Luki had said she'd seen Brood in the fog, and Homer had seen something he'd called a *qwuittcaz*, which sounded like northern tribal dialect.

Iari's grasp of spoken tenju language was entirely academic, and then only the standardized Tanisian dialect, which they mostly avoided in Windscar. Asking an expert gave her a reason to crash the interspecies conspiracy two meters away, so she did. Crossed the two-meter distance and pitched her voice low. "Corso, Notch, what's a qwuittcaz?"

They bounced a look off each other, startled. "It's a predator," Notch said. "Pack hunter. It lives—" He gestured vaguely in the direction of back and outside. "—on the steppes. You don't see them around bigger settlements. They're shy. Why?"

"They attack people?"

Notch blinked. "No."

"Well. That's not totally true. They don't attack towns," Corso said. "Or groups. A loner, though—maybe. 'Specially if the person's small." He made a face. "Was a threat, in my family. Be good or the qwuittcaz will get you. Why?"

Iari shook her head. Wouldn't meet Gaer's eyes, though she felt the weight of his stare. Heard the little hiss that meant clamped nostrils, flat jaw-plates. That information meant something to him. Well, good. She'd ask him later. For now: "What's going on over here?"

She thought, half a beat, she'd get a voidspit *nothing* from one, two, all of them. Corso opened his mouth, looked at Notch, closed it again. Gaer made another little hiss, very clearly *look at me, Iari.*

She didn't. Stared at Notch, because Notch had guilt marching around his face like initiates their first week in basic.

His eyes slid away from hers. "My rig choked," he said. "I don't really know. Comms went, then I couldn't make it move. And now I can."

"I stayed with him," said Corso. "You needed Gaer to deal with this voidspit."

Now she looked at Gaer, who tilted his head and did not, very carefully, have an expression. "But *you* know what went wrong with the lieutenant's rig."

"No." Gaer dragged the word out. "I don't *know.* I suspect. And you don't want a treatise on arithmancy right now."

No, she did not. But that told what had probably happened, anyway. "Battle-hex," she said. "From the metal mecha?"

Gaer's plates flared. She got a whiff of burnt sugar off him, the lingering scent of Gaer's fight-or-flight chemistry. "My guess. Yes. It drilled into the Aedian hexes through a break in the pattern. Through, *yes*, the damage."

These metal mecha were going to be a problem, and there was at least one more, more than that if she believed Char, which she did. "That what happened to Char, too?"

Gaer tipped his head the other way. His eyes narrowed in nothing *like* a smile. Like he was trying to drill into her head and make her understand, and like she wouldn't like it much when she did. "Yes and no. What happened to Notch is more like what happened to *you* last spring."

"Lots of things happened to her," Corso said. "Be specific."

Gaer ignored him.

Iari did, too. Lots of things *had* happened, but only one had gone after Aedis hexes, and that'd been the hexes on Sawtooth's contaminated chip. They had gone after her nanomecha, hacked into them through some arithmancy no one had quite figured out. That same hack, besides taking her nanomecha offline for a few days, had made them evolve. She'd channeled Ptah, in that cellar. Or her nanomecha had. Or something.

"You said only Notch's *rig* is showing effects, though."

"So far."

That was different. Iari's rig hadn't shown any ill effects from the invasive hexes. Then again, her rig had been so badly damaged she might not have noticed. And the transmitter this time was a mecha, not an infected riev. Maybe that accounted for the difference. "And there's no sign of this with Char."

"No."

"But you're sure this is what's happening to Notch's rig. Because circumstances aren't the same, Gaer."

"The symptoms are not the same. That which was transmitted, however, might be."

Notch was looking back and forth between them like they were speaking High Sisstish.

"What the fuck are you talking about?" Corso kept his voice low. "Iari, you know what he's saying?"

Oh yes. She understood fine. That Brood in Sawtooth had not been the thing that cooked her nano so that some voidspit hex got in. The hexes got in by themselves. And now they'd gotten into Notch, too.

Aloud, she said: "You think it's the separatists behind it? Another of Jich'e'enfe's hexes?"

Gaer hissed through nostrils clamped nearly shut. "That would track. Though whether they have several sets of hexes, or their hexes can . . . sss, evolve to exploit any arithmantic weaknesses they encounter, I can't say."

Iari watched the understanding break over Corso's face. He'd spent some time in that cellar with Jich'e'enfe. He'd seen her open tiny Weep fissures. Seen her command Brood and rip the aether with a tesser-hex to escape. And he'd also seen Iari . . . do whatever she'd done. He'd promised secrecy, afterward. Had kept that promise, too.

Was keeping it now. Corso turned to Notch. "Huh. Well. It's all right. If it's like that, what happened to Iari, you'll get over it. *She's* fine."

Corso was a good liar. Iari was thankful for that. But Notch also deserved better than half-truth dissembling, and *she* had to know. "Are you feeling all right, Lieutenant?"

Instinct, habit, to say *yeah, fine, of course I am.* Iari knew the impulse. All of them did.

Notch dragged his gaze back to hers. Locked on. "My rig's fine. The alert's gone. Corso gave me a jump with the power cell and that fixed it. My HUD says everything's optimal."

"But?"

"I feel a little off. I don't know how to describe it. But I'm good to go, sir."

Off could be first time in violent combat, coming off the syn . . . or badly compromised. And he could be—probably was—playing it down. When her nano had crashed, she'd been marching all over B-town, picking fights with Brood. So all she said was, "If anything changes that might compromise your effectiveness, you tell me. Anything. Even if it seems crazy or impossible."

Notch's eyes widened. Hazel-gold, in good light; the head-lamps bleached them colorless, except for the spreading black pupil. "Understood. I think. Sir, what happened in B-town?"

"I'll tell you later, Notch," Corso said, looking at Iari. "Not the time for it."

No, the time to talk about that had been—ungentle Ptah, *any time* since they'd gotten to Windscar. Instead, Notch had been stomping around, side-eyeing Gaer and the riev, and Iari had been avoiding him as much as she could. She didn't say that. No point to it. She just nodded at Notch, said, "Good," and eyelocked Gaer. "With me, please."

Gaer followed her across the corridor, to what passed for private. Homer and Luki were over by Iffy, talking about what they'd seen. Dodri and Llian stood at the corridor intersection, both facing right. The riev stood together, shoulder to artificed shoulder, facing left, because that was where the mecha noises had last come from.

Iari opened a private comm channel and waited for Gaer to drop his visor. "Tell me about this darkness."

"This is a very strongly worded go-away hex. It causes hallucinations, not actual damage. It is not a substance. It's an *effect*."

That . . . was oddly reassuring. A knot—one among many—in Iari's chest loosened. "Homer said he saw one of those . . . qwuitt-whatevers. Bet me he's not afraid of them."

"No, I think that's right. If your attackers see what scares them, they might just turn and run. Before you ask—I don't think it will affect the riev, not because they can't be frightened—though I have some doubt there—but because the hex manipulates living organic processes. I think it will pass right by galvanics. And I *will* bet you that the darkness is the reason all of Corso's grannytales said this cave was haunted."

Iari wished she could pinch the bridge of her nose, banish the headache, make some fucking progress. She had ten people jammed in a corridor, and every time she tried moving forward some new voidspit happened.

"Is there any way you *can't* sound like a textbook?"

He made that airless clicking that meant laughter. "You're welcome."

She snorted. And added, under her breath, "You think Notch's nanomecha will evolve like mine?"

"I don't know. Regardless, you can't send him back to the hopper alone."

No, she *could*, absolutely. But she wouldn't.

In the surge, you fought if you were upright. There hadn't been the luxury of retreat . . . there hadn't been *any* luxury. Even if his syn went offline, he had a working battle-rig. And if it failed again . . . at least it was armor, and he'd be some version of safe until someone could get to him.

"Incoming," Gaer murmured, so Iari had time to turn around.

It was Iffy, visor up, her delicate features radiating grim. "I can't find anything wrong with them. Luki and Homer. They saw things that scared them."

"K'bal battle-hex," Iari said flatly. "Defensive. Non-damaging. They good to go?"

"They are." Iffy looked from Iari to Gaer. "*You* tell me the details later."

He sketched a salute. "Sister."

"Oh, stop." Iffy looked at Iari expectantly.

Right. Time to move out.

CHAPTER SEVEN ═══════

G eneral comms, Gaer thought, were like being in a block of apartments with transparent walls. You couldn't have much in the way of private conversations. In an open-visor world, on point with Llian, Char, and Winter Bite, he should've been able to *not* hear Iari talking to Iffy. (He would have tried to spy anyway. He *was* SPERE, Five Tribes Intelligence, Special Research.) But with everyone sealed in their rigs, there was no way *not* to hear. The other templars appeared to have the same trouble. Llian stared very hard at the middle distance, not quite at Winter Bite or at Char or at the *setatir* door. The others, when Gaer had his HUD do a visual scan behind him, showed him various battle-rigs either holding far too still—Luki, Dodri—or, in Homer's case, fidgeting with the fit of his gauntlets.

The riev did better at pretending, having neither helmets nor HUDS. They had their scarily efficient and sensitive riev auditory sensors, so they weren't missing the conversation. Winter Bite's equipment was probably better than Char's, Winter Bite being one of the scout class, with that disturbing array of tentacles. Right now Winter Bite had the majority of those tentacles hovering over this newest door, double wide and solid-slab metal. He wasn't saying anything, which Gaer decided meant that his initial assessment of *I sense no movement, Ambassador* still held true.

Char had turned partway, dividing their attention between both ends of the party. When the mecha had attacked, Gaer had thought they would simply push everyone aside to get back there. And maybe, if the skirmish had gone on much longer, they might have.

Gaer, who had been, and still was, trying to get past the multiple hexes on the door panel, kept working. He loaded another set of standard *unlock this* hexes into his optic, cycled it to look into the requisite aetheric layer, and deployed them.

The panel sparked. His HUD flickered as feedback sparked (in reality, to his un-opticed eye) across the gap and crackled across his rig. The vakari battle-hexes shook it off. It was a good jolt, though. Nasty.

"That could have hurt," he said. And added, when Char pivoted to lean over him: "It didn't. I'm fine."

"Those are old defenses," said Char.

And oh, he did not want to ask how they knew that. Do *not* consider the age of Char's galvanically animated (and thus legitimately dead) organic core.

He stared at the panel instead, through his optic. Now that he'd blasted the first layer away, he could see what the problem had been. And what Char meant.

He could *see* the hexes. There, physically etched on the panel. Tiny, precise, *artificed.*

What he and Iffy had found on the mecha were aetheric traces. K'bal work. The k'bal knew more about arithmancy than anyone else; they had taught (maybe, the histories were spotty) the wichu. But the wichu had figured out artificing. How to lock a set of hexes into physical permanence—any fool could do that, *write them down*—but artificing was a way to stitch more layers of aether together. Expand a hex's effects. Gaer suspected the old k'bal voidgates had been modeled on wichu artificing, perhaps even created in collusion with them, before wichu clientage to the Protectorate. Gaer wondered if the wichu had been angry about that—when vakari came and annexed their system, and the k'bal would not fight with them. But the k'bal were pacifists, and no good at battle-hexes. That had been the wichu's problem, too, with the Protectorate. Oh, they didn't mind creating damaging hexes, not a bit; but they weren't ready for vakari war-arithmancy. Had no counter to it. Until they'd rebelled and gotten themselves allies, anyway, and access to bodies out of which to make riev.

(Never wichu bodies. Rarely alwar. Officially that was because alwar and wichu were smaller than tenju or humans. With wichu that was true, but most alwar were as big as small human adults, so the logic failed. No, what alwar and wichu had in common was not diminutive frames, it was political power, and too much sense to let themselves become riev.)

But *this* door panel had been artificed by wichu, or at least inspired by wichu technique. He noted several stylistic markers indicating that these hexes were designed to circumvent vakari defenses. Specifically Protectorate, Expansion-era defenses. And here he'd thought *Introduction to Historical Hexes* wouldn't apply to his future career.

"Char. Did the wichu and the k'bal make another alliance *after* the wichu rebelled? Do you know?"

Char hummed deep in their chest. Gaer decided that must indicate thoughtful consideration. That, or Char was about to explode.

"I have no direct knowledge. It would be possible."

And it would make sense. The vakari Protectorate had been a particular enemy of both wichu and k'bal. If there *had* been an alliance, that would explain why the Expansion had started with such violence in the k'bal Verge, and why the Protectorate had hunted k'bal to extinction.

The panel sparked again, and Gaer set that thought aside for later examination. The sparks were purely machine this time. No hexes.

"It is curious," Char said, so quietly that Gaer felt the sound more than heard it. A rumble on the edge of his senses. "All previous doors were unpowered."

Which meant there was a live power source somewhere behind the steel, which suggested that at some point, someone had decided to cut *off* that power to everything else. Gaer didn't think it was coincidence that someone had chosen a point deep enough into the hill that any emissions would (and had!) avoid cursory sweeps from Aedis patrols. Or, if this place was as old as it seemed, vakari patrols from the Protectorate. Now, whether that power cell had trundled along for a hundred years unattended, or if there were new custodians back there, well. He had to get the door open first to find out, but his bet was on new custodians.

"I would *bet* that the other mecha are waiting nearby, as well. Assuming one does not open a portal on us right here."

Someone (Homer? It sounded like Homer) gasped over comms. Gaer grinned behind his visor. Was gratified to hear Char make one of those machine coughs that passed for their laughter.

Winter Bite said, deadpan: "If a mecha appears, Ambassador, we will protect you."

"I rely on that." Gaer inserted the tip of a gauntleted talon into the door panel. He stabbed around the guts of it, scoring the artificing—easily done, with the hexes rendered inactive—and destroyed any chance of their resurrection. Then it was a simple matter of hexing the mechanism into doing what came naturally.

There came a hiss—this thing was aether-tight? Interesting—and the doors slid apart. Quietly. Easily. Not at all like ancient machines left to molder. That tracked, if there were separatists hiding down here. This door might be substantially newer than the others, even if the hexes were not.

"We're in," Gaer said. "Proceeding."

It was dark on the other side, but just plain dark, not hostile k'bal shadow-hexes. Winter Bite moved into the doorway, his hexes glowing faintly as his sensory appendages uncurled. Gaer's rig began scanning the space.

Well. His first report was not going to be very exciting. "It's a T-intersection. Go left, go right. In front, it's just a wall. Plain stone, unmarked."

"How far do the passages go? What else can you see?" Iari crowded up behind him.

Gaer wondered if she was going to ever just settle on a position, instead of trying to be on both ends at once. She'd seemed more comfortable in B-town, when it was just him, her, Luki, and Char. Then again, she'd only been able to be in the front, there. No rearguard to worry about.

Winter Bite had moved into the middle of the intersection, so Gaer answered. "A door on each end, Captain, solid like this one. They also appear to be electrically active."

"Hexed?"

"Unclear from this distance."

Gaer stepped up beside Winter Bite, so that Iari could take his place on the threshold. He suspected she'd wanted to go first, but—well. He'd just end up in front again anyway, first time anyone ran into arithmancy.

"Left or right?" he asked her. Started to turn to look back, which he didn't *have* to do in a battle-rig, there were cameras, but he found he preferred *seeing* her. And it was in that pivot that he saw Winter Bite's hexes flare up blue-white and heard Char say, "Gaer, *move.*"

You listened, when a riev Char's size issued commands. Gaer went forward, because *behind* was full of Iari and Char. He spun around to put his back to the wall, and jagged the barest bit down the righthand branch of the passage. He wasn't a bit surprised when his HUD lit up with battle-hex warnings, all around.

Char had *said* there were multiple mecha. One appeared now on each side of their party, left and right, materializing out of the dark and onto everyone's HUD.

And, oh *setat*, a third mecha appeared *behind* them, where they'd cleared the *setatir* tunnels already, where no mecha should be *able* to be.

Where it was just Notch, Iffy, and Corso.

Gaer still had his optic tuned to the third layer of the aether, and he could see the webwork of hexes on those mecha—meant to turn light, to turn sentient attention. *Setatir* brilliant defensive, concealing hexwork, evidently nullified when the mecha moved—

Or when the mecha *portaled.* He'd made the *setatir* joke, and now here it was, real and unfunny. Gaer saw a blur in the physical world, tinged with violet, but in the aether a fog of equations, which swirled and phased between layers and suddenly locked. For less than a heartbeat, they were stable. And in that fractured beat, the mecha moved, crossing from doorway to halfway up the corridor. It spread its limbs evenly between wall and floor and charged.

Last time, the mecha had gone straight for Char, arithmantically speaking; even if it had succeeded only because of Char's

Aedian graft, riev were clearly (and literally) bigger threats than a single vakar. Gaer readied a riev-trap defense.

Then the mecha crashed into him and deployed a battle-hex that tunneled through the first layer of his battle-rig's automated defenses before he managed to slap it aside.

That was—that *shouldn't* have happened. These *setatir* mecha were k'bal-era *old*, his rig was *new*, and if he did not figure out his defenses now, he would be the next in a long line of persons killed by theoretical unlikelihoods.

He'd had the riev-trap counter queued up on his optic. He diverted his attention from his distressed HUD (and the incoming, sharp metal limbs of that mecha) into the aether, where the mecha was a collection of roiling hexes, all its defenses active. This *wasn't* the one Iari had hit earlier, unless someone had repaired it. (Awful thought.) The code looked familiar, though, that mongrel arithmancy-alchemy he and Iffy had seen on the first. He tweaked a few of the trap's variables, swapped out a constant, and slapped his riev-trap-turned-mecha-trap onto the charging mecha.

It—worked? Not quite. Not perfectly. In the aether, Gaer watched the mecha's defenses flare and sputter. With his physical eye he saw it stagger and slew sideways. Not a full stop, no, but enough to make it slide off him. It fetched up hard against the wall across from him, beside the *setatir* door, and jerked its limbs like it was trying to free them from deep mud. Gaer watched his trap start to fray.

Corso had holed the thing with whitefire, hadn't he? Well. Gaer unclipped his jacta, little sidearm, nothing as powerful as Corso's longcaster—but this was point blank, too. He fired without waiting for a target-lock. The bolt hit. Whitefire spattered over the mecha's carapace, following hex lines Gaer could see in the aether. *Not* the hole he'd hoped to make, but the mecha's carapace was smoking a little as the whitefire burned through its defenses.

Iari arrived then, axe out, shield out. He started to tell her he had his mecha handled, help Winter Bite. His comms cut out before he managed her name, and his HUD turned entirely red. There should be an alarm, too, but Gaer couldn't hear it.

Because, he realized, there was no *air* in his rig. His HUD showed him phlogiston and a collection of gases ranging from toxic to useless. He sealed his nostrils, clamped his jaw-plates, closed the inner lid of his eyes. The toxic stuff worried him—mild corrosive, he'd cough blood for a day if he breathed it—but the phlogiston was *bad*. Just a little igniting hex, and he'd cook. And his rig's defenses, even if they did come back online, wouldn't help him in*side*. All he had was his optic. Some *setatir* alchemical hex from the mecha must've gotten through. It was fast, to've transmuted the air to phlogiston and corrosives. But the very fact it'd gotten past his rig's state-of-Five-Tribes-arithmantic-art hexes meant it was some old wreck of an equation no one defended against anymore. If he died in here now it'd be like getting killed with a rusty *fork*.

Gaer had no intention. Change the phlogiston back, he could do. That was a matter of a flipped constant and a reorder of functions. His optic made those calculations and deployed them while he worked up a counter to any attempts at ignition. His rig remembered at least one of its protocols and unsealed his visor. Which, yes, put him distressingly close to a two-meter-wide mecha across a three-meter-wide corridor. He imagined it regaining control of its limbs and stabbing him through the *setatir* eye.

Then Iari slammed into it, shield first, just as he felt the flick of an ignition hex. He deployed the counter-hex—messy, looked like a second-year cadet's half-hearted efforts, but it worked. Enough, anyway. A few fingers of smoke curled out of his helmet. Without his HUD, Gaer was effectively blind to his rig's reports. Well. That just meant he had *all* his attention for the *setatir* mecha—

—which Iari was chopping like firewood, as it tried to free itself from his trap. He didn't dare fire his jacta again. If he hit Iari, he wouldn't hurt her—that Aedis rig would shake off something that small—but he'd hear about it until the Weep sealed. So he turned and sighted the old-fashioned way, with his eyes and his instincts, on the mecha down the left-hand passage, and fired.

Then Winter Bite closed the distance, and Char arrived into the passage, and suddenly things were too crowded for bolts. Metal shrieked—let that be mecha, please, not riev.

"Gaer." Iari's voice echoed out of his helmet. "Get your voidspit visor down." Then she must've noticed the remnants of smoke wisping out of it. "You all right?"

"Yes. Fine." He wasn't going to argue about his visor yet. Give the battle-rig a minute, two, to collect its limited wits. He blinked past Iari into the aether. The mecha that had attacked him was dead. Many pieces of dead. Arithmantically dead. As was—yes. As was Char's and Winter Bite's, in one piece but far more battered. And—

"There was a third mecha, behind us—"

"Corso shot it. Iffy . . . trapped it in stone. Notch cut it up. They're fine. *Everyone* is fine." Iari sounded a little surprised. "Whatever you did to defend the riev, it helped."

"I didn't do anything." His voice sounded rougher than he expected. Right. Corrosive gases. He must've inhaled a little in the first moments. He coughed, then swallowed and regretted it. Like slivers of glass. "I never got the chance."

"That is not true. It was distracted with jacta bolts," Char said, without turning around. They sounded smug. "You are an adequate shot."

"Sss, *adequate*. You try without targeting. This *setatir* thing went after *me*." It was just starting to hit him, how close it'd come. "With hexes. Straight for me. I thought it would go for the riev."

"Of course it went for you. You're vakari. It probably wanted some new bones. We broke all its other babies." Iari's voice softened a fraction. "Close your visor, Gaer."

Then she was turning away, retracting both shield and axe and clipping the inert shaft to her hip. Trusting him to close his visor and not to crumple to the *setatir* floor and have an attack of the shakes. That mecha was huge. And pointy. And stank of whitefire scorch and Iari's vengeance.

For the love of all the dark gods, he'd gone face first into Brood before. This shouldn't bother him. So the mecha had aimed at him. Swarm had done that before. Boneless, too.

But those were impersonal horrors. Things he'd trained for. This was—not. K'bal had probably built that mecha, and wichu might've had hands on it too, then or since, and neither of those people had much love for his. It didn't matter that *he* wasn't Protectorate, that his foremother had been one of the instigators of the Schism, that he personally held a dim opinion of genocide. All that mecha saw was *vakari*.

Now Luki arrived, Llian in tow, and there was suddenly not enough room in the corridor, with the riev still clustered around their battered mecha, and *Iari's* dead mecha, *and* three templars and bah.

Gaer walked down the corridor, past the templars, like he had a plan. Which he did. Sort of. There was no one down the right-side corridor, and there was an unattended, closed door. He was going to open it. He went to the wall panel. He had no Winter Bite to confirm or deny movement on the other side, but—there. He coaxed the rig into sealing his visor again. The HUD showed him a list of indignities, minor damage, normal levels of phlogiston. Then it ran diagnostics on *him* and added to its list. But his visor seals worked, so he was fine.

His jaw-plates hurt from how tight he'd clamped them. The scarred one especially. He suspected inflammation from the corrosive gas along the seams where Aedis mesh held what was left his own flesh together. He tried to relax it, flexing it carefully, as he settled into a squat in front of the door panel. This lock looked very much like the last one. Same mechanism. Same hexes. He dispatched the hexes. He should wait for Iari before he opened it. Or someone in the Aedis. Or Corso, for that matter.

But the *setatir* mecha had gone after *him*. It was personal. Iari had said—*it probably wanted some new bones,* and that nagged at him. She'd been teasing. She hadn't been serious. But what if it *had*? The bone mecha must've come from someplace in here. Some facility that *made* them. He reckoned he had a fifty-fifty chance, either this door or the one by Winter Bite, of finding such a thing. A, a *crypt* full of dead vakari. Or a really well-guarded storage closet. Or, really, *anything.*

But hunches were not reasonable, and he was having one. And if he waited, it would mean he was scared. Or prudent.

He opened the door.

He did *not* get a faceful of mecha or whitefire. His headlamp punched a hole into perfectly normal darkness. This room had seven walls, counting the one with the door. Like the walls in the large cafeteria-garden space, these varied in length and width, and in the angles at which they met each other, though the height remained uniform. The wall with the door was just wide enough *for* the door. The one more or less directly across from it was the longest, lined with what looked like a bank of cryostasis tubes or coolant canisters. They didn't match, as if they had different manufacturers, or different purposes. There were tables shoved up against one of the other walls: slightly too high, oddly bowed in the center, with an attached console and what looked like a retractable cover. Several of what Gaer guessed were turing consoles on individual pillars jutted up in no discernible pattern. The whole place was . . . uneasy. Unbalanced.

"*Dammit*, Gaer." Iari sounded a little bit breathless. His HUD said she was still back in the corridor, coming fast. "I turn my back for one minute—"

He held up a hand to forestall her. "It's empty. Maybe. I need Iffy."

"You have *me*." That, said on external comms, meant for him, as she came up beside him. "Did you know it was empty?"

"No. But I thought it must be. The mecha attacked us out *there*."

"There could've been another one in *here*."

"Then you would have saved me again," he said, softly, also on external comms. He'd intended it to come out lightly, halfway to jest. Instead the words roughed in his throat, caught on the phlegm and blood. He looked at her instead, knowing she couldn't see through his visor. That she'd just see herself in reflection.

"Someday, Gaer . . ." She trailed off, and sighed. "What's in here you wanted so badly?"

"I wanted to know what it was the wichu wanted the mecha to protect."

"*Wichu*, not k'bal?"

"The doors were artificed. The k'bal *might* have known how to do that. But I *know* the wichu do. They were old hexes, but that doesn't mean there aren't new wichu. And now we see what was so valuable that they needed to lock it in. Cryostasis tubes."

One was clearly of human manufacture, shaped like an oblong box and stamped with a pre-Confederate logo and words in a language not Comspek. Another pair were clearly tenju-made, eight-sided, from the same vintage. They had ships' logos painted on them, peeled and faded with age. Another four were marked as Confederation, with that generic dimension intended to fit everyone from an alw to a tenju—but still old, before the Accords.

And there were three that were smooth, unfaceted, like capsules rather than coffins. A little smaller than the others, though still large enough for a tenju, a vakar, a human. Gaer's optic picked out the artificing, barely visible on the surface. His actual eyes picked out tiny teslas, dimmed to save power. Because there *was* power.

Wichu. Post-Accord manufacture.

Iari had stopped at the oddly shaped table. She had one hand on the cover, the other flat in the bed. "This looks like it's some kind of surgical unit. I don't see a med-mecha, though, so—it's got to be old. Expansion-era, maybe. This could've been a medical facility."

"With cryostasis tubes? That's not an effective use of resources."

"Sure it is." Iari's voice faded as she moved around the perimeter. "In the army, we used them for catastrophic trauma. Things you couldn't treat on the front."

"Not the Aedis?"

She was quiet long enough he thought she might not've heard. He tapped a private channel to her. She didn't open that either, until Gaer thought there was something wrong with his comms. Then a faint *click* and:

"Our nanomecha can stabilize most injuries. What they can't

will kill you anyway—you know. Missing limbs. Really big holes. Massive blood loss." She made one of those breathy little *huhs*. "There's a story that the nanomecha don't *like* cryo. That we don't use it because they either don't or won't work, or they won't let *it* work. One initiate horror story is that cryo actually kills them. That they just stop functioning, and you're fucked afterward."

There had been rumors for as long as Gaer could remember, both in and out of Five Tribes cadet circles, that Aedis nanomecha were . . . if not sentient, then more aware than anything that size had a right to be. It was that game of *how barbaric are our allies, really?* Gaer, who'd seen some of the classified reports, knew that the nanomecha *had* been sapient when they'd been a wichu bio-weapon. He supposed the Aedis had programmed that out of them before injecting them into templars.

Which would be a lot like genocide, which didn't *sound* like the Aedis he knew, but he was definitely not bringing that up to Iari. She'd gotten quiet again. Probably thinking about her own nanomecha, and how they'd gone offline for a brief window, before coming back somehow changed. Probably thinking about Notch's, and what they might be doing now.

"You know," he said, "the wichu made the original Aedis nano-mecha. Maybe *that* is the back door Jich'e'enfe exploited last year, to breach yours. If she had found some of that old code."

"The wichu made a bioweapon, not—what we have."

"Ah. I didn't think you knew that. I hadn't thought that was common knowledge among templars."

"It's not. I used to sleep with the Chief Chirurgeon. She liked to brag."

"Ah. Yes. The charming Sister Diran." Gaer poked along the edges of the bank of 'stasis tubes. There was power in the facility, obviously, but the individual power cells on the old tubes showed no activity. The new ones, however, were not only active, but they were *occupied.* "Iari. Look. Should we open them?"

"What? Why?" Iari had been poking around one of the turing consoles. Now she abandoned that and came back to him. He waited for her to notice the same thing he had, to make the same conclusion.

Which she did. "Those are new tubes."

"They are. And they're wichu-made."

"And there's something or someone inside." Said not with curiosity, or surprise, but flat, unimpressed distaste. "I don't suppose you see any indication of who's in there."

"I do not."

"Then no. Leave them locked until Iffy gets up here. Open an old one, if you have to open something. Mishka's tits, Gaer, you're worse than a kid during the Double Moon Festival." She drifted away again.

He eyed the occupied 'stasis tubes. There were many things that could be in there. You could freeze things besides people. Medicines. Maybe even food. That would make sense; the wichu separatists wanted to disrupt ties with the Confederation, wanted to exact a little revenge on the vakari—wanted general mayhem, which did *not* lend itself to stable supply lines, and besides, their presence on Tanis was meant to be secret. Or, if the wichu separatists were using this site, which the newer tubes seemed to suggest . . . there might be a *separatist* in there. A living one, badly hurt. Maybe even Jich'e'enfe.

But Iari was right, too: they would need the Aedis facilities to treat anything serious. Gaer set one strand of curiosity aside and indulged the next closest, next best. Open an old tube. He chose one of the tenju-made, the one that looked newest. There was no point in arithmancy here. He checked anyway, flicking through all the layers with his optic. None of the machinery worked, as expected; but there *was* something on the surface layer, so dim Gaer almost missed it. Like an aura, in that it had hints of color, but there was nothing alive *for* an aura. It was like, like the *stain* of an aura, burned into the metal.

It wasn't unheard of. You saw the phenomenon—or had, before the wide adoption of battle-rigs—on battlefields. Prisons. Hospitals. Places that took on that same resonance as the auras of the beings inhabiting them. There was a whole genre of vakari literature (in both Protectorate and Five Tribes) devoted to the fantasy that simple murders could produce them, and if an arithmancer were skilled enough, *sensitive* enough, they might discover how someone died, or who did it. But never, to Gaer's recollection—in the actual *data*, not someone's fancy—had there been aural bleeding from one person strong enough to leave an impression.

Until now. This tube held the vaguest hints of yellow, orange, sunset colors. There'd been panic, here. There'd been pain. A bruise-colored shadow that meant despair.

Iari wouldn't appreciate the significance. She'd say, *leave it shut, if you don't want to look.*

Want warred with should. But it had always been Gaer's belief that knowing a thing was better than not, so—he flipped the panel open and, after a moment to figure out the manual controls, opened the tube.

The seal disengaged with a click. The door fit into a socket, propelled by hinges that lifted it in or out; there were tracks along which it would slide after that, to allow access to the interior. The hinges weren't working. He curved his fingers around the edge, thankful for vakari talons. Rocked the door gently in its socket.

The top hinge snapped. The bottom one, more stalwart, held on as the door slid open partway and jammed.

But it was enough. Oh, dear dark lords.

He'd expected a body. Expected desiccation, skin clinging to bone. Maybe just bones. He'd had vague expectations of a k'bal, three skulls, three necks, a more usual assortment of limbs. Or a tenju. Or a human.

But the skull looking back at him had jaw-plates, and long curving bones on the side. It had teeth bared and declaring its lineage, foremother and clan, etched in a red faded mostly to grey. For a moment Gaer stared at the dead vakar. Then gravity asserted itself and, without the door against which it had been leaning to support it, the corpse collapsed out of the tube.

Gaer hopped back as the skull, several tenacious vertebrae, and a forearm slid out. For a moment it hung there, looking very much like it wanted to claw its way free. Then the frail remnants of skin tore, and the bones popped loose, and, after a short fall, shattered as they hit the stone floor. The remainder of the corpse collapsed inside the tube.

Now, with the door partway open, he could see the inside. There was scoring all along the inside of the door, where the vakar had tried to get out, hands and feet turned against impervious steel. Oh dear dark lords, no wonder at all there were aura-stains.

"Iari. Come here." Gaer was proud of how calm he sounded. How he *hadn't* just yelled.

His tone must have warned her. Iari let out a tiny hiss of exasperation, but she didn't protest. He turned as she came up beside him.

"I did not expect prisoners. Or torture." He showed her the scoring. "This person was sealed inside and left to die. Protectorate. Before you ask how I know—the teeth. That tribe never re-belled."

Iari crouched. Did not touch the broken remains on the floor, just looked, for a long moment, at what to her must be a jumble of bones. Of spikes. More death, and this time of a species she didn't know well, anatomically. Didn't know at all really, except for him. But oh, whoever had killed this vakar had known them well, exactly how to slice between spines and joints.

"We'll send someone down for them. Are the other tubes—?"

"I haven't looked." Gaer's face felt stiff. He thought about opening his visor. Letting her see the colors his chromatophores must be right now. Let her read him, and understand. Instead he said, "I don't want to look. Iari. *This* person—is missing a hand and part of an arm. Surgically removed. *Deliberately* removed. *That* is how the *setatir* k'bal were getting their vakari bones for those mecha."

Iari was looking at him. He could feel it. "What happened here is awful. But that's not the problem we have to solve right now."

It took a heartbeat to realize she was waiting for him to acknowledge that. He hissed through his nostrils. "I'm fine. What problem do *we* have to solve?"

"That was Luki on comm. Char and Winter Bite got into the other room. Luki says we need to see."

CHAPTER EIGHT

ari didn't remember Tobin running around this much when he'd been a captain and she'd been a private. She remembered him always being at the front, which—well. The front kept slagging *changing*. Either he'd delegated (which she also did not remember, and which didn't seem much like Tobin) or he'd just been better at guessing where he'd be needed. Saichi hadn't been his first field command.

It had been his last, though. Now Tobin didn't run anywhere. Maybe that would be her solution, too. Have something much bigger take her apart, and then, by the Elements, she'd sit down.

Two things had already tried dismantling her today. The syn still twitched along her nerves. She was glad of the rig, which concealed the minute jerks of skin and muscle as the nanomecha purged the excess adrenaline. That last voidspit mecha had damn near gotten Gaer. He'd *acted* all cool, but she knew him. And even if she'd got it wrong, if he was that blasé about fending it off, well. He hadn't seen it orient on him and *charge*. She had. She could've been just that little bit too late and he'd be in pieces.

What the mecha hadn't managed, though, the dead vakar in the tube had. She'd seen Gaer rattled when he'd thought Tobin might give him to the wichu for questioning, after they accused him of espionage and assassination to the Aedis Synod. One of those things had been true—he *was* SPERE—but Jich'e'enfe had been a surprise, and had damn near killed him and Iari and half of B-town. That the wichu had wanted him smacked more of politics—of a desire for vengeance against vakari, even citizens of the Five Tribes, who'd been allies before the Weep. Gaer's certainty that they'd, what had he said, *take him apart*, suggested that maybe wichu separatists and mainstream Confederation-aligned wichu differed only in the levels of violence they were willing to use against vakari.

Iari didn't pretend to understand the emotions and politics of a former client people against their patrons. But hating *all* vakari this many years after the fact seemed excessive.

Especially Gaer.

It bothered her, seeing him like this. It bothered her that there had been, still were, constructs whose primary purpose was killing vakari. It bothered her most of all that there was an active 'stasis-tube in that—what, hospital? laboratory? Gaer would say *torture chamber* and *prison* and he might not be wrong. She'd been imagining . . . ungentle Ptah, she *hadn't* been imagining anything. A body in there, alive or dead, or some other thing that needed stasis—it hadn't mattered to her. They had separatists to find, didn't they?

But it should've mattered.

She paused at the intersection where Dodri and Homer were waiting. Dodri had eyes on Iffy, Corso, and Notch, still hovering over their mecha.

Homer turned toward Iari as she came up. "Haven't seen anything, Captain."

Which didn't *need* saying. It was obvious. And it was just as obvious Homer was nervous, now that she was looking at him.

Sure. First field exercise and he'd gotten *this*. It wasn't the surge, wasn't anything like—but she could put herself in his battle-rig, couldn't she? Remember first fights, first syns. First real fear you might die.

Elements, what would Tobin have said? "Good. Thank you"— and not rank, but *name*, because she knew it—"Homer."

She touched his shoulder in passing—careful, the battle-rigs didn't like touching—and avoided his eyes as she poked just her head down the passage. "Iffy! I need you to leave that mecha and come take a look at the room Gaer just opened, please. Notch, Corso, go with her. Dodri, Homer: you stay here. Make sure nothing comes up our backs."

It probably (definitely) wasn't the most exciting assignment for a templar, playing rearguard. If either Dodri or Homer was disappointed, though, she couldn't hear it in their *yes, sirs*.

Gaer, who'd been drawing breath to make a remark, let it go in a hiss. That seemed like progress. He wasn't arguing her decision, either. That seemed . . . maybe promising.

They passed the other mecha. It was slightly more intact than the one she'd killed. A lot more battered.

"Char did that?" Gaer said, which was the first unnecessary comment since the lab (all right, that was a handful of meters and seconds ago, but for Gaer, that was an eternity). Iari decided to take it as a positive sign. "And it didn't try any battle-hexes?"

"Char and Winter Bite, and if it did, nothing worked."

"I have a theory about that."

The tightness in her chest eased a little. "I'll want to hear it, but first—" She gestured Gaer through the doorway.

More proof of his mood's recovery: he ignored her gesture. Paused to examine the door's entry pad, which dangled from a single wire from its socket. "I see we took the precision approach."

"You were busy. Winter Bite reckoned he could get it open."

"Thus, I am replaced by riev." Gaer moved past her, into the other room. Stopped almost at once.

One step after him, and Iari understood why. It was a very different space. Or rather, two very different spaces.

It was also full of dead bodies.

Wichu, four of them, in various poses of traumatic death. One had died close to the door, with what looked like a pair of bolt-holes in their chest. Two more had died near the far wall, where a modular shelf-unit had been pulled over. It had been holding crates, the sealed, insulated kind used for perishable food or medicine, which were now scattered around it, in varying states of opened or crushed or—void and dust, *melted*, with that bubbled-up texture that said it'd been some chemical solvent, not heat or whitefire, that caused the melting. Iari's HUD began cataloging possible contaminants, and advised that the whole area was a little bit toxic, please keep the visor sealed.

Luki stood just past the bodies, facing the door. When Iari came in, she said, "There's another set of passages back here, and a dead-end back room with an altar like the one we found in B-town. Winter Bite says it's not doing anything. The altar, I mean. We didn't go in there," she added. "I thought we should wait for everyone else. You know. In case."

Beside Iari, Gaer snapped into sudden, taut stillness.

Void and dust, of course they'd found another altar. That made sense. Jich'e'enfe had used the one in B-town as some arithmantic focus, her way to punch holes into the aether and do impossible arithmancy and control Brood. But it had also served as a portal-maker, and Gaer had suspected it connected to *other* altars, so—here one was.

Winter Bite stood beside Luki, facing the other direction with all his tentacles outstretched. He cocked one in Iari's direction. "There are organic traces present in this room, Captain: tenju, alwar, human. The crates contain more concentrated remains, though they are divided by anatomical function rather than species. There is also a corrosive residue in the crates that I believe was intended to destroy the organic material inside."

That took a moment to parse. Iari was almost sorry she had. The crates were full of *body parts*. Mishka's tears.

None of the dead wichu appeared to be Jich'e'enfe, which made Iari's guts both clench and relax. She'd have loved to get hands on that woman alive, on the one hand; and on the other, it would be nice to have *that* settled. These wichu, though, were strangers, and somewhat recently dead where no wichu had business being: so it was a safe guess they were separatists, and someone *else* had killed them.

That was the problem she had to solve. Who'd done the killing.

So look at the room.

The first third of it was the same precise excavation as what they'd seen so far, all the dimensions just a little bit wrong, too many angles, what Gaer said was k'bal design. There were cabinets set into the smaller wall-niches, and tesla fixtures inset in the ceiling. There was also a broad-bellied nanoforge with an old-style solid-state screen and keypad about halfway down the left side. It had been turned partway over, its screen cracked, its keypad dangling from wires in three distinct pieces. Whatever it *had* been making, it wouldn't be doing so anymore.

Across the room from the nanoforge was another of those surgical-bed-looking units, like the one from the cryostasis-tube room. Only this surg-unit's lid was entirely shut. It had been bolted to the wall, then torn violently loose, though it was still upright. The fourth wichu lay beside it, sprawled like a doll thrown down in a tantrum. A doll with a skull shattered from the impact. Char stood between the wichu and the sealed surgical bed, their hexes throbbing faintly red.

About two-thirds of the way into the space, the room itself changed. The walls and the floor became rougher. The teslas (still unlit) dangled from naked cables instead of being socketed in the ceiling. There were still alcoves carved (or blasted) into the some of the walls. No shelves, though. It funneled into another tunnel, lopsided both in shape and orientation, on the backside of the altar, trailing into the dark.

The damage had been done to the shelving unit and its crates, the nanoforge, and this surg-unit. Nothing else. Targeted, then. Someone had been trying to destroy specific equipment or— ungentle Ptah, *supplies* of some kind.

"Winter Bite—are there vakari remains here?"

"Negative. Or rather, Captain—there are *traces* of vakari material in the room, but none inside the crates. And nothing recent."

So there was *that*. Iari wasn't sure if that made it better or not. Bone mecha—vakari bone—were clearly older constructs, and maybe made *here*. Which, fine, this had been a k'bal hideout first. That made sense, no surprise. What the *wichu* had been doing with more recently deceased tenju and alwar parts, however—that was some new horror-creation.

Gaer had been ominously, uncharacteristically quiet thus far.

He panned his headlamp around the room, hovering over the seam where the obviously k'bal tesla fixtures sprouted wires and vined off across the ceiling, dropping the occasional naked tesla to battle the subterranean dark.

Iari waited while Gaer did whatever he did, probably arithmantic, deliberately unnarrated. The last of the syn had worked its way through her body. Her skin ached a little, like it'd been stretched. The inside of her rig smelled a little bit like sweat and lot more like metal and ozone. She wished she could open her face shield. She wasn't claustrophobic (you couldn't be, and wear a battle-rig), but she wanted to feel air on her skin. Wanted to smell something besides herself and the faint ozone of rig electronics. Which, given the environment—eh. Sweat and ozone was *fine*.

"Well?" she asked. "Anything revelatory up there?"

"No hexes. The patchwork between systems is artificed. Wichu did it."

"Wichu made these ugly walls?"

Gaer snorted. "Probably. The k'bal certainly didn't. The wichu are also responsible for this tangle of wires. They were splicing into the k'bal systems to power whatever they were doing in here with *this*." He took one long vakari step past her and swerved for the surgical table and stopped beside it.

Iari's scalp tightened. That kind of focused attention just made Gaer look more like the apex predator his species were. The visor's menacing silhouette didn't help. And Gaer didn't focus like that unless there was arithmancy. Char's hexes were red, all right, that was another mark in the *hostile arithmancy* column. But Char was focusing on Gaer like *he* was focusing on the table. Iari stifled an urge to deploy axe and shield and went to stand beside him.

"What?"

Gaer tilted his head a fraction, acknowledging her arrival. She thought she could hear the faint hiss of breath through clamped facial *everything*—jaw-plates, nostrils, every clampable orifice—behind it.

"Hexes." He snipped the word off. "Artificing."

She hadn't heard his Sisstish accent that strongly since . . . ever.

Luki tapped a private channel. "Is Gaer all right?"

"Nope." Iari scanned her HUD: no sign of anything toxic, no Brood, coming off the table.

"Gaer. I'm going to need a little more detail."

He swung his head toward her. The opaque visor drank the light from the overhead, inset teslas and threw back an oilslick gleam. "This is another old surg-unit, like the one we found in the other room. Like the other, this has no med-mecha. It relies on a rudimentary turing and requires someone to *tell* it what to do. Except that other unit was just *equipment*. And what I mean by that, before you interrupt—is that *this* is a wichu device. Or rather, *sss*. A device wichu have artificed from its original purpose. The other machine was probably used to remove limbs from the prisoners in the tubes. Obscene, but within the parameters of surgery. This unit is *not* for surgical purposes. It is *galvanic*."

"Captain," Char said, voice tuned down to just audible to the rig's pickups. "This unit is also occupied."

Iari's fist flexed, damn near popped the shield. She stomped the syn back. "Occupied by . . . something alive?"

"Unknown," said Char, but Gaer said, "No," in acid-soaked tones. "This is—*sss*. I cannot be entirely certain, but I think this is something one could use to make, if not riev, then something *like* them." He looked at Char. "Do you concur?"

"It is not a true kiln," Char said. "Those are much larger. And there appears to be conventional life support functional on this unit. But there are similarities, yes. I . . . it feels the same. I cannot be more specific, Captain, I am sorry."

Iari blew out a breath. Galvanism—making riev out of dead bodies—was illegal. Had been since the Accords, when the Protectorate made peace with everyone else because the Weep was the bigger threat. But even the *obvious* use that riev could be fighting Brood hadn't been enough to overcome Protectorate orthodoxy (and be fair: even the Five Tribes had balked). Even before that, though, the wichu hadn't shared the riev-making technique with their allies. Not that the Confederation had *asked*, exactly, where the big constructs were coming from, *how* they worked. The Confederation had only cared that they *had* worked, and that they'd been good at killing Protectorate troops. The actual *how* of it, though, the hexwork behind reanimating dead bodies—no one knew how that worked. The bone mecha were—disturbing. But they weren't galvanic, either, not the same way.

"It would make sense," Gaer was saying. "That wichu separatists who want to eradicate the vakari as a species would try to recreate their best weapons to do so. *Sorry*, Char. I don't mean to depersonalize you."

"When Oversight was active," Char said, "riev were one mind, and one purpose, but we were not people. That was depersonalizing."

"Someone killed these wichu," Iari said. "How do you know it's not the attackers' innovation?"

"Someone *who*?" Gaer's jaw-plates flared, then flattened. "The residents of Windscar? What, neefa herders and homesteaders who hate the Confederation and the Aedis so much they want to stay out here and pretend you lot never happened?"

"So, you're saying this level of arithmancy isn't possible from hinterlands tenju?"

"Yes, but not because of the way you're making it sound. It's a matter of power. Your whitefire shield comes from the power core in your rig. Your axe has a split processor, one in the shaft for short bursts, and the link-up to your rig—"

"I understand my battle-rig, Gaer. Your arithman-splaining."

"That is not a word."

"Iffy says it is. The point is—you're *sure* this surg-unit here is wichu-altered."

"Yes. Completely."

So the wichu separatists couldn't get a real kiln, and they made do with altering old medical equipment. That didn't tell her why all the wichu were dead, or what the second surgical unit in the other room was for. Maybe the separatists had intended to upgrade it, or it was just there to neatly dismember the dead who were now out here divided in *boxes*— Oh.

"Gaer. You said *partly* galvanic. Like the bone mecha?"

"No. Those aren't galvanic at all. Those are diff—" He stopped. Hissed, very softly. "Different, but perhaps related. The bone mecha aren't reassembling organic bits into whatever they were, but rather into new patterns. That kind of thing—nanomecha could do that. Or something like nanomecha. Proto-nanomecha. If the separatists are making *riev*, or something like riev, from k'bal technology, then—the wichu intended to use nano technology once before, didn't they? Transmutatively and with intent to do harm, on living organic tissue."

They were back to the original wichu bioweapon. Which had become Aedis nanomecha. Yes. "So what does that mean? You think there's malevolent *nano* doing the work of galvanics? In that surgical table? And transmuting what into what? You think there's something alive in there, some kind of *riev*?"

"An excellent question." Gaer snapped his hand out, stopped it just over the table's keypad. "Shall we open this and find out?"

Iari looked at Char. Nodded. Then Iari stepped back, in case she had to pop her shield to protect Gaer, and Char stepped closer, in case they had to smash something.

Gaer hovered his hand over the table's controls. Then he reached down and poked a single-stroke command with the tip of one gauntleted talon. The cover retracted, any hiss or pop lost in the sudden howl of an alarm, and the solid-state screen flashed with a single, repeating phrase in a language Iari couldn't read.

Not that she was looking at it for long, because the table's cover folded back with a sigh and—ungentle Ptah, Mishka's tears, Chaama's fucking *bones*, what was she looking at?

It was, it *appeared* to be, a naked male tenju lying on the surgbed. *Appeared*, because the head and most of the face were obscured by a dark, almost black, metal . . . cap? Almost a helmet, except that it clung to the contours of the skull, leaving just smooth metal where the ears should have been, and dipping down over the left eye, marking where it should be with a single red cabochon ringed first by a strip of bright silver, and then a wider circle of inky black metal. The right eye (closed), nose, and entire jaw were visible, the jaw slack. Both tusks were both capped with the same dull, dark metal as the helmet-cap. The tenju's right arm stopped at the elbow; below that was a gauntlet more obviously armor-like, like an army-issue battle-rig. The portion along the forearm had grooves and raised tubular fixtures, as if it covered cables or slimmer, more vulnerable attachments, running the length of the arm and tucked in under the cuff at the top of the wrist. The hand was fingerless, except for the thumb: a segmented metal mitten, curled into a relaxed fist. Where the metal met skin—on the head, on the arm—the flesh was a swirl of angry pink and spongey blueish-black with faintly weepy edges.

The right eye opened.

Bloodshot, pupil huge and round and unresponsive in the stabbing glare of two headlamps. The cabochon lit too, ungentle Ptah, must be a tesla behind it, though it flickered less like a tesla and more like a *heartbeat.*

Then the not-quite-dead man sat up, straight from the waist, and lifted the gloved right arm. There was an aperture in the palm, very much (exactly) like the business end of a jacta. Iari's HUD reported an energy build-up, whitefire, *target lock.*

Her shield snapped from her gauntlet unbidden, syn-driven, her axe a half-second later. Before she could use either one, Char's massive right hand—the Aedis limb—enveloped the dead tenju's weaponized hand to the wrist. Char closed their fingers, and Iari heard the metal crumple. Char's hexes flared red and angry, then white and blinding. Iari winced in reflex, expecting a scream— because it wasn't just metal glove breaking, there had to be pulver- ized flesh and bone, and people made noise when that happened. The tenju didn't. The cabochon-eye flashed—maybe that meant it hurt?—and then whitefire bled through Char's fingers, as the not- dead tenju's hand-weapon discharged into Char's palm. Then it swung its very flesh-and-bone fist at Char's forearm, and when that strike failed, grabbed Char's armor. Iari saw steam coming up from the white-hot hexes, imagined the smell of cooked flesh, was never so grateful for the sweat-and-stale smell inside a sealed battle-rig.

It was then she saw the faint glow of hexwork on the one-eyed helmet.

Gaer said, "It's transmitting."

Ptah's flaming *eye*. Iari snapped out her axe blade and split the tenju's skull, crown through cabochon. She expected a spray of blood. Instead, a purple-black sludge began oozing out of the gash, that the rig said was *Brood* and Iari knew wasn't. At least, not entirely. It was the same stuff that'd been in Sawtooth, back in B-town.

Then Luki was there, sword out, shield out. "What is that?"

"Familiar," said Gaer. "Except last time we saw effluvia like this, it was coming out of corrupted riev. Jich'e'enfe's work. *Wichu* work."

"This isn't a riev," Iari said, with more conviction than she felt. "It's—mostly a naked tenju. There's no exo-armor. It—was it, was he, alive?"

"Marginally. There is a whitefire weapon in the glove." Gaer gestured, and Char let go of the dead tenju's fist. He prodded through what should have been bone and flesh, what was black sludge instead. "Some of the larger riev were equipped with weapons like this. Char would have had one when they were commissioned. So would have Sawtooth. Those were weapons the wichu saved for the biggest riev because those riev had the most internal power. Riev, however, have a distributed galvanic core, and this . . . *this* person appears to have their original organs. There isn't much left of the hexwork here, but I will *guess* that this weapon was powered by the tenju's living body. That is—they were alive when this was done to them, and remained so until, well. Until just now." Gaer flicked bits of dead tenju and sludge off the tips of his gauntleted talons. "When the separatists couldn't suborn and corrupt actual riev, they decided to make some new ones. Living ones. *Half* riev."

And then Iari's comms interrupted: a squeal of emergency override from Notch, who had codes to do that.

"Captain! Do you copy?" He sounded a little frantic, and Iari winced.

"I copy. We're fine." Ungentle Ptah. Iari retracted her axe. "You said the—helmet? The cap? Was *transmitting.* Where? Like a comm transmission? It, he, was talking to someone?"

"Not speech. More like a signal, indicating the subject's status and location." Gaer sounded disgusted. "There was a burst on a sublayer of the aether, that's all I saw. It was over too fast."

Char rumbled faintly, unhappily. They looked at Winter Bite. "It is something Oversight would have done."

Winter Bite's teslas dimmed. "It was very like that. I perceived an echo of the transmission the ambassador describes, and it was familiar. Like Oversight."

"This dead person's signal was not an attempt to subvert *us,* Captain," Char added. "It was communicating with another trans-mitter. Oversight would have done that—did do that—when riev died on the battlefield."

Iari realized she'd been holding her breath, and let it go. "The altar in the next room—did this transmission go through it? Use it? Because we, Gaer, thought the altar in B-town acted like some kind of transmitter in addition to every other voidspit thing that it did."

Winter Bite's tesla-eyes dimmed. "I—Captain. I do not know. I apologize. I was distracted."

"By the One-Eye trying to shoot me with his magic glove. That's understandable." Iari coughed up a laugh. "Gaer. You think you could tell if whatever this transmitted went through the altar?"

He was picking at the cleaved skull now, bent closer over it than Iari liked. "I'd have to examine it."

"Then come on and let's do that. Luki, Llian, Winter Bite—

check out the other passages. See where they go. *Stay together.* Char, you're with me and Gaer. Lieutenant?"

"We, ah. We heard, sir."

"Good. Then that saves me repeating myself. Get everyone together, and come in here. And be careful."

CHAPTER NINE

" . . . and that's it, Captain," said Luki. "All clear." She glanced over her shoulder, further down the passage. "Winter Bite says the only place left is the, ah, altar room. One way in and out, and he and Char haven't gone in. He says it's full of organic residue, too."

Iari flipped to a private channel. "He give any more detail than that?"

Luki blew out an audible breath. "Nope. And I didn't ask."

Iari didn't blame her for it. The *organic residue* from the broken crates had been body parts, which Iffy had identified as forearms and a voidspit box of eyes. All the extra bits, evidently, from a great *many* not-quite-dead One-Eyes, none of whom were in evidence here. That was worrying—both that someone was making One-Eyes at all, but also *where* they were. And there was still the matter of who'd killed all the wichu.

This new set of passages had evidently been where those wichu had lived. They were far smaller than the k'bal constructions, rougher-built, possessed of slightly domed ceilings and more conventional angles. They were laid out in a cross: you came up from the One-Eye room to an intersection. Left and right, two shortish passages that dead-ended, several openings obviously meant to be living quarters. There were packets of food, a small store of water, rude bedding. One room with a chemical toilet, nothing like running water anywhere. Whatever had powered the teslas, they hadn't found it. Gaer had hypothesized a graft to the original k'bal power source, but that still didn't tell Iari *where* that source was.

The only positive discovery was that none of the rooms had any kind of door—not metal, not wood, not even a voidspit curtain—so it was easy to clear them. Luki and Homer had gone left, Dodri and Llian, right. Notch was still back with Iffy and Corso and Gaer, in the One-Eye room, examining bodies.

Iari suspected that trouble, if they found it, would come from the altar room: straight ahead at the end of an unbroken passage with no rooms warting off it. Even from here, Iari's HUD didn't like it. Little pings of alarm, *unidentified arithmancy, proceed with caution.*

Iari tipped her head back, let it rest on the battle-rig. They'd been hours at this already. She was tired. Everyone was, except the riev, who were waiting in front of the doorless opening, hexes crawling faintly red, for her orders.

Right. "Winter Bite—you think you can get me a rough estimate of dimensions? Maybe a layout? Can you do that without going inside?"

"Yes, Captain." He shifted more squarely into the opening. Char set themself more definitively between Winter Bite and everyone else.

Iari's HUD pinged again, benignly this time. Just an advisement of approach from friendlies. Iffy. Gaer. Corso. Llian, Homer, Dodri, and Notch. Iari had no biometrics on the riev ("Be grateful for that," Gaer had said), but everyone else was yellow stress settling back into green, except for Notch, whose biometrics said yellow pushing up into orange. That meant her people were tired, but their nanomecha were doing their job. Made her worry for Corso and Gaer, who had no implants. But vakari were physiologically formidable (or terrifying; Gaer'd lived through things that would've killed anyone else) and Corso was Corso.

"Winter Bite's scanning the altar room," she told them—which they probably already knew, if they'd been listening to comms. Corso might not've, though, so this was for him. "Once we've got a rough idea what we're dealing with, we'll go in. And I warn you: there's something organic inside."

Iffy raised one hand, let it drop. "Of course there is. I don't know if I'd rather more boxes or more bodies."

"I'd rather know what killed the wichu," Iari said, "and whether or not it's still here, *and* if it's hiding in there somehow avoiding Winter Bite's scans. And if it's not, where it *went*. And I want to know who dug these tunnels."

"Wichu separatists did." Gaer's voice could etch metal. "*These*, the little tunnels. The ones that look like they were carved by children with spoons."

Corso had opened his visor again. He peered around, narrow-eyed. "Nah. There's not a lot of wichu up here in Windscar. The villages are small. They notice *anyone* new. They'd talk. I'd've *heard* about it."

"But this cave is remote." Homer seemed a little surprised to have spoken, and more surprised when everyone looked at him. "If there were new wichu, or, ah, *any* wichu, coming up here some way that *didn't* take them through the villages . . . maybe they could dig all this and have no one notice."

Dodri snorted. "Everyone offworld comes through Seawall. Even if these secret wichu took overland caravans from B-town and bypassed Windscar-village, *someone* would notice. Unless they're just using some kind of dropship?"

"Then the station would notice," Homer said. "And the Aedis would hear about it."

"What about the altar?" Iari asked. "Could someone make a portal with it and use *that* to get supplies out here?"

Homer and Dodri looked at each other. Llian said, "The altars can *do* that?"

"Gaer. Can they?"

He hesitated. "Maybe. We know Jich'e'enfe used the altar in B-town to connect to at least one, possibly two, other locations. And then there was the tesser-hex, which just opened into void."

Corso made a face. "Helpful."

"Sss. If they were using a portal, where would the debris go? Tunnels like this take effort. Sure, you pull the material out, you make a new hill, in a few years all anyone sees is grass, but." Gaer drew up straight and still. "*Setat.* They *could* have been working up here that long. *Years.* No one would come near the caves because of those hexes. No one would *see* what they were doing. Separatists could have come up here in ones and twos, disappeared into the tundra, no one would know."

"Raiders might," Llian offered. "They've been bad lately, hitting caravans. People've gone missing from villages. We'd stepped up patrols."

"Raiders might be *in* on it," Corso said. "Pay 'em enough, they turn into your guards."

Gaer dismissed raider-talk with a flick of his fingers. "What about Brood? More fissure activity lately? Because that would track with separatists using altars, too."

Dodri and Homer looked at each other, then at Notch. (Not Llian. She'd gone up beside Luki, peering after the riev.)

"People go missing all the time. Raiders, Brood, weather. It just *happens* up here." Notch sounded a little impatient, a little defensive. "The villages keep the records, not the Aedis."

"So yes," Gaer said, "What you're saying is wichu separatists could've been working up here for the years it would take to dig out these tunnels, forging alliances with raiders, snatching people to carve up and turn into—what did you call them, Iari? *One-Eyes.* All of this, and the Windscar Aedis had no idea."

"It didn't have to be digging. Priests could make tunnels like this. I don't think that's likely, mind you." Iffy craned her head up to look at Gaer. "Other hexes might achieve the same effect, though . . . ?"

"Sss. Nothing *I* could create, or any vakari. But Jich'e'enfe proved extremely talented, and who *setatir* knows if they've found a way to transmute material like your people."

"*My people.* Priests, or alwar?"

"Both."

Corso grunted. "Yeah, okay. The grannytales talk about some of the old gods being able to change one thing into another. And shut it, Gaer, don't you hiss at me—that's what Iari sent me up here to do, listen to grannytales. Though the tales were mostly about people being turned into mushrooms or neefa or sheep or whatever."

"You're sure not the other way round? Sheep and neefa into credulous villagers?"

"No, he's right. Corso is, I mean. I remember those stories, too." Homer seemed vaguely embarrassed. "My great-gran, she wasn't Aedis."

"Lot of people still aren't, up here." Notch sounded thoughtful now. "They don't tend to talk about it around *us*, though."

Corso laid a look on Notch that would etch metal. Iari braced to interrupt, if he went on one of his Aedis rants. But then he took a deep breath and held it and glared—first at Notch, then at her—and said nothing.

Progress.

Then Winter Bite pinged her rig. The riev didn't have comms (yet; that required permission, and that was sitting on some Seawall bureaucrat's desk), but the B-town armorer, Jorvik, and Gaer had engineered an interim transmitter. The riev didn't have proper voice-comm, and she couldn't transmit anything back, but she could receive non-verbal reports.

Her rig accepted the data package and unwrapped it. A two-dimensional line-drawing map grew on her HUD. She could see that the room had six distinct sides, and one jagged alcove that was barely as wide as an (unrigged) alw that might count as a seventh wall. It was larger than anything else they'd found so far, except that first big open cafeteria space. Low ceilings, like all the rest, that reminded Iari of that voidspit cellar in B-town.

Didn't help there was a lumpish central shape etched out in the middle of Winter Bite's map. She couldn't tell what it was, exactly, but she could guess. The altar. And something beyond it, a little smaller, against the back wall.

Iari linked the map to everyone's rig, even Corso's, overriding his *leave me alone* settings. She opened a private channel—not a request, since her battle-rig had command-level permissions—and said, "You need the map. And if you're not *on* the comms, Corso, link in now."

He didn't answer. She didn't expect it. Whatever his reasons for coming out here, nostalgia and fondness for battle-rig conversations weren't one of them.

On the general channel, she asked, "Winter Bite. What are we looking at? And." Elements, she hated to ask, but: "What can you tell us about the organic residue?"

"The organic matter is concentrated on the far side of the room, behind the altar. There is nothing of sufficient mass to render an identification with accuracy. There is also a second nanoforge in the same area. It is dormant, but it does appear to be intact."

"A nanoforge, *not* a surgical unit turned riev-kiln," Luki repeated, clearly and deliberately.

"Correct, Sergeant."

"A room with seven sides again? That's got to mean something," said Iffy. "Religious, maybe."

"*Sss.* It means the wichu are terrible architects?"

But Iari heard the nerves under Gaer's snark. Iari watched her own biometrics tick up into the yellow. They were all waiting—for her, to make a decision. But also to *say* something, to settle nerves. To reassure. Tobin would've, Tobin *had*—and they'd followed him (and they'd died, but that wasn't Tobin's fault). Char didn't need comfort, Winter Bite didn't, but the rest of the templars did.

And all she could give them was orders. "Gaer, Char, with me. The rest of you, stay here."

In case walking in there triggered some firestorm of hexes or a legion of mecha or Elements knew what. Luki didn't like it—Luki made a noise in her throat that sounded like an argument strangled before it achieved volume—but she said a firm Yes, *Captain,* cool as you please. That got Dodri and Homer biometrically settled. Llian was still agitated, but Iari read that as frustrated curiosity. Notch was—Notch was *not* okay, medically or attitudinally, but at least he was quiet about it.

Gaer stopped a meter from the altar and stiffened: both knee joints locking, shoulders going rigid.

Of course. Because the last time he'd been in a room with the altar, it'd tried to open a tesser-hex and suck him through it.

She did not know what to do with a hesitant Gaer.

Char, it seemed, did. "The altar is dormant."

"Winter Bite tell you that?" Gaer's tone was spikier than his elbows, argument, but he took a stiff step forward anyway.

"Winter Bite offered confirmation to my initial assessment." Char's tone dried out, acquired edges. "I was with you, Ambassador, in that cellar, during your examinations. Surely you recall."

"Sss. I recall." Gaer cocked his head at the altar and squatted, spiked elbows propped on spiked knees. His head cocked in that *I am looking through my optic* way he had.

Then Gaer straightened up quickly enough Char twitched his direction. "There are traces of Brood. Faint, but there. This is the same altar. The B-town altar." He jabbed the point of his visor at Char. "You knew that. You *had* to know that."

"I did not want to prejudice your examination."

"I—oh. Well. It's the same altar." Gaer turned back, sweeping his headlamp over the altar's jagged surface. "It survived the tesserhex. That's interesting. And it came *here*." He crouched again. "Let me see if I can ascertain recent use."

Gaer could be the most closed-up, unhelpful neefa on Tanis, or he could spill information like water from a cracked mug. The tilt of his head told her this was going to be the cracked-mug version, if she was patient. Iari waited. And:

"Yes. The transmission we detected from the One-Eye passed through the altar, and it came from somewhere terrestrial, and I'm guessing—local. On this planet, anyway, if they're using standard notation. Here. I've sent the location to you. Are they familiar?"

Iari called up their current coordinates, set them alongside the ones Gaer had sent. "Not to me. They're just numbers. Corso? Lieutenant? Any insight?"

"I didn't get that far out on the steppes," Corso said. "There's not much out there."

Notch made an unhappy noise. "That area got hit hard in the surge. People left, didn't go back. It's probably good raider country. There are a couple small villages out that way. Ettrad, I think. Byn? Homer, is that right?"

"Yes sir. Byn's only got people in summer, though."

"So anything and anyone could be out there. Right." Iari squinted at her HUD. "With the hopper, we'd be there in a few hours, depending on weather."

That would involve an update with Keawe in Windscar, which— ungentle Ptah, might be more trouble than it was worth. It would be more efficient to go straight from here on foot—that'd make it a day, give or take—but with Notch's nanomecha potentially acting up, maybe about to go offline entirely—that changed things. He was a templar, and danger came with the job. Iari had made those same arguments to herself back in B-town, and damn near ended up dead for her judgment.

Notch, if asked, would choose to come along. Keawe, if told about Notch's condition—about any of this—might say *all of you come back.*

Or she'd say, *It's your command, Captain,* and maybe that was the real problem. Because if she were Notch, she'd want, *need,* to go along. But as the person responsible for Notch's well-being—

Sending him back would waste *hours* with the hopper, while there were dead wichu separatists here and the—what, the *half-riev.* The wichu must've made that thing, which begged asking *why*—both temporally and causally. Why now? Why *that* thing, which was an innovation on riev galvanics, which looked—to Iari's unprofessional eye—like someone had drawn inspiration from bone mecha and the dead vakar in the cryo tube, except that inspiration had been *hey, let's lop off a limb and replace it, let's fuel whitefire weapons with a live body, let's do* something *with hexwork that turns their guts into sludge.* It looked too deliberate to be an experiment. It looked *designed.* Leave that information to take Notch back? Leave Notch here alone? Or *all* of them go, and trust Notch would survive the hike?

Or set that problem aside for now. Finish this room first, *then* decide how to proceed.

Iari edged around the altar, sweeping her headlamp across the floor. Winter Bite had said there were organic traces too small to map, so—oh.

That must be what he meant.

Small fingers, pale and limp and clearly no longer alive. Iari moved closer, panning up the rest of the arm. Found a second arm, no longer attached. Found the rest of someone very unfortunate in many small pieces. Raggedy, not clean, like they had been torn apart.

"*Setat,*" she said, very softly.

The Sisstish profanity got Gaer's attention better than any shouting. His headlamp joined hers. "Sss. So when Winter Bite says *organic,* what he means is *dead.* This seems familiar. A dismembered wichu."

Ungentle Ptah, merciful Mishka, "More than one, though, this time. I count at least five arms." Iari squatted beside the first arm. "There's not enough blood for them to've died *here.* Gaer, you notice that?"

"I do. Pinjat's home was an abattoir, and he was just one little artificer torn apart by mad riev. This is, well. This is the butcher shop."

Someone—Iari thought it was Homer—caught their breath,

shock or rapidly arrested nausea. Corso grunted—audibly, identifiably Corso, rueful and darkly amused. As if he'd never been green. Or maybe because he had been, and he could remember feeling that kind of shock.

Iari just felt tired. "So the wichu weren't killed here. Or someone cleaned up the blood."

"Or, and this is *no* comfort: someone used the altar this time for its original purpose. Not a *setatir* tesser-hex into the void, but . . . as a place to offer sacrifice. The altar would have absorbed the blood to power whatever effect was intended. Potentially, a portal to those other coordinates."

Iari closed her eyes briefly. "So whoever killed the wichu—was allied with them. Or knew how to use the altars, anyway."

"*People* did this." Notch suddenly sounded much older. "That's what you're saying. Not—not renegade mecha or Brood."

"People do most of the terrible things in the multiverse," Gaer said wearily.

Iari had nothing to add. Instead, she said, "Dodri, Homer, Llian: stay in the corridor. We don't all need to stomp through here. Iffy, Notch, come in here, please. Corso, I can't order you, but I could use your perspective."

The next few minutes developed for Iari a new, grim appreciation of the term *headcount* as she worked her way almost all the way around the perimeter of the carnage. Everything else was a jumble of viscera and bone.

"I think we're looking at the remains of a separatist cell. I count seven? Plus the four in the other room. Eleven." One head in particular, blasted white by her headlamp. Lips curled back, teeth bared. In this cave, in the cold and the dry—hard to say how long since death, but not so much that the features had rotted into unrecognizable.

Iari thought about saying nothing. Telling Gaer and Char quietly later. Telling Corso maybe never. But they weren't children, were they? No one here was.

"I found Jich'e'enfe," she said.

Corso and Gaer damn near collided, rushing to see. They stood there together for too long, maybe trying to find the rest of her, which Iari reckoned impossible for anything except medmecha.

"Good," said Corso finally. "Looks like she died screaming. There's some justice."

And from Gaer, "Sss," but softly, like he'd sprung a leak. "So she survived that tesser-hex, too."

"Captain." Char had not lingered among the dead. "The nanoforge has a small generator with a power cell at one-third capacity still attached."

Not a word about Jich'e'enfe. Maybe Char didn't care, but Iari didn't think so. Jich'e'enfe had, through her machinations, made everyone realize that riev were still dangerous, but also capable of self-determination. That they were people.

So maybe Char had mixed feelings. Or Char was doing their voidspit job, because Char was a templar and a professional. Iari wasn't sorry to have someplace else to go look, and something else to look at. She joined Char back by the nanoforge. The primary controls were wichu-height, which meant short for damn near everyone else. (Iffy might only have to bend over a little, but Iffy was tiny for an alw). Iari crouched down and convinced the nanoforge to power up. It offered her an access screen with a choice of languages: incomprehensible squiggles or squared-off-font Comspek. Easy decision.

Gaer came sidling over, opened a private comm, and said, "Who did this, though? That's what I'm wondering. Both because

Jich'e'enfe was *extremely* talented, and I don't imagine she'd've died easily, and also, well. *We* didn't do it."

Now she looked sideways at Gaer—eye-level with his hips. Good view of both sets of knees, too. She tilted her head and stared up the long, alien angles of a Five Tribe battle-rig. Vakari had those spines on their chests. The rig's plating made them look a little bit like the prow of a ship from this angle.

"We, meaning SPERE? You sure, Gaer? Didn't think Karaesh't was sending you regular reports about field ops."

He stared down at her. Realized, maybe, the awkwardness of their relative postures, and squatted. "If we *had*, those mecha wouldn't have been here. They seemed very keen on vakari. And also, if SPERE *were* responsible—assassination is one thing. I won't say SPERE doesn't do that. But we wouldn't leave this kind of *mess*. It's evidence."

"What about Protectorate special ops?"

"Sss. No. The mecha argument remains. And they wouldn't've left any vakari remains behind at all, bone mecha or otherwise." He poked idly at the nanoforge screen with a talon. "Are you getting anything from it?"

"Nope. Just a list of jobs." Basic forge things, like simple tools and machine parts. The forge didn't seem to have much in the way of a turing. More automated than interactive, like a janitorial mecha. And definitely no security measures. That said either arrogance or trust or both. Iari wanted to download the data, but she *didn't* want to link her rig to systems that'd belonged to Jich'e'enfe. Not after what'd happened last time. She pried the console open. Please, merciful Mishka, the manufacturers had followed Confederation guidelines, and all the guts were in the same general places—aha. Yes. She pried the data core out of its harness. The nanoforge chirped reproachfully at her and promptly shut down.

"Data core," she said, and handed it to Gaer. "You keep it."

Iari stood up, glad of the battle-rig's support. Her stomach twisted unhappily, reminding her how long it'd been since she'd eaten. Since any of them had. There were bodily functions a battle-rig could take care of, but feeding its occupant wasn't one of them. And this was not the voidspit place she wanted to break for lunch—no, check the chrono, dinner.

"We need to investigate those coordinates." Leave Notch here with the hopper, approach on foot, try to go unnoticed. Iari expanded the private link to include Iffy, Corso, Notch. Char and Winter Bite would hear, no matter what. "So who did this? Not the Protectorate, not Five Tribes, or we wouldn't've had those mecha to deal with." She heard Gaer's faint, amused hiss. "But clearly someone could get past them. So are we dealing with two groups? Let's assume all the dead are wichu separatists, like Jich'e'enfe, and all associated. Whether they were all arithmancers or not, we know *she* was, and she was good. So whoever killed them—the wichu knew them, and let them past the mecha. Because I'm betting the wichu knew how to control all the k'bal defenses."

"So their allies betrayed them," Notch said. "Way I see it, whoever did it saved us some work."

"Yeah, great, someone did us a favor. But that someone isn't a fucking hero. They made friends with people who trafficked in Brood and tried to infect the riev and trashed B-town," Corso said with some force. "So that someone turned on the wichu eventually, great. But why now? And why like *this*? Because *this*—makes me think they're actually worse than Jich'e'enfe."

"I agree with Corso," Gaer said. "Much as it pains me."

"Revenge?" Notch said. "Maybe for what happened in that other room. The, the . . . you know. The dead person."

"The half-riev? The, what did you call it, Iari, the One-Eye?

That, it—wasn't the first attempt. There are boxes of *bits* over there. That suggests *several* attempts, because those arms and eyes were the extras, and I would bet several successes. No," said Gaer, "I think the better question is *where are the rest of the One-Eyes*. I think *that* one was left behind as a, a sentry. A guard. It was probably meant to kill anyone who opened its chamber. It *transmitted*, remember. The people who killed the wichu know that we're here now."

"So let them come," said Notch.

Iari heard Corso draw breath to retort and cut him off. A little too loudly for comms, a little too sharply: "We assumed Jich'e'enfe and the separatists were working alone up here, but that was a mistake. We *know* they didn't work alone in B-town. They had allies in the cartels. They stole local riev to experiment on. What did you say, Lieutenant? People go missing up here all the time?"

"I—yes."

"Shit," said Corso. "You could harvest people by the dozens up here in a *winter*."

"So the question is, who were they working with? And I bet we find out at the other end of that altar. At those coordinates."

That still left the problem of the altar itself. Iari knew the Aedis was largely constructed religion. Had been, in fact, designed as a rallying point for the Confederation against the vakari Expansion. The founders had done their best, on its founding, to find commonalities among every practice and religion among the founding member species, to distill them to the basics. To the Elements, which could be gods, but which could also be abstracted into ideas, concepts, for the more agnostically minded. The alwar had been relatively uniform in praxis across the Harek Empire, having solved their religious dissent before ever reaching the stars. Their adoption of Element worship had been key, and a model to everyone else. Most of the other founding people—tenju spacer clans, a few seedworlds, two separate human collectives, and a scattering of colonies—had at least *some* elements (Elements?) that could apply. Gods or spirits whose features were *like* one of the Four. Allegorical adaptations. But what the Aedis had *not* incorporated, anywhere or from anyone, had been any gods of blood and sacrifice. Hrok and especially Ptah covered violence and destruction. Bloodletting, though, for divine favor—never. But the Aedis had never tried to purge other beliefs, even those bloodier traditions. It had simply got on with keeping its promises, fighting vakari first, and then after the Weep, fighting Brood, and let people decide where to place their allegiance. Most times, it fell with the Aedis.

Pockets of native tenju beliefs persisted—on Tanis, on other hinterland planets. Of course they did. But there hadn't been, to Iari's knowledge, cults on Tanis that murdered people. Or at least they *hadn't* gone around murdering anyone since the Aedis. And now there was not only a bloody sacrifice out here on the Windscar plain, but it was linked up with wichu separatists who'd tried to start a new surge by attempting to first reestablish Oversight for every decommissioned riev and then infect those riev with Brood, while also opening tiny fissures and letting the voidspit Brood spill out. It would have been fucking chaos, if it had worked. It would have undermined faith in the Aedis, in the Confederation—in *everything.*

"Corso, Notch," said Iari. "Do any local Tanisian gods require blood sacrifice?"

Corso blew out a frustrated breath. "Yeah. Can't remember the name. A-something, Axa, Axil . . . My great-gran used to leave a bowl of blood from every animal she butchered—"

"—that you set out by the door, and no one touches it. Yeah.

My grandparents did that. Both sets of them." Notch looked at Corso. "Axorchal. That's the name. Axorchal. The, the *Reaver*. I think. No. Axorchal the One-Eyed. The One-Eyed Reaver?" He trailed off. "Fuck."

Iffy *tsked*. "You sure it wasn't Axorchal the One-Eyed, Herder of Neefa? Don't answer that, Lieutenant."

At least they could joke. Iari remembered being part of exchanges like that when she'd been regular Confederation army. When she'd been new to the Aedis, too. (Before Saichi. After Saichi . . . there had been no one to joke with.) She remembered Tobin's half-smile, his silent observation—had wondered then why he didn't join in.

She understood now.

And she made a decision. Seal this room up, get Gaer to ward the altar, and go north—*with* the hopper, at least until they got close to the second altar's coordinates. Then—then, depending on Notch's condition, she'd reevaluate.

Iari looped everyone into the same channel, clicked to open—

Dead click. No connection.

Her HUD blanked, a half-second of total panic, total *dead*—and then it came up all over alerts, direction *of course* from the altar. Iari whipped around as the whole voidspit thing lit up violet-black. There were hexes on the floor that she hadn't seen before, flickering up like there were teslas under the stone, more blue than violet and still dark enough to make her eyes ache.

Then the aether tore open in a vertical slit that started two meters above the altar and jagged its way with an audible *ripping* sound to the floor. The last time Iari had seen something like it, there'd been Brood on the other side, and aetherless void, and her HUD had gone incandescent. This time—no Brood, and no invading vacuum. But there were bipedal people-ish shapes on the other side, wherever that was, hazed by the black fog and still hard-edged enough Iari could see the red glow coming out of where one eye might be.

That answered a few questions, then—whom the transmission had been aimed at, and were there more half-riev, *and* where they were.

Then the slit tore a little wider, and Iari could just make out the ugly silhouette of a second altar, and more figures crowding into the tear.

"One-Eyes, contact!" She snapped her shield out. "Gaer! Get that portal closed!"

She knew he'd be trying, but everyone else needed to know that. Because everyone else had to buy him that time.

Then the first of the half-riev (the One-Eyes) came through the tear, from blur to suddenly solid as they stepped into the cave. (Add another question answered: did the altars act like portals? Yes, they did.) This one wasn't naked—wore armor that wasn't a battle-rig—but besides that metal skullcap and that cabochon eye, they also had one of those gloves on their right hand. That hand was coming up, starting to point.

Iari snapped out her axe, no time for the shield, and jumped as syn punched her forward.

CHAPTER TEN ═══════════

G aer had all his attention on the data core, two aetheric layers in (because sometimes you could hack the data core *without* a processor), which was why he wasn't immediately aware when his battle-rig panicked and Iari yelled his name (he *heard* her, same as he heard the alarms, but it took time to get back to the outermost layer of reality). He arrived to the screaming alarms with the echoes of "Gaer! Get it closed!" still ringing in the helmet's confines.

Close what and *the five hells is this* and then comprehension—the altar was opening (that was the cascade of data on his optic, *aha*) in a welter of complex arithmancy, hexes that could indicate an open portal, and *oh yes* there were things coming through the portal and he was crouched with his *back* to it on the far side of the room from the only exit, that was stupid, he needed to move—

He shoved upright, damn near slammed into Char—who'd got themself close enough to panic his rig *again*, who was the only reason he didn't lose his *setatir* head when a bolt of whitefire hit Char, just barely in front of Gaer's fortunately visored face. Char's armor absorbed the shot in a flare of hexes.

It was Char's left side, their original side, which had different responses to whitefire than Aedis hexwork. Aedis armor tended toward deflection, the transmutative hexes changing one energy into another. Wichu artificing absorbed whatever hit it, storing it for later: as a battery for any excess power a riev might require in battle, particularly for weaponry, which for intact riev like Char would've been a whitefire (literal) hand-weapon.

Which Char did not have. Which the things coming through the rip *did*. Gaer thrust his head around Char's shoulder in time to see that four bipedal shapes had spilled out of the vertical rip (not a Weep fissure, not a portal, some hybridized horror of each). A fifth was resolving in the tear, bleeding equations from both helmet and armor that stitched them together through multiple layers of aether. That was how riev looked to an arithmancer (except riev had armor everywhere). Unlike the naked half-riev in the other room, *these* arrivals wore armor. It was all metal bits and nanoforged plates, not a battle-rig, and the configuration was what you saw for local peacekeepers: chestplates and backplates, lighter armoring on limbs. It wasn't a uniform, nothing matched. (But that *was* a B-town peacekeeper pauldron, and that chestplate there was army cast-off). They all had jactae hanging off their hips or clipped to their thighs, too, so far ignored.

Hypothesis: jactae were for when the whitefire weapons needed a recharge.

Whitefire took a *lot* of power. With riev, weapons were powered by absorbed energy and by their own internal power core. The One-Eyes might have finite shots if they were relying on just what their living, corporeal bodies could fuel.

The best test for a theory was battle.

Which they were well and truly *in*, now, the templars from the corridor having come inside, a maelstrom of battle-rigs glowing hexwork (Gaer's HUD began organizing the chaos, tagging friendlies and marking the half-riev as hostile).

Number One had tangled with Iari, Three and Four had engaged with the other templars. Number Two—a big one, Keawe-sized, indeterminate species and gender under the piecemeal armor, the only one facing him and Char, who'd already shot at them once—fired their whitefire gauntlet again. Gaer jerked his head back, and Char's hexes flared up.

Then someone let out a strangled yelp that echoed through comms. Gaer jagged around Char in time to see a templar go down (not Iari), sparks bleeding from their battle-rig's knee, where an *absolutely* stolen Aedis axe had landed and stuck. One-Eye Three—Gaer thought it was Three, anyway—held the other end of the axe, tugging the haft with no sense of *how* to dislodge it, like someone who'd never imagined a weapon could get stuck in a body.

Like someone with very little experience. Gaer drew his own jacta, didn't wait for his rig's target-lock, *fired*. His bolt scored a line through Three's armor. They howled in pain and, when they saw who had shot them, in fury.

If Gaer never heard *veek* shouted at him again, really, it would be too soon.

(Note: *this* lot of helmeted horrors could use words.)

Then Corso drilled a longcaster bolt through the unhelmeted side of Three's skull. Gaer wished he could hear the impact. Probably a very satisfying *hiss* as the whitefire punched through. Maybe a wettish *clang* as the skull inside split from the heat.

As Three went down, Two's glove flared. Their helmet did something else that wasn't a whitefire overload. A battle-hex, the sort that turned air to phlogiston and added a spark, uncoiled toward Gaer.

(Five finally pushed through the portal over by the altar. On their heels, Six shoved into the ripped, raggedy hole. And behind them loomed another shape in there, bigger, glowing with hex-work even through all that portalish fog, glowing like a *setatir* beacon to Gaer's optic. *That* was the arithmancer making this whole business happen, *bet* it was, and they were much taller than a wichu.)

Gaer jagged sideways, intending to avoid the battle-hex, intending to draw his monofil out and cut this neefa-eater in front of Char into several pieces. He slammed into Corso instead, who'd been dodging the *other* way.

There was a moment where Gaer's rig shrieked imprecations at him—collision, *collision*—and then he bounced off Corso, because *setatir* Aedian rigs were heavier and Corso was a *setatir* brick of a tenju anyway. The bounce sent Gaer right back into the One-Eye's line of fire. *Actual* fire, this time: the aether around Gaer turned into phlogiston and ignited as the hex went off like a fireball.

Which, *fine*, his rig could handle that. Gaer tweaked a variable of his battle-rig's defenses, shifted the numbers *thus*—and bounced the hex off his shield, away from Corso (who had his visor *up*, the neefa) and back toward the One-Eye, who thrashed in the fire but neither ignited (people were harder to light than old leaves, alas) nor panicked, who was raising their weapon-hand up again.

Gaer saw Two's gauntlet's hexes glow.

Then the fire around the gauntlet flickered and turned molten, then solid. Smoking, greasy black, hardening into stone as Gaer watched. The One-Eye shrieked and collapsed, thrashing around trying to get stone-coated steel off their hand.

"Got him." Iffy sounded the slightest bit out of breath. "You both all right?"

Gaer strangled an urge to stare at her. Priests, even healer-priests (even Iffy), trained for battle. He knew that. He'd never seen *this*, but there was time to ask later.

She wasn't even looking at him. Looking at Corso, who'd gotten his *setatir* faceplate down, finally.

"Draw their fire," Gaer shouted. "Those gloves *drain* them, count the shots until they switch to jactae."

"Copy," said Corso, so at least someone was listening.

Then in Gaer's helmet, Iari's voice: "Gaer, close the fucking *altar*!"

He wanted to shout back, *I can't, you did it last time, do it this time*, but he didn't know where she was. His HUD didn't mark templar locations except as *friendly*, and he couldn't see clearly through the madness—of whitefire, of templars, of phlogiston and random bursts of flame. Of arithmancy pulsing off that altar in irregular waves. Black smoke pouring out of it, too, getting thicker, blacker, *please* Iari's Elements, let that smoke not be the hallucinatory voidspit again because no one needed to *imagine* monsters right now.

So of course right then, someone (Dodri? Llian?) yelled, "Brood!"

Gaer watched as a boneless sprang at Corso's undefended flank, no, *two* boneless, their pentad eyes glowing the same awful shade as their misaligned mouths. They latched onto his rig, spread themselves over him like a shroud. Corso did not shriek, howl, or thrash. Corso did not appear to *setatir* notice, which meant his rig hadn't noticed, so *either* these Brood were completely concealed from hexes (which had happened), or—

Gaer confirmed there was no alert on his HUD, none on his optic—and more infallibly, nothing off Char (who smashed their One-Eye opponent flat, finally, and then stomped hard to be certain) or—spin, look, *there*—Winter Bite.

Then Luki screamed, "It's not real, no Brood, *not real!*"

Luki had figured it out. Luki also sounded *setatir* terrified. Gaer took that to mean she was trusting her battle-rig, not her eyes, and that she was seeing the same hallucinatory horrors as everyone else (except Char. Except Winter Bite. Probably also except the One-Eyes, since half of their vision was artificed truth).

He had to close the *setatir* altar. Gaer dropped back into a crouch behind the nanoforge's scant shelter and deployed a defensive hex meant to bend light, the sort of *look away* that wouldn't hold up to examination or close attention, but worked well in a skirmish. The smoke actually helped. No one was screaming *veek* at him, no one was trying to cut him in half, which let him feel a little bit better about dropping into the layers of aether where the portal hexes lived.

Anchor points had to be fixed—and yes, *this* altar had those equations etched into it, which meant it was a mobile half of the gate (they'd guessed that was possible). But on the other side . . . Gaer snaked his awareness through the rip's tangled-up hexes, found that set of equations, caught them—and slid another step deeper through the aether. He had an approximate real-world location where the other side was, but he had a theory, too. If one set of coordinates was on an altar, maybe the second set was, too.

He sent his awareness slipping along the connection between anchor points. This side, the altar crusted with layers of old blood, was the destination. The power that opened a portal, and held it open, was coming from the other side (that *setatir* arithmancer). That was where Gaer needed to go in order to shut this side down (unless he could destroy *this* altar, which he could not). He was not about to go through the portal in his fragile flesh, no; he would send his less fragile mind instead, through the aether, backtrailing the threads of power. Then, in addition to cutting the connection, maybe he could figure out a little bit about what the anchor on the other side *looked* like. If it was another altar, or something more fixed.

(Fixed would be nice. Fixed would mean someplace the Aedis could find and eradicate, preferably with aetherships and artillery. *Mobile* would be a potential problem, so that's what Gaer expected to find.)

Arithmancy was the mother tongue of the multiverse, numbers and functions like an alphabet, the equations like words. The analogy Gaer liked was poetry. Arithmancy was *living* language, moving, mobile. Descriptive, but also predictive. So *predict*, create: a series of equations that predicted the lines of power between both sides of the portal. Gaer spiraled his own hexes around the portal's conduit like a flexible tube, a coil that he could follow, and that would adjust to any fluctuations—

The portal's equations rippled like water in wind. Then the power swelled from threads into ropes and shook violently.

(In reality, in a room choked with hallucinatory fog and more conventional smoke from things on fire (whitefire burned *anything* without arithmantic warding that it touched), more One-Eyes popped through the portal. Char had stationed themself in front of Gaer, both bulwark and blind, so he couldn't see for certain—but he thought the One-Eyes outnumbered the templars now, though by how much—?)

The ropes of connecting power between portal points shrank and resumed being threads. Still pulsing, still active, but . . . less. So *that* was what the portal looked like when it sent someone through. All right.

That activity was also an enormous drain on *whatever* was

fueling it. If the other side was using blood, like Jich'e'enfe had—
sss, it must be an abattoir over there to get this many people
through.

Gaer's arithmantic hands slipped on his hex, and a strand of it
broke loose. It lashed like a whip, and Gaer saw that the equation
had been rebalanced (*setatir* arithmancer), turning it from con-
nective and stable to something intended to wound. It would *feel*
like a physical hit, if it got him—like it broke skin, like it drew
blood. Whether or not it did, he'd find out when he put all the bits
of himself back in one aetheric plane. Sometimes a hex manifested
damage *on* the body itself, sometimes inside it; sometimes it confined itself to the mind.

(The mirri, who'd washed their collective hands of the Confederation and the Protectorate and everyone else after the Weep's
opening, had said some hexes could hurt the soul, but they'd been
parthenogenic mystics, so.)

Gaer dodged the lashing end of his hex, once and twice.
Caught it ungracefully on the third try and controlled it. The end
snapped at him, its solution indeterminate, fluxing along a series
of possibilities to defy any predictive defenses he meant to launch.
It was . . . sss. It was a smart and novel bit of arithmancy. It was
also flawed, and after several more passes, Gaer excised the prob-
lematic variable in the center, just cut its solutions off outright,
and restored stability to his *setatir* hex.

Jich'e'enfe would've flayed the inside of his skull if she'd caught
him with something like that. (Not good.) Instead something had
caught her and cut her into little pieces. (Good!) This new arithmancer was not Jich'e'enfe's equal. *That* was a nice surprise. He
wished he could tell Iari.

(In reality, the templars were—winning? Probably winning.
Gaer heard Iari shouting something, probably *hurry up, Gaer*. Iari

definitely would not want to hear about arithmancers. But while he was paying attention, Gaer remembered to breathe, and felt his focus several layers down and away sharpen. Breathing. Yes. One did forget.)

The portal's equations shivered again, prelude to another flex and another set of One-Eye reinforcements. Gaer rode out the next expansion (as the portal spilled more trouble into the cave), and when it contracted and withdrew, he latched on and went with it.

It was like being dragged skinless through seawater. It hurt like bits of him were sloughing away. (His skin *probably* wasn't peeling off. Probably. He *was* probably screaming a little, though.) Gaer held on, writing and rewriting his hexes to keep them steady.

Portal technology was about crossing physical space by tunneling through layers of aether. The aether at its surface layers mapped close to the physical world. But the deeper one traveled, the less representational those layers became, the more bizarre the architecture. There were layers in two dimensions, and layers in twenty, and monochromatic layers where one could only move in short, straight lines and at right angles. And then there was void—said to be the last, the deepest aetheric stratum, which early astronomers had mistaken for that space between stars and worlds (which was why they called it the same thing and confused everyone. Arithmancers knew better; void was infinite in its folds, and it was still part of aether, and the theory didn't make sense when you were sober.)

Then Gaer hit the other end of the portal, *bang*, like slamming into a steel bulkhead. *This* was the anchor point, *this* tangle of equations and battle-hexes, so many hexes, some of which he recognized in principle and some of which made his mind ache. But what he could see clearly was the rigid structure of it: matrices and grids unfolding at queasy angles, dimensions tethered by artifice and arithmancy unlike anything he'd ever seen. (Beautiful. Terrible. Oh *setat*, oh dark lords, so terrible.) But he could tell that the anchor was another altar, and that on the physical plane it would be so much metal and blood. Here in the aether, though, it was so much larger, it seemed to be *moving*—

—because there were Brood trapped in the altar's folds. Oh. *Oh.*

The k'bal had made tesser-hex gates to cross void; the alwar had replaced those with a more elegant and efficient solution. The vakari—the Protectorate then, before any Schism—had engineered their own methodology: by using a convoluted fold of the deep aether to power their passage from one point to another. And in that fold, they'd found Brood.

No one knew if Brood were the byproduct of the vakari tesser-hex engines, or somehow native to that folded aetheric layer. But Brood had fueled a voidship navy that had both the will and the means for galactic Expansion, capital E. And as the Protectorate spread, their Brood engine-fuel spread through more deep layers of aether, into void itself, until there was only a thin skin holding them back from the place where planets hung and ships moved at conventional speeds.

After the Weep, of course, no one *did* that anymore, used those engines or those equations. No one was stupid enough to draw power off the Brood-filled layers of aether. You found the equations in archives; there were endless artistic renderings in 2D dramas of what it had looked like.

And those renderings had been wrong. Because this altar, this anchor, was drawing its power from Brood just like the old vakari engines. Gaer couldn't *see* the Brood in here with his eyes (those were wide, unblinking, reflecting and absorbing the march of arithmancy from his HUD and his optic). But he knew the shape of Brood arithmancy, the awful calculus of their beings rendered equational (he, too, was a numeric rendering this deep in the aether, Gaer i'vakat'i Tarsik as integer, variable, constant). This portal was powered by Brood, power confined and channeled in the altar's physical form like it was a voidship engine.

Jich'e'enfe had wanted to use the Weep; she had made little fissures to drip Brood out where she needed them. This portal—using Brood as batteries—was just another page in that book of stupidities. And even if Jich'e'enfe was dead, *someone* had (mis) learned her lessons, because *this*—resurrecting vakari equations, *using* them again—was the arithmantic path to another *setatir* Weep.

And worst, most awful: Gaer couldn't do anything about it. The binding of Brood to a physical artifact (so many aetheric layers away) meant he couldn't unbind them *here* without, well. Without being the next vakar to doom the multiverse with an act of unwise arithmancy.

The altar had to be taken apart from the *outside*. Preferably with a templar axe.

He knew how she'd done it now, how Jich'e'enfe had escaped that B-town cellar. There must have been Brood in that altar, and he hadn't noticed them (but how could he have thought to look for *this*?).

Bet, *bet* there were still Brood in it now.

Gaer doubled back toward his body. The pulses of energy seemed to be stabilizing, the connection was becoming more solid, *that* was bad. He endured another rush of skinless-saltwater flensing, and then—void and dust, dear dark lords—he landed back on their own side, slammed into the hexes that made up the altar. Another lattice of equations, that exquisite obscenity.

And Brood. This altar wasn't identical to the one on the other side. It was . . . more brittle. Thinner. An older iteration, maybe: he could see versions of the same binding hexes, but less elegant (still so much more complex than he could understand just by looking). Variables not as precise, orders of operations and derivations not *quite* as perfect.

The power pouring into it wasn't helping this altar's integrity, either: was eroding the hexwork, like Brood effluvia devoured flesh and bone. Slowly, awfully, inexorably.

(Gaer's body was aware of Char picking him up and *throwing* him at the doorway, of the battle-rig's indignation as he landed and skidded to a stop. Of smoke and blood outside his visor, of screaming on the comms).

Gaer pulled himself out of the aether too fast, and landed back in a body that didn't feel like *his*, or like *him*, for a heartbeat. (Heartbeats were slow. Decades, generations between each thump, whole worlds turned to ash.) His skin didn't fit right. His eyes didn't work right. (Blink, idiot, *blink*; at least the second lids had exercised protective reflex and closed.) Then the blood running down the back of his throat made him swallow, then gag, then cough. He got his feet under him, shoved upright.

His HUD flooded his blurry eyes with new information. The black hallucinatory fog was still swirling around, dispersed mostly harmless by the churning battle. Char still held the ground in front of Gaer, mostly shielding him, though Char themself was beset. Their hexes rippled redly, brighter in patches where white-fire had hit. (A lot of bright patches. A lot of hits. Void and *setat*, he needed to clear his head *now*.) He registered Winter Bite— another collection of hexes that his battle-rig didn't quite trust— on the periphery, a little less besieged; but then he wasn't trying to protect the arithmancer who hadn't done the one thing he'd been asked to do, either.

Gaer fumbled his jacta off his hip, linked it to the HUD's target system. He could shoot things. He could help that way. He picked the closest One-Eye, a burly tenju with arms bare except for the glove bolted, who was coming at Char. The One-Eye raised the gauntlet, flexed the palm, and Gaer saw the convergence of hexes as whitefire coalesced, drawn from the twin sources of the living tenju and the glove itself, which—

And then Gaer saw it, how the glove worked. The bastard cousins of the altar-hexes, the ones binding Brood into service, laced all through the glove, too (and the helmet? Bet, but check later.) There were . . . Brood in the gauntlet. Some little, minor kind, maybe swarm, maybe some sort no one had seen before, slaved and serving as battery, concealed from all those Brood-sensitive Aedis hexes by battle-hexes and arithmancy.

Despair soured the back of his throat, joining the blood and iron of overstretched arithmancy.

His hand wasn't steady. His eye certainly wasn't. The battle-rig did its job (something had to) and compensated for both. Gaer planted a jacta bolt into an unarmored bit of the One-Eye and they staggered. Char didn't pause, didn't look back; they simply turned to the next One-Eye and shoved *that* one back, and made room for Gaer as he pushed forward.

"Fall back," he told Char, with no faith they'd comply. These One-Eyes weren't just bandits, or mindless like the corrupt riev or that naked specimen in the other room (it must have been a cast-off, a mistake, not a sentry at all). These One-Eyes were almost an army, in numbers and gear if not quite tactics, and the templars were outnumbered. The gloves seemed to have two modes, whitefire (which drained both user and Brood-battery) and conventionally artificed phlogiston-flame hexes for when the glove had to recharge. He could do something about the latter, at least: strangle those hexes, smother those fires. Force the aether to behave its *setatir* self.

Corso had pulled back to the doorway to give himself range, and sat there methodically pumping longcaster bolts into the room, with Winter Bite defending his position like Char had defended Gaer's. Iffy was—oh, *not* with Corso (a shot of pure panic, *where*—), Iffy was crouched down beside a fallen templar, paying no attention to 'caster bolts or whatever else might be happening. Beside her was Dodri, more or less upright, hacking at whoever came within range. The downed templar was Homer, had to be; Llian's rig was smaller and anyway *that* was her over with Luki. Two templars with swords, the only two who carried them, pinned together against the wall beside the altar, pushed there by the flood of One-Eyes coming through.

And *there*, finally: two of the larger rigs, both with axes and shields, shoulder to shoulder. Iari and Notch. They were surrounded, had been driven by One-Eyed currents away from Llian and Luki, forced to the wall opposite the nanoforge and closer to the entrance (where it was clear everyone needed to go, *setat*, withdraw).

One of half-riev—big, tenju (*all* of the One-Eyes were tenju, Gaer realized)—slapped an open-palmed glove onto a battle-rig. Whitefire burst out in crackling strands that solidified (for some version of the word) into a wave of plasma. The battle-rig's hexes flared up, all those shifting equations that Gaer could see in the aetheric layers adjusting, responding. Some to disperse, some to counter.

And then the rig's hexes blinked out. *Dead.* The templar inside it tottered and dropped to one knee.

Gaer choked on Iari's name, changed it to, "Char!" and leapt forward, intending to pull the attacker off bodily (knowing he wasn't fast enough, it was too far away), knowing he didn't dare shoot, because if he missed he'd hit an unshielded rig and his bolt would go through. The templar's armor would reboot, it *would*, take that on faith, *setatir* Aedis (gear, templars) always got back up.

Not always.

From his periphery, Gaer saw Char crossing the room.

Then the downed templar's partner spun around, synning-quick, shield first, to make the attacker flinch back, then the axe slicing behind.

The One-Eye did *not* flinch. Its glove still glowed, radiating out from the palm, like it had dipped its hand in plasma, and it slapped the templar's shield. Whitefire sizzled against whitefire.

(Through his optic, Gaer saw the equations meet, saw them mesh. Saw the shift in equations as the glove's power-draw slid out of balance. The cost for this would be suicidally high, the glove was going to *eat* its wearer from the inside—literally, because inside that glove were Brood.)

They didn't care, this One-Eye fanatic. They ripped a monofil off their belt with the ungloved hand and swiped at the fallen templar. Missed, but only because the other templar's shield held it back. The One-Eye *leaned* against it, pushed hard—

The templar's shield snapped back into its gauntlet. The One-Eye staggered, threw up the gloved hand out of reflex to catch themself. And the templar's axe descended, suddenly wreathed in hexes Gaer had only seen once before, hexes that slid down the shaft, not from the axe, but from inside the battle-rig—no.

From the *templar* inside the rig.

Gaer watched for the second time as Iari lit her battle-rig from the inside, every crack burning blue-white. Plasma ran down her armor like water (a cascade of interlocking equations, each changing the next) and collected on the edge of the axe, until Gaer could only face that brightness through his optic.

Then her axe hit the One-Eye's glove, and that glove *shattered*. Whitefire cracked off in high-velocity shards. Gaer flinched and deployed a skein of deflective, reflexive hexes.

Somehow the One-Eye (now the One-Hand, Gaer amended) was not dead yet. The blow that had destroyed the glove had not just burned all the imprisoned Brood, it had vaporized the flesh inside, burned the stump, and blackened skin all the way to the One-Eye's shoulder. But they were, had been, tenju, and tenju did not know when to die. One-Hand twisted their remaining wrist holding the monofil and jammed it into Iari's forearm to the hilt, at the seam where her shield-gauntlet mated up with her forearm.

The monofil should have bounced off, or shattered, when it came in contact with the rig's defenses. Instead the monofil's blade slid through, and Gaer realized Iari's rig was as defensively dead as Notch's. Just blank, to his optic, now that he thought to check.

But it was still moving, *she* was still moving. He could see through her faceplate, backlit by Iari herself. He expected to see that snarly grin she got sometimes when she fought, unholy delight in the violence. Instead Gaer saw with growing horror that her tea-green eyes had gone white, like all the color had been burned away. And her aura—Gaer didn't know what he was seeing. What those colors even *meant*.

Notch at least was still *Notch*, roiling reds and oranges and violent violets, scared and furious and shoving himself upright.

Then the green flooded back to Iari's eyes, and she returned with it. Her rig's defenses came back, too, in a hex-flare that made One-Hand's monofil sizzle and snap.

Iari recoiled, shook her arm, flexed her hand. Blinked at One-Hand.

Who was still shrieking, but with insensate fury, not pain. They stabbed again with the monofil's broken length, missed, and then—as Notch's rig resurrected itself, as Char arrived—jerked away from the templars. One-Hand fell, caught themself on the ruined arm, which crumpled in a very *un*-flesh-and-bone-like way, and kept moving, worming, dear dark lords, across the stone floor, still shouting actual words.

The altar. They were going for the altar. No more One-Eyes had come through recently; the monstrosity just sat there, throbbing violet-red and bleeding smoke. (Brood writing under the skin of it, now that Gaer knew where to look. How to look.) One-Hand threw themself across the altar and lifted their monofil, and Gaer realized what they intended, too late to do more than shout, "Stop them!"

Char tried: diverted mid-step and swiped, missed.

Then One-Hand twisted their wrist and drove the broken monofil into their uncovered eye with enough force to snap their head back. The screaming stopped. The body did not crumple so much as wilt, collapsing partway with the force of the death blow. Blood and something sludgier, blacker, spilled out as they slumped across the altar.

Gaer's HUD lit up with Brood alerts. Char's armor flared. Even Iari recoiled (the syn and the rig showing sense, maybe, when their templar didn't). That was One-Hand, their emanations, so much Brood they had in their system. Then the altar flared too, all the strange script Gaer remembered blazing suddenly visible, with a violet so dark it made his eyes hurt. He remembered that, too, from B-town. Fear stole his breath, locked him stiff. The altar was going to open a hole into aetherless void, a *setatir* tesser-hex, it was going to suck them all in and Iari had already spent her *whatever* that was, Ptah's wrathful gift, so she would not be able to destroy it.

Gaer's optic damn near blinded him with a litany of its own alerts. The hexes he'd seen, those brittle guardians that held the altar together, that held the Brood under its skin—were breaking. And in the eyeblink it took to see, to understand, before the reflex to shout a warning could happen (because he could not stop this, he knew that to his bones)—the altar split.

It broke like something gone rotten: a crumbling along all seven faces, the metal falling into itself like a sinkhole. One-Hand disintegrated entirely, flesh to slime to smoke and dust, leaving a hole into which the altar folded itself. Alerts burst across Gaer's HUD, aetheric rifts, fluctuating atmosphere, gravity heaving and ebbing. The altar crumbled inward and left a hole in the aether, the edges of which wept Brood slime. On the other side of that maw stood the other arithmancer, the one who'd made the *setatir* portal in the first place, who held up a gleaming, gloved hand, whose helmet burned red where the left eye should be. Whose silhouette was tenju-broad but distorted, too, jagged and angular and *wrong*.

That arithmancer held up their glove, and Gaer saw the palm flash violet-black. Then the portal imploded and tried to take everyone with it: sudden and violent summons from *here* to *elsewhere*.

Iari threw herself across Notch. Gaer felt his boots slip, dropped to his knees and *clawed* for purchase. Then Char caught him, pulled him tight as if he weren't a battle-rigged vakar, as if he were a child's rag toy. Gaer saw One-Eyes swept past, lifted off their feet and sucked back into the maw as the altar imploded. Saw one who didn't quite make it, who left half of themself on *this* side, oozing something between Brood slime and honest blood as the rip stitched itself back together.

And then it was done.

"Iari." Gaer pushed at Char. "Did she, is she?"

"Here." Char's voice vibrated through his battle-rig's skin. "She is safe, as is the lieutenant." But there was something in Char's tone that warned him *safe* wasn't *all right.*

Gaer pushed at Char's arm—like pushing a mountain, but the mountain decided to let him go. And yes, thank you dark lords, Iari was there, pulling Notch to his feet, both rigs flickering. The bisected One-Eye lay where the altar had been, where the stone itself had been melted and cooled to black glass.

Gaer started to ask Char what was the matter, but then he saw: between altar and wall, where Luki and Llian had been pinned— there was nothing. The templars were gone.

CHAPTER ELEVEN

G aer leapt to the altar's far side. He was afraid of finding broken battle-rigs with broken bodies, or worse—just a greasy smear where Luki and Llian had been. But there was—nothing. Just cave floor, not even the heat-slicked black glass, that was impossible—

No. *There.* His headlamp settled on marks in the stone that looked like the scrapes two battle-rigs might make if they were dragged. He upped his HUD's magnification, crouched. The gouges got shallower the closer they got to the altar, which suggested—*sss.* They'd been lifted up? Aedian battle-rigs?

"Sound off," Iari said, too calm to have noticed the absences yet.

"Winter Bite and I are optimal," Char said, breaking protocol and personal custom and thrusting themself to the fore. (Buying him time, Gaer realized, or delaying some other, more awful thing than *two templars just got sucked into I don't know what.*)

If Iari noticed that breach, if she cared, it didn't show. "Copy. Notch?"

"Fu—Okay. Not great."

"Dodri?"

"Unhurt." Dodri sounded grim. Sounded like she had something else to say, too, that she'd just bitten off.

"Homer?"

"Homer's down." Iffy's voice shook. "He's dead, Iari."

Oh. Oh *setat*.

Someone's breath caught. Then came a beat of silence, awful silence. Gaer swung around to look at Iari. She stood there beside Notch, having helped him upright, still with one hand on him.

"He's . . . what?" Notch sounded smaller, suddenly. Younger. "How?"

Iari jerked her hand off, then, like some live spark had traveled between the rigs. "Iffy," she said, and sliced right through whatever Iffy had been about to say. "Are you hurt?"

"I—no, but—"

Implacable as the sunset, as pitiless: "Corso?"

"Fine." Gravel-voiced, more than usual. Gaer caught peripheral movement, Corso crossing to Iffy and fallen Homer. Winter Bite followed more slowly, his attention divided between the altar and Iari, like he wasn't sure where he should go.

Gaer realized then Iari hadn't asked about Luki and Llian yet, that she should have—that, void and dust, she was the captain, she had everyone's *setatir* rigs linked to hers, she could see everyone's status on her HUD.

She already knew they were gone. She must've known when they disappeared. Or maybe her rig was dead, or malfunctioning, *why* go through this roll-call otherwise?

Because everyone had to know.

Gaer couldn't quite breathe, suddenly. The problem wasn't physical, he knew that, not lungs or throat. But when his HUD reported a clear atmosphere, no contaminants, he popped his visor. The air tasted like burned meat and ozone, with lacings of that flat iron you got after excessive phlogiston and fires.

"Iari." His voice echoed in the room, louder than he'd intended.

She turned toward him. She might as well have been Char, for all the expression she showed. (Except her aura. Oh, dear dark lords. That was a storm, a cataclysm, and let it not break the surface.) "Where are they?" she asked. "Luki and Llian."

And *that* was when the rest of them figured it out, did their own counts, reckoned the missing. Notch's head came around, Corso's breath caught. Someone higher-voiced—Iffy or Dodri—made a tiny, hurt noise. (Iffy, Gaer decided. Dodri seemed like she might be past hurt.) Winter Bite and Char looked at each other, a conversation conducted without eyes or faces. Then Winter Bite came over and stood on the other side of the blasted-glass spot where the altar had been. His chestplate retracted and his appendages emerged.

(Of course, Gaer thought, with the part of his brain that was always observing: those tentacles are delicate. He'd put them away in a fight.)

"Gaer." Not even a hint of impatience from Iari. That more than anything else told Gaer she was not one bit all right.

She needed to hear—void and dust. That Luki and Llian were all right, or at least alive. That she hadn't lost three people today.

But if they *did* live, how long that continued would rest on where they'd ended up, and that:

"I don't know, exactly." Gaer stood up slowly. "I *think* they were pulled through when the portal closed. *This* side collapsed, but the other side was still open. I was wrong. Iari, I was *wrong*. I said, I thought—Jich'e'enfe was traveling *into* the void from B-town. But she was traveling *through* the void to another altar, I think using the equations for the form—"

"Thank you. I'll take that report to mean you're fine." Iari turned toward Notch. "Your syn's offline, Lieutenant."

Notch blinked. He'd gotten his faceplate open, too, was staring between Iari and fallen Homer like he wasn't sure where he should be. His aura was roiling conflict: grief, shock, rage. Surprise splashed through his aura. "Yeah."

"Did you know that it was? That your nanomecha weren't functional?"

Before this fight, she meant. Gaer winced.

Notch realized what she was asking. His mouth opened, hung there. Then his jaw ground itself closed. "Sir. I didn't think—"

"No. You didn't." Iari looked at Gaer. "Can you get it open again? The portal?"

"No."

There, a tiny crack in her composure. Gaer didn't think anyone else here would know it, except Char. The way her jaw flexed, *just so.*

"I pulled coordinates from the other side," he said. "A physical location. Sending now. But listen. The actual anchor is another altar. I—you don't want an arithmantic treatise right now—"

"Correct."

"—so you just have to trust that I *can't* open the portal, and that it, the altar—could move."

She stared at him, and her jaw relaxed. "Dodri, Char, Winter Bite. I need you with me. Iffy, you need to get the lieutenant back to Windscar. Gaer, you go with them."

"I—what? Iari, *Captain.*" Oh, like a whip, Iffy's anger. "What about Homer?"

Gaer closed his eyes.

"He goes back with you and the lieutenant." Iari's voice was dangerously blank, dangerously reasonable. "If Gaer can't open the portal, then we have to go back out these caves the way we came in. We can leave Homer in his battle-rig. Char can carry him back to the hopper." She paused, closed her faceplate. Hummed. "These coordinates you pulled, Gaer—are you sure about them?"

"Yes. But the altar can move. Can be moved."

"So we have to catch them *now*, before they move it."

Notch had started walking toward Homer and Iffy. Now he whipped back around (and wobbled, unsteady). "You're going after them."

"Yes."

Notch squared up to Iari, a little too close. "I'm going, too."

Iari opened her visor, flicked a look at his chest—would not look up, would not bend her neck (literally or figuratively, *setat*). "You are, by your own admission, unfit for duty. You're going back to the Aedis."

Gaer took an ill-considered half-step toward Notch and Iari. He thought to get between them, say something arithmancer-ish, draw their collective ire . . .

Char stuck out an arm, not enough to stop him, but enough that he'd have to step around them. A warning, that gesture. But the look Char cast at him—cold blue teslas, a face that didn't move by design—looked (somehow) like sympathy.

Notch wasn't going to quit yet. "Luki's yours, but Llian—"

"Is *my* responsibility," Iari snapped, "same as you are."

Then Corso, who did *not* have Char to restrain him, walked over to Notch and said, "Come on. Help me with Homer, all right? We can carry him. Char's got other things to do." Corso's gaze touched Gaer's, a clear *so do you*, as Notch seemed to wilt in his rig.

Iari was already walking away from Notch, crossing toward Gaer. She stopped beside the glassed, ruined floor.

"When the One-Eye died on the altar, they yelled something. Did you catch it?"

"I heard. I didn't understand it."

Char cocked their head. An entirely new voice ripped out of them, raw and furious, in a language not Comspek or one of the primary tenju languages.

Corso had spun around when Char shouted, half-raised his 'caster. Now he lowered it again. His face said he hadn't known Char could do that, and maybe he still wished he didn't.

"Void and *dust*. That means, 'Axorchal the One-Eye receive my soul.' Or . . . spirit. It's northern dialect."

Iari nodded. "Thank you. Gaer? A word." She closed her faceplate.

Take that as a hint. Gaer sealed his visor and accepted the private comm link already blinking on his HUD.

"It happened again," said Iari. "The, the plasma. The *evolution*. Did I—did *I* do this?"

"Close the portal? No. It was that One-Eye stabbing themself in the *setatir* eye who did it. Blood sacrifice."

"Thank Ptah." Iari blew out a breath. Gaer watched the fog collect for a split second on the inside of her visor. "What are we dealing with? There are—*how* many dead One-Eyes? Ten? Twelve?"

He thought he understood what she was asking. "You were outnumbered."

"Fuck that. I mean—*what is this*?" She toed the black glass. "Who did this? 'Axorchal One-Eye, take my spirit.' That's a prayer. What is this, a cult?"

"A well-armed cult unafraid to attack templars. Formerly allied with a well-armed collection of wichu nihilists who want to bring on the next surge and reopen the Weep. I think we know who killed Jich'e'enfe. And I think I might know why. Iari, there were Brood *in* the altar. I think, somehow—they're *powering* whatever the altar does. The blood is a catalyst. I think this is what Jich'e'enfe was doing in B-town, trying to get Brood into riev like she'd gotten them into the altar. They're *dead*, technically, so—the Brood would be bound to their hardware, same as the altar. Same as the old vakari voidship engines. But—I saw Brood in the gauntlets, too. Probably in the helmet too? I don't know. The point is— this, she—they fused Brood to *people*. Or someone did. The living blood is feeding them—that's how the One-Eyes can use whitefire. Maybe that's what happened to the alliance—Jich'e'enfe hit the limit of what she'd do, and this cult killed her for it. And at least one of them—of the cult, I mean—is an arithmancer. I saw them on the other side of the portal. Not a wichu. Far too big. I didn't get a clear look, but I did see a glove and a glowing red spot."

"A One-Eye arithmancer. You're saying a hybrid *riev* did all this? Or just the neefa in charge of them? Some kind of high priest of Oversight for the One-Eyes?"

"I don't know."

"The fuck *do* you know, then, Gaer? Sorry. Not fair. I—sorry."

You wished at times like this for privacy greater than comm channels, and you thanked your ancestors back to the first egg that you didn't get that wish. "No. I'm sorry. I tried to close the portal, and I couldn't. And I mean, I couldn't figure out how, much less have the requisite skill. I was going to tell you to smite the *setatir* thing, but you'd already—I guess it *does* still work."

"Yeah. Well. Promise, Gaer. When I find the other end of this portal, I will cut the fucking thing in half."

"I need to go with you."

"No. You need to go back to Windscar and report to Keawe. Notch is a mess. Iffy isn't a templar. And—Gaer. You have to tell

Tobin. Keawe might not, but—Tobin should know. He needs to know. About—what I *did*."

"This is your report to make, not mine."

"I know. But there's no *time*. These . . . cultists. They might not know that *we* know where they are. I think Keawe's going to get preemptive when she finds out about—" She flicked her fingers. "All this. I don't want anyone else caught out like we were. Maybe the arithmancer got dumb and sent all their people through, but probably not."

It was getting hard to breathe again. Gaer flared his plates, his nostrils, inhaled past the weight on his chest. "Iari. There is an *arithmancer*. You need me."

She turned, catching his reflection on her faceplate. "Gaer, void and dust. I'm not planning to go out and *die*. I need time—to find these cultists, to find Luki and Llian. To get them out, if they're still alive. I need you to figure out how to *fix* this. The altars, the portals, this arithmancy that keeps catching us out. That keeps *taking* us out. Find a way. Gaer, if you can't, no one up here *can*."

"You need to say all this to Notch."

"I need to say it to you."

"He's your second."

"He *lied* about his nanomecha. And I knew it. I can see his fucking biometrics, Gaer. I knew he was lying about his syn, I *let* him lie, and now where are we?"

That wasn't fair to Notch; it ran right up on hypocritical, too, since Iari hadn't told Tobin about things *he* should have known. But Iari's tone said she didn't care about *fair* right now, and Notch couldn't hear anyway. (The riev could, but the riev wouldn't go telling tales. They were Iari's the same way she was Tobin's.)

Gaer wished again for privacy that didn't require closed visors. He wanted her to see his face. Wanted—sss. No. The visors were best.

"Iari. None of this is your fault."

"Don't." Light, airless, brittle. Then she turned, visor retracting, and walked back toward the other templars. Except for Char and for Winter Bite.

It was Char that Gaer picked to look at. Char's brilliant blue teslas, Char's tenju-esque face. He opened his mouth to say things Iari would hate, and hung on them, mouth open. (Thank the dark lords for closed visors, then, maybe.)

Gaer killed his comms, and said to the dead air inside his helmet: "Keep her alive, Char. Watch her back."

Char tilted their head ever so slightly. And said, in a whisper that Gaer's battle-rig had to process to audible: "I will."

It was full dark when they got out. Clouds wisped overhead, just enough to blot out the stars, not enough to obscure the swollen, sullen moon. Iari had moved fast through the tunnels—they'd been through them already and besides, *let* something jump out of the voidspit dark at her. But they'd been thorough, clearing it the first time. Nothing jumped.

Out here, though—take it slower, allowing the possibility of an ambush by more, what, One-Eyes? Cultists? Whatever you called hybrid-riev fanatics in service to (people, a person) a pre-Aedian god. Iari wasn't worried for herself in event of an ambush, or the riev, or Gaer. (Notch was—not all right. But he had Corso and Iffy to watch him, so.)

She could say she was worried for Dodri, who was, if not green any longer, still young and worried, maybe scared, maybe mad.

Definitely still in shock from Homer's death, from Llian and Luki vanishing.

And pretending *worry for Dodri* wasn't even real, was it? Because Iari meant to take her along on this retrieval, which could go wrong in more ways that she cared to count, but which would be better than going back to the Aedis with a dead templar and not much else. (The ruins, the, what had Char called it, a *kiln*—that was all information, that was all important, but Gaer could take that back. Gaer could explain it. It was still *nothing*, when weighed against Homer.)

Iari watched Dodri anyway. You never knew how the young ones would do until they did it. And when they emerged, Dodri took the textbook position she should, on Iari's flank, while the riev paired up and went first. Said *yes Captain* and her voice didn't shake, so—she was as all right as she could be, in the circumstances.

Iari wasn't as sure about Notch, who'd elected to carry Homer with Corso's help. That was guilt. That was hurt. That was . . . hah, probably partly Corso's doing, keeping Notch focused on some other hurt than how angry she was at him. Corso had done his share of hauling bodies, in the army days. She and he both had. And Notch's biometrics told her he wasn't all right, not by any measure of the word. He and his battle-rig shared miserable yellows and oranges, not a single voidspit green.

The hopper, at least, was where they'd left it. Iari had almost convinced herself that it would be gone or sabotaged. She waited for Winter Bite to confirm what her HUD already said—there was nothing moving out on the plain, nothing waiting to jump out at them. Then she let the hopper's turing scan her battle-rig. All the teslas on the hopper's hull lit up as the hatch cycled and *thunked* through its unlock protocols. Then the ramp unfolded and a rectangle of brightness spilled onto the snow.

Iari took a few steps out of that light, into the darkness. Snow started falling in Windscar in autumn; by this point in the season, it sat several feet deep, and that layer and the moonlight conspired to an illusion of smooth, unbroken beauty. The reality was a collection of plains punctuated with low, surprisingly steep hills and deep channels cut by the seasonal floods. Daylight would also reveal any tracks out there—animal, mostly, but Iari supposed there were people, too.

Behind her, creaking and thumping on the ramp. Iffy's lighter steps. The heavy shuffle-drag of two big battle-rigs carrying a third.

Iari had been just one battle-rig, when she'd carried Tobin back from behind the lines at Saichi. That had been spring, snow on the ground melted, rain falling (so much rain). That had been mud to her *knees*. But Tobin had been alive. Homer would be heavier by orders of magnitude.

She had to get Luki and Llian back. Or at least try. Find out what the voidspit One-Eyes were doing. She called up Gaer's altar coordinates and a map and did a few calculations. Battle-rigs moving at speed could cover that distance by sunset tomorrow, if they synned most of the way and didn't take many rests. That was the biggest reason she wouldn't bring Notch. Couldn't bring him. He had no syn. He would not be able to keep up. She knew from the inside what *that* felt like, how useless he'd be until his nano-mecha righted themselves.

She could reach those coordinates herself faster than the HUD's projection, but only if she synned the whole time with her evolved nano, which Dodri did not have. She could do it with the riev. They didn't need food or water or rest. They could do it themselves alone, fastest of all—but Winter Bite and Char were also templars, her responsibility (so had Homer been, see how *that* had gone), and Jich'e'enfe had found a way to hurt riev, so assume the One-Eyes had that knowledge, too. Or at least their arithmancer did.

All this was assuming Gaer had gotten the right coordinates, that he understood the hexes. Though if she started distrusting Gaer *now*, she should just go back to Windscar with everyone else.

Gaer would solve whatever this was, altars and arithmancy and half-riev horrors. Gaer and Iffy. As badly as she wanted Gaer with her, he had to go back to Windscar. And Iffy had to go with him, because Iffy would keep Keawe's suspicion off him, and legitimize anything he found out that Keawe didn't want to hear. Iffy would protect him.

Iari switched to the general comms and checked that her voice went to everyone's HUD, even Corso's, who had a habit of shutting out templar chatter if she let him.

"Is everything secure, Lieutenant?"

"Yes." Notch was brittle still, more tired than angry. "All systems check out. Soon as you're clear, sir, we'll lift off."

"Copy that. Dodri, Winter Bite, Char—with me."

Dodri and the riev had been waiting at the base of the ramp, though Iari bet Char had been watching her the entire time. There were protocols about leaving people alone in dark dangerous places. Especially captains. Especially brooding, silent captains who were planning to take a team into enemy territory, unless that captain had an attack of sense at the last.

On cue—did he read *minds*, in addition to auras? Or did he just know her that well?—Gaer pinged a private channel. "I don't suppose you've rethought this."

She flicked a glance at the little grey indicators that had been Luki and Llian. Grey didn't mean dead. It meant . . . maybe dead, but definitely out of range. And until she *knew*: "No."

Faint hiss, a sigh pushed through jaw-plates. "Notch has appointed himself pilot. We may crash."

"The turing will do all the work." Wait. "Corso's an actual pilot. Why isn't he—"

"Heading for you," Gaer said, and cut the comm.

"Iari! A word?"

Iari gestured *stand down* at Dodri, who had moved to intervene, and turned to wait for Corso. He had his faceplate open, the neefa, and *argue* all over his face.

She opened her own faceplate and set her features to *patient*. "Just say whatever it is fast. We need to move out."

"All right." That battering ram of a jaw retreated. He worked the words around in his mouth, like he was trying them out first. "What about me?"

Reflex made her want to snap, *What about you?* She kept it behind her teeth. Said instead, "If you're asking, *where are my orders, Captain?* I can't order you to do anything. I did think you'd have had enough excitement, though, and that you would be returning to Windscar."

"When I first went out looking for this place, Keawe warned me. Said there were reavers up here, hitting villages—reavers, Iari, not raiders. Bandits take *things*. Reavers take people. You're dealing with a cult of reavers who take people and make half-riev out of them. And cults attack *other* religions. Like the fucking Aedis."

Knight-Marshal Keawe had said something like that in Iari's last briefing. Iari had imagined reavers meant traffickers, moving people from remote villages to the needle-dens in, oh, Seawall. Someplace big and southern, where the PKs didn't know every cartel thug in Lowtown. "Thanks for telling me."

"You're templars. All of you. You can't just—*walk* in there. Iari, come on. Would it kill you to *ask* me to go with you?"

"I'm more worried it'll kill *you.*"

"I'm not a fucking *civ.*"

Oh, for the love of Ptah's burning eye. "You are, legally. You're also more experienced in the field than anyone except the riev and me. But I cannot *ask* you to do this."

His eyes narrowed. "Legally? Or personally?"

He was volunteering. He'd once mocked her for doing that, when their army enlistments came up, when he ducked out of the surge and the fighting and she'd gone to the Aedis. She'd thought then—or told herself that she'd thought—he didn't see wide enough. That he didn't understand that the surge and the Brood didn't care if you'd served time or were tired or whatever. They were coming, and *someone* had to do *something.* The word she'd used was *selfish,* but what he'd heard was *coward.*

And truth—void and dust, what did she know about it? She knew what *she'd* seen, as their platoon's roster changed, when Corso had gotten the promotion and the seniority that put him in charge. She'd watched him take more and more risks on himself. She'd seen him freeze, too, when Brood broke through the barriers at Soren-Woo. No one left in the village then except Confederation troops when the boneless and the skeleton-wings arrived. And after that fight: Soren-Woo still in Confederate possession. A win.

But Corso had looked at the names of the dead, and at her, and resigned.

And now he wanted her to bring him along on *this,* with her first field command with one already dead and two missing, with hexwork no one had seen before, and half-riev who screamed fealty to, and died for, gods long out of favor.

She wanted Char with her because Char wouldn't bend, or buckle, or flinch. Neither would Winter Bite. Dodri was young, but Keawe had trained her. All of them would stand.

But so would Corso. She'd known *that* since B-town, since he'd faced Jich'e'enfe and her Brood fissures unarmored and unarmed. He might panic a little in the confines of a sealed helmet, but he wouldn't run. He wouldn't freeze again.

He might die, though. All of them might. But the rest of them were templars, and this was both profession and oath. Maybe calling.

Corso was just (a civ) asking to help.

And Mishka save all of them, Chaama guard their steps—she needed him.

"Fine," she said. "I'll ask. Will you come with us?"

"Fuck. *Yes*. Let's go."

CHAPTER TWELVE ≡≡≡≡≡

A n Aedis hopper didn't *need* a pilot; the onboard turing
could handle all but the most complex maneuvers. Gaer
knew that B-town (and Seawall, and every other urban
center on the planet) had laws requiring organic pilots in the
cockpit in case Weep fissure activity wiped the turing (which
had never happened) or in case of catastrophic mechanical failure (which *had*, either because of very large Brood or very bad
weather). But the Aedis wasn't subject to civil law unless it wanted
to be. Tobin would've insisted on a templar pilot, damn sure. Keawe hadn't bothered.

Now Notch had put himself in the pilot's seat, curled into as
much of a knot as his rig would allow, his back to the rest of the
hopper's cabin. A day ago, Gaer might've thought this was a young
lieutenant having a spectacular sulk, and good riddance. Now—he
wasn't sure that still wasn't happening, though the whole hunched-
over-how-small-can-my-battle-rig-get attitude looked more like
retreat than resentment at being sent back to Windscar. Like a
man trying to get as far away from everything as he could.

Like the body of a very young templar, for instance, in a very
wrecked battle-rig. It had been easier in the caves for Gaer to look
without looking, behind his visor's concealment. In the hopper,

though—everyone's visors were open, except Homer's. (That was a kindness. Gaer knew Iffy had opened it already. Knew she'd closed it again.) Whitefire left unmistakable marks. Homer had been hit a handful of times, and though the battle-rig would've turned the first few shots, even Aedian hexes gave out.

Brood were the usual cause of templar death since the Accords and the Weep. The last time death by whitefire had been a *thing* had been Protectorate against templar. Vakari against everyone else. This time it was wichu-caused—by separatists, nihilists, sure, but still wichu. Making riev was a banned practice, and someone was clearly still practicing—someone wichu had trained, however that alliance had ended—and now templars were dying. And the wichu, so very jealous of their privacy and independence, and still so *very* dependent on Confederation, on *Aedis*, protection, wouldn't like how this looked. There would be echoes all the way to the Aedis Synod. There would be howls for reform, for integrating the wichu or ejecting them outright.

Someone else could be happy about that upheaval (someone else would be the Five Tribes embassy in Seawall, Karaesh't in particular). Someone who hadn't known Homer. Someone who didn't know Iffy, who was sitting back there (not kneeling, there wasn't room, or Gaer thought she would have) singing something about Mishka and flowing water, and Chaama and resting bones.

Gaer was trying hard not to listen. It was what priests did, in any religion: marked the passage between life and death, sang souls to wherever souls went according to doctrine and orthodoxy. He didn't believe in the Aedis version. Or the Five Tribes. Or any. But Iffy's grief made his chest hurt.

Vakari didn't cry. Excessive tears came from ocular damage, not grief. But he would bet a great deal that the reason Notch was up in the cockpit was because he *could* cry, and he didn't want to be seen doing so.

Gaer would just as soon let him, and they could fly back to the Aedis accompanied by Iffy's prayers, or by silence when Iffy's voice or obligation ended. Except *someone* needed to comm Keawe, and that someone was Notch, and Gaer knew he hadn't even tried yet.

There was grief, and then there was abrogation of duty, and if Iari's life hung in the balance, the latter was not an option.

Gaer shoved himself upright, legs wide, gripping the handhold for balance; the hopper was not a bit steady. From here, he could see through to the cockpit. Notch had set all the panel-hexes to transparent, not just the usual two in the front, but the top and the bottom as well, so that it looked like he hung suspended in aether over fast-moving snowfields, some blasted down to the (dead, rotting) grass layer by the eponymous wind that alternately howled and hummed around the hopper's contours.

Gaer hated the openness of Windscar province, the landscape. The endless sky. B-town sat on the edge of the steppes, but it had a forest crowding up on the south and west; and even if one could see a great distance north and east from the walls on a clear night—and appreciate that clarity, that perspective—there were nice comforting trees and buildings to hem in the sky. To give it boundaries.

Gaer took a better grip on the handhold, pinned his gaze on Notch, and forced himself forward. He didn't mind heights, or high speeds, but he did not like them in combination. The solid bar under his hands reassured him. He spread himself over the cockpit's opening, leaned down, ignored that fast-moving snow (there were solid panels, Aedis hexwork, he was *fine*), the dark slashes of ravine, or road, or whatever. The skies were clearing the farther south they traveled. Hints of stars through the clouds, and fingers of moonlight that bleached both cockpit controls and Notch colorless. The cockpit had a slightly domed overhead that an enterprising vakar could, with some twisting, use to see the direction they'd come. The clouds and the sky were darker that direction, threaded by flashes that might just be reflective artifacts from the hexes.

Oh dark lords, let it be only reflection.

Gaer cycled his optic and *sss*, no, of course the dark lords were ignoring him. The Weep fissure had gotten active. Emanations flickered, colors only Gaer could see rippling across aetheric layers. They were many kilometers from it—the Weep cut the planet up near the pole, sliced through the eastern hemisphere. It looked like a violet-black line most of the time, an errant thread in the garment of the multiverse. It widened sometimes, spat out physical Brood. More often it bled from the aether's deep layers, warping physics and playing havoc with comms and honest EM.

So it was possible Notch *had* tried the comms, and they just hadn't worked. Gaer glanced at the terminal. Display blank, no clue there. Notch hadn't turned his head or acknowledged Gaer in any way yet, though he had to know Gaer was standing there. You didn't *not* notice two meters of vakar a handspan behind you and looming.

Void and dust.

"Lieutenant? Notch. A word, please."

Now, finally, Notch turned to look. "What is it?"

Gaer flinched. Soft-skin faces varied in color so much, dependent on pigmentation and blood flow. He'd seen varying shades in all sorts of conditions—anger, embarrassment, fear, shock, pain. *Grey*, however, was a novel hue. And horrifying.

He sampled Notch's aura. And yes, it was polychromatic with grief, distress, anger, fear (which he expected). Also fractured and strobing with stress (also expected). But the aura was also . . .

dimmer, somehow. The colors were less intense, *flat*. Gaer flicked a look back at Iffy, got an optic-full of similar hues: more in the blue range, though, and more solid throughout. (Iffy wasn't falling apart on him, *good*, because he was going to need her.) Her colors were brighter, though, more—ah. There. That sparkle that templars and priests all had—their nanomecha—*that* was the difference. Notch didn't have it.

This was—oh. Not good. Iari, even at her most compromised, hadn't looked like this. Gaer set his concerns over comms aside. He leaned down, flared his jaw-plates and nostrils together. Tasted stale tenju, old sweat, *new* sweat, sour fear. A coppery echo that might've been blood, though Notch had no visible wounds; the syn did that sometimes, though. Except he highly doubted Notch had been *able* to syn since that first fight in the large, open room, when the metal mecha had hit him.

He could *ask* how Notch was, and get *fine, nothing*, some kind of neefa-shit. Or he could say, in his quietest voice, "There is something very wrong with your nanomecha. That is not a question."

Notch made a noise in the back of his throat. "Don't you start."

"I'm not—sss. I'm observing. You are clearly not *well*. Your nanomecha are nonfunctional. That is—very bad, Notch, do you get that?"

"Of course I get that." Notch's gaze crawled over Gaer's face. "Don't you tell Iffy. Not now."

"Tell her what? Your nanomecha appear to be dead or dying? She does need to know."

"It can wait."

"For what?"

"For the Aedis. The hospice."

"Then have you told dispatch that we're coming? Have you advised them of your condition?"

"Comms didn't work when I tried." Notch sank a little deeper into his rig. "Been a little while, though. Maybe they're back."

"The fissure's acting up. That could be why." Gaer suffered a moment's pity. He leaned forward, down, put his mouth close to Notch's ear. And lied. "Iari had this happen last autumn, with her nano. It passes."

Notch rolled a bloodshot side-eye. "Captain didn't get anyone killed, though, did she? I didn't say how bad it was, even though she told me to. Then I went down in that fight and she came to help me and if she *hadn't*—"

"Then what? Homer wouldn't have died?"

Notch's jaw flexed. "Maybe."

"You are smarter than that, Lieutenant. Or you should be." Gaer cast a look back into the hopper. Iffy was still hard at prayer. Homer was still dead. It should be Iari having this talk or, or *Tobin*. Or *setatir* Keawe. "Tell Iffy you need her help. She needs something to worry about. That's you. And go *back* there to tell her. Sing with her, or sit there and watch, or *whatever* you lot do with your dead. But sitting up here, imagining that you're going to die, and blaming yourself because someone already has? *Sss.* No. You are in command here. Act like it."

Notch blinked at him. Then he closed his eyes, visibly gathered himself. Muttered, "Back up, then, let me out," and heaved to his feet, as Gaer folded aside to make room.

Then, *finally*—the cockpit was his (and the *setatir* turing's, humming along and flying the hopper). He folded himself into Notch's seat. *First* thing, reset the opacity on the *setatir* panels, yes, there. Then he reached for the comms.

Gaer tried Windscar first, and raised dispatch through a crackle of Weep interference. He managed to convey their imminent arrival, that there were casualties. Dispatch seemed fixated on *who* was calling (Where was the captain, the lieutenant? What about Sister Iphigenia?), and after two repetitions, Gaer cut the connection. Dispatch would blame the Weep, not the vakar.

And the vakar needed the comms for another purpose. When the Aedis had seconded him last autumn, when it was clear that they weren't just going to hand him back in a couple of weeks, Karaesh't had sent Gaer a package from Seawall. Knight-Marshal Tobin did not, had not, monitored Gaer's mail from the embassy; a foolish courtesy, in Gaer's opinion, but one he tried not to abuse. (He liked Tobin. That was also foolish.)

Karaesh't had sent Gaer an updated SPERE hack on Aedis comm security protocols, ciphered into a chatty missive about the Winter Nights festival in Seawall that no one who read it would believe was genuine. Gaer had chipped out the cipher, recovered the code, loaded it into his optic. And then done nothing with it since they'd come to Windscar, because Knight-Marshal Keawe wouldn't let him near comms unsupervised, being *very* clear what she thought of the vakar asset's reliability.

So really, this was her fault.

Gaer slid into the aether, wove Karaesh't's hexes (elegant, as always) into the Aedis protocols. And waited, for a long moment, head cocked toward the back of the hopper. The singing had stopped. There was conversation, rendered unintelligible by the hopper's propulsion noise and, as Gaer cocked an eye toward the instruments, a gusty, howling tailwind. Then he hunched forward over the comms and sent his message. One quick burst, no audio, to Seawall and Karaesh't. He didn't try twice. If the Weep interference had stopped that transmission, well, bad luck.

Then he withdrew his SPERE code and keyed in the B-town dispatcher.

He half expected (half hoped) for more interference, for the

Weep to preclude all possibility of contact. So of course this time there was no difficulty connecting at all. This time he got patched straight through to Tobin, who listened to Gaer's rapid report without interruption. Who said only *acknowledged*, at the end of it, even though Gaer had just told him they had new problems growing off old ones and Iari had gone running north to solve everything by herself. Tobin wasn't the yelling sort. He'd been at Saichi. *Loss* was a thing he understood. *Cost* was. And he trusted Iari.

Which is why Gaer nearly didn't say, "One more thing."

The channel hissed, and Gaer hoped for a heartbeat the Weep had eaten the words.

Then Tobin's voice came back, patient, calm, his dread only audible because Gaer knew the man: "What is it?"

Gaer closed his eyes. His heart thumped like there were Brood after him, or One-Eyes. "Iari's nanomecha have changed, you know that. But you don't know *how*."

And he told Tobin what Iari should have, what she'd been afraid to, because *damn* sure Iffy and everyone else in that cave had seen her go all Ptah and turn the altar to glass and shut down the portal. *Damn* sure that report would get to Keawe. Tobin had to know first.

Tobin was quiet a little too long for comm protocol, and Gaer had a moment's hope-horror that the Weep had cut them off after all. But then he said, "Is this the first manifestation?" and Gaer understood *why* Iari had kept quiet. Lying to Tobin—and Gaer was a *setatir* SPERE agent, he was *good* at prevarication—felt like putting your skin on inside out.

He should say yes. He should cut the comms. He should never have started any of this. Instead he said, "No. The first instance was in B-town, when she closed Jich'e'enfe's tesser-hex. She was afraid to tell you. But this time, other people saw it. Keawe will get it in a report, which means . . . I had to report it to Seawall. And she wanted me to tell you now, so I am."

Another long silence, and this time the comm-link wobbled. B-town was far away, and emanations were mercurial.

"Acknowledged," Tobin said. And then, because he was Tobin, he said, "Be careful, Gaer," as he cut the link.

So that was—done.

Gaer spent the next few minutes altering the turing's comm-logs—terrible Weep tonight, so many interruptions—to make it look like Windscar had been his last, and only, call. If someone compared logs and timestamps, they'd find him out. Then he could say—truth—that he'd called Tobin to make a report. The transmission to Karaesh't would stay out of it.

Then Gaer realized that he wasn't hearing *anything* from the hopper's cabin. He cranked around, half afraid he'd find Iffy and Notch looming over him, having overheard everything, seen everything. Instead he saw Notch sitting on the bench, head tipped back, eyes closed, and Iffy with her little field med-mecha and tablet running diagnostics on him. Gaer watched, quiet and, if he had to admit it, a little bit worried. He didn't *love* Notch. Didn't really like him. But . . . sss. If there were hexes that could take out *templars* this completely, and those hexes had belonged to wichu separatists (who had made improvements after B-town, evidently), and now belonged to some cult of hinterlands heretics who had fused Brood with *people*, then that threatened . . . everyone. Everything. Confederation, Five Tribes, Protectorate. The Aedis had plenty of enemies. Offer those enemies a way to take out the templars, and—well. The galaxy could, might, would probably—dissolve into war.

And if the Weep happened to vomit a new surge right then, as politics destabilized, then the galaxy went down in Brood-slime. Maybe that'd been Jich'e'enfe's plan. But she was dead now, and the people who had all her arithmancy might well be worse.

All those happy thoughts almost made Gaer miss the flash from the cockpit comms. Would have, if a particularly egregious gust hadn't rocked the *setatir* hopper just then, which made him check on the turing (fine, if annoyed by the weather).

And there it was. Incoming message, blinking threadily.

By rights Notch should answer it, or Iffy, or someone officially Aedis. But he was an official Aedis asset, certainly divided in his loyalties, and also the only one here. Keawe would be livid if he answered her comm, but—

He tapped the comm. It wasn't Keawe. Iari's voice bled through the tiny speaker, fractured. "—copy? Notch? Iffy!"

"Gaer," said Gaer. "Are you—"

"Lis—." The comm cut out. Came back in a wobbly, "—issures. We have signs of Bro—."

Void and dust. "Iari, repeat, I lost you."

"Ettrad. Whole—stroyed—."

Ettrad was, if Gaer recalled Corso's hand-drawn map, a minuscule settlement, a literal dot—and now, if there were Brood, probably not even that. "How *many* Brood? What kind?"

"Unknown. From *fissures*, copy? Brood are gone."

And how would she know that, *from fissures*? That was Iari-speak for fissures that someone had made, rather than the primary Weep fissure, which spat out Brood all by itself sometimes. Gaer wanted to argue with her, because if she was right (she was right: his gut said so), then Jich'e'enfe's voidspit war-making had already escalated. Or the cultists had repurposed it. People disappeared all the time, Notch had said. Had there been an uptick in

Brood events? He'd have to check with Aedis records, if Keawe would let him.

But that was a problem for later. For *now*: "Copy. Are there casualties?" He could call Windscar and ask for emergency aid. Iari didn't even have a priest with her.

"All dead." *That* came through clear. "We're fine. Still on plan—"

The comms blanked entirely, the whole board. Gaer didn't need his *setatir* optic to say that was the Weep's doing, because the hopper juddered too, like it'd hit solid ground and bounced. Like it'd, oh, lost its *setatir* engines for half a beat.

The turing set up its own clamor for Gaer's attention, unfolding a screen and throwing up a request for a physical pilot.

"Gaer? What just happened?" Iffy's voice, and closer than he liked—she was already in motion, coming forward, *not* a good idea.

"The Weep is happening. Secure yourself and Notch. And Homer," because Iffy and Notch were not spacers, might not understand that unsecured things could become projectiles, and an unsecured battle-rig would be catastrophic.

Gaer slapped the comm board again, in case (nothing). Then he slid into the turing's code with the same SPERE hex he'd used before, and from it, into the hopper's automated systems. The Weep interference destroyed hexes, or mutated them—generally to complete failure, sometimes in interesting and potentially lethal directions. Gaer helped the turing counter those effects as the hopper bucked and rattled in a combination of Weep and wind. The buffeting was no gentler in the aether, but there was no malice in Weep emanations. They were purely environmental, no more wit than the Windscar storms or winter cold.

Still, Gaer had never been so glad to see an Aedis compound as he was to see Windscar. All compounds were patterned on pre-voidflight fortresses, the sort you found on any world that had reckoned how to work stone. Thick walls. Gates. Guard towers. A courtyard (and this was a departure from pre-voidflight architecture) massive enough to hold an aethership and a hopper hangar. The Windscar Aedis covered most of a squat hill, its perimeter wall partway up from the base. Bigger than B-town, meaner, with a much smaller town (also called Windscar, proof of this province's lack of creativity) huddled in the lee of the hill, in the Aedis's shadow. Grey-walled stone raised by priests (bones of the Element Chaama), spring-fed (water for Mishka), literal fires burning in all the corners (Ptah and an apparent desire to show every enemy exactly where the whitefire ballista were housed). Hrok, Gaer supposed, needed no special representation in a place named for that Element's terrestrial breath. In the dark, in the storm, those guard towers glowed like the headlamp on a templar's battle-rig.

The turing limped the hopper over the walls and spiraled into the courtyard, aiming for its pad, where a small cadre of priests waited with a mobile med-mecha for Notch. And where Keawe—unmistakable, battle-rigged and massive, faceplate open and staring up—waited, too, to see them home safe.

CHAPTER THIRTEEN ≡≡≡

C orso already knew there was something *very* wrong in Ettrad. The trail gave it away. Many feet tramping together—*not* reavers, who typically traveled single file, like wolves, when they went on foot—coming out of the village, leaving the road and plowing through the snow heading north. No one went north. There was nothing up there but Weep.

And it was a fresh trail, too, which also made no sense in this weather. Two instances of makes-no-sense had been enough to prompt Iari to call a rest. Which, yeah, Corso was pretty glad to get. There was sleet coming down mixed with snow, splatting hard on the battle-rig's skin. He was actually grateful for the fucking faceplate, which did *not* steam up despite his exertions. Iari had run them the *whole* slagging way so far. After all that arguing, after getting past whatever the fuck was her problem, after he *won*—Iari was going to make him run more than he had since his army days.

But then, yeah, that trail appeared where it shouldn't be, going a direction it shouldn't be, and they'd stopped.

Now Winter Bite stuck those tentacles out and waved them around and said, "Brood."

Which was almost the last thing Corso wanted to hear. And of course Iari had to investigate, being a templar and Iari.

Which was how Corso experienced his first Aedis rig Brood alert.

In the army, Brood alerts were low-tech: shouts and screams or, best case, intel handed down by command that there were Brood in a particular area, be careful. In B-town Corso had just walked into them.

This was a full-on strobe on his HUD that damn near blinded him. He acknowledged the alert—poor rig didn't know what to do, with a civ inside—and killed the flash and tried to blink sense into his HUD again. The map resolved in a shower of optical sparks.

"Where are they?" Corso couldn't get the HUD to tell him anything useful. He unclipped his 'caster from its harness on the rig. If there *were* Brood, it wouldn't be any use except as a club, but it gave his hands something to do besides shake.

"It's just residual emanations," said Iari, sounding like herself: cool and a little put out by Brood interrupting her business. "Nothing moving. No fissures. No wichu arithmancers."

Corso knew that last bit was for his sake, and was grateful for it.

"We're a long way from the fissure," Dodri said. It was almost an objection.

"Brood travel," Corso said. "But we got Char and Winter Bite. And the captain was at fucking Saichi. We'll be fine, even if there *are* Brood."

Total neefa-shit. Saichi had been a technical victory, and Iari had been there and lived, all true. One of two in her unit to make it out, and she'd carried Tobin out. Char had been there too, part of the army troops. That's where they'd lost their original arm.

As if summoned, a massive shape appeared on his HUD, *right there*, no alarm, rising out of the grass without a fucking whisper. Of course it was Char, and yeah, there, the faint gleam of hexes reached out of the swirling sleet-and-snow dark. Made you appreciate why riev spooked the vakari so badly, and why it was a damned good thing Jich'e'enfe's plan to corrupt and control riev had failed.

Corso breathed the heat back out of his face. Willed his heart *slow down*. Char wasn't worried (and they were right beside him). On comms, Iari was telling Dodri to come up, there was nothing, it was *fine*.

But it wasn't. He followed Iari onto a relatively clear, well-packed strip of snow that would pass for a road out here. An ATV lay crossways on its side. Big dim shape, just on the range of the headlamps, though the rig's sensors could pick out its edges. There was no energy signature, machine or mecha or otherwise, but Corso knew *dead* when he saw it. He dragged his headlamp over the wreckage. The ATV looked undamaged from this angle. Repulsor coils, treads, all of it looked intact.

Corso held his breath and edged around the vehicle.

Ah, there was the damage. Doors pulled open, pulled halfway off. He crept up and poked his headlamp's beam into the depths. Turned away fast. That was the thing about Brood. They didn't eat. They just killed.

"Casualties," Char said, in a voice quiet enough Corso guessed Iari was close. He remembered the HUD might show him her location, and blinked up that map just as she appeared on the road in front of them.

"There's a homestead in the trees," Iari said. She added her headlamp to Corso's. "Looks about like this. All the animals, all the people, are dead."

Dodri and Winter Bite arrived then. Corso thought Iari might warn Dodri to stay back, but she didn't. Made him remember the first time he had seen Brood deaths—the first time Iari had, too. He was starting to be damn sorry he'd volunteered for this mission.

That wasn't true. He was just sorry. Some shit you didn't need to see ever again.

Ettrad matched Corso's memories of a dozen other Windscar settlements destroyed in the surge. It was small: two parallel streets crossed by one, lined tight with buildings. That would the school, squat and square, there in the center. Across from it, the clinic dome, with the platform on top for emergency medevac hoppers. The slender two-story stack that was general store on top and the town's ATV storage below. The big double doors were open. Town this size might have two vehicles, there was one dead on the road, so—Corso let himself hope that someone had gotten away (despite the trail heading north, despite everything he *knew* about Brood attacks).

And yeah. Fuck hope. The second ATV hadn't even made it into the street, had smashed nose-first into one of the building's support pylons. The remains of a boneless was draped partway over the windshield.

Corso started forward, but Iari waved him back. She went into the building alone. He stood on the threshold as she swept her headlamp over the wreckage. The beam didn't linger anywhere, no hitch in its progress, so Corso knew it was bad in there. Iari always got smoother and colder the worse things got.

She flicked off her headlamp and came back into the street. Corso went with her. Dodri was standing out there with Char and Winter Bite, the three of them facing different directions, covering all the angles. Dodri turned as Iari came up. With their headlamps off, the rigs were darkly anonymous, matching silhouettes with tiny teslas. If he hadn't known who was who, Corso wouldn't've been able to tell them apart.

"We won't find survivors, will we?" Dodri sounded very young.

"No. Everyone who survived is walking north right now. The direction *we* were going. Where the One-Eyes came from. Anyone think that's coincidence?" Iari was staring off into the dark. Corso wondered if her rig saw things his didn't. If whatever had happened to her nanomecha gave her better vision. Or if she was seeing something from a long time ago.

"No," Corso said. And then he added, "The slagging wichu and their altar-voidspit have started a new surge."

Iari rounded on him fast enough his rig chirped alarm. "If this was a surge, there wouldn't be a trail out of here, because there wouldn't *be* survivors." Then she turned her glare into the rain and the middle distance, and he realized that fury wasn't for him. "This is like B-town. Like Jich'e'enfe's mini-fissures. Targeted hits. Only this time the target was most of a village."

Then Dodri proved she was brave, and asked, "Why didn't they come south, then? The survivors, I mean. To the Aedis? Or, I don't know, *any* other settlement? Why go north? There's nothing that way but the *fissure*."

"There's something," Iari said. "There's an altar. There's an arithmancer who sent a bunch of half-riev to kill us—bet me he's not alone up there. Bet me he's calling himself Axorchal or Axorchal's high priest and he's got *followers*."

"Avatar," said Corso. "That's the old word. The leader *was* the god, or the god's literal representative—"

"But how can they believe that?" Dodri blurted. "They *can't* believe that."

"Doesn't matter. They're going that way because they don't think you lot can protect them from Brood," Corso said, with a careful eye on Iari. "Because this Axorchal One-Eye is telling them *he* can. Or he's telling them he controls Brood and this is what happens to them if they *don't* join up."

Dodri sounded horrified. "But we haven't heard about any of this. Not the Brood, anyway. It *can't* be that widespread. People up here talk about things. *You* know that." That last to Corso, like his agreement would tilt reality any direction.

"Doesn't have to be widespread, though. The homesteads and the hamlets—they go months out of contact, no one notices. Neefa-herders are always moving. Long silences up here are normal, *especially* in summer. And the Weep fissure fucks up the comms all the time," Corso said. "Even if they sent hardcopy messages—caravans get hit. ATVs get hit. It'd look like random banditry. Keawe *said* there'd been an increase in raids. Meanwhile, if you're trying to start some kind of cult, this is the place. Up here, the Aedis isn't as much of a *thing*, Iari, you know that. Get people talking, tell tales all year that Brood are back—exaggerate what happened in B-town, say the Aedis is lying about how it went down, or whatever."

Iari sounded more thoughtful (still angry). "Using Brood on the villages could be a recent development, too. Until very recently, there was some kind of alliance between the separatists and whoever's leading this cult. Maybe to make the One-Eyes? I don't know how that all fits. Maybe when they started taking out villages with Brood, Jich'e'enfe balked."

"Jich'e'enfe didn't balk about using *Brood*. She was doing that already in B-town. If there're villages dying from Brood, that chews up Aedis reputation in the north. Let that get *out* into

B-town or Seawall—and the Aedis gets a planet-wide image problem. That would've served the wichu separatists. But *something* soured the relationship." Corso held up a hand to forestall interruption. "Maybe the cult got its own ideas. Or maybe it had those ideas all along and was just using the wichu. Axorchal's called the One-Eyed because his other eye's looking where no one else can. Into the spirit world. Into people's hearts to see if they're lying."

"Gaer said there was an arithmancer," Iari said. "All of that, an arithmancer can do. Or *look* like they're doing."

"Maybe Jich'e'enfe was dumb enough to teach someone her tricks."

"Gaer said that, too."

Then she got quiet, which—shit. "You're thinking," said Corso.

"I am. Mission's evolving. Hrok's freezing *breath*. We still need to retrieve Luki and Llian. That hasn't changed. But this—first the One-Eyes, and now active Brood? That's bigger. We need to follow these tracks. See where they're going. See if we can get in with them, figure out . . . all of it. How it connects. Wichu. One-Eyes. That altar."

Corso felt every aching joint in his body, a creeping cold in his gut. He squared a shoulder toward Dodri, like that would somehow shut her out, and pinged Iari's rig for a private channel.

He thought she wouldn't grant it, for a long moment. Then she said, "Corporal, take Winter Bite and Char and make sure the village is clear. No Brood or survivors."

Corso thought Char might argue—or crack his skull, because that was the look they gave him. Icy blue teslas that somehow bored through his faceplate and told him Char knew Iari was sending everyone away for *his* sake, right now.

But Dodri said, "Yes, Captain," startled, like she'd forgotten her rank. Like she didn't know Char and Winter Bite had more experience each than the sum of her years, and that they'd keep her alive. Maybe she didn't.

Maybe she was the smartest one of them, because she wouldn't argue with Iari.

Iari waited until they'd all walked away to open that channel. "What?"

"We're in *battle-rigs*. We can't just walk up on a bunch of, what, refugees? Cultist recruits? Because if they survived this, someone *let* them survive, you have to've thought of that—and ask, hey, where you all going? You know where that cult's hiding? Want to tell us? Can we come, too?"

Iari huffed, more amused than annoyed. "I don't think they'd like us better if we walked up to them naked."

There was a slagging image. "Guess it depends on their preferences."

This time Iari's grunt was more pensive. "We can *follow* them, maybe. Avoid contact. Let Winter Bite run surveillance."

"I might have an idea." This village had been abandoned, not razed. There'd be stuff to scavenge here, too. More edible food. Water. He'd find clothes. Corso was already halfway to the refugee-cultists in his mind, imagining how he'd intercept them, where he'd say he was from. Nowhere near *here*, everyone would know each other. Shit, tell an old truth, his family owned neefa herds, that's what he did, except something had happened, Brood, he'd heard of Axorchal . . .

So when Iari said, "So what is it? This idea," Corso knew he was hip deep and sinking.

"Send me in. Let me infiltrate the survivors when we catch up."

Another soft huff. "Not alone. I go with you."

There were so many reasons that wouldn't work. Corso drew breath to list them—and stopped. Because, truth—he didn't want to be among cultists alone, and his best objection—they have some arithmantic shit that can fuck up your Aedian nano—wouldn't affect Iari. Which she already knew.

And, *and:* something else was chewing at Corso, gnawing its way from hunch to certainty. "Iari. Listen—"

"I'm going with you. Not negotiable. You can be in charge, but—"

"Not that. *Listen.* What if someone made me when I was looking for the ruins? I did a lot of talking to a lot of people. A lot of asking. What if the One-Eyes *wanted* us to come up there? What if someone in one of these slagging villages sold me the grannytale about haunted caves and monsters, knowing I'd take it to the Aedis? Knowing I was *working* for you?"

"That's a leap."

"If the cult *is* a cult and they're recruiting out of the villages, then maybe it's not. What if word got around I was looking for stories and someone gave me one?"

"Knowing you'd take it back to us? What, were you carrying ID that said *Aedis contractor*? Don't answer that. I know you weren't." Iari's voice tipped into thoughtful. "We thought the problem was just wichu, though. We didn't think they had allies. Someone *might* have made you, but it was no one you even thought you needed to look for."

"Right." You didn't obsess about fuck-ups. Learn from them. Let them go. Readjust. And what mattered anyway was, "I think they meant to ambush and kill all of us, anyone who showed up to those caves. I think that One-Eye in the machine, that was a trap. They knew we'd open the machine. Sure, they killed one of their own, but that's tactics. They had numbers on us when they *did* show. I think that was a message to *you*. To the Aedis. If we'd been less lucky—"

"If we hadn't had Gaer, you mean. And Iffy. And Char and Winter Bite." This time Iari's grunt was more pensive. "If you're right, that means they didn't intend to take Luki and Llian. But now they have two live templars to send a message with. But what message?"

"Some version of *get out*. You know what happened up here after the surge, right? All the reconstruction, all the Confederation money, that went mostly to Seawall and B-town. The bigger cities. The population centers." Those had been the places hit early and hard, before anyone knew what to expect from a surge. Before they'd realized Brood didn't move like an army. Brood didn't occupy. They hunted. So maybe reparations to those bigger population centers was fair and necessary, but, "The money didn't come here. Not past Windscar-the-town, because Windscar-the-town had an Aedis in it. Not to the villages. Not to the homesteaders. They don't hate the Confederation up here, Iari. They just don't have much use for it."

"Confederation, or Aedis?"

"Both. Some people love one more than the other. Some people don't see a difference. Point is—this isn't B-town. The population's not going to love you. Even if they don't like the One-Eyes, they might not help you either."

"So that's the connection between the wichu and these One-Eyes. Jich'e'enfe, the separatists—they wanted *us* to fail. The Aedis. The whole Confederation. The Accords with the Protectorate, *all* of it, because they want—wanted—the vakari to suffer. All of them, Protectorate and Five Tribes."

Because some people only saw *veeks*. "That's why they're so pissed at the Aedis and the Confederation. Because you, we, forgave them."

"Ask Gaer how much we've forgiven." Iari snipped the words out. Paused, then, and took a deep breath. "So the wichu separatists, nursing this grudge—they find willing partners in this cult of Axorchal because *they* want us gone, too. And the cult's promising what, that the Weep, the Brood, the surge, fucking Saichi—all that goes away if the Aedis does. Like it never happened."

Corso realized he'd been holding his breath. Let it go. "Everyone knows what the Aedis did. Everyone knows what we owe them. But some people hate owing. There's been talk of secession since before I was born, Windscar for Windscar, withdraw from the Confederation. Tanis for the tenju." Void and dust, Corso hated to say it. "That was the neefa-shit we used to say when I was Dodri's age. We'd throw the fucking alwar *off* this planet, right? The alwar, the Aedis, all of you. And it's all shit. Most people know that. Especially with the Weep fissure right there." He pointed north. Waited, in case Iari had something to say. She didn't. Of course she didn't.

This must be how Gaer felt. Made him sympathize, damn sure. "Iari. You need to *think* about this."

"I have. I have been doing nothing *but* thinking. They attacked templars. They *took* two of us. Whether or not they meant to do that at first, and not kill us all—they did. And they know we'll respond. Either they don't care because they can handle whatever we bring, or that's what they wanted all along. Us to come at them. Or some third thing I haven't thought of."

"Well, think of this. If you go up there with me, and they make you, *they will kill you.*"

"I fucking know, Corso." So calmly delivered, so quiet, the savagery surprised him. "*I know* the safe thing to do right now is go back. Report to Keawe. Get reinforcements from Windscar, have *them* call for backup from B-town. Then the Aedis comes back in force, and by then . . . by then *what*? How long will that take? A week? Look how long *we* just argued about this. Add the Knight-Marshals and the Reverend Mothers. Ptah's burning *eye*, I report this, it'll end up in front of the Knight-Commander and the Synod. They will argue, and they will debate, and they'll summon the wichu and demand explanations. And by the time there's a decision, it'll be too late for Luki and Llian. Maybe for Windscar too." She turned away slowly, like her bones hurt. Like she'd aged all the way to decrepit in minutes. "Surprise is all we have. We go now. I'll comm the hopper. Gaer can make the report."

This was voidspit big-p politics, the kind Corso hated. The surge had felt too big eleven years ago, with generals who'd never put a foot on Tanis telling troops born here how to die. Give him cartel power struggles, give him bribery and blackmail—that made sense. This for that. Small violence.

Iari didn't care about that. Hadn't cared about anything except fighting Brood back then. At least that's what he'd thought, when she signed up with the Aedis. But no. She *was* Aedis, from skin to nanomecha. True believer. All of her heart given to a thing that couldn't love her back.

Corso was starting to understand what Gaer brought to Iari. Not just the arithmancy, not even mostly that. Gaer thought about big-p politics, he saw things she didn't, he argued. She trusted his judgement. She trusted him.

"What would Gaer tell you to do right now?"

He startled a laugh out of her. "He'd . . . void and dust. He'd point out the same things you did. He'd also tell me he needed to get eyes on their hexes. He's already furious I sent him back. *We don't know enough, Iari, sss.* He'd say that." She looked up, then, at nothing. Looking for answers in the dark and the aether, while sleet fell on her visor and melted. "He'd be wrong about that, though. They've used fucking Brood against people, Corso. That's all we need to know. It begins and ends there."

CHAPTER FOURTEEN ══════

"I 'm Corso. Corso Risar." Corso flung an arm across Iari's shoulder. "This is my cousin, Iari. She's from B-town."

Iari could feel Corso's heart banging around in his chest like an impending medical emergency. Which they might have, if the alw pointing the longcaster at them decided to fire. Suspicious, pinch-faced woman.

That was who Corso had eyes on, too. That was who he addressed. "Brood hit our homestead. They—" A savage headshake, that sent his hooked braids skittering across Iari's back, snagging her sweater. "Fucking Aedis did nothing."

Ungentle Ptah, he was spreading it thick.

Besides the alw with the 'caster, a handful of faces stared back at them. The survivors from Ettrad, all tenju except for the alw, and except for the alw, all unarmed. All a little bit hollow looking, all a little bit scared, but a not insignificant number looked suspicious, too. Those were the ones she was watching. Fear wasn't good for anyone's sense; fear and suspicion, though, that could mean violence. Iari was acutely aware that she had no battle-rig, that he didn't, that they both were wearing some of Ettrad's scavengings—shapeless sweaters, tatty coats, canvas trousers over

Aedis skinsuits. (A couple of plain metal knives, but those were in pockets.)

Finding those things had taken some time. Then Corso had talked Iari into a four-hour rest, actual sleep. And *then*, with dawn splitting the eastern sky, they'd got moving. It had taken the better part of the day to catch up to the refugees. It should have gone faster—just follow the voidspit trail—but Corso had argued go wide, so that there was a long, visible trail in the snow in case anyone wanted to look, that crossed the Ettradens' trail half a mile before Corso let them catch up.

So *that* had cost more time than Iari had wanted, and without the battle-rigs they were moving at the pace of scared civs, with boots that got stuck in snow sometimes. (Luki and Llian didn't have *time*; but Luki and Llian weren't the first priority anymore, and *that* chewed holes in Iari's guts if she let herself think about it.)

So she didn't think. She walked. She followed Corso.

He had predicted this cover story would work, thin as it was— said she was overthinking how much anyone would ask questions. ("They just got Brood-smacked, Iari, they aren't going to ask for fucking *references*." And he'd added, "Look at us. We look like we can take care of ourselves. That'll help sell it.") Corso was voidspit *sure* the One-Eyes were looking for volunteers, that the Brood were there to displace and disrupt. Fine. But assuming *this* lot was heading to join up—just because they were going north, and not Aedis-ward south—seemed too easy. (But why else go north? And why had *these* people survived? Corso had answers, or thought he did. So fine. Let the man do what he did, which was talk his way into places he shouldn't be.)

Truth was, she hadn't interacted with civilians without Aedis insignia, standard uniform-armor or battle-rig, for more than a decade—since her army days—and she hadn't *been* civ since childhood. Soon as she could join up, she had—the second decade of the surge, by then, *everyone* was expected to serve, and if you signed up you got some choice of assignments.

Now, out here, in front of the Ettradens, she was just Iari with a B-town accent and a scar on her face that might say *veteran* or *dangerous criminal.*

A smallish tenju woman, just north of middle-aged, with a knot of hooked braids like Corso's, grimaced and spat. "Fucking Aedis."

Corso's fingers dug into Iari's shoulder just a little bit harder, like he thought she was going to blow her temper and their cover. Ptah's own sake. The *fucking Aedis* comment seemed—not forced, exactly, but . . . rote. Like it was expected.

The man directly beside Fucking Aedis grunted approval (bigger tenju, with hook-studded braids sticking out of his hood) and said, "Put the 'caster down, Gel."

Gel, the only alw, and the only armed person Iari could see (except Corso), shot Fucking Aedis a hostile side-eye. Then Gel made a show of angling the 'caster's muzzle groundward. She did not, Iari noted, engage the safety.

Army vet, *bet* she was.

The rest of the Ettrad group—all tenju, notable in itself—had hung back, unwilling to involve themselves: these three were in nominal charge, and Gel had the weapon. Iari guessed *she* was the leader.

"I'm Bersk," said Fucking Aedis. She gestured at Braids in the Hood. "This is my brother, Trammen."

She didn't say *we're from Ettrad.* Maybe Corso was right about details. Or maybe they *weren't* from Ettrad.

"I'm Geltrannen." The alw was still watching Iari. "How did you find us?"

"You left a trail a blind neefa could follow," Iari said in her best B-town drawl.

Bersk looked surprised, but Trammen laughed. "She's not wrong, Gel. We did."

"There were Brood," said Bersk, a little defensively. "We had to get out fast."

Iari felt Corso steel, take a breath, then, "Been a lot more Brood, lately. You notice?"

"Always been *some* up here." Trammen gestured vaguely north. "The fissure, right?"

"True," Corso said. He was gripping Iari hard enough to hurt. "But after the surge, we didn't get more than a couple swarm or the odd pair of boneless for *years*. Now? A lot more often. Aedis is fucking up."

Iari dug her elbow into Corso's ribs. Felt, rather than heard, the grunt. He shut up about the Brood, anyway. It was *his* job, sure, getting in with the locals, and he hadn't wanted her here. But she didn't want him trying so hard that he got them both made.

"Not wrong," Trammen said again, and looked at Bersk. Something flickered between them.

Gel had gone back to staring at Iari. "Where'd you get *that*?" She tapped her teeth with a gloved finger.

Right. The capped tusk. Iari forgot about hers most of the time. Gel could be asking because a woman out of B-town—anyone coming north who wasn't from Windscar—might be running from something or someone, for reasons that would make that person unwelcome in a party of unarmed survivors.

Except Gel *wasn't* asking about Corso's capped tusk—his was newish, plain, a little shiny. But Iari's, now, hers came with an old scar, made by force rather than a keen edge, and it had the dull metal cap you got in the military.

Or in the Aedis.

Corso had said that the best lies are the ones you don't tell.

Iari eyed Geltrannen. "Fought in the surge. Visor broke. You fight, too?"

For the first time, Gel's expression changed, from suspicion to appraisal. Iari'd given her the right answer, then. "Yeah."

"Wherever you're going," said Corso. "You mind if we come along?"

Bersk looked at Gel, who nodded. Bersk relaxed. "Sure. Gel knows a place."

Oh, *did* Gel. What Iari knew was that Gel didn't seem worried about attracting Brood with group of unarmed, desperate, easy-pickings survivors, which any trooper who'd spent ten minutes in the surge should have been. *Guess* that was because Gel knew the Brood weren't coming.

Void and dust, Corso had been right. It wasn't just a crazy arithmancer kidnapping people and running hexwork experiments. There were people like Gel who *knew places.*

Trammen smiled like they were all friends now. "You're welcome to come with us."

"Great. That's—thank you." Corso's voice broke on gratitude. "Wouldn't want to spend another night out in *this*, just us two."

Ptah's *eye*, he'd turned budding thespian. Iari controlled a scowl, a grimace, a rolling of eyes. Corso's grip was leaving bruises. She shrugged him loose, locked eyes for a breath.

Then she drifted away, just a pace or two, and stared into the snow, doing her best imitation of someone who'd just lost everything, who was scared, who was worried about what was still out there.

Except she knew what, who, was out there. Char, Winter Bite, Dodri. Please, Elements, let someone be watching now, see her standing, understand. Please, Elements, that Winter Bite had heard every bit of that conversation. Then let Char's *sense* put it together, if Dodri couldn't.

When Iari turned around, Bersk and Trammen (especially Bersk) were surrounding Corso, trying to engage him in conversation. Bersk had a slagging *hand* on his sleeve.

Trammen, after a moment, walked over to Iari, wearing a smile she didn't like and an assurance she liked even less. No caps on *his* tusks. Just calculation in his eyes, mismatch for the warm-voiced, "Hey, don't worry, you're safe now."

He held out a hand to her. A *hand*, like they were friends. Like he was *saving* her. Well. A budding cult needed recruiters, didn't it. Brood had a way of making everyone instant allies.

Except Gel's hand stayed on her 'caster. Iari noticed that, too.

Geltrannen kept everyone moving through the rest of the day, then roused them up after a cold trail-ration dinner and drove them on again through the night, a trot-jog-walk cycle ostensibly to "put distance between them and Brood" (who moved faster than bipeds, which Gel had to know; they could run until their hearts burst, and Brood would be faster). The clouds had gathered into a low, flat, pewter ceiling and the wind licking out of the north smelled like snow. That Gel wanted to move meant their destination must be close; otherwise she'd dig in. Wait it out. Instead she was racing the weather.

At least the brutal pace kept everyone warm. But it also meant meant taking frequent short breaks because the civs weren't in trail-running shape, and *that* was when Bersk or Trammen—they alternated—got to work. They'd tuck in beside some panting person or three, and start yammering on about how things had gone wrong since the surge, anecdotal neefa-shit that made Iari's head hurt, it made so little sense. Every rest, every break: a litany of grievances that included stray Brood and failures of Confederation oversight *and* Confederation neglect, which were somehow both an acute problem worse than Brood, and also maybe connected to it, you couldn't trust, you know, *them.*

There was enough truth laced through it, like poison in a cup: funding that never materialized, the Confederation caring only about Seawall with its voidport and the beanstalk to the station. The neglect of the north, where the fissure was, you'd *think* that would matter to some people. Same things Corso had told Iari. None of it was new to the Ettraden refugees. There was a lot of nodding, a lot of additional complaints that had the air of things repeated many times. Like a temple call and response.

Of course, templars didn't learn Catechism sleep-deprived and exhausted, either.

Iari had not asked *how* the Aedis acted as the bully-arm of the Confederation without ever being *there* when the Brood attacked. This wasn't about logical thinking, or reason, or anything except creating grievance. Bersk and Trammen hadn't said anything yet about any Axorchal, though, or any savior, at least in Iari's hearing.

Corso might've heard something. Corso was getting the *special* treatment. Bersk made a point, every break, of carving him off by himself and having a conversation. Corso, for his part, played along with Bersk—who wore her hair in the same voidspit braids, pre-Landing tenju tribal, who whispered to him about *old ways* and *Landfall* and, when Gel wasn't looking, *alwar invaders,* even when Iari was within earshot. But when Iari wasn't—maybe there was talk of Axorchal.

Because Iari had Trammen to deal with. He worked on her mostly by filling up any silence, and by keeping her away from Corso. During his chatter she learned he and Bersk were sibs, that they were native to Ettrad, that Gel wasn't, that she didn't even live there. *Gel*, it seemed, *passed through periodically* on the caravans, which was a stock phrase so unlike anything else that came out of Trammen's maw that Iari guessed it for rote.

Hrok's freezing breath. Iari *did* ask how many alwar had lived in Ettrad (twenty-some), and found out they'd all conveniently died, except Geltrannen.

"So," she'd said, slowest drawl she could manage. "*All* the alwar died in the Brood attack except Gel? Isn't that . . . weird?"

Trammen had leveled one of those grins at her, like he thought she'd be charmed by seeing every tooth in his head. "Not really a bad thing, though, is it?"

Iari thought about Iffy, about Llian, and stared. "Take it there weren't humans in Ettrad?"

A snort. "I—no. They don't usually come up here, you know? Afraid of Windscar, of getting their little soft hands dirty. They—" The first glitch in the smile, as Trammen read something in her expression. "No. No humans."

Iari wanted badly to get a moment or ten with Corso, to compare notes and knowledge. And there was no way Bersk and Trammen were letting that happen. Trust Corso, that was all she could do. She knew she was voidspit at lying. She kept her jaw locked and looked either sullen or at least too dumb to bother with, even though Trammen seemed determined to try.

Iari did a lot of watching of the survivors, when no one was looking at *her*. They ranged from teen to middle-aged, reasonably fit, reasonably healthy, mostly male. Iari noted the lack of children and elderly early—having picked through the Ettrad ruins, that was no surprise; all those people had died. But it was odd that there were no parents or children at all among the survivors. Unless the Brood had known where to go, who to kill.

She watched Corso, too, like the sun rose and set on him—to make sure everyone *else* imagined how things stood between them. Those were muscles she hadn't used in a long time, damn near two decades. She just hoped it was convincing enough for Geltrannen.

That woman was the danger. She didn't talk to anyone. Too busy leading, sure, but also too busy watching. And her favorite subject seemed to be Iari.

Iari didn't *think* Gel had made her—if that were true, Iari was sure Gel would put a bolt through her skull (Gel would try). But the last time she'd caught Gel staring, the alw had smirked, small and nasty, like she thought she'd sussed out a truth Iari wanted to hide. It'd taken most of Iari's discipline then *not* to say something, start something, burn any chance of finding Luki and Llian and what was happening up here in favor of cracking that look off Gel's face.

Then, just as Iari thought she saw grey dawn in the sky, Gel picked up the pace. She speed-marched them up one final hill—straight up the side, slick and deep with snow, a slip-slide, breath-stealing endeavor—and then stopped. For breath, she said, a rest, which was voidspit. Iari realized that the moment she hit the top.

Geltrannen had stopped for effect.

The valley below them was small, flat, accessible by stream-beds carved between steep hills. The snow lay thick and unbroken on the edges, but in the middle, spreading dark like a bruise, like rot, was some kind of camp. Long rows of tents radiated out to the southeast and southwest. The latrines stretched off to the west. In the center stood one long tent, open on three sides. Mess, probably. The whole northern edge of the valley rose up impossibly steep, a natural barrier. An old homestead crouched at the bottom, house and barn and byre, a couple sod-sided outbuildings. Iari guessed there might be a command center in one of the buildings, the house probably. There were a couple of temporary structures back there, too, some kind of yurts. One of the sod-and-stone outbuildings sat at some remove from both house and barn, in the northwest. The byre sat at the top of a small rise to the northeast, long and narrow and trailing smoke from a metal pipe in the roof. Maybe where they were keeping her templars. Or the altar.

There were patrols walking the perimeter, but no fence, no earthworks. No defenses. No one was worried about Brood coming *here*.

No wonder Geltrannen had wanted to know where Iari'd gotten her scar. *Can you fight*, that meant.

Because the One-Eyes were building an army.

"We're home," said Gel. She stood at the front of their ragged train, her small frame bulked by coat and hood, the longcaster held crossways. Like an entertainment vid's idea of a Windscar nomad, down to the pose. "Welcome to the camp of Axorchal One-Eye."

Gel took her time walking them down to the camp. That gave everyone a chance to get a long look. Be impressed by the layout, the size. And, mostly, to give Bersk and Trammen time to tell everyone about Axorchal, no, not the *grannytale*, the *real* Axorchal. The Ettradens were exhausted, traumatized, had been prodded to anger at every step; Iari didn't think they could make a reliable decision right now about much of anything, except maybe which pair of socks they should wear. And now they were hearing how great Axorchal was, how he was the answer to Confederation incompetence and Aedian malfeasance, how *he* would take care of them, protect them from Brood, when it was clear the Aedis and the Confederation wouldn't.

It was, to Iari's mind, so obviously manipulative. But along with the exhaustion, the recent loss and trauma—with what had obviously been well-stoked resentment, with people who'd been spared (she was certain) because of their sympathy—she saw the impact. Wide eyes, slack jaws—because that camp down there wasn't ravaged by Brood, that was *order*, that was *safety*, without the Aedis or the Confederation. That camp was genuine Tanis, *real Tanis* (a phrase Iari had learned from Trammen, and learned to hate, along with Trammen himself), not some off-worlder neefa-shit.

Iari pretended to gawp with them and used her time to count the rows and the tents. She guessed the population somewhere north of a hundred, if those tents each held two people. That was a lot of homesteaders, a lot of remote villages. A lot of time and effort to recruit, to train.

Keawe had mentioned reavers to Corso, people stealing people, but Iari didn't see any sign of forced servitude. No one in shackles. No one working while someone else stood there and supervised. If reavers were trafficking people, they either weren't bringing their prisoners here, or those prisoners were assimilating. Or, ugly thought—the most resistant were the ones being made into One-Eyes.

Ungentle Ptah. All that carnage in the ruins, all those dead wichu, *clearly* that had been where the One-Eyes were made. But what if it wasn't? What if they made One-Eyes here, too?

The syn sparked in the back of her neck. It would help a little bit, if it came to a fight. The nanomecha would still trigger an endocrine response. There just wouldn't be a battle-rig on the other side.

Iari took a deep breath. She knew she was scowling. Caught Corso staring at her, and tried to rearrange her face into awe or at least neutrality. But then Corso's eyes flicked past her shoulder. Oh. He was trying to warn her. So she wasn't surprised to hear footfalls slorping through the snow, and then Bersk saying,

"Well then, Iari. What do you think?"

That was a smug tone. Iari turned slowly. Looked Bersk up and down. The manic delight in the other woman's eyes reminded Iari of Swift Runner's diseased amber teslas in a B-town warehouse cellar, right before that riev had tried to break her in half.

Iari wanted to break Bersk in half, but she'd settle for breaking the smug. "Seen camps like this before," she said, like every word required great effort. "In the army."

Bersk looked a little undone. "This isn't the *Confederation*. This is—"

"Still an army camp." Iari shrugged. "What's the difference?"

She shoved past Bersk, aiming past Corso and toward the front of the line. Slogged past the Ettradens, who were here not just because they were sympathetic (susceptible) to Axorchal's cult, but also because they were the most physically useful to a cult preaching rebellion. Soldier-fodder, the lot of them.

And gentle Mishka, patient Chaama: Luki and Llian were down there. That was affront enough, seizing templars as prisoners of an undeclared war. But their battle-rigs were down there, too, and an arithmancer could learn a lot from a battle-rig's hexes about Aedian defenses, about the syn. About templar nanomecha. Gaer had told her there was an arithmancer here. And that there were voidspit Brood in the altar, in the One-Eyes' gloves—which, if Gel knew and these poor refugees didn't, was five vakari hells of an irony.

Gel had been watching the reactions of her new recruits. When she saw Iari coming toward her, she turned and started walking downhill again, with just enough room on the path for Iari to walk beside her.

"I heard what you said to Bersk," Gel said as Iari drew even. "Not impressed, then?"

"Didn't say that." The path wasn't wide. Gel's longcaster was a lunge-and-grab away. Take it, club Gel with it, and—void and dust. And *what*, shoot Bersk and Trammen? Talk everyone else into better sense, standing over a trio of bodies? *Oh, don't worry, I'm Captain Iari, the Aedis is here to save you, sorry we didn't know what was happening here sooner, now please turn around and go back to your dead families.*

Iari made herself look somewhere else other than Gel's face. "Didn't know you were recruiting a tenju army."

She'd expected a smug acknowledgement, maybe even a boast about Axorchal's prowess or popularity or *whatever.* Instead, Gel's eyes narrowed, her mouth thinned.

Ungentle Ptah, what Iari would not give for a Gaer report on Gel's aura. But all right, she had plain intuition, use that: it looked like Gel might've noticed no alwar survivors from Ettrad. Like maybe she saw what Iari did: everyone visible down in the camp was tenju. Gel looked like a woman scrambling to conceal her reaction. Iari knew what that effort looked like from the inside: anger plastered over with unconcern.

Geltrannen couldn't make herself smile. Watching her try made Iari's skin (and the syn) prickle. "You never asked what kind of resources we had."

"Huh. Well. Camp like that means an army. That," and Iari pointed her chin at the 'caster in Gel's hands, "is an army weapon. Armies need enemies. Who're we fighting?"

She thought she'd overstepped for a fistful of hammering heartbeats. Geltrannen *looked* at Iari, same way Gaer did sometimes.

(Ptah's flaming *eye.* What if Gel was an arithmancer, reading everyone's aura?)

But all Gel said was, "Not the dull stone you pretend to be, are you? You mind fighting someone besides Brood? Say, Confederation? Or Aedis?"

"I like fighting better than farming," said Iari. "Long as I get a weapon like yours."

"Oh," said Gel. "You will. Don't you worry. You might even get something *better.* You might *be* something better."

Iari's guts clenched. And oh, she wanted to ask *what the fuck does that mean,* wanted to wring it out of Gel on the spot. But instead she grunted an incurious, "Good," and fell back. Faked a stumble, pulled off to the side, propped her boot on a rock and began adjusting the tabs.

"You all right?" Trammen asked in passing. He sounded sincere.

"Fine," she snapped. "Fucking boot is all."

Iari swore and rolled her ankle and pretended to work off a tweak until Corso caught up, with Bersk beside him like a weaselly shadow. Then she jammed her foot back down and fell in step beside him. It wasn't a wide path. No room left for Bersk, unless she wanted to try pushing back. Iari half wished she would.

Corso caught Iari's elbow like he meant to keep her from slipping (not a chance), held it hard enough to keep her from lunging (also unlikely). "Catch up with you in a minute, Bersk, yeah? Got to talk to my cousin."

"Sure," said Bersk. She bounced a look off from Corso to Iari and back. A little confusion, a little concern. Then she hiked on ahead, speeding up to catch up with Trammen.

Iari said, under her breath, "Flirt on your own time, Risar."

He let that go with a rolled eye. "What'd Gel say to you?" And louder, "You all right? Your knee acting up?"

"Fine," Iari snapped. And on the edge of audible, "She's promising weapons better than 'casters. Promising that I'll be something better. She also doesn't look happy. I asked if she liked the tenju army. Maybe she's figuring out there's no place for her or anyone except tenju in this organization."

Corso grunted. He let go of her elbow. Kept his hand close, like he meant to catch her again. He lifted his chin vaguely at Bersk, who'd leaned close to confer with Trammen. "You might be right. *She's* going on about how Axorchal's for tenju first, Tanis for the tenju. Same slogans *I* used as a fucking teenager."

"So, this camp has factions. Maybe that's why they killed the wichu. Simple xenophobia." Ungentle Ptah, she was not covert ops. Corso had been right: send him in alone, let him get himself out, report, and then they'd figure it out. And now here she was.

"Your plan?" Corso asked.

Gentle Mishka, *her* plan. Acid in her gut, ice in her chest, a mouth dry as dust. Was this what Tobin had felt like at Saichi? Everyone looking to him to solve things. And look how *that* ended.

"Hasn't changed."

Find the altar, destroy it. Find Luki and Llian, get them out alive. Figure out who was in charge down there, who the arithmancer was, if those were the same person. Kill them, which was Iari's plan if she could—she hadn't told Corso that part yet, but he'd figure it out.

Corso side-eyed her. Visibly weighing an argument, visibly letting it go. "Right."

Because it was too late to change things, even if she wanted to, which she didn't.

Please, Elements, let this work.

CHAPTER FIFTEEN ≡≡≡

C orso's gut clenched around ice and needles. He wished to the old gods, the Elements, the veeks' five or nine dark lords, that Iari would change her mind and her plan. This was *big* trouble. He hadn't been able to tell Iari everything Bersk had said to him, talking all her neefa-shit about restoring the old ways and expelling the alwar and reclaiming Tanis. It wasn't anything *new*; that kind of talk had been circulating on the fringes for years, even before the Weep. It had disappeared briefly in the first years of the surge; there hadn't been time for sedition then, what with Brood ripping people apart from Windscar to Seawall. But afterward, with the Aedis so firmly entrenched, with the Confederation administration in Seawall still so very much alwar, the talk had come back.

Corso fingered the end of a braid that'd slipped over his shoulder, pulled it straight. Counted the hooks studding its length. Those were a pre-Landfall custom. Old Ways, capitalized O and W, in the same way Axorchal was. Except the tribes that'd worn their hair braided were long gone—had been since just after the alwar Landfall (the old Harek Empire then, not even Confederation—it was *that* long ago). The custom had been reconstructed, reimagined, and served as a marker of rebellion from someone who'd once conformed. Corso had heard all the propaganda, he had participated in those early movements. Mostly people getting together and drinking too much, yelling about what had (almost certainly *not*) been glory days no one could remember. Some imagined, perfected simplicity. The farthest he'd gone with the whole business was growing his hair long, braiding the hooks into it.

Bersk, with her endless recruitment chatter, hadn't been in the army. She was just a little too young. But she'd grown up in a place where at least some people imagined a Tanis without the Aedis and the Confederation. Where people seemed to have forgotten that even if the Aedis left tomorrow, the Weep would still be there, and the Aedis stood between them and the fucking Brood.

The word Bersk used was freedom, as in Axorchal would restore the true, but freedom wasn't what Corso saw in that camp. No, that camp was order, of the sort the B-town cartels understood. Force, but also manipulation, with all the power held close to the top. If there *was* an Axorchal—Bersk thought there was, a god-touched man or a god-*become*-man, she didn't seem to grasp the distinction—that's where the power was, or standing close to them. Corso just *bet* it was the arithmancer Gaer'd talked about. Arithmancy looked a lot like magic.

Corso knew that's who Iari was after. Name, face, location. Head, if she thought she could get it. She was an Aedis-raised war-orphan from B-town, but he'd *bet* her roots came from the north. The Confederation was enforced civilization, *civility*, laws and procedures. The Aedis was there for when politics failed, like it had with the Protectorate and the Expansion, and then again with the Weep and the Brood.

And this—*all* of this, what had been wichu separatists, *terrorists*, allied with and then killed off by a cult to an obsolete god—was really just about control. About having hexes that controlled Brood. About controlling *people*—with fear, with violence, with their own slagging prejudice.

This was a big camp. A lot of people. A lot of resources. Corso bet the cult had had some initial help from the fucking wichu for more than just making half-riev One-Eyes. He knew from Bersk that Geltrannen had been staying in Ettrad since last winter, talking about Axorchal's return, how the old gods were rising. That she'd been promising to take them (and Bersk was hazy on who *them* was, if it had been everyone or just some select few) to see Axorchal when the time was right.

Which Brood had conveniently provided, by destroying anything that might entice people to stay where they were.

Corso's foot slipped. It was just a short skid before he caught himself. He swore at the trail, at his foot, at the multiverse. Looked up and found Bersk coming at him again. *Flirt on your own time*, Iari had said, and he hadn't been, but maybe Bersk thought he had.

Maybe he should start. See where *that* got him.

Fucked, that was where.

He let Bersk snug in beside him, let her talk. Concentrated on keeping his feet where he wanted them. On making his own assessments of the voidspit camp. He reckoned Iari could see the same things he did. What worried him was what the pair of them couldn't see. Hexwork could be anywhere. Everywhere.

Somewhere out there were Char and Winter Bite and Dodri. *They* would see—all right, Dodri might not, but the riev would—the army camp, its relative capabilities. Maybe even the hexwork. What they would do with that knowledge—how that would help him and Iari—Corso had no idea.

Bersk shut up, finally, as they neared the valley floor. There were several ways into the camp that Corso could see from this perspective. Geltrannen had brought them the hard way, straight over that hill and down on a switchbacking thread of a path. There was another, flatter trail that followed a creek bed winding between two hills on the northeastern edge, closer to the old homestead buildings. Corso could see big patches of flatpack made by a lot of feet. Bands of One-Eyes roaming Windscar—ha, no, more likely that was where people were bringing in the supplies. There were deeper gouges in the flatpack. An ATV had come through here, more than once from the misaligned gouges, or more than one. But most of the wear on those trails was foot traffic.

Interesting. If the ATVs were still here, that could be a help getting out.

There wasn't a front gate, no marker or arch that said *come through here*. Geltrannen marched them in across the nearest perimeter. The guards saw them—no way they couldn't. Didn't move to intercept. Acted like motley hikers showed up every day and walked right in. Maybe they did. Maybe they'd been doing just that for a long time.

Corso had done a lot of his army time in field camps. Bigger than this, most of them, but the idea was the same. There was organization behind this endeavor. Planning. *Long* planning.

"Bersk," he said, as they passed down the aisle between rows of tents—some flaps open, some closed, unmatched gear but still *matching*—"When did you meet Geltrannen?"

She looked at him, surprised. "I think it was a few years ago, midsummer. She came through with a caravan. When it came back through, she stayed a while. Made Ettrad her base, you know? She's—ah, she's a trapper, and a hunter."

Sure she was. Corso nodded. Seemed like Gel had wormed into Ettrad. Embedded there, almost, like some undercover plot on *Verge Runners*. A few *years* put it well before the business in

B-town. The cult had been around a long time. And if the wichu had been here, too, which they *had*—void and fucking dust, they'd been planning all this for a while. Which came first, though—cult or separatists? Corso wasn't sure it mattered at this point, except for the history books.

Geltrannen marched them up what was clearly a main thoroughfare toward the big tent, army surplus, that Corso reckoned for the mess. It was clearly the center of things—geography, social gathering—food, definitely, but maybe also religion. Would they keep an altar in the open? That would make it easier.

Then a—what? cultist? soldier? badly misinformed and mistaken neefa-brain?—tenju, armed with a longcaster like Gel, piecemeal armor, came trotting up out of the mess tent and stopped in the middle of the path just out of earshot. Gel sped up to meet him, and they stood there, backs turned, heads together. Gel didn't like whatever she was hearing. She jerked her head back, stared at the tenju. Eyes wide. Then narrowed.

Huh.

Then Gel spun on her heel so hard she dug through snow and into mud underneath. She waved an arm down a much narrower line of tents, a gesture that looked as angry as it did directional.

"This way!"

"What?" Bersk looked surprised. "But—"

"*This way*," Gel repeated. "Don't *argue* with me." And she stomped off on what was clearly a detour that she didn't like.

Suddenly Corso had no one minding him. Bersk peeled herself away to deal with the Ettradens, who might have noticed Gel's annoyance and who had definitely noticed the guard blocking their path and diverting their progress. When Bersk stopped to answer a question from one of the Ettradens, Corso just kept going toward the back of the line, where Trammen stuck to Iari like a shadow.

Corso shot her a look, *willed* her to notice. Caught a flash of green as she looked back. One heartbeat's eyelock, no more. Let her understand, come on, he needed a voidspit *second*—

"Ask you something?" Iari said, and Trammen turned to her like she'd pulled a rope.

So Corso walked past, cool as the breeze. He ducked into a narrow space between rows of tents and went the opposite direction Gel had.

He popped out on the next aisle over. This was a narrower thoroughfare, mostly deserted. Corso put his shoulders back and walked like he was supposed to be there, brisk and purposeful and straight toward that mess tent.

It was open on three sides, which made looking inside pretty easy. There was a firepit up the center like some ancient history longhouse and a canvas partition in back, from behind which came smoke and food smells and metallic banging. That gave Corso some hope the cooks here were better at it than Bersk, and also that they weren't cooking over that firepit. (Not that he intended to eat many meals here. Damned if he wasn't missing those food-tube horrors still stored in his battle-rig. And his battle-rig. Void and dust, what was wrong with him?) The furniture inside the tent was that crisply utilitarian cheap you got from a nano-forge. Long tables. Long benches. Empty, right now. There was also a conspicuously empty space near the rear, off to one side, with a clear patch scraped out in the dirt, where it looked like there should be another table and there wasn't.

Corso angled that direction, keeping just outside the tent's perimeter. Yeah, okay, there were the marks where a table *had* been, so where had it gone—oh. *There.* Several pieces of broken table sat in a neat pile just around the back, near the curtained-off part Corso thought was the kitchen. Corso paused to examine it, under the cover of adjusting his boot (anyone watching would think he had no idea how to fasten the tabs, since he had to do each of them twice).

Nanoforged tables were cheap, yes, but they were also sturdy. This one had been smashed in a couple of places, as if something heavy had gone right through it. Corso had been in places where the heavy things were drunk tenju, and this *was* an irregular army camp. But drunk tenju didn't tend to leave scorch marks and scoring and . . . yeah. That was blood, too.

Try half-riev tenju, instead of drunk. That would add some weight. Try—shit. Templar battle-rigs, if Luki and Llian had come through the portal here. There had definitely been some kind of fight. Maybe battle-rigged templars coming through an altar portal and, you know, being a little bit mad about that.

Maybe this was what the Ettradens weren't supposed to see. Amend that, without the maybe. Recruits couldn't ask questions, like *what broke the table.* Recruits couldn't see any break in the control and the order.

Corso stood up, swallowed his heart and his hope back into the cold knot of his gut. Now that he looked, he could see disturbance on the ground, too. There were—not tracks, exactly, but holes, deep footprints, in the snow. Grooves and scrapes and slagging *holes* that went all the way into the underlying mud. Heavy things had come this way. Heavy things had been *dragged.* Corso couldn't say for sure if those were battle-rig tracks, but he *could* say the makers of those tracks had gone somewhere behind the mess tent.

Which meant he had to go, too.

Corso looked around—no one seemed to be looking at him, he hardly saw anyone—and followed the drag-marks around to the back of the tent. The old homestead was back here, barn and house closest. To the west of those sat one of the yurts, and to the east, some sod-topped smaller outbuilding. The byre was farther away that same direction. If he'd hoped to pick up any trail back here, well, too slagging bad and no luck. The ground back here was hopelessly churned up, but it was also *busy*. There was a thoroughfare stomped through to dirt from the barn to the kitchen part of the mess tent, which had its own separate entrance hanging off the back of the larger mess tent like a boil. The whole area was just mud and snow (no blood, or at least nothing he could see in a fast glance).

But—huh again. What had looked like *one* yurt from the trail was actually two conjoined prefab units, with sliding doors rather than flaps for their entry. A twisted stick stood upright beside the entrance, like a signpost if signposts were just a little bit warped and a little bit short and, you know, missing a sign.

Something about the stick's silhouette jabbed at the back of Corso's mind. Familiar. Awful. He got a little closer and realized why. What he'd taken for a weather-warped branch was an actual pole, and the deformations were carvings that ran the whole length of it. Crude work, nothing Corso could identify clearly from this distance. But the curves, the angles—not symmetrical, not at all pleasing. It *looked* like the bastard brother of the carvings he'd seen on the altar.

Oh, what were the slagging chances *that's* where they were keeping it.

No one had come after him yet. No one had challenged him. There wasn't even a slagging guard back here. Of course he was going to look.

The door to the yurt slid open. A tenju man stepped out still talking to someone inside. Big man, broad, hooked braids. An unwholesome spiral circled one eye, sprawling across nose and cheek and ending somewhere on the side of his neck. Had to be a tattoo. That much cosmetic vanity would've smeared in the amount of sweat Corso could smell on him even from here.

Latrines, this camp had in abundance. Not so much on the showers, apparently.

The man turned around at the last second, saw Corso, and startled. He was blue-eyed, like Corso, which marked him as native (spacer tenju were brown-eyed, generally, or yellow, sometimes green; blue was a Tanisian rarity). Corso saw the recognition. Saw something in the man's face relax.

Instead of demanding who Corso was, what was he doing—questions for which Corso had prepared, more or less—Tattoo-Face just blurted a *sorry* and stepped aside. Even thrust a hand in the door to keep it from closing. Voidspit courtesy, no challenge at all.

Something said Corso belonged here. The braids. The blue eyes and the longcaster. Corso caught the door, nodded thanks. Took a breath. His answers to *what are you doing here* were about to be a lot less plausible. But Tattoo-Face had already walked off, leaving Corso in possession of a partly open door and a clear look inside.

It was a lot darker. All the light came from camp lanterns hanging from the central pole. The conjoining wall pinched together into a largish, roundish aperture, across which hung a tatty blanket. The smell seeping around it, petrichor and iron, made Corso's gut try to crawl into his throat.

The yurt had an actual floor, prefabbed and very scuffed panels. And despite the relative clutter in here—boxes and crates lined one side, stacked high as Corso's head—there was also a very wide, clear path from the front door to a fetid curtain, and a set of scrapes on the prefab floor like something very heavy had been dragged through here more than once.

Another tenju, his hair a mass of braids, was on his way into that second chamber. He had just tugged the curtain aside, and started to step through into the other (Brood-stinking) room of the yurt. Which meant the curtain was open enough that Corso could see past it, into that second chamber.

It was even darker back there, no lanterns at all. The light was dim and red like an angry riev's hexes. Corso blinked hard, squinted—and then he saw where that light came from. What squatted in the center of the second room.

Corso had been coming into the yurt. Now he arrested his forward motion, reversed it, had the front door shut between him and *that fucking thing* before he'd drawn a full breath. His whole body felt hot, cold, prickly with chills and sweat.

All right. *Don't* panic. Gaer had fucking *said* there was another altar. Iari was fucking *looking* for it. Now Corso had found it, first try! Good for him. He'd come *back* here to find it. So panicking about his success was stupid. All he had to do was tell Iari about it, and to do that he had to gather his slagging *shit* together so Bersk and Geltrannen and everyone else didn't notice—

"Corso!"

He spun around and there was Bersk, hurrying toward him from the direction everyone else had gone. He speared his gaze past her, attracted by movement, thought he saw Iari just vanishing around the side of one of the sod-sided huts.

And then Bersk cut off his view, having gotten right up on him while he hallucinated Iari. "Come on." She took his hand like she'd earned that privilege, tugged on him like a prize neefa. She was pulling him away from where Iari had gone (where he thought she'd gone). He jerked his hand loose. "Where's my—my cousin?"

Bersk made a face. "With Trammen and the others. But *you* are supposed to come with me. Gel said."

Like it was a special thing she was offering. Like he was special.

This was the fastest way to separate him from his so-called family. From a potential drag on his loyalty.

He'd argued to infiltrate this place alone, and been pissed when Iari refused him. Now he was getting his wish, and he didn't like it.

Iari needed to know where the altar was. And he needed her to know where *he* was.

But when Bersk dragged on his hand, Corso followed.

Iari was starting to think Corso wasn't coming back. That look— she thought it meant *buy me time*, and she had. Two voidspit minutes of Trammen monologue—during which he'd assured her that yes, there was room here for everyone, that Axorchal wanted *all* tenju, that it wouldn't be a problem that she came from B-town—while everyone else followed Geltrannen like blind neefa.

If Corso was off doing recon, *great*, but if he didn't get back before someone asked where he'd gone—she'd better think of something. Latrines. Sure.

But then Bersk came bouncing past like a kid on the way to a sweet shop, on some errand taking her away from the Ettraden parade. Iari turned to look. Thought about trying to follow, but then Trammen seemed to remember he was supposed to deliver her somewhere.

He took her elbow exactly like Corso had earlier. The syn

burned along her nerves, and Iari jerked away from him—harder than he'd expected, or she'd intended.

Trammen blinked. "This way, Iari, come on."

Ungentle Ptah. She shrugged and went with him. He led her back toward the northern edge of the camp, past the barn and the house, where the other Ettradens had already gone. They passed one of the sod-sided outbuildings, which—huh. There were guards out front—unarmed, wearing coats with hoods, standing side by side in silence.

Then one of the guards turned to watch her and Trammen go past, and Iari saw the metal glove, the skull-cap, the red cabochon.

Her syn prickled, shooting lightning from her needle-socket all the way down her spine.

She let her steps drag, then stop. Pretended to stare at the One-Eyes (that would be fair), but she was mostly looking at the building. It wasn't big. Four walls, a smallish door mostly eclipsed by its guards. No windows, or rather—windows recently boarded from the outside. In its past life, it might've been a work shed, or a smokehouse, or someplace to keep chickens.

What it held now was something important enough for One-Eye guards, the first ones she'd seen since arrival. Iari had a very short list of what might qualify. The altar. Templar prisoners.

Though templar prisoners would be a very new development. The building's fortifications seemed older than that, like it had been sealed up well before Luki and Llian would've arrived. That didn't mean they *weren't* inside, though. It might mean this camp had built a prison before they had caught any templars (if it was a prison), and that begged asking,

"What's in *here*?"

It came out harsher than she'd meant. The voidspit syn was still looking for its battle-rig, still trying to move her—because her nanomecha knew bad shit when they saw it, evidently, and had more sense than she did about standing so close.

The look on Trammen's face was shock turning thoughtful. Wary. He rearranged his lips into a sneer. "It's where we put troublemakers."

"So, a prison?"

"Not quite. Just say it's no place you want to be."

She wanted badly to demonstrate exactly how *little* she cared for Trammen's implied threats. She wanted to let the syn have its way, and—do that, she'd end up inside the voidspit prison herself, *or* dead.

She dropped her gaze and shrugged. "Just *asking.*"

Trammen started to reach for her arm again, reconsidered, let his hand drop. He edged closer, until Iari could smell the oiled canvas of his coat. "It's all right. I just don't want you getting in trouble, is all. I don't want you ending up *in* there."

Oh, *now* he was all gentle-voiced. Iari side-eyed him. "Who's in there now? What'd they do?"

That smile again, the one with all those teeth, the one that meant, *come along now, like a good useful idiot.* "I don't know. I just got here, too, remember?"

"Then how do you know it's a prison?" Mistake, *mistake.* She knew it as soon as she spoke. He might not *know*, might've guessed, same as she had, that guards meant something needed guarding. The difference was he'd jumped straight to thinking that something was people, and without knowing (she hoped) about templars. That meant keeping people locked up must be something he'd *expected* to find here, in this place he'd supposedly never been.

She looked up, expecting a faceful of Trammen's suspicion.

Instead she saw the first flicker of fear. He made the *start walking* gesture again, and this time she did. He tucked in behind her (but not touching, quite), and leaned close to her ear.

"You see the guards? Those are Axorchal's Chosen."

You could *hear* the capital letter. "Are they like priests? Like . . . like *templars?*"

"Feh." He made a spitting noise. "No. They're *better.*"

"Is that what we're going to be?"

"Only some of us." Trammen glanced over his shoulder, where the One-Eyes kept their post, unblinking and incurious. "Only the lucky ones."

He said lucky, but Iari heard *damned.*

CHAPTER SIXTEEN ══════

Homer's funeral began with the morning bells.
It was Hrok's time. In Seawall, where Gaer had dropped
down the beanstalk and spent his first dirtside month,
they called Hrok the Breath of Dawn, because the ocean breezes
typically picked up then for a variety of meteorological reasons that
had nothing to do with Elemental forces, but which didn't make
pretty poetry.

Of course, in Seawall, breezes were pleasant things, skipping
off the ocean and bringing welcome cool to the baking streets.
Here in the north—Windscar north, not B-town north, a distinction Gaer hadn't fully appreciated until this winter—Hrok's breath
was an act of war.

This morning the wind came thick with snow, last night's
storm finally arriving at the Aedis, which blunted some of the
bone-biting cold in favor of poor visibility and little graupels of
misery that snuck past hood and collar and stung where they met
warm skin.

Gaer could, of course, go inside. The temple was open, and
would remain so, despite Hrok's gusty exhalations. Aedian funer-
ary custom was to leave the doors open, made pretty by some *setatir* story about spirits unbound, about freely crossing thresholds

and boundaries. (The Five Tribes and the Protectorate had similar stories about what happened to the souls of the dead. Not as poetic, not as comforting, just as improbable.)

And Gaer had intended to go in. But then he had gotten to the temple doors and stopped. One of the doors *was* pushed to, concession to storm and blowing snow, but the other was propped halfway, and it was in that crack of light and heat that Gaer found himself caught. Found himself examining the doorframe, admiring the hexes he could see laced through the aether. Wards, mostly inactive, except for the ones meant to transmute cold to heat. But those doors could shut and seal, and with those hexes active, they might hold off a whole battalion of Brood.

(This Aedis, Windscar, had done so in the surge. Other Aedis compounds had done so and fallen, because even the best hexes weren't infallible.)

Perhaps there was a hex against vakari on the doors, then, because he could not step through. Tried, lifted a foot—put it down again. The aether itself might well have been solid. Or, or gravity just pulled harder on him. Made it impossible to take that step. But of course it wasn't a hex. It was a different kind of warding.

Guilt. The firm conviction he did *not* belong in there. The fear that he did.

Windscar's Mother Superior—Hesteth, the tallest alw Gaer had ever seen, and a priest of Hrok, besides—stood facing the east with her arms raised as she welcomed the (theoretical) sun and the dawn. The nave was not yet full; the vigil would continue until midnight, when Homer would go to Chaama's embrace, and Gaer understood that people would pass in and out throughout the day, as shifts allowed. That was the point of the custom, which had started when the Aedis had, during the Expansion war.

Which, being a diplomat in addition to SPERE arithmancer,

Gaer'd had to study—both war and Aedis customs. It was just that he'd never actually attended an Aedian funeral. The templars who'd died in B-town last autumn—Gaer had been in hospice when those funerals happened. Iari had attended. Gaer hadn't pried at that memory. Iari had been to a lot of templar funerals. She didn't need to relive another for his curiosity.

And truth, he hadn't been sorry to miss them. He hadn't known those templars except as faces and names. He'd exchanged two words with Lieutenant Peshwari, which was sufficient for Gaer to understand Peshwari didn't think much of vakari. Iari had told Gaer that Peshwari had come from old Seawall money, and was partial to humans, then alw, with tenju a distant third. It had been Iari's way of telling him not to feel bad for skipping that funeral, and truth, Gaer hadn't.

But Homer, now. Gaer couldn't say he'd known Homer *well.* But he was someone with whom Gaer had conversed, even if it was superficial exchanges about weather, the quality of the breakfast rolls, the latest song Kreeshan Blue had released. Homer had been someone he'd fought with—bone mecha. Hallucinatory fog. Homer had been Windscar, Keawe's and Notch's, but he was also *Iari's.* Iari would be here, if she could. (Notch would be, too, and he wasn't; that was a matter of some concern, but it could wait. It *would* wait.)

Iari would *want* to be here, which Gaer did not, but Iari was out there in this *setatir* snow running into hostile arithmancy and cultists and who *setatir* knew what, so that there wouldn't be two *more* templar funerals.

(No. There would be four more. Six, if someone managed to kill the riev.)

So. *So.* If Iari could not be here with Homer, he intended to be here *for* her and void and dust, dear dark lords, he couldn't manage to cross the temple threshold. As Iari's proxy, he was doing an abysmal job.

The bites of snow, the malicious eddies that stung exposed flesh—call that penance, of the Five Tribes sort (which always hurt), for his reticence. Gaer hadn't decided how long he would watch, yet. Through this first set of prayers. Maybe until he froze to the stone.

Then Iffy said, from the region of his elbow, "You could go in. No one would say anything."

He started, Iffy's voice (and presumably Iffy) having materialized with no warning. When he looked back, Gaer could see her tracks in the snow, rapidly filling. She was quiet, that was all, and he'd been distracted. She hadn't *flown* here or floated or hexed herself silent. (His own tracks, he noted, were long since whited out.)

He delayed answering her while a pair of templars—initiates, from the tabards over their armor, scuttled past him. One of them looked a little bit startled as she passed, recognizing him as The Vakar. The snow-covered vakar standing outside like the stupidest of neefa in a snowstorm.

The second initiate didn't look up at all.

Gaer slanted a look down at Iffy. "Oh, I don't know. Some might mind me inside."

"Gaer. Honestly." Iffy folded her arms across her chest. She wore a coat, like all sensible beings. (Not templars. Templars wore armor, all of them, even the training-initiates. Keawe had put the Aedis on alert after they'd gotten back.) Gaer supposed that armor rule would apply to priests, too, unless those priests were in occupations where armor was a detriment. Like, oh, the hospice, where Iffy's tracks said she'd come from: across the courtyard directly, rather than through the labyrinthine halls that would have spared her the need for a coat. It was probably faster, going out-side. Iffy tended to favor practical speed over comfort. It was a trait she shared with Iari.

Iffy sounded a little bit like Iari now, too. "You're being a—a *neefa.*"

Gaer huffed. His breath steamed out his nostrils and the seams in his jaw-plates, disrupting the swirling snow. "Perhaps. What's your excuse? Not my company, surely."

He felt her looking up at him. Refused to turn and meet her gaze.

After a moment, she said, "Mishka's bells are at sunset."

That took him a moment to parse. All Aedian priests served all the Elements, like the templars—but they had preferences. Spe-cialties. Iffy's was Mishka, but . . . Gaer gestured into the temple. "I see priests of all sorts in there. Mishka, Ptah, Chaama. Hrok."

Iffy blew an errant snowflake off her nose. "I have time. The vigil lasts until midnight."

"So it does. Then why are you here *now*, Sister Iphigenia? If not to attend."

"To see you." Her aura swirled, reddish and violet and un-healthy yellow. Fear.

Ah. "Notch is not doing well. His nanomecha have not responded?"

Iffy stuck her jaw out in a gesture clearly adopted from tenju. "No. But that's not the reason."

Green spilled into her aura like paint. Bright. Clear. More hon-est than she was. Gaer decided to let the lie pass, for the moment, because she still hadn't blinked, and anyone who would lie un-blinking to an arithmancer deserved his respect.

"Well. Then enlighten me."

"When we were in the ruins—with the altar. Iari *did* something. She—her whole battle-rig looked like it filled up with plasma."

Well. This line of inquiry had been inevitable, and he'd *told* Iari to tell everyone, and . . . *sss*. He'd reported to Tobin already. One betrayal was quite enough. "Is that a question? Because I am certain the battle-rig did *not*, in fact, fill with plasma."

"But you saw whatever it was happen."

"Yes."

"And you saw the—channeling effect. When Iari made that plasma go through her axe and just cut the altar in half."

"I definitely did see that, yes."

"Do you know what, how, that happened?"

Gaer cocked his head. He knew the gestured unnerved people— or rather, people who were not vakari. People who were not Iari, who didn't flinch, had never flinched. "Hexwork? Have you asked the armorer?"

Iffy didn't flinch, either. "You're not a neefa. You're an *ass*."

"I don't *know* what it was. I can guess. Iari's nanomecha responded to a threat."

"But—have you seen it before? Did you *know* that would happen?"

"Ah. *That's* what you intended to ask. Did I know it would happen. There are arithmancers who specialize in probability. I am not one of them."

"Mishka's tits, Gaer!" Iffy clapped her hands over her mouth in the next breath. No one inside seemed to hear, being focused on Mother Hesteth. It probably helped that everyone had clustered forward in the nave, away from the gusts and the snow. "What is the *matter* with you?"

"The *matter*." Gaer tilted onto his toes. Void and dust, there was even a little puddle inside, where the blown-in snow melted. It was clear water, showing him scuffed stone in its meager depths as well as the spangling of the overhead teslas (there were torches, too, *real* fire, but they were too distant to cause a reflection). "The matter," he told the puddle, "is that you are very *much* here about Notch, and I don't like where this line of questioning goes."

Two spots of anger—the same color on mammalian skin as in auras—blotched her cheekbones. "You're reading my aura."

"I am. I am *that* sort of arithmancer."

"An ass. Yes." Iffy drifted back a step. The snow began collecting on her hood. Her breath steamed out, partly obscuring her face. (Not her aura, if that was her intent. Surely she knew better.) "I wanted to know if you'd seen Iari do that before. Or, or if she'd told you she could. Because you didn't seem surprised, and—it seems like you should be."

"You might have asked Iari."

"Oh, please." Iffy tucked her gloved fists under her elbows, less as if she were cold, more as if she were trying to keep from using those fists on him. "She'd've said *later, Iffy* and brushed me off. Or just *looked* at me and not said anything."

"And so you're asking *me.*"

"You're her friend," Iffy said, so baldly that Gaer flinched. "You know her better than anyone."

"Knight-Marshal Tobin—"

"Is the Knight-Marshal. You're the one she talks to every day. Listen, Gaer." Iffy stuck out one of her hands, uncurled, and made as if to touch his arm. He didn't quite jerk away, but her hand stopped as if he had.

Her cheeks flushed again, this time not with anger. "You're right. I am here about Notch. His nanomecha aren't—they're not doing what Iari's did. They're not making that . . . that upgrade.

That evolution. I don't know *why*, I don't know if it's because that big k'bal mecha did something different with its battle-hexes, or if Notch's nano are just different—"

"Or what, if I did something to Iari's?"

"No!" She blinked. "Is that even possible?"

As if she'd just considered the idea, all bright and chirpy-voiced. Gaer would have believed her, if he hadn't been watching her aura.

"I did *nothing* to Iari's nanomecha. I did not even visit her in the hospice after the house fell on her." His jaws ached, his plates were so tightly clamped. He could barely open his mouth at all. "As for the rest . . . you are asking, Sister Iphigenia, for me to betray Iari's confidence."

"No. Yes. But Gaer—I'm asking for *Notch*."

That, at least, was aura-truth. Iffy's aura, however, was too close to Iffy's face, and Iffy's large blue eyes.

Gaer found somewhere else to look. *Up*, into the cold, honest snow. The sky behind the clouds was lightening toward dawn, black-grey with startling white flakes falling down and becoming an undifferentiated grey, out of which little stabs of cold fell into wide, unsuspecting eyes. Hrok's unkind breath conspired with gravity to rip Gaer's hood off entirely, and the cold began an immediate assault on his held-together-with-polymesh jaw-plate. He forced that plate open as far as it could go (the other, still the original material, opened more easily, and more widely). Tasted cold and snow and iron on the wind.

Iron. Huh.

He tasted nervous alw, too. Iffy's distress, Iffy's exhaustion. The part of his brain that was apex predator (and Five Tribes SPERE agent) marked those, linked them to weakness, linked them to vulnerability, exploitability. The rest of him (most of him) that was

Gaer i'vakat'i Tarsik saw the same things, and said, "When was the last time you slept, Iffy?"

"Probably the last time you did." He heard her stop herself there, a little catch of the breath, then an audible click as her tiny, blank, square alwar teeth clicked together.

He whipped around, vakar-fast, and closed the small gap between them, until he stood between her and the temple, his back to that warmth. The day wasn't bright enough to cast shadows. The temple, however, could and did, and spread his over her. "What, exactly, are you asking me to do? Besides to betray Iari."

It was very dramatic. It was (her aura told him) somewhat alarming, intimidating. Yellow and orange, green fading again. Blue-violet hope welling up. Cerulean *faith*. "Whatever you can tell me about—*that*. What Iari did in the ruins."

Gaer weighed his options. Recalcitrance now might cost him one of the only friendly faces left here in Windscar. Betraying Iari *again*, sss. But he'd already done that with Tobin, hadn't he? Because he'd known this very line of questioning was coming. Because Keawe might already know—

"Notch," Gaer said. "He hasn't made any reports yet, has he?"

Iffy pursed her lips, then licked them. Her gaze dipped somewhere near Gaer's collar. "He would have. I—invoked medical privilege." Her gaze came back up. "I wanted to ask you first—Gaer. The more I understand what happened to Iari, the more I'll understand what might be happening to Notch. Or not happening. If I can—get his nanomecha to do what *hers* did. And I need something to say when the Knight-Marshal wants an explanation for the contents of his report when I let him submit it, because you know he *will* report it."

"Tell Keawe he's seeing things. *Sss.* No. All right, *here*. I do not know what it is. I saw her do it once before, in B-town, when

Jich'e'enfe opened that tesser-hex portal." Which, now that he'd seen the portals in action—that tunnel to Brood-filled void had not been a destination, like he'd thought; it had been a route for the portal to take, to help Jich'e'enfe cross what had been a great terrestrial distance, from a B-town warehouse cellar to the k'bal ruins in Windscar. He shook himself back to *now*, and Iffy's *setatir* stare, sliding now from hopeful to analytical. "There was a Brood tunneler, or something like it, that Jich'e'enfe had summoned, and it had Iari. I had *thought* . . . I had thought Iari struck the altar, at the time, because the portal closed. But I think she struck the Brood, and the arithmantic backlash from that strike is what closed the portal. The tunneler, of course, died. I was not in a position to watch her do *anything* from the aether, you understand. And until—sss, yesterday? Was it just yesterday? She had not been able to replicate the effect. Though she had not *tried*, either, until we encountered those mecha in the ruins."

"But there wasn't—oh. I see."

"Do you? Excellent. Iari did not."

"The effect, the strike—it's something with the syn. It's something the nanomecha *control*."

"You're so sure it's nanomecha? Not, oh, the Elements' favor? She's partial to Ptah. Can't it be a miracle, Sister Iphigenia? Can't this ability, this gift, of Iari's be *divine*?"

Iffy jerked back like he'd struck her. "It—could. Of course it could."

"You don't believe that."

"No. I don't." A smile ghosted across her lips. "I think it's arithmancy. How's that for heresy?"

"From a priest of the Aedis? It barely rates."

"Well, thank you anyway." Void and dust, she *bowed* to him, a palm-curled-over-fist Aedis gesture Gaer had thought was media fiction, because that was the only place he'd seen it. "I'm trying to isolate the triggers for Notch's shutdown, and by extension, what triggered Iari's repair. And if Ptah's divine strike is a feature of that recovery, because it's linked to the nanomecha and the syn somehow—it helps to know that, too."

Any information was better than nothing. Oh, Gaer understood that. And he also knew: "You have no *setatir* idea what you're doing. Didn't they give you Iari's medical files?"

"Of course they did. But Diran's in B-town. Sister-Healer Israt is *good*, but he's not—he doesn't know what's wrong, either. I'm the expert, Gaer, and *that* is why I'm asking you, because *you're* the arithmancer."

"Well. You asked. I answered."

"You could help me—get Notch's nanomecha back online."

"I could *not*."

Iffy sent a puff of warm breath into the cold. Frowned at the cloud of it. "It's getting colder."

Gaer cocked an eye at her. "That happens."

"What if—Gaer. They're out there in this."

"Yes."

"Without us. Without *you*."

"Iari has fought Brood before without an arithmancer. So has Corso. And Winter Bite and Char, well. *Char's* fought everything."

"Not people." Iffy blew another cloud. "Riev don't kill people. Templars don't."

Anger soured the back of his throat. "Of course templars kill *people*, Iffy. It's just that they haven't since the Weep opened."

"I—Mishka's tits. Gaer, that's not what—I'm sorry."

The anger drained as fast as it'd welled up. "I know what you meant. If you want me to say *no, you're right, the templars don't understand killing people, despite what we did in the ruins,* then I will. But it's neefa-shit."

"I thought you'd want to help."

"I do. And I have. But there are limits, even for me, even if you trade on Iari's name."

Gaer decided he needed to stop this conversation. He found, being already pointed away from the temple, that it was easy to keep going that direction. Away from the light, and from Iffy. Not toward the hospice, not toward the guest quarters, either. There was no place he wanted to be *in* this Aedis.

(On this planet, if Iari didn't come back. But that was a matter for later.)

The courtyard corners each met in a square tower. Gaer headed for the nearest, and for the heavy wooden (not real, the original had been destroyed in the surge) door that faced into the courtyard. There were stairs beyond that, what must have been early and original construction: big, square, short flights and wide landings. It was meant for armored templars to run up and down without difficulty, for getting personnel up to the top of the walls in a hurry if the lifts had all failed. It worked fine for a single, unarmored vakar; he took the steps two at a time, and then three, as anger and exertion warmed him. The stairwell ended in another heavy false-wooden door, also propped, and the smell of cold, wet air. Light leaked through—the sort that came from the big tesla floodlamps on the other side, which meant eerily whitish blue at this range, eerily bright.

He pushed the door open. It was somehow even colder on the other side, Hrok's *setatir* breath slicing through Gaer's coat and all the layers underneath. He tasted iron again on the wind. And petrichor, even though it was snowing, not raining. Ozone. Something oily and bitter-sour.

Gaer stopped on the threshold (again, his new habit). His fingers curled around the edge frame. Very thick, bound with polysteel, glowing to his optic with hexes meant to stop weather and every Element and whitefire and Brood.

Gaer had spent two years, more or less, looking at the Tanis Weep fissure. Except for one personal visit, in the company of the Seawall Aedis and his own embassy, he'd done his observations with drone-borne instrument-readings, and much more rarely from the B-town Aedis walls with his optic. You had to get lucky to see the fissure, that far south. It wasn't especially active, as fissures went, or consistent in its activity.

But right now, from the Windscar walls, the fissure was lit up like the remnants of poor shattered Kreshti. To Gaer's optic it looked like a mountain range of emanations. It wasn't a surge *yet*, but . . . it was doing something.

In B-town, he would have advised—oh, Iari first, then Tobin. Maybe Tobin directly. B-town kept a nightwatch, but they didn't watch the fissure specifically. They couldn't *see* the fissure. Windscar was used to this vigil, and there were plenty of personnel up here with the instruments and hexes to see what Gaer had. The last of the Windscar nightwatch, waiting for their dawn relief, would've seen it, would be monitoring it. Keawe probably already knew.

The Windscar Aedis perched on a hill for a reason, *to watch the* setatir *fissure*. To watch the town, too, that huddled on the southern face of that hill, spilling all the way down to the base. It looked like a smaller version of B-town, except Windscar-town had walls.

Gaer didn't expect that those walls would survive an hour of an actual surge. Aedis protocols said civilians could evacuate inside Aedis compounds; that was part of the reason for such massive courtyards. But that sort of withdrawal was also a last resort. Windscar wasn't prepared for that kind of siege, anyway. And the templars up here, the priests, weren't acting like they expected one now. So the fissure was *doing something*, but no one was worried.

Gaer stepped out onto the ramparts and twitched his hood back up. He hadn't slept last night, same as Iffy, because he'd been writing a report for Keawe. Not an after-action report—that was Notch's sole purview. *Gaer* was just an arithmantic asset. He'd been matching the fissure readings taken during the time they'd been in the ruins, mapping the moments of spike and flux to the altar's activity, and the portal's. He'd been staring at those numbers long enough he didn't need to check his optic's data storage: what he saw here, however it smelled, was the same thing. Little fissures, one or several, ripping tiny little sacrileges into reality and letting Brood slip through. Not a true surge, but an attack nonetheless.

From the *north*. The direction Iari had gone (with Dodri, with the riev, with Corso. She was hardly alone). But she'd gone without *him*. She needed him to—what had she said? Solve it? And he needed her to come back alive.

So of course he'd betrayed her, first to Tobin (never mind that she'd told him he should), then to Iffy. Because *that* helped Iari, that was solving anything. Except it might, if Tobin pretended he'd known all along.

What Iari had really asked for, though . . . solving *this*, errant arithmancy and how to counter it . . . he was no closer.

Gaer started walking away from the wind, the north, the *setatir* Weep fissure: turned south, the direction of B-town. The wind plastered his hood to his skull, made him feel like he stared out of a tunnel. Snow swirled past, smearing everything white and formless. He flicked into his optic, just for color. All those Aedian hexes flickering through the aether. Wards layered on each other like sediment.

Wait. There was something out there, at the optic's limit. Something in the sky, blurred by distance and the intervening local hexes. He refined his optic, filtered out all the local equations, and—ah. Yes. An anomaly in the aether, which is to say something large enough he could detect it at range. Detect, but not *see*. The aether didn't work that way. Whatever it was, though, it was getting closer.

This, he should report. To someone. Not to one of the nightwatch, because he didn't know them and they only knew him as *the vakar* (assume they used the polite term). He could tell Iffy. He *should* tell Keawe. And if he was going to face *her*, then he wanted certainty about what he reported. He cycled his optic out of the aether and into the purely visual. Its capabilities were more restricted on this layer of reality, but it had some limited magnification—

A wedge-shaped nose like a spear point, the body's bulk swelling behind. It was moving fast, and—*Setat*. That was an aethership coming up from the south, on a B-town trajectory. *Rishi* had been moored there, last Gaer knew about it. If Tobin had sent *Rishi* north, that meant—void and dust if he knew what it meant. Keawe would know, but she wouldn't tell him unless it was the Five Tribes embassy coming to get him at last, having found a way around Tobin's manipulation of treaty. Or maybe they, the Aedis, was here to take him into permanent custody, for knowing what one of its templars could do and failing to make a report.

Gaer quashed the surge of cold panic, tucked it back into an icy knot under his ribs. Tobin would *not* arrest him. Nor would Tobin *or* Keawe yield him back to Karaesh't and SPERE. The fissure's current flare-up would provide enough cover to keep him seconded a while yet. It was *fine*.

Except—except it wasn't. *Rishi* was coming a little bit cross-ways, like it had repulsors failing, or a hurricane cross-wind—neither of which made any sense at all, since the storm was blowing out of the north straight over its prow. That skew might make sense if the nav-turing was offline. If the Brood emissions were bad. And Brood emissions might keep *Rishi's* comms from working, too. Windscar might not know *Rishi* was inbound. *Bet* they didn't: Gaer looked, saw the big aethership dock in the courtyard was dark, dormant, entirely unlit. Not expecting a visitor, no.

The templars on duty in the southernmost watchtower weren't visible from this angle. *Assume* they had noticed the aethership, they weren't fools. Though if they weren't looking—not having an optic like his, not knowing they *should* look—they might not have. They *would*, soon enough, but there would be no alarm. Aetherships were friendly.

Gaer weighed the efficiency of trying to get their attention, trying to explain what was the cause for alarm, how he knew, and that they needed to call Keawe at this hour, which nightwatch might not be eager to do. Then he turned and sprinted for the stairs. Pelted down them, three at a time, and skidded onto the courtyard, startling an initiate and an acolyte who'd been coming from the temple. They threw up their hands—both sexless, species-less, in robes and scarves and mittens.

"Ambassador?" said one of them, though *which* was a mystery. "Is everything all right?"

Gaer aborted his dash around them, spun and dug his heel into the snow and muck and hoped he did not fall. "Where is the Knight-Marshal?"

Expecting to hear *her quarters* or *her office*, or somewhere equally difficult to access.

They looked at each other, these wintry apparitions. "I don't know," one said, but the other, the one who'd acknowledged Gaer first, "I thought I saw her going toward the hospice."

"Thank you," Gaer said. He hadn't had a good destination in mind, but now he did. Even if he couldn't find Keawe there, he'd find Iffy, and *she* would understand his urgency.

Gaer was out of breath when he reached the courtyard-side hospice doors. These were more practical, modern, like B-town's: panels of polysteel linked to motion sensors, wide enough to accommodate mobile med-units and broken battle-rigs. They'd brought both Homer and Notch in this way, though Notch had staggered in under his battle-rig's power. Gaer had so far not gone inside at all, having spent enough time in Aedis hospices, *thank you.*

He took a gulp of air, and stepped into the range of the door-sensors.

The warmth hit him first, like a wall, followed by the blue-white glare of teslas. Med-mechas whirred overhead on tracks that crisscrossed the ceiling, somehow not smashing into each other on their high-speed errands. There were mobile partitions set up, their edges smoking faintly to Gaer's optic, that frosty haze that meant sound-dampening hexes were active. Gaer rocked to one side, and up on his toes. Iffy could be anywhere in there.

Gaer cleared his throat. A med-mecha paused in its transit. Gaer's optic advised him of incoming hexes, and he deployed the necessary deflections. The med-mecha twirped, affronted.

Gaer eyed it. "I need Sister Iphigenia, not diagnostics. Do you understand?"

Its teslas flickered, which might be yes, or no, or *I am going to set you on fire, vakar.* Then it let out a long, sharp trill, which was picked up by a second med-mecha.

And then, truly a miracle, proof of Aedian grace: Iffy emerged from behind a partition: hair under a hood, one glove partly peeled off. *"What* emergency?"

Then she saw Gaer. Then every scrap of color fled her face. "What, did Iari call—?"

"Is Keawe here?"

"She just left, Gaer, what's wrong?"

"Aethership," he said. "Coming in from B-town. Did you know, Iffy?"

"Did I—what? No! Who is it?"

"I have no idea, but it's coming in badly. If she doesn't know yet—tell Keawe."

"Badly? *Gaer—*"

And a second voice, Notch, low and rough, "The fuck's going on? Iffy? Gaer, is that you?"

Gaer left Iffy to answer Notch. He was starting to feel a little bit foolish. *Rishi's* arrival was a surprise to him; there was no saying it was a surprise to Keawe, that anyone needed warning at all. It was his nerves, that was all. His guilt, seeing trouble in every event.

He went back to the courtyard more slowly. By the time his breath settled—minutes, which was more than enough time for Iffy to get on the Aedis's hardline comms—the dock had lit up, strobing flashes meant to guide a ship in through the worst weather. Iffy'd advised someone, at least.

Or maybe someone had just looked *up,* finally. The aethership was a growing, obvious presence, even to unaugmented eyes. It had gained some altitude and scrubbed off some speed, but it was still coming in slightly crossways, and with a wobble Gaer didn't like.

Iffy came trotting out of the hospice, this time in a coat. She came straight to Gaer.

"What's *wrong* with the ship?" Iffy asked, like he should know. "Is it the hexes . . . ?"

It was second time today she'd wanted impossible answers, and it was barely past dawn. Gaer hissed. His optic showed him hexwork intact, all the equations swirling around like they should. Anti-grav, phlogiston-scrubbing, plasma-cooling.

"Not the hexes. Maybe they're just in a hurry."

He felt Iffy's stare scorch the side of his face. The dock began howling an alert, warning everyone to get back to a safe distance. *Rishi* began its descent, gently at first, but it rapidly turned into more of a controlled fall than a landing. The plasma coils turned blue-white with effort, the whine of them loud enough to split stone. The ship straightened out, briefly; then it slewed sideways again, and started to roll. And then the engines just stopped, all of them, and the ship dropped the last fifty meters, with a last frantic roll that missed the upthrust dock and set (slammed) the ship down more or less square on its keel.

They looked fragile, aetherships, like they were made out of silk and bone. The reality was much heavier, and much sturdier. Amalgam and polymesh on a polysteel frame, hexed for buoyancy, for durability. Those hexes were tested now.

Rishi hit the Aedis courtyard with force enough to rattle Gaer's teeth and his balance. A shockwave rolled off the plasma coils, energy sloughing off in what Gaer bet was an emergency purge. His optic lit, advising him to brace. He lurched in front of Iffy instead.

She staggered; one would *think* that, having one set of knees and being closer to the ground, she would find balance easier. Gaer stuck out an arm and caught her before she pitched over, flexing both sets of knees to absorb her weight and his. Around them a few people weren't as graceful, or as fortunate to have a vakar on hand.

Gaer straightened and set Iffy back on her feet. She tried to say something, until the aethership dock began wailing again. *Two voidspit tones, in competition: one an obvious come quick, the ship bellyflopped and the other an alert for an opening hatch.*

Still more pounding on the courtyard announced Keawe's arrival, with a speed that made Gaer think she was synning.

There came a hiss, a pop, and *Rishi's* hatch started cycling. An emergency ramp unfolded itself, telescoping until it hit something solid before hardening into a smooth surface. The hatch irised open. A gout of steam emerged, turned to fog, hit Windscar's cold and froze. Then an errant gust came and tore it apart, like scattering diamonds.

Tobin's head poked out first—which was *not* protocol, that a Knight-Marshal emerged first, but which *was* the fastest way to get everyone else to stand down.

It worked. The alarms cut out abruptly. In the sudden silence, Gaer could hear every whir and click of Tobin's mecha hip and leg as he walked down the ramp.

Keawe had her axe shaft in hand. She saw Tobin and clipped it back to her battle-rig. Opened her faceplate and yelled, "Ptah's left *ball*, Tobin!"

Tobin was too far away for Gaer to make out expressions. He guessed there was a smile, because Tobin was prone to those. He was human, middle-aged, middle-sized. Bare-headed, which in this cold had to be excruciating despite the thick brush of dark hair. He wore the usual templar armor, not a battle-rig. At least Keawe had her helmet.

"The Weep is active tonight," he called back. "We lost the nav-turing."

"I thought they might have," Gaer said to Iffy. "I did say."

"You weren't that specific." She still held onto Gaer's sleeves, not for balance, but because she'd forgotten to let go. "What's To-bin doing *here*, though?"

"I called him," Gaer said. "I didn't think—he'd send anyone. I certainly didn't think he'd come personally."

"You—what? When? Why?"

Tobin had gotten most of the way down the ramp. He must've noticed Gaer already—vakari were difficult to mistake for anyone else. But this was the first time he looked at him, and this time he was close enough for Gaer to read his expression.

And his aura.

Gaer unpeeled Iffy's tiny hands gently and straightened his sleeves.

"I'll be in my quarters," he told Iffy. "When someone needs to see me."

CHAPTER SEVENTEEN ≡≡≡

T rammen took Iari to the barn first. The big doors were partly open; the amount of rust on the hinges made Iari think they wouldn't open much wider than that. Or close completely. Iari could see the rest of the Ettradens clumped in the middle of a large open front area lined with crates and boxes. There was a loft overhead (more boxes, and a ladder of much newer vintage than the rest of the place). There were stains in the floor where a big vehicle had sat once—tractor, ATV, something that dripped fluid. Little drifts of snow, too, that had sifted down through the roof's patchier bits. A youngish tenju woman was talking to Gel, holding a tablet and stylus, frowning at the newcomers.

Trammen herded Iari inside, then went to talk to Gel. Iari thought about ducking *back* out, then let that idea go. She had to play along. She had to trust Corso. She had to find her people.

Then she spotted a filthy tarp in the corner, a pile of irregular angles and shapes that could be a pile of junk. Except (blink) the barn floor around those shapes showed signs of disturbance, scrapes in the wood planks from something heavy and large dragged across them. She pushed through the Ettradens, crowding—eh, what was his name? Radin, Raden, the one who'd said earnestly all templars should be sent offworld. Raden shot her *a look*, then crossed her gaze and flinched and sidled away.

Closer made it obvious. Yeah, those were battle-rigs. She picked out the distinctive curve of a chest piece on top, another matching curve jutting out sideways. Of course they were disassembled. Iari had left hers in similar condition with Char, Winter Bite, and Dodri (still in her own rig).

Fear hit like a battle-rigged fist to the chest, like it would punch a hole right through breast and spine. She couldn't breathe, couldn't see. The syn came to her rescue and burned through, getting air back into her lungs. Cold air, dusty. Maybe a little bit metallic, like blood or hot polysteel.

Or Brood.

She realized she'd made fists, that she'd rooted in place, when Geltrannen said, "Something wrong, Iari?"

Obviously something was. Iari gathered her scattered wits. It *wasn't* bad news—Luki and Llian were *here*. Somewhere. Alive or dead—but *here*.

"Those're battle-rigs," said Iari. "Under that tarp."

Gel was standing a prudent meter away, balancing a smile against wary eyes. "Yeah. They are."

Iari squinted at the alw, trying to look—oh, void and dust, *not* like a pissed-off templar, *not* smarter than she'd pretended. Like Corso's stone-dull cousin. She pointed, sketched the line of the chest plate with her fingertip in the empty air. "Those are *templar* rigs. I know the shape. Those, they—they were all over B-town last fall, with the Brood. They're not like army rigs."

"No," said Gel. "They're not."

Raden had turned around at the word templar. Now he joined Iari in peering at the tarp-covered pile. "Templars? We killed templars?"

Iari held her breath against Gel's expected smirk, the smug, *yes we did*.

But instead Geltrannen dropped her smile entirely, and there was—fear? Anger? Both?—in her eyes. She rounded on Raden. Said, in a voice chipped from ice: "*We* didn't do anything, did *we*? You just got here. Those are templar battle-rigs. That's all *you* need to know."

"I—but—"

Where are the templars? Iari damn near choked on the asking. She swallowed it down. Managed a "huh," and, "That'll piss them off. The Aedis."

Gel pressed her lips flat. "We can deal with them."

Trammen arrived then, beaming, from wherever he'd been. Talking up the young tenju woman, maybe. "Gel, we—what's going on?"

Raden pointed. "Templar battle-rigs. Iari saw 'em. You never said we'd get to kill templars."

Trammen scoffed. "How'd you think we were going to chase them offworld?" But he side-eyed Geltrannen. "Gel, quartermaster wants—"

"If we're killing templars," Iari said, "we need whitefire weapons. When do we get those?"

That got Raden's attention. Now Gel had three sets of eyes on her, expectant. Her smile hardened. "In time. When we're sure you're ready."

No, that wasn't ominous.

Iari grunted. "Better not take too long. *That*"—she jerked her chin at the lumpy tarp—"will bring the Aedis running. We ready for that?"

"We don't fear the Aedis," Trammen said, trying for bravado and sounding like a third-rate B-town bully boy. Iari ignored him.

Gel hesitated, clearly (to Iari, at least) torn between a loyalist retort and her own misgivings. She glanced around at her audience. Then she dug out one of her smiles again. "Come on. We need to get you settled. After rest and a meal, we can talk."

Iari wasn't really surprised when all the Ettradens got herded back out of the barn—it wasn't a place you kept new recruits, was it?—and up the little hill to the byre. Of course, *that* was appropriate. Recruits were just *like* neefa, eating whatever crap Gel shoved at them. But the byre made tactical sense, too, as a holding area. A little bit distant from the rest of the camp, single entry, not conveniently accessed except by a narrow, neefa-wide path with no cover. Its roof seemed in far better repair than the barn's, at least. It also smelled a little bit like neefa still, as they climbed the little hill to it. Or maybe everything stank of shit.

This time it was Raden who balked at the door. "We're not *neefa*."

Iari bent her grin into a scowl before anyone saw, as Trammen spluttered and tried to explain that it *had* been a byre, but now it was just newcomer quarters, and, whispered confidence, it was maybe better than the tents because it had a solid roof.

"It's just temporary," Trammen was saying, "until they can work out our permanent assignments."

Until, Iari reckoned, they knew who was worth keeping and who wasn't. Who'd make a good useful idiot out in the camp, who'd go out and recruit, who'd make a good One-Eye. Who might've asked too many questions about templar battle-rigs.

She stepped around Raden, cut Trammen off, and walked into the byre.

The Ettradens weren't the only new arrivals. A half-dozen others *there*, clustered in one corner. Another three or four milling around on the opposite end. There was no one wearing a gauntlet or a helmet. No one even armed. Iari stopped just inside, let the rest of the Ettradens push past her (having decided, like neefa, that where one went, so should everyone else).

They'd left the stalls intact, just removed the doors, so the place looked like partitioned barracks. The stalls were stuffed with nanoforged cots, the smell of too many people and last century's ventilation. There were beams overhead, maybe three meters up, and a half-floor on top of that. Iari eyed the ladder. That might've been storage for feed or hay up there once. Now . . . probably not, if the thumping meant anything. There were people moving around up there.

The chill on the back of Iari's head said the door was still open. She turned and there was Trammen, and with him, some double-wide tenju she hadn't noticed, who stepped in front of the door and pulled it shut. Gel was still outside. Double Wide wasn't wearing a uniform here, but he had a badge pinned on his jacket: a stylized single eye with a jagged pupil, like a lightning bolt or Elements knew what.

(Corso would know. Corso wasn't here to ask. Her gut couldn't knot any tighter.)

"Nuh-uh." Double Wide held up a finger the size of Char's. Shook his head. Smiled like they were friends. "Need you to stay in here. Don't want you wandering around out there until *later.*"

"Latrine," said Iari.

"Chem toilet." Double Wide pointed toward the back of the byre. "Enjoy it. Once you're out in the tents, it's just ditches with a plank across."

Trammen was staring at Double Wide's badge with a mixture of awe and envy. "I'm with Geltrannen," he said. "I helped bring these folks in. And Bersk? You know her." He tried to edge past.

Double Wide cocked his head. Smiled wider. His tusks were

intact, and large like the rest of him. His braids were shorter than Corso's or Bersk's, and glittered with hooks. He looked Trammen over and chuckled. "You're staying in here, too."

Iari nudged Trammen. "Don't worry. Bersk's with Corso. They're *fine.*"

He looked gutted. "She's. I."

Iari left him there. Found the chem toilet, in case Double Wide was watching. (She doubted it. Trammen started whining before she'd got out of earshot. But still: play the part.) It was tucked in a back corner near a window with open shutters and two missing panes of glass. Iari waited in the inevitable line until she reckoned Double Wide had forgotten she'd asked about it. Then she stepped out and took a walk around the byre's interior. Stone walls, solid, no windows within reach except the narrow one near the chem toilet. There were windows higher up, loft-level, but she couldn't see what and who else was up there from this angle. She reckoned she'd have the same luck with the ladder she'd had with the front door. Double Wide was lurking between ladder and door, like he meant to guard access to both.

Hell if she knew how that hierarchy worked around here. Double Wide had a badge, but he was a normal tenju guard with a 'caster. The One-Eyes were . . . One-Eyes. Gel held some kind of rank or status, but she clearly hadn't been happy about templar battle-rigs (and presumably the templars that came with them), and no one *else* seemed all that bothered. Trammen was in here with Iari, while Bersk, whom Iari had taken to be Trammen's rank, was loose out there with Corso.

Iari circled back toward the door. Trammen had given up. Double Wide was still there, arms folded, surveying the room's inhabitants. The shock of recognition hit her in the chest like a fist. She'd looked at Keawe's troops that way, picking templars for this mission. Measuring, assessing—who'd do well with the riev, with Gaer, with Corso. Who'd adapt to the B-town command structure, who'd be Keawe's first.

Double Wide's gaze found her then. Locked. *Assessed.*

Iari had to look somewhere else, fast. The wall. The floor. *There*, an unoccupied cot that would catch every draft from the voidspit door and be *just* the wrong angle for Double Wide to see easily from his post. She scuffed her way over to it like someone who'd never had to march. She turned her back to Double ·Wide (and most of the room, made her skin prickle). She sat, bunching her coat up in her lap, shoving her hands deep. She found one of her knives she'd brought from Ettrad and slid it up her sleeve.

No one looked at her. The people in this *holding cell* were all concerned with their own situation. Knots of discontent, muttering about—oh, probably the Aedis. Iari had seen this look before. Void and dust, Blessed Four, too many times during the surge, and after. The hollow-eyed shock. The frantic anger. The need to blame. *Then*, blame had mostly landed on the vakari, regardless of affiliation; but then, too, there hadn't been vakari around to punish. Now—now, everyone was set on the Aedis. The whole Confederation.

If, *if*, she was right about someone using Brood surgically on the villages, same as Jich'e'enfe had in B-town for the cartels— then it was only the people who'd react like this—with anger, with blame—who would've survived. Who would have been *chosen* to survive. The dangerous ones.

How would they—the command staff? The arithmancer? *How* was this slagging camp organized?—pick the One-Eyes, though? Gaer said there were Brood in the gloves. That was one kind of horror. If they were really half-riev, or something like, then there'd be a version of Oversight. That had been Jich'e'enfe's intention.

Restore Oversight, infect riev, get a Brood-fueled army she could direct. Maybe she'd been running parallel with this cult all along—because damn sure, you wanted the Aedis distracted, you wanted the Confederation's attention, you loosed a Brood-fueled cult on a hinterlands planet with a Weep fissure.

Oh. *Oh.* That made sense. Jich'e'enfe, the separatists—they'd never intended to loose riev on the Confederation at large. They'd've used them on the vakari, on the Five Tribes in Confederation space. And the cultists here would be starting an uprising that would get the Confederation involved, that would make the Aedis do what it *never* had, in all its history, and do violence to Confederation citizens. A two-sided attack. Or more, if there was voidspit like this other places, other planets.

She wanted to—jump up and pace. To shout. But really, she wanted to tell Gaer. Ptah's unblinking *eye,* she wanted to tell him. The syn was tingling along her spine, under her skin. That's how agitated she was. Better calm it down or she'd get someone's attention. Nanomecha, the syn—sometimes it acted up (lately, since the evolution) if there was something to worry about. Or she liked to think that they did. The nanomecha weren't *divine,* she wasn't that credulous; the Catechisms called them a blessing, but what they meant was an upgrade to standard biology. Everyone *knew* that.

But they were still little machines, and once they'd been sentient—and none of this was useful to think about right now. What *was:* remembering how to fight without a voidspit battle-rig or any armor at all. She hadn't outside of training. And sure, she *trained* often, but not against people with 'casters, and never against half-riev abominations.

Fight that battle when she got to it. For now, *first,* she had to get out of this byre.

The walls were all stone. Iari put her hand on one, intending to what, push? See how solid it was? She palmed the rough stone and—

Her hand spasmed. A tiny arc of electricity followed it, and a faint smell of ozone. Ungentle fucking *Ptah*! Reflex jerked her hand back. She managed to control both the urge to swear and her syn, which tried to come online to defend her. She pretended nothing had happened instead, looked around. No one appeared to have noticed.

She opened her hand slowly. There were no burns. No marks at all. The walls were warded, somehow. Arithmancy. Clearly not meant to injure, but to contain people—

Not clearly. You assume.

Void and dust, Ptah's burning eye, she had an inner Gaer. He was probably right, too. There were other bunks all along the slagging walls. If the wards zapped everyone who touched them, then the mood in here should be a lot more agitated than it was. A lot more whining and yelling. And there shouldn't be people, oh, *leaning* on the stone, either, unless they had a pain tolerance higher than Char's.

The wards reacted to *her*, no one else. It was pretty obvious what the difference was.

That added a new layer of *oh shit* to the situation. No, several layers. Why ward a holding area in the first place, and then—how many other places had hexes on them, and how many would Aedis nanomecha set off? (Assuming it was *all* Aedis nano that would react, not just her special sort.) It made sense to ward storage, or wherever they were holding the templars, the altar, maybe, against casual contact from all but the highest-ranking—but why hex a place holding people at all?

Unless the hexes weren't *just* wards. Unless they were something else. Something you'd want all your newcomers exposed to.

You could use alchemy or arithmancy to affect a person with no nanomecha. Obviously. That was how you made templars and priests in the first place. It took hexes to fight hexes effectively . . . but if someone *had* no hexwork, then someone had no defense.

She had no way of reading these hexes. She needed Gaer, and she didn't have him.

She was just one in of a roomful of people. Anonymous. Woefully ignorant of the specifics of arithmancy, but—no, this was a good thing. Double Wide was the only guard in the place, and his primary task seemed to be to stand in front of the door. He didn't act like someone worried about a riot. He wasn't armed like someone prepared to handle one.

So—the expectation was for docile refugees. Which, given the propaganda and speeches Iari'd heard on the way from Ettrad, seemed optimistic. In Iari's experience, *scared* and *angry* didn't stay docile for long. If that *was* the expectation . . . why?

The hexes.

She scanned the room until she found Raden again. He seemed to've forgotten his complaint about byres and neefa. Beside him sat Trammen, with the rest of the Ettradens. They were talking, all huddled together, and Trammen's hands waved around periodically. But they weren't looking around like people getting ready to *do* something. They weren't looking for her, either.

Good.

Iari drew her legs up, boots on the cot, which was something a templar would *not* do, let people think that. She tilted her knee sidelong, like she meant to rest it on the wall. She felt the chill coming off it first, Windscar winter throbbing through the stones. And then, maybe a centimeter from the stone—a static buzz on her skin, through trousers and skinsuit. She stopped, held position. Looked at the wall. She couldn't see anything obvious, no crackling little web of lightning. She moved her leg a fraction. Then another. Then—void and fucking *dust*, there: a visible arc and flash. This time she made herself hold position, hold the connection. She'd expected—well, lightning. A flash of connection, then gone again. That didn't happen. The lightning stayed, a clear bridge of *something* from arithmancy in the walls to the arithmancy in her blood. Like the walls had a current of some kind that just flowed, and if it had a place to go—like her nanomecha—then it'd take that path and keep that connection.

Okay. Useful to know. If she couldn't figure another way out of here, maybe she could overload the wards with enough physical points of contact, assuming hexes worked like current. Too many connections, she might blow the whole wall, building, however far the hexes reached.

Or it would overload *her*.

Whatever happened, if she did that—damn sure everyone would know that Iari from B-town wasn't just flesh-and-bone normal.

Still—keep that idea in reserve. It was terrible, but it was *something*. In the meantime, she could wait. Observe. Just don't touch the voidspit walls.

CHAPTER EIGHTEEN

Bersk spent the morning dragging Corso around, getting him billeted, pretending to act as a guide. It was pretty clear pretty quick she'd never been here before, that she was operating on Geltrannen's directions, and Geltrannen's authority. *Geltrannen said, Geltrannen sent,* every time they had to interact with anyone. Gel's name worked like a slagging ID pass, which was useful to know. Interesting, too, since there weren't many alwar around.

The camp quartermaster was one of them. Corso had expected the quartermaster to be in the barn, but instead Bersk led him behind the mess tent and into the second of the prefab yurt-structures (not the awful double-wide altar-yurt, thank any god listening). Bersk ducked inside first, already announcing *Geltrannen said*, and Corso stepped cautiously after her, blinking to make his eyes adjust. The room was an arrangement of boxes and crates, all in varying stages of open and empty. Supply yurt, then. He could hear a generator humming in the second room, but the interior remained dim, lit by the two battery-powered lanterns that hung off the central support that arched across the expanse of the ceiling. That would've been weird, except he could smell dust and hot amalgam. That generator was running a nanoforge back there. There wouldn't be enough power left for teslas.

Bersk got all the way through, "Geltrannen says we're to get our kit from you!" before she realized there wasn't anyone standing there to take her order.

Corso craned his head around, peering into the crates without moving. Looked like blankets and piles of clothing. Trousers. Shirts. Sweaters. Coats. A whole crate of boots. Well, sure. The cultists recruited from ruined villages, and refugees didn't have *stuff.* Though, ugly thought, most of this *stuff* probably came from those same destroyed settlements.

"Hello?" Bersk sounded a little lost. Corso drifted sideways, trying to get a look into the yurt's second room.

"I hear you," said a collection of shadows, and then the quartermaster emerged from behind a stack of crates taller than he was. Even so, he was still taller than most alwar: slate-black skin, eyes the color of the storm clouds overhead. He was holding a tablet and stylus and wearing a scowl and a dark-metaled badge pinned to his collar. It was a single eye with a lightning-bolt pupil. Looked like an Aedis thing, almost, except Corso knew Ptah's left eye didn't rate its own iconography.

That had to be some symbol for Axorchal One-Eye. Void and dust. The cultists had *insignia.*

Bersk launched into her Geltrannen-laced speech again. Corso grunted when he was introduced, and mostly divided his attention between the quartermaster and the back room of the yurt, which did *not* have a divider, and so Corso could see the winking teslas of the nanoforge. It was bigger than the one in the ruins, which probably meant it was newer. He could just make out the edge of the beleaguered generator and stacks of weaponry, which gleamed and looked far newer than the dusty clothes on offer in the front room. 'Casters didn't come oiled like that unless they'd just come off assembly. *New* 'casters meant—well. That meant someone was smuggling, probably through B-town. Cartel-boss Tzcansi had been into smuggling weapons, before she'd crossed Jich'e'enfe and ended up Brood food. *Bet* these cultists had been her clients.

The quartermaster didn't seem to notice where Corso was looking. He was more interested in Corso's 'caster, which he examined. Then, grey eyes sharp, "You want a newer one?"

"Nah."

That got him a grunt, a blanket, and a mess kit still warm from the nanoforge. Corso fingered the utensils. Metal was stronger than forge-fiber, more durable (also what the army had issued, back in Corso's day). Metal was cheaper, too, if you had access to factories, which these people didn't, though it was hard to imagine a box of forks would be missed before a crate of longcasters.

Bersk was telling the quartermaster that Geltrannen had brought in some more recruits (she actually used the word), that they were in the byre, that they were all tenju, that none were armed. (So *that* was where they'd taken Iari.) Corso watched the quartermaster duck into the back room, emerge with a 'caster, hand it to Bersk. (Who at least knew how to handle it: checked the load, the charge, didn't point it at anyone).

"And here." The quartermaster scooped a pair of badges out of one of the crates. He set one atop Bersk's pile, in the middle of her blanket. He handed the other to Corso. The metal—and it *was* metal—felt cold, to Corso's bare hand. Felt . . . slick. Not like oil. Like slime.

Corso resisted the urge to drop it and scrub off his palms. He stuck it on top of his own stack instead. And then waited while

Bersk got their billet numbers. (Please, any listening gods except Axorchal, they were not assigned somewhere *together.*)

Then they were out and done, *finally.* Corso took a lungful of cold and snow and side-eyed the badge. Even out here, in grey daylight, it seemed to suck up the light.

Bersk was standing on one slagging foot, her pile of kit balanced on her raised knee, already pinning the voidspit thing to her coat and grinning like a damn child.

Corso wanted to throw *his* into the snow. Or at Bersk. He watched her fumble with the clasp. He could offer to help, maybe he should, but he knew he'd rather touch fucking Brood.

"Corso? You okay?"

He blinked. Bersk was staring at him. "Fine. Just thinking, is all. Where'd the nanoforge come from?"

He knew it was a bad question the moment he asked it.

Bersk shrugged, then got a look like she hadn't thought about it, didn't see why she should, didn't see why *he* should. A gleam of curiosity lit her eyes, and oh, Corso didn't want *that.* "I don't know. Does it matter?"

His turn to shrug. "Nah. Guess not," he said, and watched the gleam go dull.

His billet turned out to be one of four cots in a tent close to the mess tent, but *not* the same tent as Bersk's. His tent was mercifully empty; one bunk had a blanket unrolled on it. (And mussed. They might have army rows and army latrines, but they did not have army discipline.) The other three were frames and naked, very thin pads. There was a little camp heater in the rough middle of the floor, its solar charge blinking a miserable yellow.

Corso picked a cot on the other side, closest to the tent flap. He dropped all of his gear in a stack and stared at it. *Long* fucking time—since Ettrad—since he'd slept more than snatches. But he didn't have time for a nap. Then he ducked out the flap.

Bersk was still chirping at some poor fucker next door (*only* next door, not the other side of the camp). He turned away and slipped down the narrow gap between tents. He'd had enough of Bersk in every sense, and he couldn't do his voidspit job with her trying to herd him.

He crossed two rows of tents and ducked into the latrines before stopping. There, he got the badge out of his pocket, stomach crawling up the back of his throat—less from the stench than the badge. It felt cold through his gloves. And sticky. And there was something about the eye he didn't like. There was something wrong with it, like hexes or a genuine grannytale curse. Void and dust, what he'd give for *Gaer* right now, which was just proof how fucked everything was.

Gaer would say *oh, Corso, a curse is just the neefa-brained way to say hex.* So he decided that this badge was . . . hexed. Or felt hexed. Too bad. Corso stared at the clouds (at least it'd stopped snowing) and kept his teeth clenched and fastened the badge to his coat by touch.

He had to pass among these people. This badge would let him do that.

"Corso?" His name floated up from the last row of tents. Void and dust, *nowhere* was safe from that woman. Corso tugged his coat collar higher up, yanked his hood low, trotted down a long line of latrines and out at the far end, close to the perimeter. He stopped and looked back, no sign of Bersk. Yet.

He had to keep moving.

Iari hadn't been wrong about Bersk's interest in him. Potentially useful, if Bersk had anything like status around here. Corso wasn't sure that she did—Bersk relied too much on Gel's name. Corso hadn't figured out yet why Bersk was out here loose in the camp, while Trammen was—wherever Trammen was. With the rest of the Ettradens, presumably, locked up in the byre. With Iari.

He'd asked Bersk about that. The conversation had gone something like:

"Oh, not *locked up*, Corso. Geltrannen says it's just until they get settled."

To which he'd asked, "Isn't that what we're doing? Getting billets and kit? Why can't they do it this way?"

"We're different." And then she'd leaned in. "We're *special*."

Special never meant anything good. Here, take this hexed badge, and then—and then what?

That was the question he had to answer. He definitely knew where the altar was. That left two missing templars and a slagging arithmancer to locate. Start with Luki and Llian. Then he needed Iari out of that byre. Though, truth—at least he knew where she was, and without a good story to get her out or burning their cover outright, she would have to stay there for now. The other two parts of the mission, he could handle alone. (Had meant to do that all along, but Iari was stubborn; maybe sitting in the slagging byre would teach her to let him do his slagging job.)

(It wouldn't. She'd just be that much more pissed when she got out.)

First thing, then—walk the camp's perimeter. Corso cut around the far end of the latrine line, found a narrow path stomped through the snow, followed that to another packed path that ran around outside the rows of tents. Corso paused, under the auspices of adjusting his coat. The corners of the camp were marked

by floodlamps, the mobile sort that came with their own generators. They were off, at the moment. One pole per corner. There
were two patrols on each of the paths between floodlamps, except
the northern edge, which relied on the steep rocky ridge for security. (Neefa might get up that. Riev might, and templars. No one
else would.) The guards moved in threes, armed, walking halfway
up their side, turning around, walking back. That'd make the mid-
point between lights the darkest place once those lamps were lit.

Corso waited, still tinkering with the fit of his coat, with the
way his longcaster hung off the strap, while an approaching patrol,
well, *approached*. And passed. (Two men, one woman, all tenju,
all armed, all badged.) They didn't call out to him. Didn't even *look*
at him, being busy with an argument about which kel'arkh team
was most likely to make the finals this year, and whether Tanis
would *finally* get a sector title. Didn't sound like people who
wanted to slag the Confederation, but then—Corso didn't think
"hey, let's drive the Aedis offworld" had translated all the way into
"that means the Confederation will kick us out of their kel'arkh
leagues." (He was pretty sure there were people who *had* thought
of that, and at least some of them were dead in the ruins of Ettrad.)

What he was sure of: the guards weren't worried about perimeter breaches from either direction. No one knew they were
up here, except the people already here, and *they* were all . . . if
not volunteers, then at least willing to stay. And they sure as *fuck*
weren't worried about Brood. Pretty slagging clear the Axorchal-
arithmancer had control of the Brood, same as Jich'e'enfe had.
Maybe better than she had.

Which left wondering where that arithmancer was. Corso
guessed either the house or the barn, since he hadn't been in either
one yet. Probably the house. Unless he'd been in the yurt with the

altar, but—nah. Evil arithmancers brooding over their evil artifacts didn't happen except in fiction. Reality likely meant the evil
arithmancer was walking around the camp looking like everyone else.

There was a thought. Corso knew the arithmancer wasn't
Bersk, Gel, or Trammen. That still left a lot of suspects.

Corso finished adjusting his 'caster, then walked the perimeter
farther—sticking closer to the tents, not walking the path where
the guards did—until he got what he hoped was far enough from
the latrines to have ditched Bersk for good. He looked at the ridgeline they'd come down this morning. (Felt like forever ago, and
also just a few hours, and he really needed to sleep at some point.)
The camp sat not so much in a valley as a confluence of dry river-
beds, protected by natural earthworks, but also hemmed in. No
training grounds, which probably meant people were hiking out
to some other place to do target practice. He wasn't *hearing* any
'caster-fire, but sound was tricky out here. Or they might be practicing hand-to-hand.

Somewhere out there were Char, Winter Bite, and Dodri.
Corso bet they'd set up on the north side, at the top of that impossibly steep ridge. He wondered (hoped) they could see him. That at
least one of the riev had optics on him.

One thing he *did* know: templars in Windscar would mop this
place up like spilled beer. These cultists, insurgents in training,
wouldn't last against battle-rigs. The hybrid riev One-Eyes *would*,
but Corso hadn't seen them yet. Assume the One-Eyes were elite
troops. Assume they *didn't* live in the common tents. That left the
permanent structures for their quarters. The byre already had occupants, so—one of the others. Barn. House. Or that smaller
outbuilding.

Or, hopeful thought, which meant it was probably wrong: most of the One-Eye supply was already dead after that attack in the ruins.

Corso cut down another lane of tents, heading back toward the center. There were more people out now, emerging from tents, talking, all heading more or less toward the mess tent and the increasingly pungent smells of camp-cooking. Corso's stomach gurgled. He'd spent the whole morning walking around, and now it was what, midday? He should eat, at least, if he wasn't going to sleep. They'd have some kind of liquid stimulant in the tent. Tea at least. Armies, templars—*everyone* ran on that shit. He let himself get swept into the general tide flowing that way, sorting itself into lines. Communal meals were also a good place to listen and learn. He might get a few names that way. Get some idea who the arithmancer was. Where the One-Eyes were. What the split was between malcontents and actual believers.

Bersk might find him again. He'd maybe rather starve.

Or, better plan: take mealtime's distraction to poke around places he shouldn't.

He slid out of line, making faces like he'd forgotten something, how stupid, and ducked around the side of the tent. The long tables inside were starting to fill up as people got their bowls of steaming whatever. Meat-smelling, though Corso bet it wasn't close to real meat. Supplies for this many people would cost, and they'd be hard to haul in here. He hadn't seen anything like functioning roads, either. You could haul in sacks of flour or spoils from the dead villages—that was probably *most* of this camp's supply source, the winter stores of the dead—but without organized hunting—and he'd seen no evidence of it so far—he'd bet the nanoforge was feeding people, too. Which . . . okay, you know, never mind eating. The joke in Corso's army days had been army food tastes like shit because that's what it's made from, and while he knew that wasn't exactly how a nanoforge worked, there was also some truth to it.

He had tubes of that Aedis goo in his pocket. He could subsist on that until they got the fuck out of here.

The crowds were definitely thinner on the kitchen end of the mess, though there were people filing out of the barn and the house. Corso marked faces while he tried to look like he had somewhere else to be, or some reason to be standing there. Gel came out of the house, in hot conversation with a tenju man, so Corso whipped around and meandered the other direction. That same move spared him Bersk, whom he saw pass on his periphery. She looked unhappy, eyes darting over the thickening line. Corso hunched, pivoted, tried to look like someone on kitchen duty, which would mean finding the—

Kitchen. Right. It was just the back edge of the mess tent, partitioned off, banging noises, voices, smoke leaking out through a vent in the canvas top. The flap snapped open, and a young tenju staggered out holding a crate too big for her arms. Her fingers—bare, red from heat or cold or harsh chemicals—clutched at the scuffed polymer. She paused, tried to balance the load, then gave up and set it down.

Now Corso could see what was inside. Bowls, spoons, several fat-bellied thermal containers that were no doubt why the crate was so unwieldy. It looked like a food delivery. And there was one place Corso could think of where the occupants *weren't* free to walk down to the mess on their own.

The young tenju was swearing under her breath, hands on hips, breath steaming. She looked . . . voidspit. Too young.

Anger curled in his belly where hunger should be. It was one thing to suck in the Bersks and the Trammens. But she wasn't much more than a damn kid, and damn kids were just—dumb, sometimes. Couldn't see that far into their futures. Or didn't think they *had* one. He'd been there once. Iari had.

See how that had turned out.

Corso pushed his hood back a little, then walked over. She didn't see him approach, being too busy wrestling with the canisters in the crate, trying to restack the bowls. She dropped three of them when Corso leaned over and said, "You want some help?"

Which gave him excuse to scoop up the bowls, brush the snow off, hand them back.

The young woman blinked. Void and dust, she looked like Iari. Green eyes. Reddish hair. Her skin was a little bit lighter, more golden than sepia. Though Iari had never, in all Corso's memory, looked that close to tears.

"Thanks." She took the bowls and slammed them back into place, as if force would help. She visibly steeled herself, then squatted and started to wrap her arms around the crate again.

From this angle, she was going to fall on her ass when she tried to stand up. Corso didn't have to fake his wince. "Hey. Is this for the—" He jerked his chin at the byre. "I can take it."

He was ready for questions, had the answers lined up. But all she did was blink. "Would you?"

That was the *easiest* question to answer. "Sure. No problem."

The crate *was* heavy. Corso figured that out in the first heave, and for half a beat, he thought he'd drop it and ruin his big, competent rescuer persona. But he did *not* drop it, and after a hitched adjustment, he cocked a grin at her. "Got it. I'll bring the box back here after, leave it here, and you can take it in? Take a rest in the meantime."

"I—yeah. Thanks. *Thanks.*" She beamed at him, then balled her hands up and stuffed them into her sleeves.

Which was how Corso ended up kicking the byre door—because *hell* if he'd put the crate down again, never pick it back up—and coming face to face with the biggest, widest, most massive tenju in the history of *ever*. Bigger than Keawe, for fuckssake. A badge that was as creepy and wrong as Corso's leered off his collar.

But he didn't have a 'caster, so, "Here," Corso said, and shoved the crate at him.

Reflex made the guard reach for it, and Corso took advantage and *shoved* the crate into the other man's arms. The containers inside slid around, which shifted the weight, which made the guard step back to counterbalance.

Corso got a faceful of overwarm air that smelled a little bit like chemical toilet and a lot like too many underwashed people. The sound, though, was oddly muted—he could *see* mouths moving, he could *hear* conversations, but for the volume of people he thought the actual volume would be louder, too.

"Lunch," he said loudly, in an effort to punch through that weird muffling. "Here ya go."

The guard rolled eyes at him, somewhere between hungry-greedy and annoyed. "You could've brought this shit inside. Table's right *here*." He waddled toward *here*—a small table, looked like it would *just* hold the crate, to the side of the door—which left the doorway vacant.

Corso saw Iari immediately, mostly because she'd already seen him, and the sudden motion as she stood up drew his eye. She looked both fine and furious, the latter obvious because Corso knew her, and knew what it was taking for her to walk slowly across the room, even as everyone else noticed him, and the crate of food.

It really was a byre. Or had been. And it was hard to avoid

comparisons with the residents, as everyone stood up and began moving toward the table. The big guard said, "Hey, a little help?"

He meant Corso, obviously, but three other people volunteered, and the guard found himself brushed aside by sheer mass of people. (Not quite a stampede, but . . . yeah, okay, a stampede.) Corso stationed himself in the doorway, looking important and officious, but no one tried to get past him.

He looked for Iari again, but she was—where had she gone?

"Corso," low-voiced and *there*, right beside him.

"The hell," he breathed, and bit off *how did you get over here that fast*. Her pupils flexed, just a little too wide, a little too black. Oh. Right. That was how.

Iari bounced a look from his face to his badge, then back. Raised both brows. Matched his pitch. "The hell . . . ?"

No way he could answer that question. He hadn't *planned* to extract her (not rescue, you didn't rescue Iari). He'd planned to . . . what, make sure he knew where she was? Voidspit. He just hadn't thought he'd have a real chance to succeed at getting to her, and now here it was.

Corso raised his chin, his voice, at the guard. "Got to take this one back with me. Geltrannen says."

And then, without waiting for argument or agreement, he backed through the door. Iari came with him, and they slammed it shut together.

CHAPTER NINETEEN ≡≡≡≡≡≡

K eawe summoned Gaer just after Ptah's bells. It was longer than he'd expected to wait, even allowing for Tobin's
precipitous dawn arrival. Almost two full days elapsed.
Gaer *knew*—from a careful watching of hoppers leaving the
courtyard—that Keawe had already sent a team to the ruins already, to bring back who-knew-what yesterday, almost as soon as
he, Notch, and Iffy had landed. Then Homer's funeral the very
next dawn, when *Rishi* had come crashing in, and then—and then
waiting. The rest of one day, during which Keawe's team returned.
Most of this one.

The turing net was working just fine. He'd had multiple messages from Iffy, mostly updates on Notch's condition (it had not
changed overmuch) and two invitations to join her for meals, all of
which he'd ignored.

Keawe, however, had not sent him any messages, nor had Tobin, until now, when she had sent an actual, physical *messenger* to
retrieve him. A tenju, like most of the templars, *armed*, like all
templars, even though they wore an initiate's tabard. This poor
child still carried the remnants of adolescent mammalian bodyfat
in the roundness of cheek and jaw. They stared up at him—because
Gaer was *up* for everyone, except Char—with that baby-soft jaw

set and only a little doubt in their yellow-gold eyes as they tried not stare and failed miserably.

This was the first time they'd seen a vakar in person, no doubt. Or at least from this range. Or maybe it was just honest dismay at the rumpled state of him.

"I trust," he said, voice gone rusty, "that this summons isn't immediate."

The initiate blinked. "The Knight-Marshal said, ah." Another blink. The faintest wince. "As soon as is convenient."

"*Which* Knight-Marshal said that? No, don't answer. Unless you're instructed to wait and escort me, Initiate, you may inform the Knight-Marshals"—Gaer laid particular emphasis on the plural—"that I will present myself at Knight-Marshal Keawe's office within the hour. I think we can both agree I need to clean up first." If Keawe had issued instruction to wait in the corridor for him, or to insist he go now, then—

Then he'd force this poor child to tell him so, and shortly after he would arrive in Keawe's office smelling of unwashed vakar, and she could suffer through it.

"Ambassador." The initiate managed a credible bow, involving chin, neck, and shoulders. "I will tell the Knight-Marshals." Less emphasis, but still a clear plural. They appeared to teeter on the edge of further comment.

Gaer was, had been, an ambassador. "Is there anything else?"

The initiate's chin came up. "Can you say, sir—do you know . . ." Their eyes slid away, then snapped back, suddenly hard and bright. "What happened to everyone else? Llian and Dodri? And . . ." A flush crawled out of their collar, up their neck, across their cheeks.

Oh, dear dark lords. This initiate from Windscar didn't know their names.

"Sergeant Luki and Captain Iari? Privates Char and Winter

Bite?" Gaer couldn't quite keep the edge out of his voice. "I know what happened at the ruin, but I know you wouldn't be asking me *that*, because if it's not common knowledge all over the compound already, then it's *restricted* knowledge, and you are not on the list to know it. If you are asking how those particular individuals are *now*, I cannot answer, because I do not know. If you are asking how they were when I last saw them—" He clipped his teeth together. "They were all alive, and in pursuit of the individuals responsible for Homer's death." Truth, partial truth. Good diplomacy.

Grant the initiate a measure of courage, anyway, and courtesy. "No sir, I—thank you, sir." They bowed again, took a step back, started to turn. And then looked back, eyes narrower now, and thoughtful. "You aren't what I expected, Ambassador."

It was Gaer's turn to blink, both sets of lids, and by the time he'd finished—well before he'd decided whether he should ask what that meant, much less gotten the words out—the initiate was in full retreat. He backed into his room, let the door close. Then he turned and leaned against it, both palms and his forehead. It was cool metal, modern, two polysteel halves that met in the middle, controlled by hexwork and lockpads.

You could *slam* a door on hinges. He hadn't thought he'd miss that. He hadn't thought Windscar wouldn't *have* that. B-town's Aedis was rife with hinged, wooden doors.

Then he reminded himself that Brood had breached Windscar's walls during the surge—briefly, but Brood-slime would chew through wood like it chewed through flesh and bone. So once, Brood had breached *this* doorway.

What had happened to the people inside—sss. What almost always happened, when Brood crashed through doors. *There* was a comforting thought.

Bathing didn't take long, nor did finding clean clothing. The

Aedis janitorial mecha were thorough. As he chose what to wear, Gaer touched every garment he'd brought from B-town. Then he settled on solid black: long tunic with too many buttons, the thick, flexible trousers most vakari wore. The only pair of indoor boots he owned. (*Oh Elements*, said his inner Iari. *Boots. This must be serious.*)

The effect at the end was vaguely menacing, but also reminiscent of the SPERE uniform Gaer hadn't worn for over two years now, since his ostensibly diplomatic assignment first to the Seawall embassy, then to B-town's Aedis. SPERE wasn't exactly a hidden branch of the Five Tribes military, but it wasn't a publicly celebrated one, either. His membership was also not publicly acknowledged, but the Knight-Marshals knew. They would understand the message.

The Aedis might have seconded him, but he *wasn't* theirs. He was Five Tribes. He was—vakari, with all that meant.

(*What does it mean?* Shut up, Inner Iari.)

Gaer switched his terminal off, which was a little bit petty. It would slow down anyone searching the turing's local memory for his notes on the ruins—analysis of hexes and both kinds of mecha and the *setatir* hallucinatory smoke. But that data was automatically synced to the main Aedis turing, and he would be surprised if priests hadn't already been at them. His tablet, which held the same data and additional notes in both Sisstish and cipher (therefore useless to anyone else), he brought with him. He left both his monofils, and his jacta, in the center of the bunk nearest the door. Templars went armed out of custom. No one else did, even vakari assets. Maybe especially vakari assets.

Then he had to go back across the room, boot up the terminal again, and search for Keawe's office, because that *wasn't* a place he'd had reason to visit yet. All their meetings had been conducted in Iari's temporary office, *with* Iari, and—

Gaer had to stop and lean on the door again. The last he'd heard from Iari had been that garbled message about finding Brood in Ettrad on the hopper's comms. Then the *setatir* fissure had acted up, and *Rishi* had come plummeting in the next morning, and it had been most of a *day* since and no one was acting like there was a surge happening.

Therefore, Iari hadn't been eaten by Brood. Neither had Corso, or Dodri, or Char, or Winter Bite.

Unless *that* was the reason for this summons. To tell him—

Oh, *setat.* Don't be stupid. Tobin would come here in person to give him *that* news.

He figured out where Keawe's office was. Got ready to switch the terminal off again and then—no. It was at best a futile gesture of defiance, and likely no one would notice, anyway. Instead, he tapped out a message to Iffy, telling her he'd been summoned. She might already know. She might already be there. She might need to come rescue him.

Because she would, even if he'd been a neefa to her. She was Iffy.

This time, when he finally managed to get past the doors, he left the terminal on.

Windscar's Aedis, like B-town's, like every other planetside Aedis Gaer had seen, kept its administrative offices together in a central area. Keawe kept her office at the crossroads of two side corridors, one which led to the armory (appropriate), the other, the barracks (also appropriate). It was a corner location that had clearly *not* been intended for use as an office, having two outside walls that would render it vulnerable to cold and potential breaches. And standing in front of the door—a single, massive polysteel panel—Gaer was reminded again that Windscar *had* been breached. That this room had. He found himself missing (again) Tobin's archaic hinged wooden door. The smell of wax and polish. Some clue how to signal his arrival. One *knocked*, in B-town. Here—

Ah. *Here* there was a camera set over the door like a baleful eye. (Like a cabochon in a One-Eye's helmet, which made his skin twitch). Gaer scarcely had time to stop in front of the door before it slid open. The cold hit him first. Then the smell, stone and leather and incense, slid over his tongue through his open jaw-plates. He could see a wall to his immediate left, naked, empty (not unmarked: there was scarring on the stone, from claws and whitefire). The wall directly across from him had a single window tucked into the corner. Weak winter light bled through it, grey with a touch of yellow, which suggested the sun might've clawed its way through the clouds.

"Ambassador." Keawe's voice snapped around the corner. "Join us."

Gaer made note of the plural. Took hope in it—of, if not an ally, at least someone who valued Iari. Then he stepped inside.

Oh ho. Someone had a warding hex up. Gaer's optic flickered advisement, not warning—it was a very benign sort of ward, the sort that turned everyone's auras the color of oatmeal. Tobin had one of those in his office. Gaer supposed it could be a standard Knight-Marshal feature, though it could as easily be meant for him. That was both flattering and . . . prudent, honestly. Which Tobin, more than Keawe, tended toward.

Gaer turned right, since the main space of the room lay that way. He saw the chairs first, three of them, wide-bottomed and vaguely barrel-shaped. Those were pure Windscar design. Knight-Marshal Tobin had claimed the one nearest the inner wall, farthest away from the window. He offered Gaer a nod, no smile; but that wasn't a bad sign, with Tobin.

Keawe offered no smiles, either (that was just mercy). She sat behind a desk that was pure spacer: polymer and polysteel, a gleaming expanse that belonged on a tenju drakkar. That might *be* from a tenju drakkar. Keawe was, Gaer recalled, from the spacer tenju clans, exiled to Tanis either because she was very good at training recruits and fighting Brood or because she'd offended someone better placed in the Synod and been dumped off in the Weep-scarred hinterlands. Maybe both. Keawe kept her desk spacer-spare, too. A terminal. A keyboard. A tablet. A desk-tesla, switched on. Everything stored if it wasn't in use.

A small, sparse bookshelf sulked in the corner. On the wall behind her—a *setatir* axe, a real one, metal, double-headed, wooden haft, meant for two very large hands. It was mounted so that the blade hung behind Keawe's shoulder like a threat. Or a promise.

She *did* smile at him, finally, but a smile from her meant the same thing it did to a vakar. She gestured at the remaining two chairs.

Gaer hesitated, weighing the marginally warmer position of the middle chair. Then he chose the one farthest from Tobin, and dragged it out of line with the others, away from the desk and Keawe and toward the cold-bleeding wall.

Gaer crossed Keawe's stare and peeled a smile of his own. "Knight-Marshal." To Tobin, "Knight-Marshal."

"I read your preliminary report." Keawe chewed the words like day-old bread. "Turns out, that is the *only* report we have, at the moment, about an incident that resulted in one dead and eight missing templars. Sister Iphigenia has been too busy to write one. And Lieutenant Notch, *I am told*, is too unfit for duty to either write a report *or* submit to an interview."

Oh, Iffy was up to her little alw wrists in Knight-Marshal-grade politics, making Gaer the only source of intelligence. Keawe knew it and she didn't like it. Tobin, damn sure, was protecting Iffy just by being here. That, and Iffy was a priest and a healer; she might have some protection from Windscar's Mother, too.

Gaer had no protection without Iari. (Maybe Tobin. Maybe. But he trusted that protection like ice underfoot.) He chose to act like he'd misunderstood Keawe's complaint. "I apologize that I haven't yet sent a more comprehensive report. I thought that, between Corporal Homer's funeral and the recovery team's mission to the ruins, I had more time. If you don't mind a few unpolished sentences, I will submit what I have now to both of you." He didn't even wait for an answer: tapped the screen of his tablet, directed the message, and sent.

Sending his report to *both* was a little bit of an etiquette breach. Windscar was Keawe's command. By rights, Gaer should've sent the report only to her and left it to her discretion whether or not to share it with Tobin. His presence in the office suggested she planned to share, but Gaer hadn't given her a choice, either.

The sour look on Keawe's face said she understood very well what he'd done. Her eyes flicked to her terminal as the report arrived in her queue.

"Thank you, Ambassador."

As if there was anything ambassadorial about his position right now. "I am not certain how helpful it will be, actually. I am working with very limited data. I assume," Gaer added, "that the team you sent to the ruins, Knight-Marshal Keawe, retrieved some samples from the individuals who attacked us and killed Corporal Homer."

A muscle jumped in Keawe's jaw. "They *did* bring back some samples."

"If we could arrange access for me, I could be of more use. I have my initial readings and data, but a more thorough examination would be useful." *Daring* her to say it was classified, above his clearance.

"We can try," Keawe said, through stiff lips. Which meant not in any vakari hell would he get near those artifacts. That she probably had the local wichu artificer, Su'seri, working on the problem. That was frustrating, to Gaer-the-arithmancer. That was a *setatir* relief to Gaer-the-SPERE-agent. He did not have to report what he did not know.

Gaer inclined his head. "My thanks. Of greater concern, however, than the half-riev's creation, or even how many there are— and I know how unlikely that sounds—is the portal."

Keawe made an impatient gesture, *go on*. Tobin offered a tiny, half-hitch of a smile. *Go on, please.*

"The transit passes through layers of aether inhabited by Brood. That is not normal. It's relevant information because I think this is how Jich'e'enfe was able to make those small fissures and bring the Brood into B-town last autumn. I have no idea how she controls the Brood that come through, or rather, how she *controlled* them, or if the arithmancer we encountered in the ruins is equally able to direct Brood attacks. I'm assuming they *can*. I—"

Keawe cut him off with a gesture. "Do we know how many other altars there are?"

"The one destroyed in the ruins, and the one on the other end of that portal. Those, we know for certain. If there are others . . ." Gaer flared his fingers, spacer shrug that he knew both Keawe and

Tobin would recognize. "I have delayed submitting a more comprehensive report, Knight-Marshal, because I have been trying to answer these questions, and to be able to offer solutions."

"And . . . ? Do you have any?"

Gaer drew his jaw-plates in close. The scarred one was starting to ache as the polymesh soaked up the cold. Served him right, didn't it, sitting so close to the wall. But he wanted distance between himself and the Aedis; he *needed* that distance and that discomfort.

"My training is practical. This is . . . highly theoretical. There are more skilled and experienced arithmancers in Seawall. My own supervisor, Karaesh't, among them. If I could consult with her—"

"You mean talk to *SPERE*."

"Yes. Not officially, but—"

"You're *already* reporting to them."

"Per the terms of my seconding, yes, I make periodic reports. Which, as you are well aware, do not include data that could compromise the Aedis. *This*, however—"

"These portals are pretty slagging compromising to the Aedis."

"These portals, and their probable link to *actually summoning and directing Brood*, are compromising to everyone signatory to the Accords. Including the Five Tribes, which of course includes SPERE. Knight-Marshal."

"No. For what it's worth, no permission granted, *Ambassador.*"

Void and dust, she could make that title a curse. "I take it that, then, is an order? I am not to report, discuss, or otherwise seek help from persons—"

"From *vakari*."

"—from *persons* more knowledgeable, for our, *your* benefit."

He could feel heat under his skin. Suspected his chromatophores were betraying him. Well. *Red* was a cross-species indicator of anger. Let Keawe see it.

Keawe set her jaw. "As I understand the terms of the treaty, and your . . . presence . . . you cannot divulge that which you learn in pursuit of Aedis business *without* express permission, even *after* the terms of your service. But I don't believe for a Ptah-shitting minute you won't tell your superiors everything the moment you can."

"And until then, you'll strangle my ability to help at all, and endanger Aedis personnel in the field unnecessarily."

Keawe's face had darkened so much that Gaer thought she might burst a vessel. Or, more likely, syn across the desk and snap his unarmored vakari neck. (Let her *setatir* try.) "Captain Iari did that on her fucking own."

"Gaer." Tobin spoke for the first time. Measured, quiet, unfailingly courteous. "Thank you. We appreciate your assistance. If you don't mind, I do have some further questions."

Emphasis laid on *I*. Tobin was even sincere in his thanks. And his courtesy.

The invocation of Gaer's first name, though, meant something. There was an intimacy to untitled first names that Keawe refused, that Tobin usually did. In the Aedis, the only name you *had* was the one. Using rank was polite social distance.

And because Tobin had used his name, Gaer had to look at him. Which he had been avoiding. Which he did not want to do, even now. Tobin was unremarkably human, medium height, medium build, dark-haired and dark-eyed, with skin more olive than brown. The most notable thing about him was the mecha prosthetic that replaced one hip and part of his thigh. That was a legacy of Saichi; that mission had killed all his command except one, a Private Iari who'd carried him back across enemy lines and sat with him after, reading him Jareth's *Meditations* on the cold hospice floor.

That was what Iari meant to Tobin. That was the loyalty.

So for her sake: "I'll do my best to answer, Knight-Marshal."

Tobin's mouth smiled gently. His eyes said *you'd voidspit better.* His voice, still courteous, quiet, even: "Your preliminary report mentioned two things of interest to—to us. As I understand portals, they require two anchors. Or at least two. In B-town you retrieved coordinates from the altar there, before Jich'e'enfe escaped with it. Did you manage to do that during *this* encounter with it, as well?"

Gaer sat up a little bit straighter. "I did. Though that information may not help. Let me explain portals, Knight-Marshals. There are the geographic coordinates, which change according to where the anchors might be. Those, I can derive, if I am on one end of a portal and that portal is currently active. And then there are the arithmantic designations of the anchors themselves, their individual hexes, if you will—which are useless as physical coordinates unless you have another anchor to connect to them. That is how I could recognize the altar in the ruins as the same one we saw in B-town."

Keawe shifted on her chair, a rearrangement of muscle and metal and bone. And anger. "There was no altar in the ruins."

Gaer controlled a hiss. "That very smooth section of volcanic glass that I am *certain* your priests noticed, because I indicated its location in my report, was the altar. The same one we found in B-town. Which I also indicated in my report."

Keawe frowned. "So one of the physical anchors you say are needed to make a portal is destroyed. And the other anchor can move, and you can't actually say *where* it is for sure unless it's open and there's an open portal. So you don't actually *know* where the other side of this portal is in any meaningful way. Ptah's fucking *eye.*"

Oh, he could let Keawe believe that. Let her believe it and walk out of this office *now.* Gaer kept himself still, unblinking.

"Gaer." Tobin pulled on his name like a string. "Sister Iphigenia indicated that Iari planned to go to the altar's last-known physical coordinates to retrieve Sergeant Luki and Private Llian. She also indicated that *you* were the one who supplied those numbers." He smiled, very gently, and his eyes were like chips of void. "You must have been certain."

Gaer clamped his jaw-plates tight, and said through his teeth: "At the time of the portal's destruction, I obtained both the arithmantic identifier and the actual terrestrial coordinates for the other altar. Those numbers, I gave to Iari. That physical location *might* have changed, if the One-Eyes and the arithmancer—I don't know. Retreated someplace else. I told Iari that."

"But you did not include these coordinates in *your* preliminary report. Either set. Physical or arithmantic."

He risked a look at Tobin. "Iari's trying to get Luki and Llian back. *If* they're alive, she—she needs time to extract them. If the Aedis comes in hot and attacks the last-known location of the second altar, then there is a greater chance the cultists will kill their prisoners and melt back into the steppes and disappear, dragging that altar with them. They have been evading us for some time. That's obvious."

"That's what Iari said?" Tobin asked, but Keawe talked over him.

"One-Eyes. Is *that* what we're calling these heretic bastards?"

"That's what Iari called the half-riev specifically," Gaer said, because Keawe's question—because Keawe—was easier to confront. "Because of the cabochon on their helmet. You know—since you read my first report, you *know*—that Iari commed the hopper when we were en route to Windscar. She reported a village destroyed by Brood."

"Ettrad," said Tobin. "Yes. You think the Brood that did that came from one of these small, directed fissures? That someone is doing in Windscar what Jich'e'enfe did in B-town?"

"I do."

Keawe sputtered. "So Iari's walking into—what, a fucking campful of these half-riev with an arithmancer and an altar that can pull Brood out of the void and aim them like fucking *artillery?*"

"Yes. She is. And she's got Corso with her. And Dodri, Winter Bite, and *Char.*" Who had promised to get Iari back alive. So.

"Gaer," Tobin said. "Did Iari *ask* you to delay your report of her location? Or did she *order* you?"

And oh, *that* was an out. Call it orders, and Keawe might stand down. Call it orders, and Tobin might—Tobin wouldn't believe it. Not of Gaer. Not of Iari, either. And then Tobin would *know* Gaer couldn't be trusted, that he'd lie to save himself, and that wouldn't help Iari.

Gaer tipped his chair back, so that he could look at both Keawe and Tobin at once. The cold throbbed at his back. His hands clenched on his tablet. He made them relax, talon by talon, before he said, "She didn't order me. She *asked* me to convey the urgency of the situation. It has been *less than two full solar days*, Knight-Marshals, since we got back from those ruins. If I had come back with the coordinates, if I had *told* you at once, Knight-Marshal Keawe, you would have gone out there, possibly overshooting Iari's team, and attempted a retrieval or a strike. We would lose any intelligence Iari could get from observation, anything Corso could get from—whatever he does, *anything* that might tell us how deep this Axorchal cult or whatever it is goes."

"That is *not* your decision, vakar."

"Clearly I made it my decision. Iari *setatir* asked me to *solve all this*, do you see? The hexes, the arithmancy—and I have not *done* that. *You* will not allow me access to people, to resources, who could help me solve it. Nor can you help her, if you go charging out there right now. That arithmancer is more than *my* equal."

"And Iari's supposed to defeat him and destroy the other half of the portal with the personnel she has? How will she do that?"

Gaer saw the trap then. The one Tobin had laid for him, the one he'd walked into. He tried to sidestep anyway. "She destroyed the altar in the ruins. Presumably she could use the same technique. I *did* report it."

Keawe's eyes were fixed on her terminal screen. "All you said in your first voidspit report was Iari'd destroyed the altar. Sister Iphigenia didn't mention anything about what happened. I assumed it'd vanished like it did in B-town, and that you . . ." Keawe rubbed her hand across her face. "You didn't exaggerate your report. Or fabricate it. You're saying Iari really did destroy the fucking altar with some kind of—" She rounded on Tobin. "What do you know about this?"

"Only what Gaer has attested in this report: that Iari destroyed the altar with what appears to be some kind of enhanced syn reaction."

Gaer reminded himself that he'd already told Tobin all of this on the hopper's comm. That he'd already *written it down* and sent it to both Knight-Marshals. It wasn't a betrayal for him to confirm it, with Tobin looking at him expectantly, and Keawe looking at him like she wished he'd spontaneously combust.

"It looked like her battle-rig filled with plasma, which then traveled through her axe and into the altar." Gaer closed his eyes, remembering the brightness, the sheer impossibility of it. "There was no residual heat or physical effect that would indicate *actual* plasma, or what happened to Iari's body, except the damage to the altar. I assumed some kind of evolution occurred with her nano-mecha and the syn."

Keawe forgot to scowl. She leaned onto her forearms and pinned Gaer with an intensity that made his plates flare. "And do you have an idea *how* it worked?"

Gaer had actually made some progress unpicking this arithmantic knot. He had all of Sister Diran's notes on Iari's nanomecha, and two personal, firsthand observations, and a skull full of battle-arithmancy with a special interest and emphasis on fighting Brood, which the Aedis was best at doing. He was one of the foremost experts in Aedis hexes *in* SPERE by now. And he understood more about riev than most, no, than *any* vakar ever had.

None of which Keawe wanted to know. What she wanted—what Tobin wanted, too—was a far simpler, naked, "Yes."

Tobin and Keawe traded a long look. Their hands moved in something like SPERE gestural cipher, except it was Aedis, and spacer, and designed to exclude Gaer. Which, well, that was fine. He would like to exclude himself, right now, from this whole *setatir* interview.

He made himself look somewhere else. At the axe on the back wall. At the few artifacts on the bookshelf. A 2D in a frame, tilted out of his sightline. A broken shard of armor, blackened on one end, pitted with Brood-slime. A few piles of books, actual bound things, with a mixture of languages on their spines. He fixed his gaze on a title he recognized, block-font Comspek spelling out *Meditations* on a cover that looked much less worn than Tobin's copy.

"I want to go on the retrieval mission," he said. "To get Iari. I assume you're going to send one."

Silence. He slanted a look sideways, saw that they were both looking at him.

Then Tobin said, "I cannot speak for Knight-Marshal Keawe, Gaer, but I would welcome your assistance, if we decide to go north."

Gaer had been assembling, in parallel, arguments for his inclusion, in case of a *no*, and reasons why they should wait until he'd examined any One-Eye remains Keawe's team had retrieved. He forgot all of it, fixating instead on: "What do you mean, *if.*"

Keawe looked unhappy. "Truth is, vakar, if you're right—about the portals, the small fissures, all of that—then these cultists, or insurgents, or *whatever*, are a major threat. What do you reckon the range on those altars is for opening little fissures?"

Gaer tasted iron on his tongue, bitter in his throat. "I don't know if two altars together can achieve greater range, but I am fairly sure one alone is very limited. Ettrad was on the way to the other altar's last-known coordinates, which were within a day of the ruins—assuming battle-rigged people moving at speed, and good weather. Certainly the distances in B-town were much shorter between altar and fissure, but that might have been intentional."

"So they're *that* close, and they're mobile." Keawe looked at Tobin. "Windscar is a training garrison. We have templars, but not much combined experience. My *priests* are all senior. Every one of them served through the surge. But I have only a handful of templars who can say that. That's why I agreed to let your captain lead this mission in the first place."

"So all that," Gaer said, "demanding the coordinates—and you had no intention of going after her, or mounting an attack at all?"

"We did. That's why *Rishi* is here," Tobin said. "But we cannot"—with a look at Keawe—"destroy a site where there might be templars operating. Or templars being *held*. You just confirmed that Iari is probably at those coordinates now, or about to be. So . . . at this moment, no, we can't act."

Keawe pressed her lips together, tight as her tusks would allow. "You might regret that, Tobin, if Brood come at our walls from a bunch of little separate fissures. Or the *big* fissure starts another surge."

Tobin tilted his head, *perhaps*, and smiled without warmth or humor. "I will regret far more killing our own because it's *easier*. But, Gaer—to your point, we will try to rendezvous with Iari if, when, she comms us. And you will be welcome."

Gaer unlocked his tablet's frame and began to roll it into a spiral so tight he threatened to crack the polymer. "Then I will, with your permission, return to my quarters until—something changes, and someone needs me."

"Funny you should say that." Keawe's voice pushed him back into the chair. "About Lieutenant Notch. Sister Iphigenia says you might know how to help him."

Gaer slid the rolled tablet (still intact, by some miracle) into the long pocket on his sleeve, running wrist to elbow, that ran along the seam between plain fabric and the reinforced panels that covered his spikes. That took all his attention, every bit, so that he did not have to look at Keawe. So he could say, calmly, "I told Iffy I couldn't help Notch."

"The word she used was wouldn't. Ambassador." Keawe leaned onto her elbows, hands folded. "You said you understood how Iari's new syn worked. Doesn't that mean you can duplicate the effect of the, what, the hexes?"

Oh, teach him to give simple answers. He should have drowned her in jargon. In numbers. In *setatir* theory until her eyes popped. He knew his jaw-plates were flat. That his nostrils had sealed down to slits. That Tobin, at least, would know what that signaled.

(Void and dust, Keawe probably did, too. She hated vakari enough to have studied them.)

"What exactly are you asking me to do, Knight-Marshal?"

"Can you replicate what happened with Iari's nano?"

"I don't know."

"Is it *likely* you could?" He hissed, and she nodded. "I take that as a yes. Then I need you to do that. Turns out," she added, when Gaer only stared at her, "templars *need* functioning nanomecha or we die. We're—what was the word, Tobin?"

"Symbionts." Tobin's own expression had locked down again. His gaze traveled around Gaer's face, careful and probing and too wise by half.

Keawe nodded. "Right. Symbionts. That means—"

"I know what it means, Knight-Marshal."

"Then you know that Notch is dying. Iffy says he *will* die if someone doesn't do something. And you're our someone."

Void and dust. "Knight-Marshal, what you're asking—"

"I'm *asking* you to save my lieutenant. Which it is in your power to do."

Gaer held up his hand to forestall her next retort. It was . . . *setat*, it was shaking a little. Teach him not to eat. Teach him to argue with two Knight-Marshals at once, in a cold room, while one of his friends got herself killed, and the other betrayed him, and he couldn't keep faith with anyone. "What you're asking—if I do this, you *cannot* let me go back to Seawall. You cannot let me take the knowledge of how to restart—and by extension, *stop*—templar nanomecha—back to SPERE. And that is not an advisement on my part, Knight-Marshal. It's a prediction. You, the Aedis—will have to keep custody of me."

Keawe cocked a brow at him. Tobin said nothing. Only watched.

"Why don't you ask Su'seri? He's wichu. Or second *him* into the Aedis?"

"He's wichu. He's provisionally Confederation. Can't second him. The Aedis is volunteer only. That's in the founding documentation. I did ask. He refused."

"I didn't think refusal was an option."

Keawe eyed him. "So refuse, Ambassador."

And oh, he wanted to. Spit *no* at her, walk out of the office. Except he'd already admitted, *like* a damn neefa, that he understood Iari's nanomecha. A simple yes, when he should've said—oh, a thousand opaque things. "Say I do. I say no, and then you'll what . . . send me back to Seawall anyway, even with your suspicions? You have said yourself I will tell my superiors everything I learn here. SPERE will know how to unmake a templar."

Keawe bared a tiny, unkind smile. "What do *you* think I'll do if you refuse?"

"I think you'll send me back to Seawall in a turing-piloted hopper that crashes into the *setatir* steppes, that's what I think."

"Don't be so fucking dramatic. You know good and *well* Tobin here wouldn't let me do that. Refuse this request—and it *is* a request, not an order—and we will release you from your service. We will trust you to keep to the terms of the treaty, and refrain from sharing proprietary Aedis information with the Five Tribes. You will be on *Rishi* within the voidspit *hour*, and back in Seawall within a *day*."

And off the *setatir* planet a short time after that, once Karaesh't got him back. He'd sat on the same data once before, in B-town, until Iari and Tobin had figured out a way to second him, so he had some cover: a way to say to Karaesh't, *by treaty I was an Aedis asset, under Aedis orders, I cannot divulge this information.* But if they let him go . . . if he *told* Karaesh't no again, and cited the same provisions, then she, all of SPERE, would see an abuse of his loyalties—that they had given the Aedis use of one of their arithmancers, and got nothing back for it—and that would bounce back on the Aedis. Erode confidence between the Confederation and its allies. Erode SPERE's confidence in *him*, too. And there was no guarantee at all that they would not try to *take* that knowledge.

This way all the neefa-shit landed on *him*. Betray the Aedis to Karaesh't—give up his intel, that was his *job*—and he put every templar in jeopardy. What he could do, other arithmancers could replicate. And once he filed a report—sss. It would travel. Up SPERE, into the Five Tribes. Into the Protectorate, eventually. Or he could lie to Karaesh't, or sabotage his own data. Betray SPERE and the Five Tribes. Live with that.

Or. *Or.*

Gaer pinned his stare on Keawe. Through her. "If I do what you ask, and help the lieutenant, and I somehow do not die in a terrible, convenient accident, you *cannot* release my service."

"So you say."

"Don't be so *setatir* coy, Knight-Marshal. *When* you refuse to release me, the Five Tribes will protest. You, and Knight-Marshal

Tobin—the Supreme Mother herself—may dance through the treaties for a time, but eventually there won't be a legal hold on my person. My question for you is what *then*."

Keawe looked at Tobin. Who said, still gently, "Do you have something in mind, Gaer?"

And without taking his eyes off Keawe, Gaer said, "I do."

CHAPTER TWENTY ═══════

And somehow, suddenly, they were outside, the door shut. Iari stared at it, half convinced Double Wide would slam it open again and challenge, protest, or otherwise try to prevent Corso from just walking out the door with her on the strength of *Geltrannen says*. There was commotion on the other side—raised voices, one sounded like Trammen—but the door stayed shut.

"Told the kid at the mess tent I'd bring the box back. Guess I'm not doing that." Corso took his hand off the latch carefully, like he expected it to grow hands and grab for him if he moved too quickly. "That was *not* my plan. I was going to find Axor—you know who. But then there are these fucking *badges* and I saw a chance to get to you, so I did."

Iari looked at him then. Really looked. He was sweating hard, grey on the edges, pinched around eyes and lips. Corso wasn't the sort to sweat under pressure. Attack him with Brood, drop a Brood-eaten body in front of him—maybe then. Fast-talking his way past Double Wide should not even rate as a challenge. "Are you all right?"

He licked his lip. Side-eyed the door and shook his head. "Am

I all right. Void and dust, I wasn't the one locked up in a *neefa shed.*"

"Like a neefa. Yes. Which suggests something about my status here. This makes you a neefa-thief." She looked around, didn't see anyone watching them, but of the people she *did* see . . . Yeah. They all had badges on display. "Is that the badge? When did you get it?"

"Issued to me, along with my fucking kit. Come on." Corso threw his shoulders back and started walking—swaggering—away from the byre. "We stay here too long," he added, through mostly closed lips, "stand around too long, Bersk might spot me. We don't want that."

"Okay. But we go *this* way." Iari leaned into him, shoulder to elbow, and nudged. "There's a building I want to look at. One-Eyes standing guard in front. I think that's where Luki and Llian are. Trammen said the One-Eyes are called Axorchal's Chosen, and they're for dealing with troublemakers, who they keep in that shed. That sounds like templars to me."

Corso shot her a look full of questions. But he adjusted his course, and hers, and steered them toward the worn path between byre and barn that some long-ago farmer must've used to whack a few steps off their chores, rather than the direct path across the old farmyard. It wasn't the most direct route, but it wasn't very populated either. "I haven't figured out where they're keeping the One-Eyes. Maybe that's who's in your shed."

"With *more* One-Eyes out front? Nah. Besides. Trammen said it was for troublemakers."

"Trammen might not've had any idea. *He's* still in the neefa-house."

"Yes. Yes, he is." Iari kept leaning against Corso, as if sheltering against wind and cold. "The byre's hexed. I don't know to do *what,* maybe just warding, it reacted to my nano—but I don't know why you'd ward a place full of civ refugees you're trying to convert."

"Because you're not sure you've totally succeeded yet. Or because they have to do something to earn their badges."

"Yeah? What did *you* do?"

"Impressed Gel. Void and dust, I don't know. Maybe she likes my braids."

"Maybe she does." Iari huffed softly. "You're good at your job. She trusts you."

Corso blinked like she'd kicked him instead of saying something nice. "Huh. Well. I think it's because I have my own weapon, too. I'm already a fighter."

"To fight who—"

"Sss." Corso hissed like Gaer and stopped. Pointed with his chin.

Someone—roughly Iari's size, so probably tenju, features concealed by a hat and a scarf—came out of the bigger of the two yurts. That person paused, staring up at the sky for a few moments, drawing on a pair of fat, fur-lined mittens. Then, still eyeing the sky, they headed slowly toward the other yurt.

Corso crouched slowly, drawing Iari down with them. She winced as his knees popped like snapping sticks. "You know them?"

"Huh."

"That a yes, Risar?"

"That's a no, and shut up and be patient a minute. I don't want to be noticed."

Fair. Smart, even: movement drew attention. Not that they had any cover here. Someone looked, they'd see two people crouching down on a dirt path. Iari closed her eyes and took deep breaths of cold air that burned the inside of her nose and her throat, all the way to her lungs. The syn was still pacing her skin's confines like something trying to escape. She clenched and unclenched her fists.

She opened her eyes to Corso's wrinkle-browed stare. "Are *you* all right?"

"The hexes in the byre were . . . hostile. They damn near set off my syn. I thought it'd get better out here, but it's not. Is the person gone?"

"Yeah. Went to the mess tent. Didn't even look this way. This place is *not* worried about security. You'd think we hadn't just blown up an altar and killed a bunch of them."

"Maybe that's not widely known." Iari shifted a little, rising up on the balls of her feet like that was *any* help seeing. "What's in the yurts?"

"The smaller one's got the quartermaster. He's got boxes of 'casters in there. And blankets, and a nanoforge. *And* the badges. But that big yurt? The one that tenju just came out of? The altar's in there."

Iari had been expecting an *I don't know*; the syn *had* been on its way to a nap. Now it came roaring back, so that Iari had to catch her breath and push both hands into the snow, like she could hold onto the ground.

"You're sure?" she asked the snow. (Fresh, but already dusted with dirt. Ash from fires? But she hadn't seen any. Or smoke. So—)

"I'm sure," he said. "I saw it. Didn't see the arithmancer, though. Or maybe I did, and I didn't know it."

"Tell me," said Iari. "All of it. Everything since they separated us."

Corso did. " . . . and then I saw this kid behind the mess with a box too big for her, and . . . here we are." He pushed up on his toes. Grunted and then stood, still slowly. It looked like it hurt. Like he was feeling every flex. And while yeah, sure, they'd been pushing hard the last—how long had it been? A day and a half, two days?

Gentle Mishka, they'd have buried Homer yesterday, if Gaer and Notch and Iffy had gotten back alive.

That made her chest hurt all over again, nothing to do with the syn. She looked up at Corso. He cocked his head, then offered a hand. She took it, let him pull her up. He overbalanced a little, stepped back, pulled her with him. She caught them both, jerked *him* back to balance—and they bumped together, chest to chest. His badge, relegated to the edge of his collar, slapped forward and hit her coat. Brushed her cheek in passing.

The jolt this time was visible, audible: an arc of blue-white, from the badge to her skin, *through* her skin. The syn stopped asking permission and happened, a flood of adrenaline that made her breath short and tight. Her senses expanded, until she could see a footprint in the snow by the voidspit *barn*; until she could smell Corso's skin and the dust in his coat, overlaid by the mess tent's concoctions; until she could hear her breath, his, and . . .

Someone was yelling. Luki, she thought. She didn't say it. She didn't want the argument, and Corso would argue. He was already looking at her, horror (at his badge?) finding new focus.

"Your *eyes*."

"What?"

"They're. Yeah." He looked at the badge again. "Did *it* do that to you?"

"What happened? To my eyes." She shook her head (heard the scrape of her hair in her hood, the rasp of sweater against coat). "They change color or something?"

"Or something," Corso agreed. "Look at me. Yeah. They're getting more normal. They'll pass."

"It's the syn. I'm usually rigged. The, it, the syn—usually goes through the rig." She blinked. Her vision *seemed* fine. "That badge is hexed."

"Yeah. Not surprised. It . . . it feels *wrong*. Bad." Corso had pulled his head as far from his badge as neckbones would allow. "I can't take it off, though. It's . . . shit. It's how we're walking around."

"We're not walking around. We're standing here tripping over arithmancy that Gaer could probably counter without a blink." Iari squeezed her eyes shut. "I can't let them give me one of those badges."

"That's going to make it hard to blend in." Corso started walking again, stomping like he wanted to make sure the ground didn't get away. "This shed-prison where you think they've got Luki and Llian—you said there're One-Eyes out front."

"Axorchal's Chosen."

"Then we have to draw them off, if you want in there. I don't think they'll let you in without a badge."

"I do want in there. I want my people *out*. But that altar." The words caught in her throat. She forced them through. "The altar's the priority. I think I'm the one who can deal with it, *and* with the arithmancer."

"Not unarmed, even with your syn." Corso changed direction abruptly, aiming across a short stretch of trackless snow and toward another path leading into the main body of the camp. "Let me think about how to get kit for you. I mean—stealing works, but that's going to be noticed. And we can't stand here. You need to walk around this place, same as I have."

"Yeah." She'd ridden the worst of the syn out by now. She tugged her hood tighter around her head as they stepped into a lane between tents. Dropped her chin and hunched and hoped no one was checking for badges.

They spent the next hour or so walking. Corso showed her the mobile floodlamps and their generators, the general layout, how the patrols moved. He kept his tactical observations to himself. Didn't say the obvious, *there's two of us, and a couple hundred of them, so we won't win a fight.*

Which saved her counterargument: that couple hundred might not even be entirely armed, and those who were had conventional weapons. That no one had armor worth mentioning.

But then she had to consider any remaining One-Eyes, the arithmancer, the altar. She had to consider Brood. Opening small fissures in the camp would make chaos. Even if the arithmancer had fine control over Brood, and could direct them, people might panic—but if the arithmancer *did* have fine control, she and Corso could be boneless food very quickly.

And there was no telling what those badges did. No one else seemed affected by the ubiquitous badges, either. Maybe it was just Corso's unluck. Or maybe people got *used* to those hexes, whatever they did. They could be some kind of identification to Brood, like *do not eat this one.* They could be transforming their wearers into One-Eyes *without* the mecha grafts and wichu artificing. They could be, what, some kind of Oversight, and she and Corso could find themselves surrounded by one hundred–odd people all *acting* like Brood, in concert, taking orders from Axorchal himself. (Or the arithmancer. Probably the arithmancer. Maybe they were the same.) Probably, *probably*, the badges weren't anything that formidable or that impressive . . . except *her* nano-mecha hated them.

They ended up by the latrines just as mealtime was ending. There were more people streaming out of the mess, going back to tents or to the solid buildings. There was also a small troop climbing a hill to get out onto the plains. That gave Iari a moment: she trickled to a stop, staring up at them, until Corso realized he'd lost her and circled back. Then he tucked in close, so it looked like they were having a private conversation (which they were). But all he said was, "Iari."

"Those people marching out, on that hill. Look. All of them all armed. Every one of them has a longcaster." None of them had much idea how to march, but most of them navigated snowy hillsides all right. Iari reckoned everyone had some outdoors experience, at least. You'd have to, in Windscar. "Are they hunting? Or training?"

"I have been here as long as you have, and no one's given me any briefings, either. Though I don't *think* there's any herds large enough here to feed this many people."

"Not food hunting. Templar hunting. Or practicing to hunt templars, at least. You hear anything about that?"

Corso frowned. "What, you mean *our—?* No. Dodri's greenish, but she's got the riev to help. Shit, Iari. They're probably watching *us* right now. Char and Winter Bite, anyway. They won't let a bunch of neefa like *this* catch them out."

"Huh." *That* was . . . a good point. Iari turned, scanning the northern ridgeline. Fingers of sunlight poked through at tentative intervals, turning patches of hillside to glittering white before the clouds cut them grey again. Of course she didn't see anyone. But she'd lay bets they were up there.

"You see any long-range comm arrays since you've been here?"

Corso side-eyed her. "Nooo. Why, you want to call in an aerial strike now?"

"No. Well, maybe *yes*, once we have Luki and Llian. Mostly I don't want *them* calling for help, either. If there's an array, we need to take it out *before* anything else."

"Iari, look around. This is not a place that can call allies. Or keep them. Look what they did to the last ones they had." Corso's voice dropped to a near-whisper. "Try smiling, yeah? At least *acting* like you're not assessing the place for weaknesses?"

Smile. Sure. Iari rearranged her features appropriately. Maybe. (Corso rolled his eyes.)

"Point," she said. "That might've cost them their supply of One-Eyes, if they were relying on the wichu to operate the machinery. You said you saw a nanoforge in the quartermaster's yurt. Nothing like that surgical unit we saw in the caves, though?"

"I haven't seen anything particularly medical at all."

"Good. All right." Iari glanced around. "Walk with me—this way. I need you to give me your 'caster. No, *listen*. I'm going to run after that group going up the hill. Pretend like I'm supposed to be with them. No one's going to notice I don't have a badge if I'm running like I'm late and flustered. I won't *actually* catch up, don't look at me that way. Once I'm over the ridge, I will *stop* chasing them and try to circle around and find Dodri and retrieve my battle-rig. I need *you* to be near that prison shed at sunset. I'll send the riev to make a very loud distraction. Dodri will meet you there; *you* extract our templars and then get *out*. I'll go for the altar."

"At sunset." Corso was sliding his hands along the 'caster's sling, back and forth, like he was memorizing the shape. Like he hadn't decided to give it to her. "We don't *know* for sure Luki and Llian are in that shed. What if they aren't?"

She almost told him then that she'd heard Luki screaming during the last syn. But there wasn't time for more argument, she had to go now, and there was only one answer that mattered anyway. "Then I've fucked up, and it's on you and Dodri to find them."

"While you're fighting an arithmancer and destroying an altar. Alone. That's *not* templar protocol."

"No. But we're going to have two templars in unknown condition. Let's assume *not good*. You're going to need all hands to extract them. And—come on. Two riev crashing around in this camp? They might not even notice you and Dodri. Or me."

"Dodri's going to be in a battle-rig. They'll notice her. And you. This is a terrible plan."

"Yeah. You got better?"

"No."

They'd gotten almost to the edge of the camp. The group they'd seen walking out had almost gotten to the top of the hill. Now that she'd had time to look, Iari pegged it for some kind of training. There were easier ways up; the person leading them had picked the hardest route. Her luck, it'd be Gel in charge; but that'd be okay, too. She had no intention of actually catching up.

Then, before she could ask again, Corso slid the 'caster off his shoulder and thrust it at her.

For an eyeblink Iari was seventeen again. Same sullen grey sky, same wind, same latrine-whiff on the wind. Corso had handed her a 'caster then, too. Maybe *this* 'caster. Then, he'd been watching her closely, worried for a green soldier on her first fight against Brood. Now he was looking everywhere but at her. For Bersk, for Geltrannen. For anyone watching them.

She hung the strap across her shoulder, settled the weight. "Luck, Corso."

He looked at her finally. "I'll want that 'caster back."

"Sir. Yes, sir."

"Fuck you. Pray to your Elements. That's better than luck." Then he turned and strode off like a man with somewhere to go, someone to see. Iari turned, too, jogging for the perimeter, contorting her face into obvious distress.

Hrok who moves unseen—

Iari trotted óff toward the perimeter, aiming at the gap between guards, ready with a story if they stopped her, hoping they wouldn't.

Let us move unseen with you.

CHAPTER TWENTY-ONE ════

Keawe escorted Gaer straightaway, personally, to the vaults under the Aedis where they were storing the salvage from the ruins. The big metal mecha looked as Gaer remembered them; they took up most of one side of the vault. The workbench held the remains of the One-Eyes, or at least the bits not obviously organic. (Those were in jars in the hospice, maybe. Or Keawe hadn't brought them back at all) Most of hardware, though, was fragments. Only two gloves intact enough to examine *as* gloves. Only *one* helmet.

Of course there was no Brood emanating from any of it.

Gaer looked, while Keawe stood there watching him, while someone else went to find Iffy. He walked around the gloves. The helmet. He (annoyed Keawe intensely, and on purpose) handled each and every *setatir* piece the templars had hauled out, even the fragments. Then he had arranged both gloves and the helmet in front of what he had decided would be his workspace, helmet in the middle, gloves on each side. The effect was a little like a dismembered body reaching for him, if that body also had two right hands. By then Gaer had a *theory*, and all he had to do was test it.

At that point Iffy arrived, out of breath, struggling with a case of blood-filled vials and trailed by a portable med-mecha clicking along on too many limbs. "Samples from Notch," Iffy said by way of greeting, and hefted the bag onto the counter beside Gaer's arrangement of One-Eye technology.

Keawe, with a muttered oath to every Element, left.

So it was only Iffy watching when Gaer put one of the gloves on.

She squeaked, reached—stopped, as he poked his fingers into the cuff. "Gaer. We don't know how those work. *Do* you?"

"Not exactly. But I know Notch didn't get infected by the mecha," Gaer said. "He got a *rig* breach from the mecha. Whatever infected him got in that way, and got into *him* through the implants and the needle-socket in the battle-rig. This is what comes of filling your bodies with tiny machines. Iffy, for the love of your Elements, look. This glove is meant for a *mammal*. Five fingers. Not enough joints. It's not even going to fit over my hand."

"Then *why*—?"

"Because I want to test my hypothesis."

Iffy gave him a flat-lipped stare, then, but to her credit, she let him work the *setatir* thing over his fingers.

Of course it was all over artificing. It had been a wichu creation. He *expected* to find elaborate hexes that stitched several aetheric layers together, that opened a conduit to the void-layers of Brood. Maybe some kind of ward that *held* Brood in place. He expected to find some kind of internal bloodletting mechanism, too—the gloves needed their wearers to power them, and the standard biopower was blood.

And yes, there were tiny needles thinner than hair ringed round the wrist, which did not manage to pierce Gaer's skin despite a valiant attempt. He might not have noticed the attempted pricking at all—that's how tiny they were—except that their hexes flared up in his optic.

He spent some time tormenting the mechanism, making it

spring, watching the data stream through his optic. And then he understood what no other vakari had, since the first riev crawled out of its kiln.

No one knew *how* wichu made riev, exactly. There were theories. And despite Gaer's protest to Keawe that he was an arithmancer of practice, not theory—he was well-versed about riev. There were hexes, *obviously*. Artificing, *obviously*, because that's how wichu did arithmancy. It was clear to Gaer now that the most morally (to vakari) offensive part of making riev, the necrogalvanism, was *deliberate*. The half-riev were proof you could make something *like* riev with a live body. But making riev out of corpses guaranteed that the subject deteriorated so fast after second-death that a nosy vakari arithmancer couldn't learn much.

Now—*now*, one nosy vakar had proof that it wasn't contact with Sawtooth's Brood-rotted effluvia that had caused the changes to Iari's nanomecha. It had been *other* nanomecha. The nanomecha in Sawtooth, the nanomecha that *made* Sawtooth. Because that was, at least in part, how the riev worked.

There had never been templar riev. Iari had told him once that templars couldn't volunteer their remains to be riev (when riev had been legal, and the Confederation at war with the Protectorate); something about the Aedis nanomecha prevented the transformation. Well. Now Gaer knew what. Incompatibility between nanomecha.

Gaer had not asked for Aedis data on the long-ago wichu weapon that inspired the Aedis nanomecha, before it defected and repurposed itself. That information was probably classified, and— *sss*, he didn't need to know. Not really. Wichu had created nanomecha. Invented the whole *setatir* field. And what he understood *now* was that riev and the One-Eyes were just later editions of the same bioweapon concept. The basic *idea* was the same: directed mutation of tissue into something else, with the infusion of alchemical hexes and arithmancy.

"There are nanomecha in this glove," he said. Waited, while Iffy interrupted her own profanity-laced mutterings (presume her research was not going as well, had not been, would not—because she wasn't what he was) and parsed what he'd said, then stared at him.

"What?"

"Cousins to *yours*, I imagine. *That's* how the wichu make riev. *Nanomecha*, infiltrating dead tissue and keeping it animate. We never knew quite how galvanism *worked*, exactly, and no one wanted to know; the wichu sure as *setat* never told."

Iffy blinked. "Galvanism is banned. It's part of the Accords."

"Yes, because Jich'e'enfe seemed the sort to respect the law, didn't she? But *banned* probably also means *classified*. The One-Eyes are alive, obviously. But a living body on its own cannot support a whitefire weapon. Too much energy. Organs degrade, bodies overheat. That's *why* the riev were built with galvanics in the first place. Use the electrical systems already in place, take out the unnecessary organs to make room for a power core—Sss, all right. The point. The Brood we keep finding in the gloves, in the altar—*they* act as an alternate power source. That's all. That's what they were to the Protectorate in the beginning, too—*power* to feed the tesser-hex drives of voidships. Sss. Never mind." He flicked his talons across his tablet. The hexes weren't *hard* to solve, once he knew what to look for. A final flick, and he sent the data to Iffy. "This will work. Feed the hex I just wrote here to a sample of Notch's blood and run a simulation. See if that restarts his nano."

"That's . . . it?" She peered at the tablet. "That's just. . . ." She squinted up at him. "You're sure?"

"I am. Run the simulation." He understood her hesitation. The change he was making looked so very minor: a few variables changed, code excised and inserted, so that one minor hex among hundreds was different. A simple change, but sometimes the most dramatic changes were simple. This one granted—or restored—a level of agency to the nanomecha. *Choice.*

He waited for Iffy to ask what the new hex would do, but she didn't. She trusted him. Trusted that his fix would work. Nodded at him instead, and scooped up yet another of so *many* samples from an exsanguinated Notch. Gaer straightened, while Iffy slotted the sample into the med-mecha and waited, watching the display as the med-mecha did the analysis for her. She was operating on faith and technology, which was the Aedis distilled to its essence.

"Mishka's *tits.* Gaer!" Iffy jumped back from the display. Jumped at *him*, grinning, arms outflung. Then she seemed to recall that vakari were unsuited to mammalian hugs, having spikes in all manner of places, and settled for making a pair of delighted fists. "It works!"

"I did say it would."

Iffy's smile fell a little. "How long have you known this?"

Of course she would ask that. *How long did you let Notch suffer.* Gaer breathed carefully past the knot in his chest. "I didn't *know.* I've been in my quarters since Tobin arrived. I had time to work on it, but I couldn't *know* without access to this vault and these gloves." Which was true, and also not all of the truth.

Iffy's eyes narrowed. He didn't need to read her aura: blame marched over her features, anger, and he'd bet the last joint of two fingers she was blaming Keawe for the delay, for Notch's suffering. That she was imagining he would have helped sooner, that she'd convinced him in the snow outside Homer's funeral to save Notch.

A better person might correct that misapprehension. Gaer kept his jaw shut. Pushed back from his place at the bench and gathered up his tablet.

Iffy was staring at him. "Where are you going?"

"You've got to go give this to Notch."

"I—no. *We're* going to do that. *You're* going to do that."

"The hexes are *here*." He pointed at her tablet. "Your med-mecha can replicate them. You no longer need *me*."

"I do," Iffy said. Her smile folded and flattened. "Notch does. *You* did this, Gaer, everyone needs to see that."

Ah. So this was a public display: march the vakar into the hospice, show everyone that he was benign. Helpful, even. Or—"Do you have orders not to leave me down here alone? What might I *do* among all these devices, I wonder, that I did not do already when I was part of the team that discovered them."

She gestured at the helmet and its two matched, detached hands. "Make unsettling displays?"

He stared at her, head tilted, so that the optic pointed squarely at her. He wasn't reading her aura—for once—but she didn't know that.

A flush crawled up her cheeks. "There are two templars outside. If I leave, one of them will come into the vault to, um."

"To guard me. Or kill me?"

"Gaer!"

"Sss, all right. Then assuming I leave, and I choose *not* to go to the hospice—one of those templars will walk me back to my quarters, then? And remain outside to ensure I don't wander loose?"

The flush settled into stubborn blotches. "Notch doesn't have time for this, Gaer. Come with me. Make sure I get it right."

Gaer almost said *I don't care about Notch*, tasted sour and spite in the back of his throat. Swallowed it. Iffy didn't deserve his temper, and it wasn't true. He did care. Obviously, stupidly, to his own detriment and damnation.

"You will get it right. But I will also go with you and I'll—do whatever it is you think only I can do. But Notch won't thank either of us for it. Me, especially."

"Oh, Notch will thank you," Iffy said. "I'll make sure of it."

He'd better, Gaer thought. *Because I am going to need a favor.*

CHAPTER TWENTY-TWO

C har wondered—had discussed with Winter Bite—whether anyone had predicted, as a consequence of decommissioning riev and deactivating Oversight, that the *we* of riev would become many *I*s. Winter Bite contended that no one had because riev had not warranted that much consideration. Certainly the wichu would not have predicted one of their constructs crawling through snow on the Windscar steppes on their elbows while conducting reconnaissance.

And if they were honest with themself—which Char always was (not for lack of imagining untruths, but because it was stupid to live by them)—they had thought to crawl the whole camp's perimeter because they had seen the evolution of warfare, and remembered the days when crawling had been a necessary tactic and the enemy had been vakari.

Char was not sure vakari weren't *still* enemies, with exceptions: the Five Tribes, by legal treaty; and Gaer i'vakat'i Tarsik, because he was their . . . friend. (Truth could be uncomfortable. This truth was.) The Accords were a matter of necessity. The Weep and the Brood required alliance with the vakari Protectorate. That did not erase the causes for the initial conflict.

Char remembered that change in Oversight's programming,

the shift from *all vakari* to *just those over there* to *no, never mind, just the Brood.* Oversight's dissolution, in addition to granting Char access to themself, had conferred the agency to decide who was friend or enemy. To choose their associations.

And to, as Iari put it, *show initiative.*

Thus, Char crawled the perimeter, elbows and belly, until they found a small depression and allowed blowing snow to cover them, even though Corporal Dodri had made no such order. She had not, Char supposed, even thought of it.

It was Char's experience that the inhabitants of battle-rigs counted *prone* as a disadvantage, a sign of lost balance or limited vantage or blocked access to weapons. Certainly, *prone* was a terrible idea when confronting Brood. It was an *excellent* idea when sneaking.

Though Char was not certain how much stealth was required in this situation. The commanders of that camp did not appear concerned with security. There were guards walking a clear trail around the perimeter, and at appropriate intervals. But they were only armed with conventional 'casters, there were not many, and none of them were the gloved or helmeted half-riev that Iari had designated One-Eyes. The brightness of the floodlamps in the camp (based on Char's estimation of the size of the teslas, the generators, the likely energy output) and the regularity of their placement bespoke a greater concern with illuminating the events occurring *inside* the perimeter than outside.

That was—good, from the perspective of someone likely to attack that camp from the outside. But it was not good for someone inside trying to get out.

Char was already worried. They had seen—because even Gaer did not realize the acuity of their optics—the woman Bersk separate Corso from the others, while the man Trammen had taken Iari and the other refugees from Ettrad into the byre.

That division seemed to Char to be strategic. Though Bersk had shown favoritism to Corso (an alchemical attraction, from Bersk's physical posturing), Char did not think that drawing him off had been sexually motivated. Char had not spent decades around sapients without learning the signs. Even with Oversight, maybe especially then—Char had *seen things*.

Char watched as Corso and Bersk moved around the camp, Bersk pointing at things and waving her hands. Ironic, that the enemy was aiding Corso in his own reconnaissance. Char was not sure what he had done to ingratiate himself, though they suspected details about his demeanor had communicated something to the insurgents. The majority of the tenju population Char observed (there were sapients inside the tents whose surface details remained undetectable) wore their hair in a similar style to Corso's. There were few alwar, and no humans or wichu at all. The latter's absence Char found not at all surprising; the violence with which Jich'e'enfe and her associates had been dispatched suggested a degree of hostility. Any wichu located here would have met a similar ending. The absence of humans was more surprising, and made Char even more uneasy for Sergeant Luki's situation.

Char did notice one universal feature among the camp's residents, at least those not confined to the byre. They wore badges that looked like single eyes, which Char supposed must represent Axorchal One-Eye. The badges were a sign of loyalty. *Affiliation.*

Char did not reach up and touch the Aedis sigil on their own chestplate. (Tactile reassurance was unnecessary, and besides, they needed both elbows to prop themselves up.) When they had first joined the Aedis, that sigil had been paint. It was later, after successful initiation, that the armorer Jorvik and Gaer had engineered a way to make the sigil a permanent feature without compromising the integrity of Char's hexes. And—this had been Gaer's particular contribution—that sigil had been hexed to permit limited nonverbal transmission *to* templar comms, and full reception *from* them. Winter Bite and Char had discovered by accident that after the sigils' installation, they could also transmit to each other—not as immersively as Oversight had allowed, but more efficiently than verbal speech. That discovery had been the subject of some debate, whether Gaer had intended it (they agreed *not*), whether they should tell the captain. Winter Bite and Char had so far agreed *not* on that decision as well. Either Iari knew already and did not care, or she did not know and might feel compelled to tell someone if she found out. Char knew that Knight-Marshal Tobin would not object to private communications between his riev templars, but Char was not sure how *other* templars might feel.

Now Char wished very much that they *had* told Iari. The sigil had been meant to facilitate communication between comm units. It was not meant to transmit or receive on the deeper layers of aether. But Char's sigil (or perhaps Char themself) had been receiving aetheric signals since the ruins, ever since Gaer had taken Char briefly offline. (Gaer called it *killed*; Gaer was unnecessarily sentimental, but Char thought it was rather sweet.) The captain's nanomecha . . . glowed, though a visual descriptor was inadequate. Char was *aware* of them, anyway, within a range that included the width of this camp, though Iari's presence was a mere flicker now that she had been confined to the byre.

But Iari's confinement freed Char to observe not just Corso's movements, but also the comings and goings of personnel in the central buildings. With one exception—Geltrannen—that leadership was tenju. Gender presentation and sex seemed unimportant, but all of the tenju had worn braids and hooks. That affectation was likely a partial cause of Corso's acceptance, and Iari's rejection, by that leadership. They were assuming something about him, perhaps.

Char had not yet identified a leader. Though Corporal Dodri had hypothesized a council, or some sort of anarchist collective form of governance, Char believed that because *Axorchal One-Eye* was not a collective power, but a singular entity, a cult in his service would employ a singular leader. Char was sure (Gaer would call it a hunch) that the leader must also be the arithmancer. To Char's annoyance, they had not identified him-her-them yet in the camp's population. Winter Bite, however, had discovered that one of the yurts (the one Corso had briefly entered), the byre, and one of the sod-sided outbuildings all possessed significant structural artificing. He had used that word specifically, and though Char did not think the corporal understood the significance, Char did. Wichu had been involved in the construction of those hexes.

Winter Bite had confided in Char, on their private channel—a burst of mecha language that Dodri would have called static, if she had been able to hear it, which she could not—that he suspected the altar was housed in the largest yurt; Char had advised him to report that to Dodri. ("It is not confirmed," Winter Bite had objected. "It is only supposition." "It is a hunch," Char told him. "Other sapients are encouraged when we have those.")

Dodri *had* been encouraged. And worried. And *more* worried when Winter Bite reported (again with Char's encouragement) that he believed there were multiple mammalian heat signatures inside the sod-sided outbuilding, though it was difficult to be precise through the mesh of hexes how many there were. The half-riev

(One-Eye) sentries at the door suggested important inhabitants; Dodri had wondered at first if it was the arithmancer's quarters, but Winter Bite's report had convinced her the templars were inside.

Not that they had a way to confirm that hypothesis.

Char shifted their weight slightly. Their perspective was necessarily limited, this close to the ground. Winter Bite and the corporal were set up almost directly across from Char's position, at the top of a steep ridge on the northern perimeter. They had a far better vantage. Char weighed the wisdom of contacting Winter Bite for an update. He would, Char knew, tell them if there was information they *needed* to know. But Winter Bite did not always grasp that sometimes one *wanted* to know things for one's own comfort, even if they were trivial.

Chaama unyielding, grant patience.

Char's awareness of Iari sharpened suddenly. So Char was not terribly surprised when Winter Bite sent a burst of mecha code that meant: *Corso has retrieved the captain. They are in motion.*

Char adjusted their optics, aiming at the neefa byre. And yes, there they were, Corso and Iari moving down the path together. They paused, looked at the ridge, and then moved with greater speed into the camp. Char lost visual contact with them as they ducked among the rows of tents, reacquired it as they moved past one of the floodlamp-generator units.

And then Char noticed something else. *Personnel gathering near the southern perimeter,* they sent back to Winter Bite.

A pause, while Winter Bite (probably, this was another hunch) adjusted his sensor array and confirmed Char's report *and* relayed it to Corporal Dodri. Winter Bite had initially expressed discomfort at first with the idea of claiming Char's observations as his own, but he had soon realized the strategy.

Winter Bite felt blue on the channel, cold and sharp and clear. *Go on.*

Armed. Disorganized. Single tenju in command. They are proceeding up the hill with purpose.

Acknowledged. Then Winter Bite's cold silver-blue presence winked out. He would be able to describe the more general movements without Char's assistance. And, truth, Char had new things to concern them.

The tenju leader had directed the armed group to proceed two abreast almost straight up the hillside. It was similar to the path Geltrannen had taken when she led the Ettradens into the camp. It was an unnecessarily steep path, which suggested to Char some sort of trial or disciplinary exercise. Another hunch. They transmitted that to Winter Bite. Then they ceased all external movement. The group would not pass especially close, but organic eyes—weak in so many respects—were acute at detecting motion.

Then Char's sense of Iari flashed like a lens flare.

Char felt an unpleasant jolt of surprise, then guilt. They had been too focused on the approaching detachment of cultists. That was an unfortunate consequence of becoming an *I*. Char kept one optic focused on the group still toiling up the hill and trained the other on the camp, searching for Iari and—ah. The captain had crossed the perimeter, moving quickly, though not at synning speeds, in the wake of the departing group. It appeared as if she were following them, though she was neither calling out nor waving nor indicating that she wanted them to slow down. She was not, in fact, acting like she wanted them to notice her at all.

Char widened their focus.

Iari remained unnoticed by: the group climbing the hill.

Iari had been noticed by: (confirmed) two patrols, each approaching the same southern corner of the perimeter. One patrol was waving and pointing (and shouting, though Char did not spare the resources to attempt to discern the exact words); they were most of the way up the western edge of the perimeter, and could only see Iari cutting across the hillside. It was probable that because of the topography, that patrol could no longer see the group nearing the top of the hill. They might assume Iari was attempting to leave without permission.

The nearer patrol, the ones closer to Iari's crossing point, could see both Iari and the climbing group. Those guards were nudging each other, and one was pointing, but their attitudes were relaxed.

Then, without warning, the climbing group reached the crest of the hill and stopped.

Ptah, blind their sight.

Several of its members were hunched over, exhaling clouds of steam. The leader (tenju male body, gender unknown, tagged Leader) was threading through them, slapping shoulders. The group was approximately seventy-five meters away from Char, who probably looked like a small drift over a rock if anyone had noticed them at all.

Chaama, make me one with your bones.

The first guards had begun to run, still waving. They would see the group stopped on the ridge in a few seconds. Char calculated the probability *high* they would assume both that Iari's flight was intended to intercept that group, and that the group had stopped to wait for her.

Char did not think (another hunch) that Iari actually *wanted* to catch up with that group, and—indeed. Iari had slowed down significantly, an expression of dawning horror on her face.

It was too late. Leader noticed Iari, became stiff and alert. (Probability: potentially hostile.) Leader pushed through the group to emerge on the side closest to Iari, at the same time shifting the long-caster out of its shoulder sling.

Now, as Iari continued to approach—more much slowly—Leader gripped the weapon with both hands.

Char tightened their focus. Even at this slower pace, the captain was running like someone who ran all the time, easily and unbothered. Her features were disorganized, suspended between exaggerated distress, which Char knew must be false, and an eye-darting appraisal of the surrounding terrain.

With another unpleasant jolt, Char realized Iari must be looking for *them* (plural)—Winter Bite, Char, the corporal. Then Char realized that was *wishful thinking*; Iari could certainly not know that Char was near this location. Iari began altering her course toward an obviously shallower patch of hillside, as if she were tired or seeking an easier ascent. Char thought that this was a ruse: Iari was putting more of the group between her and Leader (and also moving away from Char).

Iari also had the entire group's attention now; Char scanned all the faces twice, to be certain. Their expressions were curious, mostly. No one seemed suspicious, except Leader, who was already pushing through the group to intercept Iari as she achieved, then crested, the ridgeline. She ran another ten meters or so before stopping, so that she would no longer be visible from the camp.

Leader, realizing what she had been doing, also moved over the ridgeline. And like a herd of neefa, the rest of the group followed.

Leader's grip on the 'caster shifted again, from loosely two-handed to business. Char heard the whine as he-she-they primed it.

"Stop there! Right fucking now."

Char decided they needed to show some more initiative. They muted their audio feed to all but emergency alert. Then they moved for the first time in eighteen hours, shaking the snow off their armor like diamonds.

This wasn't going to end well.

Iari stopped (right fucking now). Stared past the business end of a longcaster and at the guy holding it. Some snaggle-toothed tenju, unshaven, threadbare braids full of hooks, swaggering with delusions of drill sergeant. Iari had heard him yelling on her run up, little snatches of abuse caught on the wind. He *might've* been ex-army, but her bet was he'd watched too many war dramas.

She had everyone's attention now. Exactly *not* what she'd wanted. A dozen pairs of curious eyes. At least it looked like everyone had followed her over the ridge. If Snaggle shot her here, Corso wouldn't see it.

She flicked her gaze around. Lot of nothing back here, open snowfields and rolling hills. She had been hoping for a culvert. A convenient fold in the hillside. Somewhere to drop down and hide. All she saw was a flattish area with a berm set up on one end—a practice range, probably this lot's original destination, and it was on the opposite side of the group from where she was. She could try turning around, hoping for a convenient culvert, and make a run for it. Probably get Snaggle's bolt in her back if she tried it.

Right. Try talking, then.

"Sorry I'm late, Geltrannen sent me." She raised her hands with exaggerated slowness. "Geltrannen," she repeated, and then remembered to gasp like she'd run out of breath. "She. Sent me?"

Snaggle stepped away from the group, still pointing his weapon at her. "What's your name?"

"Iari."

"Iari. Iari. I-ar-i. Nope." Snaggle smirked. Lifted the 'caster to his cheek. "Gel didn't mention you, *Yar-ree*." He put a Windscar accent on it, like he needed her to know her name was southern, three syllables instead of two.

That was when Iari decided he was performing badass for his audience, that he didn't mean to shoot her as much as he did to scare her and probably humiliate her. This neefa-shit was her cue to gibber and apologize, and his cue to yell more abuse at her.

Sure. She could do that.

Or she could syn the short distance between them, take the fucking 'caster out of his hand, and feed the first bolt to him.

Iari beat the syn back, gulped a breath, tried to look dismayed. "But she said—I'm supposed to go with the group leaving after meal for 'caster practice? That's you, yeah?"

Snaggle's expression said she hadn't quite sold it. (Because she wasn't Corso.) "That's us. Yeah."

They stared at each other. Iari heard wind, the whine of a primed 'caster. One quiet voice in the faceless group say "oh shit" with undisguised anticipation.

And then: "Wait, no, Fergil—I know her. Hey, Iari."

Elements bless. Or curse. That was Bersk's voice, and Bersk pushing her way through the crowd, all cold-flushed skin and manic eyes. She looked—huh. Curious. Intrigued. Because, *right*, Bersk's Iari had been taciturn, Bersk's Iari would've just stared at Snaggle instead of offering up excuses.

Corso had been right. *Terrible* plan. So much for Hrok's passing unseen. She could try Ptah's fire and mayhem.

Iari let her hands drop. The knife she'd shoved up her right sleeve slid down a little. Not enough. She pulled her fist into her coat, began working the sweater cuff. She'd wanted that voidspit blade to stay secure and *not* come falling out, and it was doing exactly that, and *fuck.*

"She came in with Corso," Bersk was saying. "I *told* you about Corso. Iari's his cousin, from B-town. She's a surge-vet, too."

"B-town. *B-town.*" Snaggle said the name like it tasted bad. "The fuck we need a *southerner* for."

Bersk trilled a laugh. "Oh, come on, Fergil. She can shoot. Corso said—"

Fergil stood there, making doubtful noises every time Bersk took a breath. Iari avoided his gaze and stared instead past him, the whole group, while she kept working at the knife. The last time she'd crossed this terrain, she'd been marching after Geltrannen. Her impression then: a winter's worth of snowfall made things *look* smooth. The buried reality was bumps that caught toes and surprise dips that sank you to your hip, then tried to steal boots. Daylight (greylight) didn't improve her opinion. But it did look like just over this ridge, to the west, that flattish area she'd seen— either had very regular, even snowdrifts stretching one side, or a series of snow-covered berms. Looked like a place that you went to shoot 'casters. To the southwest, a steep-sided creek bed trailed out of the camp valley. That was a place she could hide. If she could get to it. Which she wouldn't, because even if she talked Snaggle into letting her join this party, she'd never talk him into letting her walk away again.

Yeah. Terrible plan. She'd tell Corso so, if she lived through it.

And she also didn't know where Dodri, Winter Bite, and Char were, and that was starting to worry her. Either they were *very* good at hiding, or they weren't here at all. She had visions of Brood coming at them, leftovers from Ettrad, and—

Snaggle lunged at her.

Iari dropped her hips, bent her knees, started a deflective

shield-arm deflection before her brain caught on that she was probably supposed to act startled. Maybe trip and fall backward. Instead she fought the syn back to *stand down* and stayed where she was, left arm outstretched. The movement was enough to *finally* dislodge the voidspit knife in her sleeve. She felt the sheath slip, and the handle bumped into the heel of her curled right hand.

Someone in the group said, "Heh."

"See? She can fight, too." Bersk looked thoughtful. "I think Corso said she was cartel, back in B-town. Right, Iari?"

Oh Elements, had Corso said that? Iari hitched her shoulder, noncommittal. The syn kept trying to focus on Fergil, reading him as the threat. And then it caught a new motion, dragged Iari's attention that way—

Ptah's burning *eye.*

Char burst up out of the snow just below the crest of the hill to the east and started running toward Iari. No, *charging.* Silent, though, like a snowslide, if snowslides ran across and up hills.

Iari snapped her gaze back to Fergil.

Who sneered, "Huh. Well. All right, but where's your *badge,* Yar-ee?"

Iari made a decision. Terrible plan, getting more terrible.

"Templar!" Iari said, and pointed, left-handed, at Char.

Everyone looked.

Iari shoved forward, slammed her right shoulder into Fergil and sent him reeling, same time she grabbed his 'caster with her left hand, close to the stock, and jerked it out of his hands. She reversed direction and cracked the butt into his face. Fergil fell back—dead, unconscious, didn't matter, just bleeding and blessedly *quiet.*

The group had not been tight to begin with; now they were spreading out more as they saw something running at them.

Templar had gotten a couple to prudently drop onto one knee, trying to sight their 'casters on Char. Maybe a third of them had elected to charge, baying like wolves after a wounded bear. The rest weren't sure what to do. Milling, looking at each other and the approaching Char, who was beginning to take on bipedal dimensions.

Except Bersk. Bersk was looking at Iari, and her eyes were hard and bright.

"I knew it," said Bersk. "I *knew*—"

Iari didn't wait to hear what Bersk knew. She threw Fergil's 'caster at Bersk's head, drew the knife out of her right sleeve, flipped the blade and folded it against her forearm. She followed her throw and slammed into Bersk, bore her over. Coats and sweaters were no kind of armor, but they'd tangle a blade. Iari jammed her right forearm into Bersk's chest, slid it up, caught Bersk's chin and pushed it back. Then they landed, Iari on top, and Iari flipped the knife again and buried it under Bersk's jaw.

Fast. Quiet. No one even turned around.

Iari left the knife there, shoved to her feet. Someone had started firing; she could hear the *pop* of 'casters, *please* they couldn't hear that down in the voidspit camp, or she'd have the whole place rushing up here. She swung Corso's 'caster off her shoulder, and then she let the syn go and charged right at Char.

The snow wasn't any less grabby on her boots, she still sank deep, but it didn't matter. The syn protected her from fatigue, carried her over the hollow awareness of how long it'd been since food or sleep. She had a bad moment where, in the churned-up clouds of snow, she thought that it *wasn't* Char coming at her. That it was some other riev, mad-eyed like Sawtooth, rotting with Brood. But then she saw the polysteel graft that was Char's right arm, and the red flash of hexwork on Char's armor as the 'caster bolts slewed off and burst in the snow. As she got close, Iari dropped onto her hip, digging up snow in a furrow and sliding, scrubbing off speed and staying out of the line of stray bolts.

Char pounded past her. Behind her, Iari heard stray yelps of "Riev!" quickly, ominously, cut off.

Then friction did its work and Iari twisted and flipped back onto one knee, primed Corso's 'caster. Raised and sighted and *fired*, just as Char met the first line of attackers.

Swift-running Mishka.

Iari had joined the army during the voidspit surge. You trained to fight, sure, to kill, *sure*—that's why there were sims. It had been Brood on the other end of her 'caster then, and Brood had a way of warping the best shots out of true. The Aedis trained you to fight more than Brood, but even then—you had to get spaceside postings, patrols in the void wastes where pirates and smugglers hid, to meet *people* in combat. She never had, until the ruins; and then she'd killed in the battle-rig, with her axe and her shield, like they were Brood. Bersk had been her first hand-to-hand fight. And these very *clearly* people were the first she'd ever shot.

But the sim training held. Mishka's mercy, she didn't flinch, didn't miss.

She had a moment's panic for Char; riev couldn't kill *people*, the wichu had artificed that directive after the Accords—but Char didn't seem to be struggling with it. Maybe the templar oaths counted as their primary programming now. Or the wichu had lied. (Gaer would say that, when she told him about this.)

(No. Gaer would say the riev had been *made* to kill people. His people.)

Char was not having trouble, and Iari's hands and eyes knew what to do. They did their work, picking off those in the rear, the ones who'd come late to the charge. The ones who realized that there was a riev, and they should go back and get help. The ones who finally realized one of their own had turned on them.

At least this had happened *over* the ridgeline. The only person left alive now was Fergil, limp in the snow. (Maybe dead. Maybe she'd hit him that hard.) And he could stay there and freeze.

CHAPTER TWENTY-THREE

C orso told himself he wouldn't look back. That Iari could handle herself. That she'd be *fine*, even if the whole of her plan rested on finding a place to hide when she crested that hill *before* the people she was pretending to chase saw her coming. The hiding part wouldn't be easy; Windscar was a lot of empty. But it was the part before that had him worried.

So he kept stopping every few meters and finding an excuse to look up and back. Which meant that he saw when the exiting group stopped on the ridgeline, *right* on it, so that no one who looked up could miss them. He swore under his breath and made himself walk a little more before he looked back again. Iari had made contact, which she hadn't wanted to do; now she'd have to talk her way through, which—oh ancestors and Elements. Iari wasn't a talker. But she was marching right at the group, so maybe she'd at least get them over the ridge before anything happened.

And there was not a voidspit thing he could do from *here*.

At least the guards walking the camp's perimeter who'd been yelling and pointing at her had stopped; they'd all gone back to their business. *That* was something.

The first 'caster shot made him jump, and he looked *again*— but the group had moved over the ridgeline. There were a couple more shots, but no one down *here* seemed upset, and beyond that, he had no idea. The 'caster fire continued: methodical, regular, like someone practicing shots. Which . . . all right. Maybe that's what was happening. It didn't sound disorganized enough to be shoot-at-a-fleeing-Iari.

Corso turned around again, *last time*, jammed his hands into his coat, dropped his chin. As for *his* plan: keep walking. Go back to his tent. Shit, he'd given up his 'caster. Everyone *else* had a 'caster. He weighed the wisdom of going back to the quartermaster against seeing if anyone here was stupid enough to leave their weapon alone and untended. Bet on the latter. He'd seen cartel needle-dens with more discipline that this place.

He tried his assigned tent first. Got his nose in the flap and realized the place was occupied. He retreated, and no one called after him.

The 'caster-fire had stopped. No one seemed concerned. No one came running over the ridge. Whatever had happened over there, it was over. Iari was *fine*, and when they got out of this, she'd tell him how her terrible plan had worked, and he'd pretend to be irritated but really, he'd be fucking ecstatic.

Corso spent the next hour or so prowling the camp, trying to avoid anyone who might recognize him—Bersk, Gel, the poor kid at the mess—and generally trying to look like he had places to go and was going there. What he learned was the whole camp of Axorchal One-Eye looked like it was coming apart. Not physically, but—there was a distinct lack of people in charge doing people-in-charge things. A lack of structure. Too much idle time for the people *in* the camp. There were a lot of dice games. Card games. People just standing and talking, wandering around, drifting into and out of conversations that Corso heard in snatches.

Some of it was the same voidspit he'd heard from Bersk and

Trammen—anti-Aedian, anti-Confederation. One woman expounding at length about the time she *met* Axorchal, which got Corso to stop and listen. It sounded mostly like neefa-shit, until she described the altar, and how she'd seen a great hole open up over it, and seen people on the other side. She'd claimed to have seen her brother over there, beckoning to her—and *he'd* died in Rusak when a pack of boneless attacked. ("He was a believer, he was," and she clutched at her badge.)

That sounded like a portal, though Corso had doubts about the risen dead on the other side. Unfortunately True Believer's Sister didn't have much to say about Axorchal himself, except her admiration for his power. Corso wanted to ask if she knew how those portals opened—that the altars ran on *blood*, and unless there were a bunch of neefa or goats around here he hadn't seen yet, that blood was probably *people*.

He didn't, of course. He drifted away from that fevered recounting and attached himself instead to a dice game conducted on a crate in the alley between rows of tents, like people were trying to hide, but not really.

He watched a few games. Then, when he was pretty sure no one was worried about him, he leaned down and asked, "You know what's going on?" like he expected them to know what he meant. (That worked more often than it should. Either people *did* know, or what they *thought* he meant proved instructive.)

"Nope," said the winner, who was busy counting the coins in their palm. They cocked a dark eye at him. "All I know, the watchers aren't watching." They tapped their left eyebrow.

Okay. Guess that could indicate a One-Eye helmet. Corso repeated the gesture. "We know where they are? I mean, did they *go* somewhere?"

Winner shrugged. Loser snorted. "Into Axorchal's yurt a

couple days back, and they didn't come out, so I hope they're ripping the *shit* out of Windscar right now."

Because a handful of mutant tenju would take down an entire Aedis. Then Corso thought about Homer, and hoped he saw Loser again later.

And shit, he still needed a 'caster. He was going to walk away then, when one of the other spectators said, "Yeah, but *someone* came back. I heard yelling in the yurt. And then they dragged people out. I think they were templars."

"Neefa-shit," said Winner. But his eyes sharpened like spears.

"Templars?" Corso dragged the word out. "What, in their *battle-rigs?* That'd be heavy. And anyway, the fuck would they even get here?"

"If we got 'em," said Winner, clearly not interested in the *how* of things, "I wanna see 'em staked out and dyin' slow."

Corso drifted away then, leaving the dicers and their audience to argue about what one should do with captive templars. The cold knot he'd been carrying in his guts thawed a little. Iari thought Luki and Llian had survived, but now Corso had found someone else who thought they had, too. That didn't explain how two presumably pissed-off templars been moved from the yurt to the outbuilding (if that's where they were; that was still Iari's hunch he had to confirm), or where their battle-rigs were. And yeah, the whole story could be voidspit, but—he didn't think so.

He stepped out from the shelter of the clandestine dice game into a gust of shit-smell. That put the wind coming out of the northwest, which probably meant another storm coming. He cocked an eye at the sky. Pewter-grey, solid clouds. That knot in his gut tightened up again. Storms in Windscar were normal in winter, constant. No reason this storm should mean anything except a few hours to a day of latrine-stink as a harbinger of more slagging snow. Except it didn't *feel* right. None of this did.

But wait. If someone was going to leave a 'caster unattended, the latrines might be the place.

Corso was coming back from the latrines with his new 'caster when the first alarm went up: yelling from the south end of camp. The direction Iari had gone *hours* ago now.

Shit. *Shit.* Corso jogged that direction, acting like someone intending to See What Was Wrong and Deal With It. A few people joined him, but most stayed where they were, craning necks and rising up on toes but not running at the crisis.

Might be a problem, Corso thought, if Axorchal ever meant to attack an *Aedis*. Maybe that's what his half-riev were for. A cure for cowardice.

He was half-expecting to come around and get a look at the hillside and see Iari and Char and Winter Bite and Dodri charging down, even though it was still daylight and they were supposed to wait for dusk. Instead he saw a pair of camp guards running downhill as if boneless were chasing them, slipping, falling, getting up again. Yelling the whole time, both of them, though the closer they got, the more Corso thought that yelling was alarm, not fear. And there wasn't anything chasing them, so—they'd seen something up over the ridge that upset them. That they'd gone up there at all broke all the patterns Corso had seen so far.

So just *guess*: that group that Iari had chased up there hadn't come back when they were supposed to, and someone had gone to check, and now—

An alarm, an *actual* alarm, ripped through the camp. Corso had no idea where *that* was coming from, didn't matter: that siren got people mobilizing, diving back into tents and coming out with 'casters. Some of them headed toward the mess tent, others toward points on the perimeter.

It looked like an emergency drill rather than a muster of troops—that kind of urgency, eyerolling and moving not a bit too quickly. Corso took some comfort in that. But nothing about this situation was *good*: either Iari's awful plan had succumbed to entropy (Corso's prediction), or there was some new, fresh voidspit about to come down on them.

The good thing about camp-wide alarms was no one thought it was weird when you ran places. Corso circumvented the mess tent (way too many people) and came around to the east, trotted past the farmhouse, took a hard turn and sprinted around to the back of the barn. He glanced up—the byre doors were open, probably meant the Ettradens were loose in the world—and nearly smacked into a tarp-covered ATV. He dodged around it, dropped down beside it. He briefly considered ducking *under* the tarp, but hiding wasn't the goal.

Yeah, okay, but what *was*? Iari'd said she'd attack at dusk, and this wasn't. This camp-wide alarm also might not have anything to *do* with her. (It did. He'd bet both tusks on it.) If she waited for sunset, or—or *darker grey*, because what sun?—the camp would already be alert. Corso wasn't sure they'd be ready for charging riev (because no one ever was), but they wouldn't be caught playing dice, either.

Iari'd told him to wait, but—maybe he could get to Luki and Llian *now*. Or get into Axorchal's yurt. Or *do* something besides wait for somebody to find him back here. Corso scooted around the edge of the ATV (snow all around it, snow on the tarp, this poor thing hadn't been out in a while), then continued along the barn wall. He paused at the corner and peered around.

From this angle—ugh. He couldn't see the front of the yurt, but the altar had been in the back half, and that was the side facing him now. He wanted to get close to that altar like he wanted to wrestle a pack of boneless *naked*, but too bad for him.

He sprinted across the snow (leaving tracks, could not be helped) and tucked up against the back of the yurt. You would *think* that someone styling themselves Axorchal One-Eye, who was promising to reclaim Tanis for the tenju or some neefa-shit, would've made an old-style yurt. Hide. Bone. Not nanoforged polymer. Corso slid one of his monofils out of his boot, slung his new (inferior) 'caster across his shoulder, and crouched down where the yurt met the snow. He prodded with the monofil's tip. Puncture resistant. Tear resistant. He *could* cut his way in, but it'd take a while. The yurt was probably not proof against 'caster bolts, though.

Or whitefire axes. Or riev.

Which, okay, *fine*. The altar was Iari's problem. He stowed the monofil and slipped along the side of the yurt. The peaked roof kept the snow from collecting up there, but where traces had melted, the water had beaded, then frozen. In a few places it had dripped down into daggers of ice.

The alarm was still howling. When Corso stuck his face around the edge of the yurt, the sound hit like a physical blow. So did the latrine smell; the wind had picked up, and gotten wetter besides. Definitely another slagging storm, sooner than later, and a big one.

He soft-footed around the corner, ready to cough up some neefa-shit story why he was back there. No one came out of the yurt. No one passed by the front. No one back here at all. He could hear, between alarm blasts, the swell of voices from the mess tent.

He could see movement that way, too. That was the central meeting place where everyone seemed to be gathering. That was probably where Axorchal, or whoever was pretending to be Axorchal, would show up and dispense divine orders.

Let that *not* be where they sacrificed their templar prisoners to feed the altar to open the Weep and bring on another surge.

Void and dust, he wished he hadn't thought that. In a vid, that's exactly what would happen. Dramatic villain speech, then dramatic murder, interrupted by the heroes (or not, if it was that kind of story). Corso couldn't see inside the mess tent from here. Just the canvas kitchen walls, steam leaking around the flap. The Suspicious Shed, Iari's alleged prison, sat by itself another few meters west. There *was* a conspicuous path between the altar-yurt and the shed. Not footprints, exactly. More like something, or someone, had been dragged. Gouges, furrows, partly filled in by the last snowfall.

Iari'd said there were One-Eye guards out front. Corso leaned to look. Nope. Not far enough. He leaned farther, getting down on his knees in the snow and walking his hands out. He could see the front of the shed, but there wasn't anyone outside. It was . . . unguarded.

Wait, Iari had said, but her terrible plan wasn't going to work now that the camp was alert (though it would never have worked). And he might be able to get in that shed and . . . do something. Besides wait for someone to catch him.

Corso looked both ways like he was crossing a voidspit street in B-town, and then darted to the shed. Stone-and-sod walls, old, more authentic than polymer yurts, and probably miserable inside. He edged along the side, toward the front.

The alarm cut off suddenly, and Corso's heart damn near climbed out his throat. His ears rang in its absence. The wind had picked up, humming and whining around any barrier, however small. It snatched Corso's breath, scattered the steam of it, and hissed around the contours of the badge on his collar.

No one came running out of anywhere to challenge him.

The clouds had darkened even further. The floodlamps lit up suddenly, with a hollow pop and the low grind of generators. Their light didn't stretch this far back. Wouldn't, even if Corso got round to the shed door. Which—he held his breath, locked his jaw, and moved—he just had.

The shed lay in shadow, and *he* was in shadow, and maybe the Elements were paying slagging attention.

The shed door looked as old as the rest of the building. Wood bound with metal, both pitted and scarred. It had a latch and an actual metal padlock, the kind that needed a key. Corso couldn't see any hexes, but he was sure they were there; you didn't trust important things to a *padlock's* security.

Void and *dust*, this was stupid.

He drew the monofil again, wedged it into the padlock and twisted. You had to be careful with monofils. They'd go through damn near anything with a little patience, but they were brittle. The padlock came off in Corso's other hand. He dropped it into his pocket. Stowed the monofil. Then he grabbed the latch and pushed.

The smell hit him first: a cloud of shit, piss, vomit. Blood under that, metallic and rank. It was completely dark in there. Black and *beyond* black, and the open door wasn't letting anything in. Or the dark was pushing the light back.

Yeah. Hexes. Definitely. Like the ones in the fucking ruins. The hallucinatory fog.

He thought he heard murmuring in there, the rasp you got when you had no spit left, just sand and dust in your mouth. *Two* voices, though he couldn't make out any words.

The wind coiled past Corso's legs, blowing into the shed, and he found his mouth very dry of a sudden. He swallowed. Managed a quiet, "Hey. Who's in there?"

Which would go down as a stupid question, because unless someone answered *I am the ghost of Jich'e'enfe* it didn't matter who they were. Corso wasn't going to leave anyone in there.

The murmuring stopped. Someone's breath caught in that darkness. Someone else let a breath out, hard.

Then out of the dark: "Corso? That you?"

Luki. Hoarse and raggedy and shaky-voiced, but alive. Corso almost sat down, the relief hit so hard. "Yeah. Llian with you?"

Luki caught her breath. "Oh Elements, Mishka's mercy—yes. *Yes.* Wait—this place is hexed, stay out! It's . . . bad. Like the tunnels. There's someone else in here, I think they're dead. They were screaming, now they're not. We're in a cage. Me and Llian. Don't know where the rigs are."

Corso winced. "How many cages?"

"I don't know. It's just *dark.*" He heard the threads of her control strain. "The captain . . . ?"

"On her way." Though not fast enough. Corso wasn't going to leave Luki and Llian in *cages.* Fuck that, fuck the hexes. He'd lived through Jich'e'enfe and her voidspit Brood. He wasn't afraid of the fucking *dark.*

Corso took a breath, held it. Slid a foot across the threshold. He braced for something—cold, shock, pain. Nothing. He edged a little farther, sliding along the solid weight of the door. His left leg disappeared to the knee. Then his left wrist, forearm, elbow—

A tiny flash caught the corner of his eye. He looked, saw that it was the One-Eye badge on his collar, gleaming like an oil slick in sunlight. Nausea rolled over him, heat and cold under his skin. He tasted petrichor, acid, blood.

He wanted to—wait. He *should* want to rip that badge off and run screaming. And the expected fear did surge up, for one brief, cold second. Then it turned hot, red-and-white rage wiping it away. He wanted to rip *something* apart. He wanted to hurt something, someone, he just needed, he needed—

He shoved off the door, rage warring with panic, and slammed himself face first into the frame on the other side. He heard the crack of wood into flesh-covered bone first, *then* he felt it: stunning pain, splitting skin on his forehead.

The rage blew away on a gust of pain. Corso reached without thinking, grabbed the badge, tore it off. *Hurled* it into the snow.

Hexed, everything, some voidspit *witchery*. The slagging *badge*. The shed. He wanted to peel his skin off and scrub it clean from the inside, which—no, *no*, that wasn't rational. *Breathe, you neefa.*

"Corso?" Luki's voice slipped out of the dark.

"Yeah. *Yeah.*" He wiped the back of his mouth. He didn't know if it was the badge that'd done that, made him killing mad, or the hexes inside the building, or both. He *did* know that if Luki and Llian were still talking (at least Luki was), it was probably because their templar nanomecha were working their own fucking magic.

"I'll be back. Luki, I *swear.*" Corso pushed the door shut before she could answer. Turned and walked carefully along the gouged trail toward the yurt. The marks weren't deep enough to have been made by battle-rigs. They must have stripped Luki and Llian *before* they moved them. So the rigs could be in the altar-yurt. If he got one, he could—put it on. And, and *use* it to go back in there with protection, with the helmet sealed.

Corso knew he wasn't thinking very clearly. Fucking hexes. This was a dumb idea, up there with Iari's terrible plan for sheer terribleness. But he couldn't just leave Luki and Llian.

He heard a groundswell of new noise from the mess tent, pushing against him like a wave. A lot of people yammering at once. And then shouting, the sort of cadence that said *your attention, please.*

At least he had a distraction.

Corso got to the yurt's door. It was unguarded, like last time. And—that made no sense, did it? Leave the altar unguarded? Except who'd fuck with that thing? Or, awful thought—Axorchal was in there. The arithmancer pretending to be Axorchal. He was staying in the room with the fucking altar. That would make a better guard than some brain-rotted One-Eye.

The noise from the mess tent had changed and solidified again, into voices united and chanting . . . a name? Oh, *ha,* Axorchal the arithmancer wasn't going to be in the yurt. He was going to be in that mess tent, doing what pretend-gods did, which seemed to be getting people to chant at him like he was some kind of celebrity and they were his fans.

Or he was going to come out of that yurt *right now* because that chanting was his cue. Corso froze, hand over the latch. Then he drew a deep breath. Held it. Let it go. Fucking *settle* his shit, shake it off, do not *lose it.*

Corso closed his eyes. That dark helped.

And that was why he did not notice Geltrannen until it was too late.

Dodri had stashed the battle-rigs almost five klicks outside the camp, in the middle of a thicket of thornleaves. It was a smart place to hide them. The soil around was rocky, and also wind-scoured, so tracks wouldn't show. And the thornleaves themselves were proof against casual snooping. Even if the cultists *had* wandered this far out, they would've avoided the trees.

"I will retrieve the rigs," said Char, and pushed their way inside. The eponymous thorns dragged across Char's armor like slicer claws, like boneless—a sound that set Iari's teeth grinding, and made her very glad Char had insisted on coming with her.

("Just give me directions, Char. Dodri and Winter Bite—"

"Do not require my assistance, Captain. You do.")

Iari had let it go because there wasn't time to argue, with a dozen bodies cooling and congealing on the backside of the hill right now. Because, truth, she had some doubts she'd survive alone. She and Char had dispatched the patrol and then made clear tracks *away*, traipsing through one boulder field and a hot spring-fed *marsh* to disguise any tracks, Char carrying her for that last bit, because riev didn't mind getting wet and people died of it in Windscar winters. That was when Iari had tried the second time to send Char back—because by now someone *must* have investigated the 'caster fire, or noticed that people hadn't come back from target practice. Someone *must* have found the bodies.

Char had not even argued that time. They had simply stomped on ahead.

And now they were looking just the littlest bit smug, as Iari got into her battle-rig the way templars did in the field, without racks and harnesses and, oh, solid *floors*. A lot of separate panels, a lot of swearing and shivering, honest-to-Elements *gratitude* for the lessons of the surge. She'd done this same thing in freezing rain, in mud, on voidspit battlefields while people died around her. In front of a copse of thornleaves in the middle of Windscar, during winter—that was easy. It wasn't even snowing.

She wasn't at all sure that Corso could perform the same

miracle. She divided his battle-rig up anyway, between her and Char, to bring back. Even if Corso couldn't get into it, Luki could. Llian might be too small, so Iari brought her salvaged clothing back, coat and sweater, trousers and boots. Those would be too big, too, but at least they'd be warm.

The return to the camp was far easier. Warmer, *faster*. The syn tingled happily, reunited with the needle-socket and the battle-rig. It was like the syn was getting a personality.

There was an idea she didn't want to examine.

Iari followed Char's lead around a circuitous, tortured perimeter, half a klick away from the camp, that never got within sightline. She couldn't see what was going on down there, but she *could* see that the floodlamps were lit, even though it was still (technically) daylight. That—might be nothing. Might be a response to the lowering gloom. Or it might mean they'd found the slaughter and gone on high alert.

Iari wasn't a bit surprised when her comms didn't work the first time she tried, or the second, or the third. Battle-rigs had a range, and Brood or fissure activity could significantly shorten it. But she asked Char anyway,

"You sense any fissures?"

"No." Then, "Winter Bite reports that Corso is in jeopardy."

There were a couple things wrong with that statement. Well. One thing wrong—Corso in trouble, Ptah's burning eye—and one thing unexpected. Winter Bite shouldn't be able to *say* anything to Char, because Winter Bite didn't have transmitting comms, except to battle-rigs, and *she* hadn't gotten data.

Iari stared hard at Char's back, pounding along as the riev broke trail. "Dodri okay?"

"Yes."

"What's happened to Corso?"

Char hesitated. "Geltrannen has made hostile contact. There is significant aetheric interference from the camp; Winter Bite believes it is the altar, though he cannot identify its location."

"I know where it is. Can you tell him it's the western yurt? The one closest to the place I think they're keeping our templars?"

A beat. "Yes. He acknowledges."

So the transmission went two ways. Huh. "We're going to talk about this later, Char. How you two are conversing."

"Yes, Captain. Dodri does not know."

"Understood. Do you want to tell her or—"

—and then Dodri's voice burst through the comms in Iari's helmet, and Dodri's biometrics lit up. "—tain? Do you hear me?"

Oh blessed Elements. "I'm here. Report."

She got Dodri's version, significantly less compact than Char's. Iari let her talk. She reckoned a young corporal needed that reassurance that she wasn't alone in command. That whatever went sideways from here, it wasn't her fault.

Oh no. It's all mine.

Terrible fucking plan, all the way.

By the time she and Char got to Dodri's position on the northern ridge, Iari knew that the camp was on high alert. That Fergil, of all fucking people, had managed to drag himself over the slagging ridge and far enough down the hill that one of the perimeter patrols had noticed him. *Then* the alarm had gone up, which had involved a siren and all the floodlamps coming on, and a mass gathering of what appeared to be everyone—even the byre's residents—under the mess tent.

(Iari could hear *that* situation herself right now, trickling through the ex-comms. Chanting, raggedy and enthusiastic, like it was a stadium full of spectators at an innebande match. Ax-orchal. Merciful Mishka.)

Corso (Dodri said) had gotten himself to the shed, gotten the door open—and retreated. And then he'd gone for the yurt with the altar (Iari had sworn, hearing that. What in five vakari hells was he thinking?) and been caught on the threshold by Geltrannen.

"She took him east," Dodri said. "Behind the farmhouse, behind the other yurt, like she was trying not to be seen. They went into that last line of tents. She's got a weapon on him—Winter Bite thinks it's a monofil—and he's not fighting back."

"You see *which* tent?"

"First one on the right. First one in the row." Dodri's voice was anxious. "I didn't want to break cover to interfere."

"You did right."

Iari amped the magnification on her HUD, like that would help at all. Just a tent. Corso was definitely in trouble. But—she switched focus—he'd also left the shed door ajar. She could see the broken padlock. And there was that voidspit altar—

"Captain," said Winter Bite. He had his appendages extended. "Movement at the altar-yurt."

Huh. Look at that: two tenju came out, holding a crate suspended from two long metal poles. Looked heavy: the poles bowed toward the crate, and the crate itself barely cleared the snow. And behind them, a beat later: a figure emerged, tall even from this distance. Robed, or maybe just a long coat: something skirted, anyway, that hid their legs. No hood, no hat; long dark braids glittering with hooks hung down their back. They wore a single metal glove. An asymmetrical helmet, more elaborate than the others Iari had seen. Probably a cabochon on the front, masquerading as an eye.

Oh, just *guess* who this neefa was.

Insurgents with delusions of godhood. Small wonder their wichu allies had balked. The wichu as a people did not trust religion, having long memory of life under the Protectorate's orthodoxy. They didn't trust the Aedis for that same reason, for all that they worked alongside it—and those were the Confederation wichu. The insurgents like Jich'e'enfe might've *thought* it was smart to fight religion with more fanatics, but someone claiming actual godhood might have changed their mind.

But *someone* had to have trained this Axorchal mock-up in arithmancy. The godhood wasn't real. The skill *was*. Jich'e'enfe might've taught him, but this kind of skill—the kind that Jich'e'enfe had possessed, the kind *Gaer* had—that took years. More than a handful of years, anyway.

The hexes on Winter Bite's outstretched appendage began to glow, first faintly, then furiously red. So when he said, "The altar is in that crate," Iari was not surprised.

But: "Gaer said you couldn't move portals around."

"It does not feel like a portal," said Winter Bite.

"Can you be more specific?"

"No . . ." Winter Bite cranked his head around to look at Char.

Who said, "It feels more like the altar in B-town, *when* it was in B-town. Not like it felt in the ruins."

"So more like it's going to open a Brood fissure than operate a portal," Iari said, for Dodri's benefit.

The situation had been urgent. Now it was just getting worse. She'd counted on Corso to help rescue Luki and Llian while she handled the altar.

But now . . .

"Char, I need you to get down to that camp there and start wrecking things. Let's interrupt *whatever* Axorchal's up to in the tent. Dodri, once Char's engaged, you and I are going to see if we can retrieve Luki and Llian. Once we have them—Dodri, you bring them up here, to Winter Bite. Get someone in Corso's rig. Then get out. All of you fall back to Windscar. You do *not* wait for us. You go. Is that clear? I'll go see about Corso."

"Yes sir." Dodri didn't sound happy.

"You want me to wait here?" Winter Bite didn't either.

"You've got perspective. You keep"—Iari waved at his appendages—"those on alert. Help Char avoid any mobs. Guide them. If it all goes bad—you get out, *your judgment*, and make sure word gets to Keawe. Any questions?"

Dodri audibly clipped off asking *how* Winter Bite would guide Char. Which, fine, it was a fair question, but now wasn't the time.

"No, Captain." Winter Bite sounded happier.

"No, sir." Dodri didn't.

"Captain." Char made it both acknowledgement and query.

"Go," Iari told them. "Break things."

"Yes." And Char melted away, entirely too fast and too quietly for someone as big as they were.

Then it was wait, wait, until a dull *boom* rolled across the base camp. It sounded like one of those round metal drums Iari had heard a million times at one of Gaer's live music events, the kind that shivered through your guts and bones.

Or like the sound a power cell might make if it ruptured. The southernmost floodlamp died.

But then—nothing happened. One minute, two . . . slagging *nothing*. There seemed to be very few people still moving around. Everyone really *did* seem to be in that mess tent.

That seemed bad. Blood powered altars. If everyone was in there—that was a lot of blood.

Iari's guts fell. She swallowed dust and asked, "Winter Bite? What *are* they doing?"

The hexes on his appendages were steadily, furiously red now. "I believe the altar is no longer crated. Its aetheric presence is much stronger. There are also new fluctuations in the aether which are *not* like a portal, but which I can otherwise not identify. Perhaps they are a fissure. Also, there is chanting. A single name. Axorchal. The chant commenced when the arithmancer entered the tent. The spike in aetheric activity began shortly thereafter."

Iari wished again (forever) for Gaer. "Is there *any* response from *anyone* to what Char's doing?"

"Very little. The perimeter guards nearest that floodlamp are responding, but they are not moving with urgency."

"Probably think it's just a blown generator." Generators were hexed to avoid catastrophic explosions, but still, someone should've noticed. Blame the nominal daylight, when the absence of flood-lamps wasn't a crisis. Blame shit discipline.

Iari stood, glad of the rig's support. She was *tired*. Nothing like real sleep for days now, just the syn holding her upright. Dodri, at least, had gotten some rest up here (had admitted it, looking guilty). She had hoped for mayhem to make a distraction. At least for that mess tent to empty out a little. At *least* for the other three quadrants' patrols to move toward Char's position. She didn't doubt the battle-rigs' ability to get her and Dodri down that very steep hill fast and intact. But getting back *up*, especially with wounded . . . Iari looked at Corso's battle-rig, which she and Char had brought back from the stash-point. She was counting on Luki to be healthy enough to wear that slagging thing. If Luki *wasn't*—

The second floodlamp popped, this one on the eastern quadrant: *boom* and a burst of sparks just like the last one. This time

Iari could actually *see* the perimeter guards react; one set began running (jogging, really) toward the second floodlamp, which suddenly exploded in a fireball that ignited the pole and everything else in a couple meters' radius.

Dodri let out a little whoop.

Time to go.

"Move," Iari said, and then led by example.

Don't die, Corso, you neefa. I'm coming.

CHAPTER TWENTY-FOUR

G aer perched on the wall of the Windscar Aedis, partly because he could do so unescorted (that surprised him) and partly because it meant anyone wanting to talk to him had to work for the privilege. That was almost certainly why Keawe hadn't come up here yet (and not that she had nothing to say to him). *Certainly* why Tobin hadn't. Which was unfair: Tobin absolutely would climb to the top of Aedis walls if he needed a conversation. He clearly did *not*.

But if Gaer were honest with at least himself, he was up here to do what he'd come to this voidspit planet to do in the *first* place: observe the fissure. He was—no, he *had been*—an ambassador officially, but part of those duties—again, officially—had included his expertise as an arithmancer. That had been the *setatir* draw of this miserable planet. A fissure to observe firsthand. The whole jagged, fractured line of it, with its offshoots and its tendrils. It—that fissure—had made the rest of this hinterlands posting bearable.

Until Iari. That, she—he had not expected a friendship. Not with a templar at all, much less *that* templar, who preferred cats to people and for all her reverence for Jareth's *Meditations* did not seem to understand that fear was a necessary component of courage. He had fretted (briefly, when he'd imagined a posting *after* B-town's Aedis) that he would miss her and her long-suffering escort around B-town's deficient nightlife. (Would she miss him? Ah, hard to say. Probably. She might name a cat after him.) His seconding to the Aedis had seemed, if not permanent, at least a way to prolong their association.

Now she was going to get herself *setatir* killed, and there was no *setatir* point in being *here* if she was not.

Which was why he'd asked Notch to come see him: to collect on those promised *thanks* and leverage them into actual, useful action. Gaer wanted Iari back alive. That, and because this way, Notch had to climb a great many stairs. That was a little bit unkind on the surface (and a part of Gaer reveled in that), but it was also a firsthand opportunity to see how his newly evolved nano-mecha were working. If Notch collapsed on the stairs, then Gaer had been wrong, and Jich'e'enfe was *still* the better arithmancer, even dead.

(If Notch collapsed on the stairs, Iffy would march up and throw Gaer off the wall herself.)

And here Notch came now, out of the hospice doors—Iffy having wrangled a discharge, Gaer wasn't sure how. (*Trust me*, she'd said, and he had.) The lieutenant clomped across the courtyard, past *Rishi's* now-righted bulk. The aethership's repulsor coils glowed with dim power sufficient to keep her upright. The gangplank stretched down from the primary hatch, though the hatch itself was closed. *Rishi* could get to the k'bal ruins in half the time it would take a hopper. *Rishi* could get to the altar's last known coordinates in about that same time.

Where Iari must be, by now, and probably up to her chin in trouble. And hexes. She had Char and Winter Bite, sure, and Corso, *fine*, but they weren't arithmancers.

Notch went into the stair-tower, and Gaer turned his attention over the wall, to the north. The Weep fissure was visible tonight, though not to a naked eye. A wall of clouds stood across the northern horizon, significantly closer than the fissure, blocking the view. It looked like another of Windscar's ubiquitous storms. It also looked like that storm had stalled out over what Gaer's consultations with local maps told him was a small valley that, come spring, would spawn a few run-off creeks until the snow melted. There had *been* (this was according to an older atlas, attached to a land survey attached to an archive from the surge) a farmstead up there, some wealthy neefa-herder who'd refused to evacuate. A flyover afterward hadn't shown signs of life, and neither Aedis nor army nor locals had sufficient personnel to investigate further.

Gaer relied on his optic to see the Weep, where *see* meant a march of numbers that described its emanations through all the aetheric layers. Right now the permanent fissure was currently very active. That was not unheard of, or even particularly unusual; Brood crawled out every so often, after all. That was the *reason* for Aedis compounds and their watchtowers, for patrols and drones.

Nor were all Weep emanations created equal. *This* batch didn't look like the kind that made extra Brood. This batch was more concentrated in the deep layers of the aether, the ones Gaer had learned through hard (scarring) experience linked Brood-layers and void. If he had to guess—these emanations were related to little fissures opening up. Or having been opened, if he was especially optimistic and conservative (neither by nature) and attributed all Weep-associated disturbance to the arithmancer and the altar in the ruins, with all this activity being just after-effects.

The tower door banged open with deliberate force. The templars lining the walls—more of them, since *Rishi*'s arrival—that were closest to that door looked, but without much alarm. They lost interest immediately when they recognized Notch.

Gaer cycled his optic from *look at the Weep* to *look at that templar* and adjusted the magnification. He could not *see* Aedian nanomecha at work. But he could see Notch's aura just fine— sunset hues, mostly, there was nothing settled or content about Notch—and it glittered and flickered like Iari's. All Aedian auras glittered with nanomecha and arithmancy; Iari's was *more*, and now Notch's was, too. And Notch was moving like someone fully recovered. Long strides, boots stomping down like the stones had offended him. He wore regular armor, not a battle-rig, like templars did in B-town, and unlike every other templar Gaer could see around him, on the walls or in the courtyard.

Maybe that was Notch's version of convalescence.

Gaer waited until Notch was within easy earshot, but still too far away for polite conversation. He gestured at the armor, called, "Are you . . . restricted duty?"

Notch scoffed and called back. "Not exactly. My rig needs repair, though, and it's not at the top of the list."

If the Weep decided to go into a full surge, Gaer had no doubt Notch's rig would be ready for battle in very short order. He supposed Notch knew that, too.

Notch stopped in front of Gaer. Looked both ways on the rampart, noting where the next-closest templars were, how likely they were to be able to hear (as far as Gaer could get from them, and very likely). Then he said, "You don't make it easy."

Gaer turned and leaned back against the wall. His coat— because although he was not restricted from his own battle-rig, he knew wearing it to just *walk around* would trigger all manner of suspicion—warded the worst of the chill from the stone. It helped, too, that he was tall enough that he could rest his hips against the rampart, so that his dorsal spikes did not force him to tilt one way or the other. He leaned back on his hands so that his ventral ridge pushed with axe-blade prominence against his tunic, where the coat front hung open.

Notch's eyes flicked to that ridge, and Gaer said, "I set a low threshold of difficulty. If you weren't willing to climb the stairs to talk to me at all, then you won't be willing to listen to what I have to say."

Notch pulled his eyes back to Gaer's face. "I *meant*—to say thank you. You don't make it easy."

"Is that why you think I asked you come? To demand *thanks?*"

"No. But I figured I better get it out of the way before you say anything else. So—thanks for making sure I didn't die. Iffy says it was all you." Notch went and leaned on the wall, beside Gaer and facing the other direction, balanced on forearms and elbows. He squinted into the wind. "Now, what did you want to talk about?"

Some of the red had leached out of Notch's aura. It was a roiling violet now, streaks of agitation like lightning. Gaer had rehearsed versions of this next bit that were more diplomatic, manipulative, flattering. He discarded them all.

"I want to go get them."

Notch had been pulling at his gloves, tugging at fingertips and adjusting the fit of the armguards over the leather. Now he stopped and made two careful fists and looked down at them. "Go on."

"I had—have—the altar coordinates. I know where they *were*. I don't think they've gone very far since, if they've gone anywhere at all." Gaer spun around on the wall, bringing himself closer to Notch. He propped himself up on his hands—elbows being spikily inconvenient for leaning. Oh, *now* they looked like a conspiracy. Which, to be fair, they were. Gaer lifted his chin toward the storm. "I think *that* is where *they* are. The fissure's very active. I think it's partly causing that storm. There are—do you care about meteorology?"

Notch actually laughed. "No." And then, sober again. "How sure are you?"

"My life on it. *Iari's* life on it."

"No one else matters?"

"They do. Not as much. I expect it's the same for you with Dodri and Llian."

Notch blew out a long, slow plume of breath. "Yeah. Okay. You told the Knight-Marshal."

"I told both of the Knight-Marshals."

Notch side-eyed him. "I'd heard Knight-Marshal Tobin was here. That's Aedis protocol if one Knight-Marshal's going out in the field. I *thought* he was here was because Keawe was going to retrieve them."

"She wants to take *Rishi* out, find the location of that altar, and turn it into a crater. Tobin won't risk killing templars. Yet."

"Huh. So he's refused to take command of Windscar, then." Notch's eyes narrowed. He had golden eyes, Gaer noticed. Almost lambent. "What's the *yet?*"

"If the permanent Weep fissure surges. Or if there is sufficient disturbance to make it *clear* the altar is being used to open temporary fissures and flood the province with Brood. That is my educated guess, based on, *sss.* Based on what I know." Tobin had asked about Weep fissure activity, was it a surge, what did Gaer think. Then Keawe had sent more templars to the walls. "When the cultists use the altar, I . . . have told the Knight-Marshals that I can find it."

Notch cocked a brow. "That true?"

Gaer flared his plates. "Not precisely. But an aggregate of aetheric disturbances does leave a mark."

"Hrok's stinking breath, I don't need a lesson in arithmancy. You asked, the Knight-Marshals said . . . no, or not yet. And you want to go now anyway."

"Because *yet* will mean there are Brood present, and I don't think that helps their odds of survival. Do you?"

Notch rubbed his face with both hands, left them there and said between parted palms: "What are you asking me, Gaer?"

"Get me a hopper. Get me *into* a hopper."

He expected Notch to say *you mean steal.* (Iffy had, when he'd floated the plan to her. Then her eyes had gone distant and she'd said, "I have an idea," which she had refused to tell him.)

Notch said nothing at all right away. His aura darkened to plum, with cerulean creep on the fringes. "You know I'm going with you, right? When you do this. When *we* do this. When are we doing this?"

Gaer flared his plates. The wind tasted faintly of petrichor. Of ozone. He didn't have to check his optic; he did anyway. The emanations were stronger now. "I was not going to ask. Or assume."

"I wouldn't help if you wanted a whole squad. Or if this was an actual surge. I wouldn't endanger this Aedis for—anyone. But this is a *retrieval.* And you say it will work."

"Oh, I make no such prediction. I know roughly where they are. I don't know what we'll find. There might be Brood there already. There are certainly cultists, and those half-riev abominations. There *will* be an arithmancer of formidable skill wielding an altar, and *that* is my concern. Kill him, and the altar is no longer an active threat."

"And if there are two arithmancers?"

"Kill them both." Gaer looked at Notch. He was younger than Iari, yes, but not inexperienced. Not anymore. "I did not simply *repair* your nanomecha. Did Iffy tell you?"

Notch's aura fractured with yellow, like lightning in a storm. "They're working. That's what she said. That, and *go thank Gaer.* I assumed that meant you did to me what you did to Iari. Why her syn let her sling plasma and slag the altar."

Oh, interesting. And so very wrong. *"I didn't do that to her. Her nanomecha made that adjustment on their own in circumstances I had no part of creating. Yours, however, did not make that adjustment. They needed help. I gave them that help."*

Notch blinked. The yellow fractures turned orange, then red, then dimmed to magenta. "I thought what Iari can do is because of some deal command worked out with your people."

"Oh, no. *Sss.* No. Until you, Lieutenant, my hands were well *out* of Aedis hexes. And now I am in up to my elbows. Which is why I reckoned I would not simply repair you, I would improve you. Give you what Iari has."

Oh, *those* were some pyrotechnics in his aura. Notch swallowed visibly. "Does Iffy know?"

"She does. The Knight-Marshals do not."

Notch went back to squinting at the distant, and to him invisible, Weep. "So if *we* go to get them, *I* can slag an altar like Iari did."

"Yes."

"And you wouldn't have told me I could do that if I hadn't volunteered to go with you?"

"I think Iffy might have, when she tried to convince you to reconsider. And speaking of—"

The tower door had just opened, spilling torch-colored teslalight onto the rampart. Iffy stepped out, robed and wrapped in a coat, looking more like an animate bundle of cloth than a person. She took a half second to orient. Then, for the love of all the dark lords, she *waved* and stepped out of the doorway.

Which made room for the person behind her to emerge. Knight-Marshal Tobin stepped onto the wall. He *was* rigged for war, as much as he could be: the battle-rigs relied on the syn, and the syn relied on the nanomecha, which couldn't live in his prosthetics; you could artifice around that, for small injuries, but Tobin's hip and leg were not that. Instead he wore his rig in pieces: a breastplate and gauntlets and greaves and cuisses. Gaer could see the shimmer of Aedian battle-hexes.

No helmet though. Bareheaded Tobin, following bareheaded blithe traitor Iffy along the ramparts like they were out for a *setatir* stroll.

"Shit," said Notch. "I thought you said the Knight-Marshals didn't know."

"They didn't." Gaer thought—briefly, not seriously—about jumping over the wall. This might be his best chance to escape.

Iffy's aura was bright cerulean triumph. Tobin's was . . . darker blues, steady, so much like Iari's it made Gaer's chest hurt.

Iffy held up her hands. "Don't say anything. Give me *one* minute." She paused, closed her eyes, moved a couple of fingers—extraneous theatrics for an arithmancer, but Iffy wasn't, she was a priest, and the hex that flared across Gaer's optic was an Aedian heresy. His optic parsed it out anyway, broke it down to its code.

"There. Privacy." Iffy opened her eyes, beaming. Met Gaer's stare and readjusted her smile. Softly, to Gaer, "I *said* I had an idea."

And that idea had been *tell Tobin*. If Gaer jumped over the wall, he would take Iffy with him.

"At ease, Lieutenant." Because Notch had snapped upright, saluted—turned the color of oatmeal again, all the color leaching out of his skin and into his aura. If Gaer wanted to jump and take Iffy over the side, he might have to wrestle with Notch for the pleasure. Tobin's eyes flickered and settled. "Gaer. Thank you for what you did."

"Sss." He clamped his plates tight. "I suppose she told you everything."

"She told me enough." Tobin set hands to his hips and turned toward the courtyard. "You don't need to steal a hopper. We have *Rishi*. She's much faster."

Notch choked. He looked as if he might throw *himself* off the walls. But Notch didn't know Tobin. And if Tobin was here with Iffy, if Tobin had climbed the stairs and come out to the wall, then Tobin was part of that *we*.

Gaer took a breath of Windscar that tasted a little of distant petrichor, of cold that made his scar ache. Of slightly agitated alw and very agitated tenju and one human not agitated at all. He wanted badly to know if Keawe had agreed to this. What Tobin had done to convince her. If Tobin was just . . . stealing an Aedis aethership, going rogue. (Tobin wouldn't. Tobin might. Oh *setat*, there was so much old business between Tobin and Iari.)

But what came out of Gaer's mouth was:

"The Weep fissure is very active. *Rishi*'s turing had trouble with Brood emanations just coming here. If the arithmancer starts opening fissures—which I think he will, if he has not already—then they will be worse where we're going."

"We didn't have an arithmancer or a priest with us last time." Tobin smiled faintly. "And this time, the turing won't be the pilot. I will."

Gaer blinked, both sets of lids, and Tobin smiled wider. "Let's go get our people back."

CHAPTER TWENTY-FIVE

"This way," Gel said. "Come on, Corso."

She made it sound like an invitation, all sultry-voiced. The hand on the small of his back, her chin tipped up so he could feel her breath on his cheek and neck. The monofil in her right hand, though—that was all promise, too, but the menacing kind. She'd already cut the 'caster's strap with it, and in so doing sliced through his coat, his sweater, every layer all the way to skin. Sliced *that* too: just a sting, just a hint of wetness.

If she leaned on that blade, she'd cut him in half. Which she knew.

He froze—that was sensible, she'd expect it—and turned just his head to look down at her.

"Hey, Gel." And when she did start to push, just a little, "Where we going?"

"For a walk." She shoved him around the corner of the shed, marching him along past the front of the barn, this time, past the farmhouse. For a second he thought she was aiming at the byre, but then she turned back into the main body of the camp, into one of the aisles he'd taken for command quarters: bigger tents, fewer of them. She picked the first tent and steered them both through the flap.

Corso was half hoping for occupancy, for a moment's shock in which he could act. But of course not. Gel wasn't stupid.

The tent was empty, its owner no doubt out there in the mess tent with everyone else. Corso noted the single cot (unmade) and the single battered footlocker (open, guts spilling out like a child had gone looking for a favorite toy). This was someone important enough to rank their own quarters. Someone too important, and too undisciplined, to clean the fuck up.

The tent flap slapped shut. The overbright floodlamps bled through the walls like moonlight's ugly cousin. The shit on the floor could be a problem, but not as much as Gel's monofil. She hadn't killed him yet, or yelled, which told him she had some questions to which he'd better have answers.

"Gel, *Gel,* wait, wait." He pretended to trip. She could let him go, or fall with him.

Or kill you, neefa-brain.

She chose the first option, adding a little push as he staggered. He went with the momentum and dropped to one knee.

"You *know* those templars," she said, cool and flat as a frozen lake.

That was when Corso knew she was going to kill him. She was skipping past all the shit he would have tried to deny, assuming guilt already.

He scrabbled away from her like a man trying to decide between getting up and getting away from the nasty alw with the monofil. Held up his left hand and hoped to Iari's fucking Elements that Gel didn't take it off.

"Sure I did. *Fuck.* I told you! I do private recon, you knew that, I told you I did some work for the Aedis in B-town before we came up here. Gel, come on, that's why we *left,* why we came up *here,* me and my cousin. Aedis shit." He panted like a man panicking. He might be overselling it.

But she stopped coming after him. "You *never* said that."

He couldn't see well in the dark, couldn't tell her expression, but he thought he heard uncertainty. At least hesitation. He let his breath out gently. Crawled another pace away from her, pushing his hand along the tent floor. Slagging *mess* in here, clothes all over. He was counting on the owner's carelessness with all their possessions, not just garments. Maybe there was a knife under here, a monofil. A loaded jacta.

No, no, and no. But he did find a stray shoe, the sort with hard soles, *city* soles. He wrapped his hand around it and stayed crouched and cowering.

"I told *Bersk*. I thought she told you everything."

"She left some things out." Gel hissed a breath through her teeth. "That doesn't say what you're doing wandering around. Didn't you hear the alarm? Everyone's supposed to go to the tent, when that happens."

"How was I supposed to know that? No one *ever* said that. I went to look for Iari, then I saw the byre was open, so I reckoned she was in the camp someplace." He swallowed loudly. "And I *was* on my way to the fucking tent. Then I heard someone yelling in that shed, so I went to check. I didn't expect there would be fucking *templars* in there. Void and dust, Gel. Why we keeping templars?"

"Not for us to ask, you and me. That's Axorchal's business." But Gel sounded a little more grim. Her silhouette settled a little, like she'd come off her toes. "Some of ours died. Group of recruits out for target practice. You know about that?"

His heart tried to climb out his slagging throat. "I—no. The fuck happened? Gel, what *is* this?"

She stood there, not answering. Looking at him, or at least pointing her face his direction. Then: "Get up. Void and dust. You're not—"

Corso didn't wait to hear what he wasn't. He threw the shoe at her. Aimed at her head, expecting to miss (yes), expecting her to duck (yes). And in that distracted moment he launched himself at her.

She was quick, give her that. She ducked the shoe, whipped around, sidestepped and struck out, like she expected him to try and tackle her and she meant to gut him when he did. Which he *was* trying, and she almost succeeded. He did his own twist, threw himself sideways. Hit the tentpole and bounced. Gel's monofil hissed through his sleeve, through skin and muscle—not to bone, not that deep. Then his shoulder hit her in the chest, followed by the rest of him, and they went over with him on top.

He landed on her weapon-arm, pinned it to her chest. Heard the breath gust out of her, and a squeak that said she'd meant to yell. Corso wasn't worried. Whatever was going on outside, it was getting more organized. Some sort of chant now, that was probably *Ax-or-chal* or some voidspit. He'd flirted with the old ways, studied them, gone so far once as to make a Winter Night offering. *No*where in the books had they talked about a slagging *rally*.

He planted an elbow on Gel's chest, insult to breathless injury, and when he was sure of topography, slid his forearm up onto her throat. Then it was a matter of mass and force and waiting. She tried to switch hands with her monofil—smart—but he'd been (smarter) waiting for that, too. She tried to get a knee up, tried to eel free. He just held her there until she stopped moving. Until experience said she wasn't going to move, ever again. He levered off her. Checked her pulse and then, because his hands were shaking—broke her neck and made sure.

Corso took her monofil. Thought about replacing his coat, and decided better. There wasn't time to play dress-up. Not with *Ax-or-chal* throbbing outside. He used the monofil to slice off a strip of cloth, wrapped it around his forearm. The cut on his ribs was shallow. His shirt had already stuck to it. His sweater would, too. That was bandage enough. He traded Gel's 'caster for the one he'd stolen; hers was an old one, army-issue, familiar.

He breathed through the worst of the shakes, then went to the tent flap and shifted it aside.

Somehow no one saw them: two templars in battle-rigs slide-running down a slope made for neefa and goats. The snow was deep, mostly unbroken (no goats or neefa here; the biggest track was a rabbit). Iari's rig sank to mid-thigh in the first jump, which prompted a redirection; she aimed at high points, rocky outcrop-pings or unfortunate shrubs. The revised path down was going to put them closer to the barn than the shed, which put them farther from the goal, but also gave them more time to reconnoiter.

Except—no, *no* time. Her HUD flashed alert: someone, some-ones, was leaving the mess tent, heading toward the outbuildings. All they had to do was look up, and they'd *see*. Except people didn't look up—civs didn't, especially, and maybe they were distracted by the fire spreading through the camp. Iari couldn't see flames from here, but there was definitely smoke rising up, greasy black against the stormy pewter. Everyone should be running that way.

And these—two, the HUD confirmed—were not. They weren't even running. They walked quickly, efficiently, apparently un-moved by the mayhem behind them and unaware or unconcerned about two templars pelting downhill.

Iari hit the bottom first. She waited for Dodri to catch up (one beat, then a ground-shivering *thump*) before bolting across the perimeter and straight to the barn's broad backside. There was just enough room between a tarped ATV and the barn's corner for two templar rigs. Iari tucked in closest to the corner, slid to a squat, then poked the barest sliver of her faceplate around the corner.

Fresh tracks trailed from the edge of the barn to the now altar-free yurt, then around again, and—she amped her HUD's magnification—toward the prison shed. Corso's trail. Right. Iari motioned to Dodri *hold still* and amped her audio feed. She could hear the noise swelling out of the mess tent.

Her rig wasn't flashing Brood warnings. Just the presence of— what, *targets*? Those people weren't soldiers. They were *civs*.

Civs with longcasters. Civs who had to know what they had in the shed, *who* they had. The moment those people had linked up with the wichu insurgents, even *if* they thought they had good grievance to do so—they'd put on those hexed badges, hadn't they? And they'd agreed to kill templars.

So yes. Targets.

Then Dodri upended all that careful reasoning. "Captain, those are *One-Eyes* going to the shed."

Oh ungentle Ptah. Iari pulled her attention back to the void-spit *job*: and yes, two One-Eyes, gloved and helmeted. They would *have* to notice that Corso had been there. Iari could see his tracks clearly, and the One-Eyes would cross right over them. And even if they missed the tracks—the door was slagging *open*.

A third floodlamp exploded into another fireball. Bigger this time, more smoke. It might not *be* dusk yet, but between smoke and incoming storm, it was dark enough to count.

The One-Eyes didn't even turn their heads at the explosion. Did not miss a step. Nor did they appear to notice the tracks. They marched up to the shed like . . . like the riev Iari remembered from the surge. Before decommissioning, when they'd been under Oversight, when they hadn't had (hadn't been able to have) names. When they'd been machines under someone's command, machines with a soldier's reflexes and muscle memory.

Iari wondered if the One-Eyes still had names. Wondered mostly—who was *their* Oversight? Axorchal the arithmancer, *bet* on that—but *how* was he transmitting? How were *any* of these people communicating without comms?

Dodri's voice was steady, strained. "They're going to kill Llian and the sergeant."

There was no guarantee it was Luki and Llian in there at all. Just a guess. Just a hunch. Just a hope. "No," said Iari. "On my mark—follow me."

And this needed timing. Wait . . . *wait . . .*

The One-Eyes passed out of view as they marched up to the broken shed door.

"Mark!"

Iari sprinted to the yurt, following Corso's tracks. She reached cover in time to hear Luki yell from inside the shed. *Yell*, not scream: hoarse, ragged, *anger* rather than fear. Iari pinged Dodri's rig—*eyes on me*—then gestured around the back.

She waited, and as Dodri sprinted around the far side of the shed, Iari whipped around the corner of the yurt and charged. From this approach, she couldn't see the front of the shed. Couldn't tell where the One-Eyes were, or Luki. The syn wanted to help; Iari pushed it down. She needed her wits; the One-Eyes had whitefire, but not much for armor, and Luki had none of either. Luki's next yell dissolved into coughing, and Iari skidded around to the front of the shed in a cloud of snow.

The One-Eye—only one outside now—was facing away from Iari, into the partly open shed door. Luki dangled from its glove like a broken doll. She'd been stripped to her skinsuit, but she had all her limbs, nothing visibly broken or bleeding. Her face was darker in patches than normal—bruises, maybe, or dried blood—and her hair stuck up in dark spikes, steaming with sweat in the cold. The One-Eye kept jerking her off her feet, raising its arm while her feet scrabbled for purchase. She clutched her own arm, just below where the One-Eye held her, like she was trying to pull loose. Her breath came in plumes of vapor, in ragged raw coughing gasps.

Then she saw Iari. Shock burst over her features, then relief, then dawning horror: "Another—!"

Inside, yes, and thanks for the warning, except now the One-Eye holding Luki knew there was something behind it. It started to turn, and Iari let the syn go.

She didn't bother with her axe. Snapped her shield out of her gauntlet and sliced out with the rim instead, hoping to shear the One-Eye in half before it could come around. But Ptah's fucking *eye*, it was too fast, syn-fast: it dropped its hips, dropped its arm, spun and slung Luki like bag full of rocks. Iari jerked her shield aside, sacrificed balance: missed Luki but ended up with her void-spit *back* to the One-Eye as momentum spun her around.

She heard Luki shout again, just before the One-Eye's shot punched her square in the back. Her HUD flashed red—yes, *yes*, she'd been hit, she knew that—but no breach. That told her the One-Eye had dropped Luki, at least, if it was using its glove to fire.

Iari continued her spin, snapped the shield up, deployed her axe and started a cut—higher, trust Luki to go flat and get out the way. She caught the One-Eye's next shot on her shield point-blank just as she came back around—which made the shield shudder and flicker and flare bright enough her faceplate blacked itself opaque.

Iari had only fought blind in training sims, and this felt just like that. Disorienting, frustrating, with sour dread in her throat (but there was the difference: to fail in a sim was embarrassment; fail here, and Luki might die). It was only for a few seconds, a blind finish to the axe-stroke she'd started, that ended in the hitching impact of whitefire blade into something, *through* it—

—and then out, just as her faceplate cleared.

She'd sheared off a part of the One-Eye's unaugmented shoulder. The whitefire had gone through part of a chestplate, through flesh and bone after that, cauterizing as it moved. Steam curled out of the wound, and stubborn oozing.

That would've dropped a regular person. The One-Eye only staggered. Below the half-helmet and that throbbing red cabochon, its mouth—young, strong-jawed tenju, gender unknown—twisted into a howl of insensate fury. It jerked its glove up, started to raise it like a longcaster.

Dodri rounded the corner of the shed in a synning sprint, axe and shield ready, just as Luki shouted, "Inside, *inside!*"

Iari twisted toward the open door, jumped that direction—imagining the One-Eye inside would fire at her and intending to catch the blast on her shield (if she got lucky) or her armor (less lucky). Dodri could handle the one outside.

Iari's headlamp snapped on automatically as she crossed the threshold.

And it didn't help. It was too dark in here. *Lightless* dark, when there should be a least a patch leaking in from outside, maybe slivers through the half-rotted roof. Iari's HUD flared with unspecified hex alarms: hostile arithmancy, nothing it knew how to counter, but familiar. The same stuff as the ruins, that black fog that had made people see terrible things. That had been a k'bal defense, but in a closed place like this, it would be torture.

And that dark was also something Iffy had handled, and Iffy wasn't here. Iari went forward anyway, shield held in front, axe cocked and ready. Her syn flared, too, searing her vision white on the edges. It felt like the hexes on the byre walls, that same pain, that sense of something *wrong*. But she had to go in, Llian was in here. The other One-Eye was, too, and—

The shot took her full in the faceplate. Iari staggered back onto her heels as the visor blacked again, protecting her eyes; then the HUD flared bright as the voidspit whitefire and blanked entirely. Iari felt the rig shudder as systems failed and fell back on redundancies. The alarms kept working. Damage-alert chirps and the wail that meant breach.

A tendril of very cold air kissed her cheekbone. Yeah. Breach in the visor. *Open*, she willed the faceplate, except you couldn't issue commands with a dead rig. There were manual releases, but you needed a free hand, and hers weren't. She still had the syn, and the syn was linked up with the rig—the needle burned in the base of her skull, that was proof the rig wasn't *totally* dead—but it wouldn't do her much good if it didn't reboot its systems. Or if she took another shot to the voidspit *face*. It wasn't the first time her visor had shattered—one had broken her tusk that way, in her army days. But that'd been a slicer-strike, not whitefire.

Didn't matter, did it? The next hit could kill her.

That had always been true.

Iari dug in her heels and braced.

The explosion sent Corso staggering—*fuck*, Gel's monofil had gone deeper in his forearm than he'd thought. He dropped to one knee as a wall of living heat washed over him, as the concussion rattled every tooth in his head. That was—huh. Not artillery. Not big Aedis guns, either.

And then it was suddenly dimmer—not *dark*, because sunset hadn't happened yet—but all the little strung teslas were dead along the lines of tents. Then Corso realized what had exploded. The floodlamp. Or rather, from that boom—the floodlamp's generator. He looked around, looked up: there had been four brightnesses over the camp not so long ago, one floodlamp per quadrant that had lit up when the alarms had gone off. Now there was a dull orange glow throbbing both to the south and to the west, and a spreading black curtain of smoke. There were two light sources left: the easternmost, which was closest to his location; and the northernmost, closest to the mess tent. The mess had *been* the epicenter of activity before Gel had grabbed him. Now—now, there were people starting to rush out of that tent toward the fires, shouting about buckets, about water, just shouting.

Because fire in a place like this would spread fast, without preventative hexes or running water. Someone hadn't thought about that in their planning. Or rather—Corso bet all the safety hexes were back in the kitchen tent, where the live flames were supposed to be. Most people who lived up in Windscar understood losing grid-power, understood lanterns and safety with emergency gear. The explosion hadn't been someone's camp-stove error. Generators came with safety hexes. And they didn't, as a rule, explode at all.

Corso guessed Iari's hand in the mayhem and shoved to his feet.

The ground vibrated underfoot. He heard canvas tearing, crashing, from the next tent-row over, and saw the spines of the tents buckle as something punched through them. It looked like a ripple of chaos. Like a ripple of *Char*: the riev appeared suddenly, in a gap between tents that they had left otherwise unmolested. Hexes crawled over their armor, silvery-blue instead of the angry red Corso usually saw. Their Aedis prosthetic was blackened a little, hand and wrist, as if Char had dipped it in ash.

Or as if they'd put that fist through a generator.

Char saw him, too; they jerked to a stop. They were, had been, cutting east, toward that floodlamp. Now they pivoted toward him, and took a step. Said, "You are bleeding."

"Yeah. Where's Iari?"

"Attempting to retrieve the templars." Char hesitated. "Do you need assistance?"

"Nah. I'll find her. You—" He waved a hand.

You had to appreciate riev. They didn't argue. Char drilled a look at him (it felt like a drill, even if their eyes were teslas and all they did was glow), then sprinted away. *Quiet*, which was disturbing, both for the havoc Char had caused so far, and for the sheer size of them.

So Iari was going for Luki and Llian. Right. Corso started that way.

A small mob of cultists surged into the aisle of tents where he was. Five, maybe six of them, badged, carrying 'casters like they were hunting a whole pack of wolves.

They spotted him, of course they did. He had no badge, he had blood all over him—but the coat was dark and so was the blood, so maybe they wouldn't see.

Which they would not, if they did not stop to talk.

"Riev!" Corso said. He pointed a direction Char hadn't gone. "That way! Big one!"

That worked: the leader waved, and they ran past. At least they didn't ask him to come along. They were young, all of them, tenju, all of them, and far too young to know running *at* riev was a bad idea. Even the vakari hadn't done that.

Then Corso ran back the way he'd come—which was also a bad idea, *and* uphill, so it hurt—onto the path between byre and farmhouse. He was hoping for relative solitude, and yeah, there was no one else back here. All the activity was down in the camp. From the slight incline, he could see more people milling around the mess tent, collecting into small groups like the one he'd just seen. Little hunting parties. He marked who seemed to be directing things. Thought about giving Gel's 'caster a try, see how it shot.

Right, and *when* the cultists came charging up to find the sniper, he'd say what?

The third floodlamp exploded. This time a fireball rolled up the pole, casting everything briefly red. Char was getting more dramatic.

More people came running out of the mess tent, scattering toward the new fire, the old fires. A few seemed to be heading for the northernmost floodlamp, like they'd just figured out what the targets were. Corso couldn't tell how many people were left inside. Where the altar was, or the arithmancer. (Bet they were both still under there. Axorchal wouldn't run around and put out fires.)

Corso stopped in a square of shadow in front of the farmhouse to catch his breath, to look around. He didn't need to charge face first into something else today. And what he'd charge into was relative darkness, it looked like. All the teslas in this part of the camp were dead. Except for right around the mess tent and the strings of lights around the latrines, *most* of the camp was dark, and likely to get a lot darker when night arrived, and the snow. Corso could smell the wet in the air, but he wasn't feeling the bite of wind yet. It might just be a *lot* of snow coming down, instead of a blizzard, which would still make things hard for everyone except Char and Winter Bite and anyone *not* in a battle-rig.

Corso threw a half-focused look at the farmhouse door. It was probably open. Go in, look around, maybe find that comm array Iari'd been asking about, maybe find something useful to help—

Like what? Another coat? A list of plans, of names, a fucking roster of insurgents? Not likely. There wasn't *time* to investigate, he knew that, it was just—his last encounter with that shed hadn't gone well. That was the problem.

He'd opened the door and then turned round and *run away*. Left Luki and Llian in there, in who knew what condition.

Fucking hexes. Char said Iari was there now, *hope* she was with Dodri, but if not she'd need help. (She wouldn't want it. Wouldn't want *his*.)

And that didn't matter. Iari was at the shed, so that's where he needed to go.

Corso had to push away from the farmhouse—physically stick out an arm and shove—to make himself leave its shadow. He paused again at the front corner of the barn. *Those* doors were wide open. He was just about ready to cross in front of their gaping dark when the last floodlamp blew. No fireball this time, though there was fire: Corso saw the fingers of flame and greasy smoke reaching up. The whole camp blinked dark.

Corso headed up the side of the barn, around the back. In the failing light, he could make out the new tracks. Two battle-rigs, following his old trail; now he followed theirs.

He heard them first. Whitefire made a sound like a bagful of wet cats when it hit something *else* made of whitefire. So unless Dodri and Iari were fighting, someone else had whitefire down there. One-Eyes, had to be.

Corso had been trotting along with his arm tucked tight to his side to slow down any bleeding. Now he peeled it off so he could hold his 'caster in both hands. He ran the checks without looking, without slowing down. Gel had kept the weapon in good shape. The clip was full of bolts, and now—without even a whine—it was primed.

The sky dimmed again, like the sun had just given up. Corso blinked. The smoke was getting bad, thick like fog. The temperature had just dropped, too, a lot—which it might do sometimes right before a storm. He must've guessed wrong; the storm must've been closer than he'd thought. He took a careful breath through his nose, felt the burn. Tasted petrichor on the back of his tongue, and ozone. Which was *weird*, you could get thunder-snowstorms, but he hadn't heard any—

And then the realization hit like a blade in the back of his skull. That wasn't smoke. That wasn't a voidspit *storm*. There was an altar in the tent, and an arithmancer. That was *Brood* smell. Brood cold. That fucker Axorchal was opening a slagging *fissure* in his own camp.

And Corso had, what, a monofil, a 'caster, no armor. And he was bleeding. This was like B-town all over again, that fucking cellar opening fissures all the fuck over, except this time there were no templars coming to save him.

This time, he had to save *them*.

CHAPTER TWENTY-SIX

T he next shot didn't come. Iari's helmet stayed dark. Her battle-rig shuddered into a reboot, and for(ever) a very long ten seconds there was just . . . nothing. Absolute, breathless stillness. The battle-rigs had vents to prevent overheating, mechanical redundancies meant to be proof against arithmancy. So she did hear the tiny clicks followed by trickles of cold air and feel that unnatural, hex-driven darkness. She wondered if the rig would come back online before she panicked, or if she'd be held, inert and unable to move. If she'd see Brood coming at her, random swarm or boneless or tunnelers.

No. If some malicious battle-hex wanted to scare her, it needed to resurrect Saichi: render the deep ravine she'd climbed up with Tobin over her shoulder, with his blood leaving trails for the boneless. How she had kept slipping, how she'd had to claw her way up with one hand while the other held Tobin steady. How her skin ached from the inside from too much synning. How her HUD had kept up a steady flash of *Brood* and scrolling damage reports. The falling levels of her power cell. The ever-decreasing distance between her and the Brood in pursuit. She'd shut her rig-to-rig comms off, because Tobin made little noises, even unconscious, when she jostled him. And if he woke up—she wasn't afraid he would scream, exactly, but she was sure he'd say leave him, *that's an order, Private.* Or worse, *where is everyone else?* She'd kept external audio because she had been hoping to hear artillery or 'caster fire from the army lines or *something* that said she'd almost gotten them home. She'd never hear Brood. They ran silent.

Iari could *hear* quiet, panting sobs that sounded like Tobin had. Except *no.* The sounds came through her external comms. Lighter, higher, that was Llian. Hrok's freezing breath, she did not need to do the fog's work *for* it and imagine herself into panic.

And where was the voidspit One-Eye? Why hadn't it shot her yet? Assume it could see in the hexed nightmare dark—*Char* had been able to—that its cabochon was more than just decoration. But it wasn't coming after her.

Iari's rig came back with a little jerk. The HUD flickered, its display pasted across the visor's shattered polyalloy. She still couldn't see *out*, blame the fog for that. But she had enough command of the rig to release the faceplate lock and raise it. It retracted in little hitches and machine whines. Her vision turned from spidered HUD to hexed, black fog. Her cheeks stung, not with cold, but with pinpricks of electricity. It was so much worse in here than the byre's wards.

Outside the shed, whitefire sizzled. There was smoke, too, and—

Oh ungentle Ptah. That was *not* petrichor. Please, it was not. That was the *hex.* Lies in the fog. Not Brood.

Her needle buzzed in its socket, all the warning she had. She angled the shield to intercept (what? *where?*), kept her feet planted, stayed in the doorway—

Whitefire slammed into her shield, flared into a corona that made her squeeze her eyes shut. Right, no visor, *keep* them closed. The next shot might skip over the top. Or the side.

"Fall back!" Corso's voice, hoarse, from behind her. "Fucking fall back and *get down!*"

For a split second she thought *he* was a hallucination, that the fog had ripped her back before Saichi, before the Aedis, to her army service. Then she slid a foot back, felt the wind hit her cheek—saw the first hazy edges of life outside the fog-hex. Another slide-step, she was out: the haze now was smoke and frail twilight.

She saw the glowing red cabochon coming at her, even as she began to duck, to crouch. Where the One-Eye's glove was, it didn't matter (it would, if it shot at her again)—because the One-Eye was holding Llian, not dangling from her own wrist like Luki had been, but hanging limp from the back of her skinsuit, hands and feet dragging the ground.

"It's got Llian!" she yelled. Then she did what Corso had told her: ducked behind her shield and dropped low.

The next whitefire blast hit her shield at an angle and slewed up. It would've taken her face off if she'd still been upright. And before the crackle of it faded, a longcaster boomed from very close by.

The cabochon exploded in a gout of something darker than blood, something thicker, the smell of which clotted the back of Iari's throat like Brood stench.

The One-Eye managed one more step and then crumpled across the shed's threshold. Ichor pooled under its face. Llian lay partly under it, unmoving.

Iari started to reach, remembered axe and shield, paused to retract them. But by then Dodri had shoved herself into the doorway. Iari got out of her way. Straightened and blinked and saw Corso standing there.

"Fuck," he said, and lowered the 'caster. For a heartbeat they stared at each other. Shock and relief chased themselves under Iari's skin like the syn. Corso had blood all over his coat and one sleeve. Some of it was his. Most of it wasn't.

And she didn't look a bit better. Corso's expression said that. Then he broke eyelock and turned and offered the less bloody arm to Luki.

"I'm sorry," Corso said to her. "I tried to go in and get you, and I couldn't."

Luki took his hand and pulled herself up. "You came back. That's what matters." Her eyes snapped to Iari. Bloodshot, bruise-blue all around—but aware. Alert. "Captain. Syn's offline. Mine and Llian's. Is she—?"

"She's alive," Dodri said. "I can't say much else."

The hexes in that shed had killed Aedian nano. Or neutralized them. Ungentle fucking *Ptah*.

Dodri dragged Llian out from under the One-Eye. She had been stripped to her skinsuit like Luki. Hers had more visible damage: a scorched patch in her mid-back that must've happened while she was still rigged, several long tears that had happened after. One eye was reddish-purple, swollen shut. Blood had dried on her face from a cut in her scalp, and her knuckles were bloody.

"She fought when they took her rig." Luki's lips were white. "She was already hurt when we got here. Rig breach at the ruins. There was water. A bucket. I was afraid to drink it. No food. We weren't the only people in there, but the other, the others? Are dead. There's something on the *walls*. I think our nanomecha protected us for a while, but then it hurt when—it hurt. We said Catechism. That's all we *could* do."

"Sorry it took us so long to get to you." Iari's chest hurt, twin spikes of hurt—relief, that they'd been on time, and rage that this had happened at all. She forced her voice even, calm. "Winter Bite's waiting on the ridge. You ready to go?"

Luki's eyes opened again, and this time they were clear. "Yes, Captain."

Iari crossed stares with Corso again. "How bad are you?"

"Bleeding some." He hitched a shoulder. "Why?"

"Because I have an extra rig at the top of the hill and Luki's in no condition."

"Huh. I can wear it."

Echoes of Sergeant Neem, back at Saichi. *Private, you carry the captain. You're in the best shape.* Maybe not the best memory to have now. "Dodri, you help them get up that hill. Fast as you can. At the top—help Corso into the battle-rig. One of you carries Luki, the other carries Llian, and you *go.*"

Dodri had picked Llian up, cradled across both arms. "I've got her."

"Not like that," said Iari. "Put her over your shoulder. Pick a side. She won't like it if she wakes up, but you need a free hand."

Dodri's head jerked. Iari imagined her expression behind the faceplate. Shock, rising argument, training abruptly recalled. She arranged Llian carefully over her right shoulder.

Corso pitched his voice low, like Luki wasn't still holding onto him. Like Dodri wouldn't be able to hear. "Where are *you* going to be?"

"You know where." Iari jabbed her chin at the mess tent. "The altar's in there. The arithmancer, too."

"Yeah. The temple of Axorchal's having services. Or it was. Char's breaking things. But, Iari, listen: I haven't seen any more One-Eyes, except *these* two."

"Good." Maybe they'd gotten them all, between the ruins and the shed. The southernmost fire seemed to've stopped, where the wind had blown it toward empty snow and no fuel. The ones in the east and west were still burning cheerfully, pushed across tents and gear. The smoke was getting bad, but: "You smell it?"

Corso's eyes narrowed. "Yeah. If they're opening a fucking

fissure, then we *all* need to leave. Your rig's a fucking wreck. You don't have a *visor.*"

"I do. It's just cracked. Listen. You saw Ettrad. I can *get* the altar. Then *Gaer* can deal with the arithmancer."

"Gaer is not here—fuck. You do *not* go alone. Luki, you're gonna have to wear the rig and do some running—"

"I won't be alone." Iari slid her eyes off him, past him. A familiar silhouette was just coming around the barn. There was soot smeared over Char's armor, and gore. Iari caught another whiff of ozone, not the Brood kind this time. The kind that came from hot metal and angry riev.

Iari looked at Corso. Who sighed and shook his head. "You better make it."

"You, too," Iari said. Then she went to meet Char partway.

CHAPTER TWENTY-SEVEN ≡≡≡

Iari sprinted toward the mess tent and the altar. Smoke was thick on the ground, getting thicker. She held her breath and tried to close her visor. The faceplate made actual noise as it closed, and the seal wasn't perfect—she could still smell smoke—but the HUD came up with only a little flicker and spidering that told her the material itself was cracked. The rig's filtration surged to clear the interior.

The HUD did its own version of clearing the smoke: showed her the hard edges of things, etched in green. Tents. Cables on the ground. It mapped off a topography, rather than heat or some other EM. Which was good, because whitefire played hell with infrared.

Plain fire played hell with infrared, too. Iari's rig reported high levels of phlogiston in the aether, which fire needed, but which fire also produced. Cause and effect. Except *cause* this time had been Char and a lack of protective hexes. Maybe some luck.

Mostly Char.

The riev met Iari halfway between the edge of the tent line and the shed. "With me," Iari said, and Char spun in place and retraced their steps, while Iari side-eyed Char's armor and hexes and tried to gauge their condition. There were still blank spots that hadn't come back since the ruins. And it didn't matter. No one was in ideal condition at this point. Char was better off than any of the other templars except Dodri and Winter Bite, and Char was the one Iari wanted anyway.

"Head for the back of the mess tent. The, the kitchen. Our objective is, destroy that altar," Iari said, trusting that Char would hear her. Trusting Char would understand what that meant. Maybe that wasn't textbook command procedure, but Char was old. Char had been at Saichi. "The arithmancer is secondary. He runs away, *fine*. Let him run. The altar is priority."

Then they hit the first wave of the smoke. The effect was immediate: everything smeared grey, everything gone dim. The rig tried to turn on her headlamp, and Iari overrode it and navigated by the HUD's green-lit map. She had already retracted both axe and shield. The battle-rig was distinctive, if someone got close enough to identify it, but the shield's hexes would blaze through the smoke like a beacon. That was the point, on a battlefield, when Brood brought their own fog. You needed to see where your people were, but Brood always knew.

She hadn't seen any Brood around here yet. She'd smelled the petrichor and the ozone up by the shed and nothing since the visor's closing. The battle-rig's HUD reported no emissions, nothing, but that had happened in B-town, too. Invisible Brood—to her hexes, to Char's. Please, let that not be the case here and now.

"Char," she said. "If there's Brood—if you can't see them— listen, if I tell you *go*, then you go."

Char's hexes were a rippling red defense. Char's optics were two spots of bright, icy blue. Like Corso's eyes, without the blink and bloodshot and weary fear, flicking sideways for a moment. Char raised a hand, made the gesture for *acknowledged*.

And that was all the conversation they had time for.

The kitchen end of the mess tent loomed suddenly in front of them, swelling out of the smoke and the dark. Iari stopped, turned her external audio feed up as far as she could. Then she poked her axe shaft out, triggered the blade, and sliced a careful line through the canvas. Steam puffed out—honest water, nothing noxious—and beaded immediately on Iari's gauntlet. That much steam meant, what, pots unattended? Or deliberate obfuscation by some battle-hex or another.

Anyone inside that tent wouldn't be armored like she was. Iari waited, and when no one slung any 'caster bolts at her, she sliced the gap wider and followed her axe blade inside.

More steam collected on Iari's visor, gathering in the cracks where the defogging hexes failed and dripping down. They'd laid down some kind of floor in here, cheap plates of nanoforged alloy that flexed under the battle-rig's weight. Iari stayed in the hole she'd made in the tent, let the steam rush out around her. She risked the headlamp; green hardline maps were *fine*, but actual eyes on was better. The kitchen had been abandoned. There were several pots left unattended on fuel-canister stoves; they were the source of the steam. Dead tesla strands sagged off the tent poles like rotting thread. There were two massive coldboxes; neither of them had a power signature. There were cables collected in bundles along the edge of the tent, also showing no current. A terminal sulked in the corner, balanced on a food preparation surface beside dirty cutlery and a bucket. The display was blank.

Iari slid inside, Char at her heels like a giant, angry shadow. Iari's HUD flickered with undefined warnings. Open flames and phlogiston, that was standard risk, but it squeaked something about Brood, the faintest warning it knew how to give. She already knew there wasn't a fissure close by because there was no frost. No creeping black fog. (Brood fog didn't cause hallucinations, just obfuscation. For once, that was a relief.) No, in here it was just the smoke, getting thicker now that the fires were taking hold among the tents.

There was no *sound* either, besides boiling pots and intra-camp chaos. There had been chanting not long ago, from the other side of a very thin layer of canvas. That implied a lot of people had been in the main mess. And sure, some of them might've gone running off to fight fires, but—all of them? There had been One-Eyes coming from this location to fetch Luki and Llian. That suggested someone had sent them.

Oversight. Axorchal. No *surprise*, that, but still: Iari watched her biometrics creep toward the yellow edge of optimal. The syn, for once, seemed content to wait for her signal.

Or she'd burned it out for today. Wouldn't *that* figure.

The kitchen opened into the back of the mess tent from one of its corners. Not a door, not even a flap, but a series of off-center, parallel panels, so that people carrying tureens and pots didn't have to push anything out of the way, but also so that there wasn't a straight line of sight from the kitchen. The dividing panels didn't reach all the way to the ground. Anyone looking would see her boots. See Char's glowing feet. Anyone set up with a 'caster or a hex would know where they should aim through those panels.

Iari traded a look with Char. The riev gestured a clear *let me go first*. Iari gestured *no* back (and heard Char and Corso together disparaging that decision).

She turned external comms off. "Be ready to haul me out." Her voice echoed in the helmet. "Or back me up."

Char's teslas gleamed briefly brighter, and they dropped back.

Iari slashed a path straight through the panels and stepped into the mess tent.

There had been a gathering recently, obviously, and not a meal, either. The tables had been pushed all to the edges to make a large central space, but also a barrier along the perimeter; several of those had been overturned or just shoved aside. The altar lurked, unattended, in the center of the tent. Sigils crawled up the asymmetrical sides, a violet so dark they looked black, or maybe red. But it didn't *appear* to be doing anything.

Of the arithmancer, Axorchal, there was no sign, unless that was—no. There *was* a body on the other side of the altar, mostly concealed except for an outflung, metal-gloved hand. Huh. Iari couldn't see the signature cabochon helmet from this angle, but— assume that was a dead One-Eye. She couldn't be lucky enough to hope it was the arithmancer.

Iari's gut clenched. This layout was so *much* like that basement in B-town (except not a basement, except ambient light, which was an improvement). Altars were for sacrifice, and this One-Eye was also *recently* dead. Its blood, its *goo*—was still steaming.

And, *and* . . . the altar's hexes were still crawling. Getting brighter. Something was happening. *Arithmancy* was happening, so *where* was the voidspit arithmancer? Prudence (maybe fear) said fall back, *find* him, he wouldn't have left this thing unprotected. But the tent was empty *now*, and it wouldn't stay that way. People would come back. One-Eyes might, too; they didn't know how many were left, and Iari didn't trust they were all safely dead. Or maybe that altar was opening a portal, and One-Eyes—or worse things—might come *through*.

Her whole body felt hot and cold at once, skin pebbled and electric. She clenched her fingers around the axe with both hands. Thank you, Elements, that the gauntlets did not care about slick palms or shaking fingers. She took a breath, held it, and *reached* for the syn. The battle-rig's needle tingled in the socket on the back of her skull, just a filament, just a thread, such a tenuous bridge to the tiny machines in her blood and bones.

Ungentle Ptah, lend me—

The syn uncoiled and crackled under her skin, through her nerves, before she could finish the prayer. It pushed fear to the edges (pushed sense with it). Iari dashed the short distance to the altar, raised the axe up and chopped. She was already shifting her weight, anticipating the flash, the explosion—

Let the visor hold, Elements—

—and then the axe *stopped*, a jarring collision of *not* whitefire, of the solid alloy shaft and something else equally solid that sent shockwaves up all the bones in her arms. Then her HUD flared *proximity* and *whitefire* and *Brood* all at once.

Then it died.

Blank, black, quiet in her helmet. Panic shocked through her; she shoved it down (the syn shoved it). The rig hadn't died around her. She could still move. She ripped the axe back, shifting it to one hand, lashed out with the other. The shield snapped out, and she *shoved*. Almost fell when she pushed through empty aether, as whatever had blocked her strike wasn't there anymore.

Her HUD was still blank. She battled to get the visor open—there were protocols, safety measures, things she had to circumvent with eye-flicks most times. She kept trying those, in case the voidspit thing could sense them. She didn't have a hand free to use the external release. The visor wasn't moving, if she had to take off the fucking helmet, she was going to die right here—

And then she was glad of her failure. Something grabbed hold of her cracked faceplate—Iari heard the slap of impact, felt the shudder, heard the sharp-edged scrape as something locked on. That gave her a target to swipe at with the axe, anyway. The blade bit something, shivered in her grasp and *hissed,* and she realized she could still hear over ex-comms.

Char had to know she was in trouble, but she shouted "Char!" anyway. She fell back a step, shaking her head. "Open visor, open visor, come *on* you neefa-shit *setatir—*"

Whatever had a grip on her faceplate still had it. She sacrificed her shield again to get a free hand and clawed at the helmet's release.

Which was when something hit her mid-torso, big and wide and *heavy*: it lifted her up and threw her back as if she were a kitten instead of a battle-rigged templar. The helmet's malfunction spared her a shrieking alarm (small favor, thank you Ptah). The syn still had control of the rig, second favor; she crashed into something that broke apart when she hit it, but the syn had her feet back on the ground. Only then did she realize that she'd dropped the axe, *where was it—*

Whatever had hold of her faceplate still had a grip (how?), and now it tugged, *wrenched*, like it meant to break her neck. She still had a hand on her helmet release, so she triggered it. Seals hissed as it tried to uncouple from the rig and jammed. Cold air flooded in. Too cold for her memory of the storm or the weather.

Brood, slagging *Brood*.

Petrichor and ozone filled her nose and throat, and acrid, honest smoke. Iari's faceplate made a muffled *crunch* that said it was buckling, rather than bursting. The slagging thing—some kind of Brood, had to be—had climbed up her rig, put all its mass on her helmet. It was either going to come through the broken faceplate or it was going to tear her head off outright.

And then a pair of hands—metallic *clang*, grinding grip, that was Char—seized her helmet and pulled.

Iari blinked in the sudden flood of light—which barely qualified for the name, it was a maelstrom of dark smoke and black Brood fog and Windscar-storm grey. The tent top had torn loose (had been torn) and flapped like a cracking whip overhead, keeping time with the gusts of Hrok's freezing breath.

Her vision was clearing. She'd been thrown almost the width of the tent. Char had already turned away. They swung Iari's helmet in their fist like a weight, like a weapon.

And Iari saw then what had grabbed her. A hand-shaped shadow, except wet-looking, like oil-slicked ink, bigger than even Char's hands, flexed through the snow and the fog. Five fingers, a wrist, and then a forearm that stretched to impossible thinness. Violet-red smoked off it, and tangible cold.

And petrichor. Iari gagged on the stench. Brood didn't *have* hands. It was—clearly not impossible, *there it was*, but it was no arithmancy, no battle-hex Iari had ever seen.

Gaer would *love* this.

The Brood-hand recoiled from Char's bludgeoning, its fingers curled; its forearm seemed to grow thicker as it receded, like someone was reeling it back on a spool.

Someone probably was. *Bet* who was holding the other end.

Iari's syn surged again, bullying the battle-rig to spring forward (thank all engineers that the needle was in the collar, not the helmet, or she'd be slagging *useless* right now). She sliced at the slenderest bit of the arm with the rim of her shield, hoping to sever it. For something without any sense organs at all, it knew where she was. It pivoted at the wrist and raked at her face, ignoring Char.

Mistake, *mistake*: the riev dropped Iari's helmet and grabbed the Brood-hand with both of theirs. Char's hexes flared crimson, and the oil-slick hand began smoking. The fingers flared stiff with pain (except *whose?*). Then it made a fist and jerked and tried—failed—to escape. Char began to twist their fists, and to pull them apart, and the hand with them.

The Brood-hand burst.

Iari remembered to flinch (no helmet, no visor, bare skin), but it was the syn that moved her fast enough to throw up her shield arm. Effluvia spattered across the shield like oil in a hot pan, catching fire in little violet bursts. When the hissing had stopped, she dropped her arm and peeked over the rim. Char stood there, hands open, the last of the Brood slime still burning off (and still burning; some of that steam was Char's armor). Their Aedis limb glowed brighter than the rest of their hexwork. Newer, maybe, but also different. Attuned against Brood in a way that riev aimed at vakari had never been.

Cold chewed at Iari's ears. At her cheeks. Her throat and eyes burned, cold and Brood emanations together. She was standing in the middle of broken tables, cheap nanoforged alloy against which her axe haft was an obvious, visible artifact. Iari scooped it up, shook the blade out. Snow—because that had started, *here* came the storm—sifted down through the hole in the tent and hissed to death on the whitefire.

Then she looked back at the altar. She was half expecting a curtain of fog. Half expecting an open maw into the void, with Brood spilling out and the arithmancer's silhouette on the other side. (What if there was a *third* altar? If Gaer had missed it?)

The altar was just where she'd left it, bleeding violet and rust. Beside it, a little in front, was a tear in the aether. A fissure, but not like the others she'd seen. It wasn't full of roiling violet-black, it wasn't smoking. Instead it was filled with the same oily ink as the hand had been made of, and it . . . oozed. Dripped. Petrichor and ozone and something dead and sour collected in the back of her throat. The corrupted riev in B-town had bled a substance like this. The One-Eyes had, too. This *stuff* was what had damn near killed her nanomecha that first time.

What had Gaer said? Brood slaved as batteries that powered the One-Eyes' whitefire. So this was *dead* Brood, which Iari had seen plenty of. But dead Brood liquefied and smoked into nothing. It, they, didn't make *limbs*.

Brood were everything Iari had thought of as *wrong*, but this—whatever it was—redefined the word.

Then she saw the cabochon's glow, red and sullen, peering out of the tear, and realized she'd found the arithmancer.

He stood *in* that tear, *in* the aether. His helmet might have been polished metal once; now it gleamed slickly. The cabochon shone wetly, too, like a real eye. Iari felt the weight of its stare. Then the arithmancer stepped out of that tear, trailing rivulets of liquid wrongness, and Iari saw that one hand was missing, that one arm dangled and dripped and, as she watched, began to reform.

Whatever the arithmancer *had* been—tenju and mortal—they were something *else* now. Brood and flesh, stitched together out of void and arithmancy. *Like* the riev, but without artificing; *like* the One-Eyes, but without the hexes to bind Brood as power for whitefire. There *was* no whitefire. Jich'e'enfe had summoned Brood with fissures, and this arithmancer had, too. But Jich'e'enfe had been alive and this person—wasn't.

Call them Axorchal.

Iari's weapon hand buzzed and tingled, and she thought for a second the rig was failing, that it had taken too much damage. Then she realized it was the *axe* vibrating, and that it was starting to glow from the inside. That her rig was, too, except it was *her*, not the hardware. It was her syn, and the nanomecha driving that syn. It was Ptah's fucking *eye*, except bound in her flesh.

Evolution, Gaer had called it.

But maybe it was a blessing, too.

"Char," Iari said, as a warning.

Then she lunged toward Axorchal, axe raised like she meant to cleave them. Axorchal did not have their slime-hand regrown yet, but they came at her anyway, peeling themselves out of the tear like it was part of them. They were vaguely bipedal—legs, torso, that one-eyed head with the long black braids that had become tentacles. They moved like Winter Bite's appendages, but there was no detail. Just oily black, smooth and featureless and more awful because of that.

Axorchal looked like a voidspit boneless, if a boneless decided to stand on two feet and play person and have one eye instead of five.

(Jareth said it was fine to fear things, that fear was part of courage. Good, because she was afraid.)

Then Char moved, fast as any syn (maybe faster), whipping around Iari, past her, slamming into Axorchal with their Aedis fist. Lightning arced from Axorchal, burnout-black, as Char struck, and spidered along the floor. Arced into the altar. Arced into void itself, and tore it open.

Iari marked that peripherally, in that heartbeat before she rode the syn forward. She slewed around Char, spun, brought her axe down—her axe that glowed like living plasma, that *was* living plasma—on the altar.

Lightning met plasma, and everything exploded white.

CHAPTER TWENTY-EIGHT

aer saw the explosion in the aether. It splashed across his optic in a cascade of equations, a burst and tangle and arrangement that said it had come from a place almost as deep as true void, that it was tearing through the layers on its way to visible.

Time ran differently there, slower the deeper you got in the aether. Distance got strange, too. *Rishi* was moving at aethership speeds into the teeth of a storm, fast as Tobin could push the engines. Gaer's optic-view of the aether showed him clarity at a distance and blurry smears up close. So to him now, the Weep fissure was *setatir* crystal clear on his aetheric horizon, a shimmering ridge of emanations spiking into the aether. It was agitated. Not as bad as it had been during the surge, but worse than, say, last autumn in B-town.

But the *explosion*—a flare of equations that bent his mind even *looking* at them—meant Axorchal-the-arithmancer was *doing* something and Iari was in the middle of it.

Gaer opened both eyes and at once regretted it. Time-dragged equations lined up beside a *setatir* wall of storm clouds just starting to spit fat white flakes out like teeth. He dug the talons of both hands into the back of Tobin's chair for balance (the seats in here were not designed for vakari physiology, but vakari battle-rigs had mag-boots, so) and rasped, "Something's blown up."

"What has?" Tobin sounded as calm as if Gaer had announced there was tea in the galley, did anyone want a cup.

Notch, in possession of the copilot seat, and as useless up here as Gaer, twisted violently enough that his safety harness tried to strangle him. It failed (Gaer had mixed feelings) because his battle-rig prevented it, but the harness did arrest the twist, so that Notch was only half able to look at Gaer. "Where? I don't see anything."

"There." Gaer unstuck his talons and jabbed his hand out, between Notch and Tobin, toward the horizon. What happened in the aether would catch up eventually. *Soon*, eventually.

Notch looked. "I don't—oh, oh Hrok's freezing *breath*."

A column of what looked like ink geysered out of the Windscar plain, solid-looking but also very much *not*. A second column split the first, that was blue-white—not heat, not plasma, mostly light but not *only*. It seemed to burn the ink, or devour it—but it was sealing the aether, closing the hole, becoming briefly the brightest thing in the cockpit. By the time that the windscreen's hexes intervened, darkening the polyalloy, the ink column was gone, and the blue-white one was fading, sloughing off streamers of translucence as it sank back toward the plain.

Which was, by Gaer's reckoning, a geographic depression in the plains, between some of the sad little lumps of dirt Windscarrans called *hills*. And close. And a match for the coordinates he'd given Iari, then Tobin.

Notch jerked the secondary display terminal over and answered his own question. "That's—that's where *we're* going."

Of course it was. Gaer answered Tobin's question: "That was the second altar, I think."

"*Iari* did that?" Notch turned around more slowly this time, no less appalled. "Could I—can I do that now?"

"Probably and probably, if there is another altar on which you can practice. Let us hope there is not." Gaer bit the words off with precision. Behind his optic, the explosion had already faded. He realized belatedly that there would be shockwaves, that he should've warned Tobin—

Rishi shuddered, then slowed. The turing, relegated from primary pilot to overseeing all secondary systems, chirped and threw a list of complaints onto the primary display. Speed was decreasing, there were stresses on the hull, the engines were *trying*—

To *brake*. Gaer peered at the display. Hissed. "Something is *pulling* us?"

"Yes," Tobin said. "Not significantly yet, but it seems to be getting stronger. Can you say what?"

Gaer cycled his optic. It was—oh, *setat*. His scar ached, every filament, all the way to his skull. "I see no gravity effects. If the altar had opened a portal somewhere into void, and Iari closed it with force, I'd expect a shockwave rolling *out*. What I see"—he gestured at his optic—"is radically different pressures trying to equalize."

"It's not a tesser-hex or we'd see atmospheric effects." Tobin's hands slid across the controls like he'd been born to pilot. He was spacer-born; perhaps he had been. Though why he had chosen templar infantry, dirtside ground forces—a mystery that didn't matter. What did: Tobin absolutely knew what a tesser-hex looked like, even if *Rishi*'s dirtside-dwelling turing might not have.

Notch made a frustrated noise. "Does that mean the portal's still open? And going where? Into what, *void*?"

"It's closed. Closing," said Gaer. "But wherever it *went*—whatever passes for atmosphere there—is what's upsetting *Rishi*."

The display yelped again, and this time Gaer knew what the

alert meant. Brood. Probably a new altar-made fissure, or several. Tobin didn't waste breath on announcing the obvious. The deck tilted suddenly, steeply. Tobin was bringing *Rishi* down, but too quickly for the turing's comfort. An aethership was not meant to skim quickly over varied topographies, city streets or forests or Windscar's endless steppes. That's what hoppers were for. The turing, disapproving, chirped louder.

Gaer had some sympathy for it. The ground had not been visible for most of the journey. Now it suddenly was, rushing past in a white blur. The storm overhead was grey, getting darker as night collapsed on them; but there was a greasy blackness on the horizon. Smoke. Where Iari was, it was burning. Or had been. The smoke could be residual.

The Brood emanations, however, were not. They were fresh, and getting more pronounced.

Tobin eased back on the throttle, which was exactly the opposite of what Gaer wanted. Of what Tobin wanted, too, bet on that. "Prepare for drop. Notch, go tell Iffy. And when you get down there, Lieutenant—strap in."

"Sir." Notch escaped from his harness, stood up, which squeezed space to a premium. Iffy would have been a better choice to ride topside—she and her rig together were two-thirds of rigged Notch—but she had been willing (and able) to wait in the cabin.

As it was, Gaer had to take his eyes off the smoke to facilitate Notch's passage. They shared a moment of eye contact. Then Notch eeled past, and Gaer reengaged his mag-lock.

"You should go with him," Tobin murmured. *Rishi* was descending more sharply now, and more quickly. Either Tobin had found a good place to let them off, or he was going to crash the ship. "I assume you'll want to accompany him."

"Yes." But Gaer didn't move. It was irrational, looking for her at this distance. Gaer knew that. Iari wasn't going to come running across the snow. If she'd survived (she had), then she was where that explosion had happened. If she had not, then he'd be looking for—pieces. Whatever he could find. And it was too far away to see *that*.

Gaer started to turn, to follow Notch, when three tiny blue blips crossed his optic. He blinked, cycled, nothing—and then he saw it again. And realized, dear dark lords, that the blip was not *in* the aether. It was his optic picking up hexes: battle-hexes, *riev* hexes.

He shoved himself over to Notch's vacated chair, leaned across it, gestured at the display.

"Knight-Marshal."

"I see," Tobin said, and took a hand off the controls long enough to engage the display's magnification. The blips resolved into bipedal, oddly lumpish figures: three of them, moving fast. Tracks stitched the snow behind them.

The comm crackled, hissed, and then: "Aethership, this is Corporal Dodri, Windscar Aedis. Do you copy?"

"This is Knight-Marshal Tobin on *Rishi*. We hear you." Tobin's eyes flashed to Gaer's in the windscreen's reflection. "Dodri, who's with you?"

"Everyone but the captain and Char, sir. They stayed behind. Sir, Luki and Llian are bad, and Corso's bleeding—"

Crackle. Spit. "I'm fucking *fine*. Tell me you got Gaer up there."

Tobin gestured *go ahead* with his eyebrows. Gaer fluttered his plates—that was pure nerves—and said, "I'm here."

"Good. Fucking *listen* . . ."

It took longer than Gaer wanted, all of it. To drop *Rishi* down to a hovering height, to extend the ramp. For Notch and Iffy to descend and be waiting when Dodri, Corso, and Winter Bite finally arrived, the riev breaking trail for the others. Corso and Dodri each had a passenger: Llian slung over Dodri, evidently unconscious, and Luki half-clinging to Corso, who was holding a long-caster and wearing a long coat crusted with snow and frost and blood. Iffy was already shouting for the mobile med-mecha, which clattered up from the sick bay in a flurry of limbs.

Gaer waited until Iffy and Notch were down before he descended the ramp; at the bottom, he waited with Winter Bite while Iffy took custody of Luki and Llian, while Dodri babbled at Notch. No, that wasn't fair. She didn't babble. She tried to get everything out in a rush before Notch could ask questions, until he took her rig by the shoulders and leaned his helmet against hers.

Gaer didn't want to watch that. He turned his back on it, so that he stared at Corso—and they had already conversed, Corso had made his report, nothing left to say.

Then Winter Bite said, "I cannot hear Char or the captain," very quietly.

Clearly Winter Bite wanted Gaer to rationalize that silence with some arithmantic explanation. To give him *setatir* hope, which Gaer couldn't do.

But it was Corso who said, "You can't hear anything back in the camp, that's what you told us. You *said* it's some kind of fucking hex off that altar. Or, or Brood shit. That's still *happening*, Winter Bite, of course you can't hear them."

Which was supposed to be reassuring, Gaer knew that, but which sounded instead like everyone might be dead.

"Gaer," Corso said.

"Yes. Hexes. Brood shit. I heard." The aetheric contraction had stopped, at least. Though what that meant—sss, he would find out soon enough.

Corso made a disgusted sound. "Listen to me. She had to send you back. I see it on your slagging *face*, you're thinking none of this would've happened if you'd been there. Tell you what, Gaer, you'd be dead by now. We wouldn't have gotten *this* far. And that arithmancer would be opening *more* fucking fissures or whatever he's fucking doing, and you wouldn't be here to deal with that."

"I'd be dead, too," said Notch. He'd finally prodded Dodri up the ramp; she had been arguing to come back with them—oh yes, she was another *setatir* Iari, that one. Stubborn, loyal tenju. As was Notch, who was barely recovered from hospice and prepared to charge into battle. Because if everyone *wasn't* dead down there, it was going to be a fight.

I'd trade both of you for Iari, Gaer did not say.

Corso knew it. Wrung out a grim little smile for Gaer as he climbed back up the ramp. "She said you should take out the arithmancer."

"I have every intention." He glanced at Winter Bite, and Notch. Didn't ask if they were ready. It didn't matter.

They left *Rishi* hovering, Corso standing sentry in the open hatch, with a longcaster and a templar battle-rig and no hope at all in his eyes.

The explosion rolled out of the altar like a wave, knocking Iari back and off her feet, flat on her voidspit back as it rolled over her. But it was force more than heat, no light at all, neither blinding nor burning. She entertained a flash of panic—no helmet, no faceplate, she was going to lose her *head*—but no, she could breathe. Probably all phlogiston, with her luck, that would ignite in her lungs if there was even the tiniest spark. For a long pair of seconds, she lay there, marveling that she hadn't died and trying to guess how far she'd been thrown. A few meters?

The fog still hung thick in the air. Iari couldn't see much, but she could see *something*. Lumps of less dark in more dark. Not helpful, but at least she hadn't been blasted blind. Over her shoulder, around her, in the periphery she heard the hiss of something burning on Char's hexes, the whine of a riev's straining armor. That was Char (please Ptah) pounding the *shit* out of the arithmancer.

Then something grabbed her leg and jerked her across the floor of the tent, back the direction she'd come. Iari didn't waste breath yelling. She tried to flip instead, retracting her shield and rolling onto that arm while she swung the axe toward that patch of ground *there*. The plan was to stop, then deal with whatever had her. She hadn't even gotten a look yet—

But then *another* something grabbed the axe at the top of her swing and damn near jerked it out of her hands. This time she could see what had her, the same thing on both ends and *shit*. A coil of that same viscous inky oil, the same stuff as Axorchal's hand. Except this wasn't anyone's *hand*, this was—coils (of one tentacle? a whole creature?), wrapped around her axe shaft everywhere her gauntlet wasn't. The coils flexed and ripped the axe out of her hand with force enough to hurt, even through the gauntlet, and reeled it back into—

Misha's left *tit*.

The fissure-tear hadn't closed when the altar cracked. No, of course not: it had grown wider and taller, and *something* was reaching through, something that *looked* like a cross between a tunneler and a boneless. The presence of both cold and the petrichor-smell argued it was some kind of Brood. But the color wasn't right. Brood had a violet glow to them. This didn't. Brood didn't eat whitefire axes, either. And Brood had voidspit *heads* (most of the time) or *eyes* (most of the time) or some other indication which was part was front.

Brood also did not like Aedian battle-hexes, and this thing would not let go of her. One coil, tentacle, *long slimy thing*, was wrapped around her leg; it had paused in its tugging. The other, in possession of the axe, flowed up over it—the shaft, pausing briefly at the whitefire head. There was sparking, hissing, *surely* the void-spit thing would let go; but then it surged over the axe entirely, covering—no, *devouring* it.

Oh Elements. Oh no, that was bad.

The coil around her leg was smoking. She could feel the throb of battle-hexes from the inside of the rig, through the needle socketed in her neck, drawing off the battle-rig's power core. And because they were linked, she and the rig, through the needle—drawing off her voidspit syn and all the nanomecha.

Then she realized she'd gotten it wrong. The hexes in the byre, those arcs of energy, that *pain*—she'd thought she was overload-ing *them*. That her nanomecha, all that arithmancy, was going to win any contest it entered. Because she was the templar. She was *Aedis*.

But Luki and Llian had gone *offline* in their prison, and they were templars and Aedis, too. Their nano had *lost* that arithman-tic contest. But still she'd been thinking that she was different, her nano were different. That she couldn't lose.

And she very much could. This voidspit (literal) monster was going to overload her, if she didn't stop it. Force her out of the syn, slow her down—or burn her rig out, and maybe her nanomecha with it, and either way then she'd be dead.

Iari called on the syn again, and on panic, and used both of them to twist and sit up. That was awkward, battle-rigs didn't fold well at the middle, but at least the momentum rolled her into an awkward crouch. She snapped her shield back out and hacked at the coil around her leg. It didn't let go, but it flinched away from the shield rim, thinning, stretching. Iari entertained a brief idea of shearing straight through to her rig, trusting the hexes to repel its own weapon's whitefire.

The coil jerked again, like it knew what she meant to try, and tipped her back onto one hip. A *third* coil shot out of the fissure's maw, then a fourth: they each seized a limb, and now she was held on *both* arms, *both* legs. Iari reached for the syn again—which hurt, it was like rubbing raw skin, except from the inside—except this time it *fizzled*. The battle-rig was drawing too much power, straining as it tried to break free of the coils. She switched tactics, tried to help the rig: lunged backward, dropped her hips, and *sat* and leaned all the way back and dug her heels deep—

She began to slide toward the fissure.

Please, Chaama, swallow me now, don't let it drag me in there.

The ground did not open up. But something hit her square in the back. Metal shrieked. Iari took half a beat to connect the two, and her battle-rig sent a jolt through the needle, a warning of breach and ruin.

Except that wasn't ruin—

"I have you, Captain."

—it was Char.

CHAPTER TWENTY-NINE ≡≡≡

G aer ran.

A vakari battle-rig was built for, well, *battle*, not protracted sprints across Windscar. One had to mind where one stepped. The plains were not nearly as flat as they seemed, when one had to cross them on foot. But vakari had been apex predators, terrestrial avian sprinters; the feathers were gone, but the physiology remained, and the battle-rig just had to deal with it. Gaer was faster than Notch, anyway. (Tenju were not built for running in any environment.) Gaer was slower than Winter Bite, but then—the riev were the arguable pinnacle of wichu artificing (wichu horror, wichu heresy).

And honestly, if there was trouble, Winter Bite was their best warning. The riev's battle-hexes crawled along limb and torso, that banked-ember throb that could mean both Brood or more mundane hostile hexwork. The One-Eyes had seemed to be both at once. As for the contents of that new fissure—assume that it had contents, and that they were leaking out into Windscar and, of course, that they were hostile, too.

The aetheric contraction they'd felt in *Rishi* had either slowed down significantly, or the effects were not as strong on the ground.

Gaer could still sense a subtle pull on the rig, confirmed by a much less subtle parade of readings across the HUD.

"You getting Brood?" Notch sounded less out of breath than Gaer felt. Of course. Notch had his own Aedis brand of wichu heresy helping him run.

Gaer wished in the ever-expanding treasonous corner of his heart for a needle-socket and templar nano. Those nano would probably kill him. He might deserve it.

In the meantime, however, he bit off the words—

"Something *like*. You?"

—between breaths and hoped Notch did not want a *setatir* conversation.

"Same. What the hell?"

"You see what I see, Lieutenant." A sprawl of dark smoke that was still pale against a greater, more complicated shadow behind it. That greater darkness looked *like* the Weep, but it wasn't quite. Some fresh novelty, then, conjured out of the aether by some wretch of an arithmancer.

Rather than continue a conversation, Gaer sent his data directly to Notch. Regretted that in the next breath (yes, that quickly), because now Notch would ask even more, *bet* he would.

Except Notch didn't, and for long enough that Gaer had to glance back and make sure he was still back there. (Notch was.) Gaer turned back in time to see the tumbled ruin of a stone wall stretched in front of him, materialized out of apparent nowhere— another of those duplicitous rolls in the steppes, where you couldn't see something until you stepped on it. He cleared it easily, discovered a more marked slope on the other side, going down much more steeply than he'd expected. The next few slithery meters and moments were spent negotiating his balance and momentum, and when he looked up the camp was *right there*: smoke-shrouded tents, flames poking up like flickering teeth.

Gaer matched what little he could see against Corso's description. They had come down off the ridge on the eastern edge, hitting the dry creek bed that Corso said was also a road. So the byre with all of its hexes was *there*, up a short, shallow hill. Gaer risked disaster to glance that way, couldn't even see to the top. Jerked his attention back to where he was putting his feet. Corso had *also* said that the camp had maybe a hundred fifty people on site, but Gaer hadn't seen anyone yet. Even with the fires, the arithmantic upheaval, there should be something alive—

Sss. And there something was. Gaer's HUD reported movement in the canyon of shadows between the barn and the farmhouse. He thought at first it was a boneless—it was the right size, more horizontal than vertical, and at first glance the right number and dispensation of limbs. But then he realized it had no head, which even boneless needed to navigate. That meant it also had no eyes and no mouth, which rendered it even more awful than an actual boneless would have been.

And its color was wrong. Gaer could see that detail even uphill and through spitting snow. Brood were a purple-black like deepest void. This was . . . slipperier-looking, oily, greens and pinks and an unholy sheen. It appeared to be watching, observing—pointing one headless end at them, while its limbs braced against the barn, three on the wall, two on the ground, the size of a small human or a big alw.

"Notch. Do you see that?"

"I see. It's not Brood. But it . . . is? At least it looks like a boneless." Notch thumped to a halt beside him (a block of hexwork and a newly deployed whitefire shield and axe). His voice scaled up sharp, accusatory. "Winter Bite! How'd you miss this?"

An excellent question. Gaer was aware of Winter Bite doubling back (a block of outraged hexes on several layers of the aether), of the riev's agitation (aura bright as that fire, with none of the smoke). Just then his optic finished its preliminary analysis of the new fissure. It fed that data to his HUD's larger display, which earned a hiss and a hard blink to banish it—and a more rapid blink to call it back. He stared, then flashed a look at Winter Bite in the third layer of aether, came back—

Oh *setat*. That pseudo-boneless was as much Brood as Winter Bite was a living mammal. The difference was not of *kind*. It was of *state*.

"—is it? Gaer! My rig's saying Brood, but also no Brood emanations, is this something with the new syn—"

"No. It *is* a boneless. But it's a *dead* boneless. Like, like a riev. But not galvanism. Don't even ask me what's animating it, Notch, I have no idea."

Gaer braced to repeat himself—*what?* was a rational response to the irrational—but all Notch said was, "Okay. Can we kill it again?"

"Let's find out." Gaer unclipped his whitefire jacta—which had nothing like the range of a longcaster, but would be lethal enough across a handful of meters—and fired a bolt before the rig could link up its targeting. He did not miss. He *would* have, if the boneless had been Brood: Brood could warp physics, apply new rules. Gaer's bolt struck and drilled a coruscating hole that began burning like whitefire did when it struck something organic.

And then whitefire sputtered and died, and the hole and its surrounding carnage filled in and smoothed over. The headless, dead boneless shuddered. Then it gathered its back three legs under it, crouched down on the front two. Gaer raised his jacta again—

And suddenly there was Winter Bite in front of him, quicksilver and glowing hexes and an aura on fire.

"Lieutenant. Amba—*Gaer*. My last contact with Char and the captain is this way." He pointed the direction they had been going.

Which was when the not-boneless flowed out of its cover and leapt at Winter Bite's unguarded, distracted back.

The riev whipped around, caught the boneless on a cross-block and flung it away. Then he surged forward and *stomped* on it, and kept stomping. Sparks and effluvia sprayed through the air, ate through the snow. Where it struck Winter Bite, that effluvia stayed, spreading across the armor, trailing smoke as the hexes burned it away.

More corrosive guts than Brood had, then.

"Hrok's freezing *breath*." Notch sounded somewhere between horror and awe. "That's what the One-Eyes are doing? Making new monsters?"

"So it seems." And Gaer needed to close that fissure before any more of them got out. Which meant he needed to actually *see* it with his eyes and not just his optic.

Corso had described the mess tent, and Gaer supposed it must be there behind the smoke and the fog. The subtle aetheric contraction continued, less than it had been, but still steady, like a slow-bleed hemorrhage, and *that* was not an image he liked. His optic had sifted the numbers. The fissure to whatever hellish aetherscape the reanimated Brood came from lay directly ahead.

"The fissure's still open, which means there might be more of these things. Winter Bite, may I suggest staying behind us and watching for them? Lieutenant, you first."

Notch cut him a sharp look, glint of faceplate and the tiny teslas around it. Then he took point and started for their destination. And while Gaer wanted to rush past him—he also wanted to catch his breath and sift through his data and *not* be ambushed by riev-Brood (which wasn't entirely accurate; it was not clear if the dead Brood had been repurposed, or if this was some new abomination of arithmancy, alchemy, artificing—but that was also true of riev, so). He stayed a close second to Notch, with Winter Bite crowding his heels.

Fog—aetheric, cold and fathomless grey, dark because there just wasn't light, wasn't anything—seeped out to meet them. Curled around their rigs and shrank visibility down to mere meters. Notch swore and stopped. Gaer could see the faint glow of his shield, the flicker of his axe.

This fog was a battle-hex; *this* was something Gaer understood. He initiated a counter-hex, and the fog began rolling back, revealing a wasteland of collapsed canvas, shattered poles jutting through like bones in some places, and buckled in others, leaving draped folds of material hiding whatever lay beneath. Some of the bulges were large, and right-angled: one of the kitchen's coldboxes, maybe. A stove. There were rents in the canvas, too, with blackened, curled edges, as if something corrosive had rested there— like reanimated Brood, *riev*-Brood, on their way out of the fissure and into the camp. Gaer still could not *see* people, but now that he'd pushed back the concealing fog, he could *hear* them. Whatever was happening out there, it sounded as bad as any conventional Brood attack. Screaming, the pop of 'caster-fire.

Let that mean the controlling force, the arithmancer, was already dead. *Let* the cultists die of their own stupidity. He wouldn't mourn them.

Except it wouldn't be only them. The riev-Brood would keep coming out and they would spread, unless he got the *setatir* fissure closed.

Which destroying the altar should have done. Which *Iari*

should have done, so either it hadn't worked, or the arithmancer was still alive, or—

Gaer shut off that panic. "Altar first," he told Notch. "If Iari didn't destroy it, then you need to finish it."

"I fucking know." Notch ventured onto the tent's collapsed landscape. "You deal with the fissure. Close *that*."

"I *setatir* know," Gaer muttered, and followed him.

They found the altar first, or its fragments, scattered as if from an explosion. Then more shards, then a largish slab that Notch poked with his axe blade. It looked like blackened metal, that was all, except for the twisted shapes carved into its face. There was no aetheric signature. No glowing hexes. The force of the explosion had cleared a rough circle: it was frozen mud underfoot here, and crisp fragments of tent.

"The altar is dead," Gaer said, reading his optic. "*Real* dead. No hexes functional."

"Copy that." Notch stepped over the shards. "There's something organic up here. Also dead. Gaer . . ."

Dear dark lords, dear Elements, *let it not be.*

Then Gaer took a breath, held it, and went to see who, what, Notch had found.

The arithmancer—assume that's who it was—lay in a tangle of tent-cloth and their own splintered armor. There was single metal glove extending up the arm, it was snapped off at the wrist. The helmet Gaer remembered from the caves—that confection of metal and spikes, with that signature Axorchal One-Eye cabochon—was missing, along with the head inside it.

"Char," Winter Bite said, icy riev rage comingled with satisfaction. "*They* did this."

That Char's body was not immediately evident seemed promising. That there was no sign of Iari's, either—

Then Gaer's foot hit something solid, something metallic, under the tent's fallen skin. He squatted down, plucked at the canvas. The one time he needed a hole, and there wasn't one. He snapped the jacta back onto his rig, drew his monofil, made the cut.

A templar helmet stared back. Cracked visor. Scorch marks. Badly damaged and conspicuously *not* part of a battle-rig. Oh *setat*. Gaer snatched for it, hesitated—then hooked his gloved talons around the edge and pulled it free. He was ready (he would never be ready) for there to be something inside (someone, Iari).

But it was empty.

He held it up like an offering to Notch.

Who said, with only a little tremor, "She must've taken it off."

The shattered visor suggested a *why*. The *where was the rest of her* was another conundrum. Gaer consulted his HUD. The primary aetheric disturbance, the fissure, was either a meter or five *that* way—his rig couldn't be more precise. Gaer stood up, still holding the helmet, and strode toward the disturbance.

And found it.

The fissure was vertical, like a gap between reality's curtains that stretched like a three-meter wound. It had been partly sealed, or had partly sealed itself: there was tent material stuck to the edges like cloth on a weeping wound, bits of detritus Gaer didn't want to examine too closely that looked organic in origin (his HUD confirmed it). The edges were slicked up with sludge, viscous stuff that might have come from the One-Eye half-riev dead by the shattered altar, and an inkier slime that looked like a partly dissolved tentacle of tunneler-sized proportions. There was a distinctive one-eyed helmet partly under that tentacle. Axorchal's *head* had ended up over here. Which meant Char had been here, too.

The faint aetheric contractions were coming from the unsealed portion of the fissure, a slit in the middle that gapped and flapped like a curtain drawn over an open window. One of the deep layers of aether leaked through the slit: oily light, like being deep underwater, or looking through a badly scratched faceplate.

Something moved behind the slit, that Gaer's HUD and Gaer's optic could only describe with equations. A large disturbance, though whether or not it had physical form—what that even *meant* on that layer of aether—Gaer did not know. This fissure was very much like the Weep itself: a portal that had gone horribly wrong, except Gaer thought this one had been intentionally opened.

Not a recreation of the original Weep, but a *revision*.

Maybe that was why Jich'e'enfe had balked at the alliance. Inserting Brood into riev was one act of terrorism against the Confederation and its vakari allies. Making Brood *into* riev was another kind of horror. Creating a whole new and different Weep, a whole new sort of surge, the effects of which were happening out in that camp right now—maybe that had been too far even for her.

Or maybe the cultists had killed her because she was wichu and foreign to Tanis. Maybe it was just that simple.

Or maybe the arithmancer had just seen a way to drive the templars off his planet and reckoned he'd sort out the mess later. Or he'd thought he could control it.

"Can you seal that?" Notch asked softly.

The Weep was beyond arithmantic repair, but the Weep had been a cataclysm, hundreds of vakari arithmancers together, portals linked across all Protectorate space. This fissure was a single insult, made by a single (dead) arithmancer. Gaer knew the equations. The theory. But the *practice* of that, the *skill*—

"I don't know."

Something crashed very near by—or not near. The fog deformed sound, distance, perception. Gaer wasn't sure the sound had been real, until Winter Bite said, "Contact." He had opened his delicate sensor array, and the appendages groped through the fog. "More of the riev-like Brood. Approaching from the south and west. At least five, perhaps six."

"Hrok's stinking breath. Try with the fissure," Notch said to Gaer. "We'll deal with *this*."

Something was coming.

Iari knew it because Char's hexes lit up again. Dull red, getting brighter, sigils suddenly burning visible where there had been only smooth armor a moment before.

Char was past saying as much. Char hadn't said anything for—an hour, a day, forever, ten minutes. Without her HUD, Iari couldn't access the battle-rig's chrono. Wouldn't have helped anyway. This rig was finished. She had been on the wrong side of a tunneler once before (the bottom), and she'd lost that rig, too, *and* nearly died.

Although, then, the tunneler had pulled a whole house down on top of her and Brisk Array, and Jich'e'enfe had blown everything else up with fire, and Brisk Array had died. This time, she wasn't on fire (yet) and Char wasn't dead (again, yet). Iari *was* buried again, but she couldn't tell under what. She couldn't see well enough to tell with only the tiny teslas left on her rig. She had Char's Aedis arm braced in front of her, which was the only reason her uncovered head wasn't paste, and which also gave her light from Char's hexes when they lit up and a good close-up-view of Char's grafted arm. Whatever she was under, whatever its composition, there was space enough underneath for one templar in most of a battle-rig. Char had flung Iari under it, then thrown themselves on top. A bulwark against the tunneler's suction, so that she wasn't pulled into whatever layer of the aether it came from as it died. She'd heard metal shrieking, heard things break, and thought about all the heavy equipment in the kitchen, and what might be flying around out there. She knew she'd be dead, too, except she'd had Char between her and whatever it was. So she'd stayed down and waited.

That might have been a mistake. She didn't know if that arithmantic voidspit was over or not, but the hexes on Char's arm said there was trouble incoming, and she was in no position to meet it.

If they caught her like this, pinned, no helmet—it'd be quick, but it would be ugly, and *no*.

Adrenaline jolted. The syn tingled, and Iari lost her breath with the shock of it. It felt like nails in her spine, like every tooth in her head had cracked open, the kind of pain people told secrets to stop. But the battle-rig twitched, so—that was something. There was still power in the voidspit thing. Or it was pulling power out of her nanomecha, which she reckoned more likely but who slagging *knew* anymore. Didn't matter. She needed to get out, get up. Defend both her and Char, if it came to that.

It took work to inhale against the crush of the battle-rig, bent and dented with Char's weight, and she wanted to cough with the cold of it, but, "Char." Her voice sounded like gravel. "Char, you hear? I'm going to try and get out. Deal with whatever's coming."

Char did not answer. Char certainly didn't move. Char also

wasn't dead. Their hexes wouldn't be working if they were. *Bet* that voidspit Axorchal had done damage, fine, but he hadn't killed her templar. Not yet.

Iari closed her eyes. Licked her lip and tasted blood. Probably from her nose; no teeth felt broken. She didn't have much for leverage. She had her left arm, but Char had collapsed on her right one, rendering it pinned and useless under Char's torso. Iari reached forward and tugged experimentally on Char's wrist. Whatever the riev was braced against, it was solid.

Iari hadn't tried moving her legs in a while, had been afraid to—but now she did, and they moved, and it hurt—but that just meant all the parts were still there. She used Char's arm to brace, dug a knee into the ground, pushed her other boot in something that shifted against her weight—that made her sheltering wreckage shift, too, and creak. *Char* shifted, their weight sliding over Iari's back, and something on the back of Iari's rig *cracked*. But then Iari's right arm slid free, and there was no new pain, and there was space to maneuver where there hadn't been. She coaxed her right arm into bending so that she could brace elbow and shoulder and push herself just a little bit up. All right. *That* hurt, too.

Faintly, *faintly*, she could hear an alarm going off in her rig. Faint maybe because all the backup systems were about to die, or because the pounding of her own pulse was too loud.

Ungentle Ptah, she did not want to open her shield unless she was clear. She'd shear off Char's voidspit arm *again*.

There came a crack from somewhere she couldn't see, and the sharp smell of rot and petrichor. Bile backed up in Iari's throat— that was *them*, they were close. She was not, *could* not, get caught like this by Brood.

She shoved back hard with both hands and bucked and it *hurt*, but she managed to slide partway free. Icy air touched her back

and her ribs, freezing the sweat in her skinsuit. Oh. Ha. *That* was
the reason for the alarm in her rig. A breach. A voidspit rig-breach,
back near the power core, probably where Char had grabbed hold
of her in the first place.

Another crack, and a howl that made her bones ache—and the
sizzling *snap* of whitefire cutting through something unlucky. The
ground under her shivered with a massive impact.

Char's Aedis arm flared blinding white, Ptah-white. Iari blinked
on reflex, and shoved backward again. Fought her way onto both
hands and knees. She had to go *faster*.

She reached for her syn—screamed and rode it all the way to
standing, snapped her shield out as she spun (ha, as she lurched)
to face—

—someone in Aedis armor. Templar armor. Shield, axe, whitefire bright. A coruscating light coursed through the seams of their
battle-rig. Not Ptah-white, but bluer. Colder. The templar wasn't
looking at her—facing three-quarters the other direction, slicing
at slimy, oily, stinking horrors that looked like a slither of slicers
(except wrong, even by Brood standards—these were oily pinkish
green). The axe sliced through and ignited whatever it touched,
and it glowed with that same icy blue fire, and where it touched
them the boneless just . . . smoked and dissipated.

It was Hrok's breath, blowing the monsters away.

Then the templar spun around and faced her, and that was—
that was *Notch*. She knew before he opened his visor, the neefa.
She couldn't make sense of the look on his face.

"Brood," she croaked, and actually hearing her speak seemed
to shake something loose in him.

"I—they're not Brood. Mostly. They're already dead."

"*All* of them?" That would be every drop of Mishka's mercy.
Her vision was tunneling in on the edges as her syn ebbed.

"No, I mean—they're *already* dead. We're killing them twice."

Iari blinked. And then Winter Bite emerged from the fog in a blaze of battle hexes. His arms were smoking and smeared to the elbows.

"The cultists have scattered. There are more of these mutant Brood, but they are moving toward the south." Riev couldn't sound breathless, but he gave that impression. "They may have detected *Rishi*."

"Knight-Marshal Tobin will handle it." Notch side-eyed Iari. "He's not *on* the ground. *Rishi's* got weapons, and Iffy's there, so—"

Iari raised a hand. Tobin *would* handle it. (Tobin was *here*. Tobin had come for her. It was already so hard to breathe.) "Char needs—help." She didn't like the way her voice cracked on that syllable.

Winter Bite shoved past both her and Notch—very gently—and began to pull the debris off Char. Oh, Elements, you could *see* the damage. Winter Bite's hexes burned like vengeance. Char's glowed, but so dimly, and in patches, as Winter Bite uncovered them.

And there was absolutely nothing Iari could do about it. She hung her attention on Notch. Took a breath and spat it out in a rush. "The fissure. Closed?"

"I don't know. Gaer's dealing with it." Notch turned his head reflexively, and showed her the direction she wanted to go.

Iari staggered past him. Two uneven steps, three. She couldn't hear anything but her battered rig, trying to do what she asked. *Whir-click* and *thunk*. (And her heartbeat, pounding in both her ears and her throat.) Her skin stung in the cold, like tiny shards of broken glass, freezing and scraping at the same time.

One more step, and she saw the fissure. Still a vertical slit, taller even than Gaer—but narrower, now. A web of sinople light stitched over the gap, drawing it closed like a wound. Gaer stood facing that crack. One arm hung slack at his side. The other cradled her helmet. Reflected light shimmered across his visor like an aurora, collected in the cracks of her shattered faceplate like liquid. Fog from the fissure whirled and roiled around him as if he was himself a savage wind.

Which he probably was, on some layer of the aether. Here, he was a just an arithmancer.

No. Not *just*. A vakari arithmancer. They were the best in the multiverse. And he was *Gaer*, who had figured out every equation he'd run up against so far. Who understood the Weep.

Iari's chest ached from the inside, but it wasn't fear this time. It was pride. It was *faith*.

The fissure seemed to suck the fog back as Gaer pulled the edges closed. Iari felt the gentle pull on her skin, on her eyes, on the frozen spikes of her hair. Then a less gentle, tugging on her breath, pulling it out of her mouth, of her nose, of her lungs. She clamped her lips tight. Held her breath, eyes slitted, just *held*, while Gaer did work that she could not see in places she could not look and the fissure pulled back its murderous cold and its fog and its malice.

Gaer wove his equations together, wove the fissure together into a writhing line. And then—gone. The sinople light lingered a moment more, and then it, too, smoked away.

It was full night, and the snow was falling, and the fires still burning in the camp bounced a dim orange glow off the clouds. Warmth—or at least cold less lethal—melted the frost off Iari's cheeks, her forehead. She blinked her eyes clear.

"Well done." Ungentle Ptah, that was more of a croak than a compliment. She swallowed, tried again. "That was—"

"A miracle? Yes. I think so, too." Gaer turned slowly, like he wasn't sure of his balance. "You're alive."

"*Not* a miracle. That was you. Your arithmancy. Yes, I'm alive." Unless that was what he'd meant by miracle, her not-yet-deadness, which—was a fair point. He was holding her helmet now in both hands, like an offering or a talisman. She could guess what he'd thought when he found it.

"Gaer. I'm okay."

He took a step, still careful, like he wasn't sure of his footing. He was close enough now she could see the damage to his battle-rig, pitting and scoring that might've happened in the k'bal ruins. Or that might've happened here, or at any point in between. Then his headlamp winked dark, and his visor peeled back. There was blood running out both nostrils and his optic seemed hazy. She smelled burnt sugar and hot metal, which meant stressed and sweating vakar, which meant *Gaer.*

He was close enough now that she had to look up, and his eyes looked like star-hung void.

"Good," he said. "So am I."

CHAPTER THIRTY

ari stood in front of Chaama's sigil, north-facing wall of the temple, a few feet of wall between her and the Windscar weather—imagining the wind on the other side, the snow—and wished she were out in it.

It was Chaama's hour. The least popular for templars on day-watch. The one nightwatch templars skipped on their days off, when duty did not oblige them to be up all night. Priests of Chaama attended, the odd templar—initiates, mostly, on one vigil or another. Windscar was full of initiates, and home to several high-ranked Chaaman priests. Sister Maralah had been here every midnight Iari had, but Maralah was out with Keawe right now, scouring the steppes for any stray mutant Brood that might've escaped the cultist camp (and any cultists who might have fled and survived; they were harder to find). The initiates found themselves standing watch instead of temple vigils, on the ramparts instead of in the temple, doing duty for the templars out with Keawe.

Notch was out there right now. *Dodri* was. Even Winter Bite. Luki and Llian were in hospice, fine, of course they wouldn't go. And Char was with the armorer, which was as close to hospice as riev got.

Iari wasn't out there, because Iari had totaled her battle-rig. That was Keawe's reason. *Tobin* would have—

Tobin *would* have—Tobin *had* in the past—expedited repairs on her rig, had issued a new one, had bent about every rule in Aedian administration to keep her in the field. He wasn't bending them now. And if Keawe herself tended to rule-bending (which she did; Iari'd had a few long talks with Notch since their return), then she wasn't going to bend them for Iari.

It was hard not to read a reprimand in that refusal.

Truth: the Windscar Aedis was still roiling, active and acting, but Iari had no duty assigned, no *place* in it.

Iari dragged her focus back to Chaama's sigil. Attending prayers didn't count if you didn't pay attention. She usually chanted with the priest. Tonight, it was just her silence and the very junior priest, a young alw, taller than Iffy, angular, with white-blond hair bound up tight and skin darker than Gaer's and an accent Iari could not quite place. Not Windscarran, anyway. Maybe not even from Tanis. She moved around Iari, chanting (alone, low-voiced, mostly steady) and arranging the stones and sand and clay—Chaama's bones—in front of the sigil with the absolute focus of someone terrified to make a mistake in front of an audience.

A silent audience. A big, scar-faced tenju officer who wouldn't even *mouth* the words to the prayers and clearly was thinking about other things.

Void and dust, ungentle Ptah, she should just—go. Let this poor priest finish her prayers and rake her patterns, unobserved except by Chaama.

She could try to find Gaer again; *he* had proven remarkably elusive, for someone two meters tall with a spiked silhouette. She hadn't expected him to come to the hospice—she hadn't been there long anyway—but she'd looked for him with Char several times, and he hadn't been in the armory. He *had* been, Char said, but he'd gone. She wasn't sure *why* he was avoiding her, but he clearly was.

The young priest concluded the prayers. Stood there, caught between Iari and the arrangement of stones and raked sand, with bits of dust and clay clinging to her cuffs and her fingers. Clearly, *clearly*, she was waiting for the templar who hadn't sung a note, who'd just *stood* there, to leave. If Iari didn't move, the priest wouldn't either, bound by ritual Iari knew very well could keep them both standing there until Hrok's priest arrived with the dawn.

"Thank you," Iari said, which was *not* ritual, which startled the priest enough that she actually *looked*, wide-eyed, an intimacy Iari dodged by staring instead at the sigil, making the appropriate gesture to Chaama. Turning to go.

Oh ungentle Ptah.

Tobin stood by the door, just inside the threshold. Watching her the whole time, he must have been. Iari felt heat crawl under her skin, hot and sudden accompaniment to the hit of adrenalized nerves. The syn didn't like endocrine competition. It jolted up her spine, down her limbs, until she settled it with deep breaths. That Tobin was at midnight services did not surprise her. That he had not come in—

Well. He might have been late, seen a novice priest and been reluctant to interrupt. Sure. It must have been kindness that made him come find her here, in a place he knew she would be, rather than summoning her to some borrowed office to have a conversation. Maybe he'd just had no time until now. Or maybe he really was *that* angry at her for keeping secrets.

Iari uncurled her fingers from their reflexive fists. Took another breath and walked to meet him. Her boots made almost no noise on the stone. *Boots,* not a battle-rig; the leather creaked a little, the tabard whispered over the polysteel breastplate and the antiballistic tunic underneath. She still had her axe, the haft hanging off her hip. Its weight was a comfort, even if the rest of the uniform was not.

She got close enough to hear Tobin's prosthetic hum before she said, "Sir," and stopped, saluted—

Tobin waved the salute aside, before she'd even got fist to shoulder. "Walk with me, Iari?"

It was her turn to startle. Templars only had one name; they gave up family affiliations when they swore their oaths. (She'd never had family; the name she'd given up came from parents dead before memory.) Tobin didn't use hers often. Not without her attached rank. So either this was a personal conversation—and she could count *those* with Tobin on both hands—or she was in *that* much trouble.

"Sir," she said carefully, and he winced. But he didn't say anything else, just gestured at the door. She pushed it open (got a faceful of spiteful snow), held it, straddling the border of hexes that kept warmth *in* and cold *out.* Tobin sighed audibly and walked past her.

"*With* me," he murmured. He limped along a blank expanse of perimeter wall, aiming at the distant shelter of the templar garrison. Iari matched her stride to his, stayed between him and the worst of the wind. "As much as we can, let's dispense with formality."

She strangled the reflexive *sir.* Tried "all right," instead, and did not like how her voice sounded. Thin, tired, strained.

Scared, like she would not be if there were Brood coming at her, or Axorchal, or a phalanx of One-Eyes.

For a few moments it was just the wind and the faint hum of Tobin's prosthetic. Then Tobin blew out a plume of warm breath that the wind tore apart and scattered. He peered at her sidelong. "How are you?"

He didn't mean physically. Oh, she could answer the question that way, it would be safest, and he might let it go. But she'd already lied to him for the last time.

"I got Homer killed. I almost got *Char* killed. And I let two templars get taken. Luki says she'll be fine, and Llian says she already is, but . . ."

"But you don't believe them?"

"I believe Iffy. She says they'll recover. Physically."

Tobin looked at her sidelong—not a glance, but a measuring gaze. He was going to say something, she could *see* it, and she wasn't brave enough to hear what.

"That shed. That prison," she blurted. Iari had written the report. Damn sure Tobin had read it. He'd know what she meant. "What was that *for*? Was it meant for templars? To, to burn out their nanomecha?"

Tobin frowned into the middle distance. "Gaer doesn't think so. Neither does Sister Maralah. That may be the only thing those two can agree on. The prevailing theory is that that those hexes— the ones in the shed, and to a lesser extent, the ones in the badges— were meant to break down a subject's resistance. Possibly to break minds outright. Char suspects a kinship between that prison and a riev-kiln, though of course we can get no confirmation from Su'seri or anyone *else* in the wichu hierarchy about what a riev-kiln contains. *Maralah* thinks prospective One-Eyes were first put in that shed—maybe the resistant, the rebels, or the fanatics— and then, when sufficiently broken, subjected to whatever medical interventions you found in the ruins." He took a deep breath. "Iari, listen to me. You didn't *lose* Luki and Llian. You will not want to hear that you saved them, and I don't blame you. But you *did* retrieve them alive, and they *will* recover. You do need to hear that. Homer did *not* live, that's true. But he did not die because of you, either."

"He was my responsibility."

"As your unit was *mine*. But what happened at Saichi was not my fault. And what happened in the ruins was not yours."

He said it with more force than was Tobin-typical, and the words seemed to hang there in the snowfall. He didn't ask her if she understood. She did. Of course she did. Jareth's *Meditations*, at its core, was about how to face things beyond your control. Some things you endured. Some you overcame. Some you avoided.

And others you charged at, head on. "How much trouble am I in?"

Ungentle Ptah, that was the *worst* way to ask *are you angry at me, have I disappointed you*, because she didn't want to hear *yes*. Because she would not believe *no*.

Tobin was quiet a handful of steps, as a pair of battle-rigged initiates trotted past on some errand. Then, just as they passed the aethership dock, lit with floodlamps and empty, waiting for *Rishi's* return, he said, "You're in less trouble than *I* am. But Keawe can't do anything to me. She can insist that you're confined to the compound, relieved of all duties—which is a *medical* hold, one that Iffy supports. And, to be fair, even if Keawe was feeling forgiving— you did destroy another battle-rig, we have a potential surge, and Char's got priority from the armorer."

His tone was dry, unbothered, gently amused; Iari felt some

of the tightness in her chest unknot. Keawe's spite, she could handle.

But, "That isn't what I meant."

Tobin nodded. "I know. I wish you'd told me about your nanomecha when it happened. I understand why you didn't."

This was the place to apologize. Beg forgiveness. She'd rehearsed it a hundred times, and the words dried up and died in her throat. She would do it again. All of it. "It was never about you. Trusting you, I mean. I did. I do."

"I know. I *do* understand. In your place, I would have done the same thing." He offered her a smile that was mostly eyes, only a wry ghost on his lips. "Gaer was most thorough explaining your reasons."

Gaer. Right. The tightness returned to her chest, her gut, her throat. "Iffy said Gaer repaired Notch's nano."

She heard Tobin's smile fade. "He did."

She'd asked Gaer to tell Tobin, do *her* work, and he had. She'd told him to *fix* the arithmancy, to *solve it*, and he had. But this—

"Ungentle Ptah, *why*?"

Tobin was quiet for long enough Iari thought that they'd reach the voidspit doors before she got an answer. That she might not get one at all: that Tobin had remembered he was Knight-Marshal of B-town, acting Knight-Marshal of Windscar, and she was just a captain.

Then, very quietly, "Keawe asked Gaer to save Notch. Gaer refused. So she." Tobin sighed. "So she threatened him."

Heat flooded under Iari's skin—anger, and guilt for that anger, because she was afraid Tobin had earned some of it. The syn rippled, offering its support, buzzing under her skin. Slowly, carefully, "What did she say?"

"That she would release his service immediately."

Her anger evaporated. Left cold in its wake. That made no sense. Had the Five Tribes classified Aedian tech, the nanomecha *hexes*? That was treason. Keawe would never—

But Tobin had said letting Gaer go back to SPERE was Keawe's *threat*. Because Keawe thought Gaer didn't want to return? Or that he wouldn't betray the Aedis to SPERE? But he would, he would have to, if he went back.

Or. No. Because Keawe had figured out Gaer wouldn't betray *her*. *Oh, Gaer. You neefa.*

Tobin was still talking, softly, urgently, like he almost never did. "Listen, Iari. I was there for that conversation, and I didn't try to stop it. If it had been *me* with a templar down and dying—if it had been *you* in Notch's position—I would have asked the same thing. I would have made the same threat."

Except if it had been her dying—Gaer would have volunteered. Tobin had to know that, too. Iari found her hands curled into fists again, and this time she left them. "So what happens to him now?"

Tobin stopped, turned, faced her. "Gaer hasn't told you *any* of this yet?"

So she stopped, turned, faced *him*, while snowflakes cut impatient circles around them. *I haven't seen him, I've been worried about other things, there hasn't been time, I don't know what to say*—all that distilled to the simpler truth. "No."

A line appeared between Tobin's brows. But all he said was, "There will be a meeting when Keawe returns, and it will include Gaer. I'll see that you have an invitation. And in the meantime—I can't get you a battle-rig. There aren't enough. But you don't need one to stand nightwatch. If you want to return to duty, get yourself onto the wall. Sergeant L'Brek's on duty up there, north tower— see where she needs you. Tell her it's on my orders."

Corso found Gaer on the ramparts during daylight—*actual* daylight, which didn't happen often in Windscar winters—with a sky so sharply blue it could cut you, with a wind (always, *always*, the slagging wind) that cut in a whole different way, blowing out of the north in little unpredictable gusts like someone laughing.

Hrok, probably, though Corso wasn't sure the Elements could really laugh. Or be happy. Or be anything. They weren't people, far as he understood, which wasn't that far. The Aedis Catechism wasn't a book he'd had much cause to read, and given his new habit of keeping company with templars and priests, well, any questions he had, he could just ask. So far the emotional state of the Elements had not been one of them.

You could see the storm coming, though. A towering wall of clouds, bruise dark where they collided with the blue. That would land on the Aedis tonight, maybe sundown, maybe sooner. That meant it would hit the cultist camp before that. Keawe was out there right now, hunting for leftover cultists and leftover Brood, with a fully-crewed *Rishi* and a unit of templars. They were all *hers* this time, except for Winter Bite, who Corso reckoned had gone along on the insistence of Notch and Dodri.

Corso knew that reports came back at regular intervals. He'd made friends with a couple of templars in dispatch, who wouldn't let him *read* the logs or anything, but who'd give him a rough summary.

Better than them, though, was Char—who had some kind of way to talk to Winter Bite and vice versa, which Corso suspected wasn't quite sanctioned. Tobin knew, Corso guessed—*maybe* Keawe (maybe that was the real reason Winter Bite was out in the

field). But no one else was talking about it. Certainly not his con-
tacts in dispatch.

So Char was a regular stop (sometimes multiple stops) on his
daily routine. Char had been bumped to priority repairs, but
Windscar's armorer had no voidspit idea what to do with riev, and
Char wouldn't let the wichu artificer Su'seri near them. So it was
Gaer doing the work, around Gaer's other duties, which Corso
reckoned suited both Char and Gaer in some weird and improbable way.

Gaer had been *busy*. Keawe hadn't taken him north, no, but
she hadn't wasted him, either. (She'd taken Iari off duty entirely—
that was probably partly Iffy's doing, but it was also spite by Corso's reckoning.) Gaer had been dividing his time between Char
and whatever Keawe had down in the vaults. *Labs*, Iffy said, and
research, and *things above both of our security clearance, Corso,
stop asking.*

Which meant arithmancy, which meant hexes, which had
something to do with the rumors about Notch's new *blessing*,
in which Gaer was involved up to his jaw-plates. Corso didn't
give a dead neefa for Aedis secrets, but he did worry some about
Gaer.

All right. He worried a *lot* about Gaer. Not in the least because
no one else seemed to have time for it—Iffy had Luki and Llian
and, until her escape from hospice, Iari to fret over. (She was probably still fretting over Iari. Corso wasn't fond enough of frustration to join her.) Tobin was acting Knight-Marshal, and *again*—Iari
came first. (A thing Iari would hate if she knew, which she would
if she thought about it for more than a minute, which she probably
had and *that* was why Corso was staying out of her way.)

But *worry* for Gaer wasn't why Corso was up here. Conversation was. He climbed the voidspit stairs to the rampart—because lifts were just boxes on strings and strings *broke* sometimes—and there Gaer was, halfway down the rampart, facing north. He wasn't wearing his battle-rig: long coat, hood *down* (maybe vakari ears didn't get cold), hands braced on the top of the wall. He looked almost native, except for all the bits that stuck out of his coat. Except that he could look *over* the top of the crenelations, which no one else could except Char. You didn't see vakari up north. Gaer was the only one in Windscar. Hell, the only one outside of Seawall.

Corso dodged a mecha holding two shovels in twice that many appendages that was pitching the last of the snow over the wall. The ramparts were down to the thin layer the shovels left, a veneer of slick white in some places, where the sun hadn't reached yet. Where the sun had, there was just steam as the snow skipped the whole melting part. Solid to gas. (Chaama to Hrok, with a little Ptah in between. Did Mishka feel left out? Another question he wouldn't ask.) Corso kicked his toe hard into that snowy remnant, chipping bits of it out. Kept kicking, throwing bits of snow, until the mecha noticed and came over, chirping and furious, to clean up.

Which got Gaer's attention. The vakar watched as Corso escaped the mecha's vindictive shoveling, head cocked, plates flared only as far as the damaged one could.

"The fissure—*the* fissure, the only one we're supposed to have on this wretched planet—has gotten very quiet," Gaer called, by way of greeting. And added, as Corso got close enough that he did not have to shout: "It did this after Jich'e'enfe's performance in B-town, too."

"Performance? That's what you're calling what she did?" It

wasn't what Corso had intended to say, or what he intended to talk about, but Gaer's word choice surprised him.

"I think it might have been."

"Okay. Performing what, and for what audience?"

"The what: testing arithmantic theory, opening those little fissures—B-town is a good size for small acts of terrorism. Do it in Seawall, you'd get too much attention. Do it up *here*—no one notices. Obviously. Do you know how many Brood-gutted homesteads they've found, now that they're looking? Disappeared people?"

"Yeah. I do. Dispatch gets reports, but all they have is locations. Winter Bite, though—he tells Char what *he* sees. Char tells me, and between us, we can usually suss out the name of the place, and from there, I can dig through the records. Some of those places have been deserted for years."

"That's my point," Gaer said. "I think they were operating—the wichu separatists—for years in Windscar. I think their alliance with the cult was never the goal, but I think it was an opportunity. As for who Jich'e'enfe performed *for*—the cult, I think. Proof of the usefulness of their alliance. Proof that she could control Brood from the fissure. And she definitely performed for other wichu— the ones in the ruins. Maybe other cells on other planets."

Corso's sudden chill had nothing to do with the wind. "Which you think there are."

"Sss. I don't know. I think we have to imagine there are. So yes, Corso. A performance. A *demonstration*, in B-town, of what she could do. Which we thwarted. Which probably did not *help* Jich'e'enfe's standing with either her cell or the cultists. I hypothesize—her failure in B-town is what soured the relationship. Relation*ships*."

"Why're you telling *me* this?"

"You asked what I meant by performance. I answered. Why are *you* here?"

"I wanted to find you. Alone. Something I want to run past you before I write a report."

Gaer shifted over to make room for Corso between crenelations. "That sounds ominous. Or like the beginning of the plot of a terrible drama."

"Both of those. First, though, got to ask—you know about Char and Winter Bite, yeah?"

Gaer side-eyed him. "That they are . . . riev? Templars? Up for field commendations?"

"Huh. Didn't know the last one."

"Char only just found out today. Evidently Lieutenant Notch is responsible." Gaer cocked his head. "If you mean, do I know Char and Winter Bite have some sort of comm contact that passes outside of Aedis channels? I do. That *you* also know suggests that Char told you, and that I don't have to throw you off the wall."

That startled a laugh out of Corso. "Char did. Yeah. Who else knows?"

"You. Me. Iari. The Knight-Marshals, because Keawe is making free with that ability. Turns out riev comms are more reliable than Aedis equipment for communication when there are Weep emanations. *Which* any vakar could have told her, based on wartime intelligence. Anyway. Why do you ask?"

"Because Keawe's had me running down IDs of everyone in the camp. And I got a hit that I thought was interesting. So I asked Char to ask Winter Bite to run a scan for me on tissue samples. And he did. We, I, have an ID on Axorchal. The arithmancer, I mean. Name's Maldon Kyrl. Tenju. Born in Windscar province in a hamlet called Utrik. I hadn't heard of it, so I asked Char. *They* said Utrik was close to the fissure. It was one of the first casualties when the Weep opened. Mostly kids and old people escaped. Kyrl was one of the children."

"So it is one more *setatir* tragedy in a surge full of them, and this Maldon Kyrl, stricken with anger and grief, sought revenge on the Aedis for failing to prevent the destruction of his home. That's . . . not necessarily a terrible plot, but it is somewhat cliché."

"Interrupt me again, vakar, I'll pitch *you* off the wall."

Gaer snorted. Waved apology with one hand, flick-flick with those overlong fingers. "Go on. Maldon Kyrl."

"Maldon Kyrl joined the Aedis when he got old enough. He was a *templar*. Served here on Tanis during the surge. Then he went MIA at Saichi and was presumed dead."

Corso had Gaer's full attention now: black eyes without whites or pupils, narrowed and drilling down. The frosted translucence of Gaer's optic did not a damn thing to uncreep the effect. "*Not* one of the members of Iari's unit," Corso added, because it was obvious Gaer was thinking it. "Kyrl was, he'd be—Keawe's age, maybe a little older. He was stationed here at Windscar before *she* was. Point is, MIA, presumed dead—that's pretty standard for templars in the surge. No one would've looked for him. No one would've thought they had to. Fine. But he was a *failed* templar. He had demerits all over his record. Serious shit. Discipline, but also something I'd never heard of, that I figured you'd appreciate. *Apostasy.* Axorchal's really an apostate templar."

Vakari faces were mostly thick hide over bone, not much for expression; but Gaer's chromatophores flickered like live coals. His nostrils tightened to slits. "And then his apostasy became delusions of Axorchal. This *is* a tale of vengeance."

"Yeah. Maybe. Listen. I did some digging in the records—they have actual *hardcopy* here, you know? In that voidspit library."

Gaer cocked his head, one of those short, sharp gestures that made Corso's skin prickle. "And?"

"And nothing. No *mention* of apostates at all, as a classification or a charge or anything. But the word is on Kyrl's record." Corso licked his lip. Winced as the wind bit into the wetness like teeth. "You really think the Aedis wouldn't . . . I don't know. *Deal* with its problem templars? Or priests? Like, permanently? They sent Kyrl to the front."

"They sent *all* templars to the front. Even the well-behaved ones. I can imagine the Aedis being pragmatic enough to assign its difficult members to dangerous posts—Keawe is *here*, after all—but I cannot imagine them *executing* someone. Consign them to a prison somewhere, or a medical facility—perhaps. Why? What are you thinking?"

Corso turned and put his back against the rampart. Folded his arms across his chest and gazed out over the courtyard, like he wasn't looking at Gaer at all. (Though he was.) "You think Kyrl's the only one?"

"The only templar with delusions of godhood?"

"Yeah, that. But also—the only templar to turn on the Aedis. He went *bad*. He got power, and he fucking used it. Listen. I know you're down in the labs, working on whatever data Winter Bite sends back through Char."

Gaer heaved up a sigh, theatrically dramatic. "The details of that research are classified. And you wouldn't understand the minutiae, anyway."

"I don't need to understand the minutiae. I just want to ask— Kyrl was an arithmancer, right? *He* was the one directing the fucked-up Brood to take out the villages? Don't look at me like that. That story's gotten *around*. What I'm asking is—did Kyrl's nano *help* with that? Did they . . . did they change, somehow? Like Iari's did? Or were they already dead, and he somehow survived when they died?"

Gaer got that unfocused look he got sometimes, like he was reading a message from the multiverse only he could see. "That is an excellent question. I have been looking *at* hexes on badges, hexes on byres, hexes on prison sheds—but not looking *for* evidence of nanomecha. I will ask Char if they can convince Winter Bite to extract some data for me. I understand the templars have recovered Axorchal's head. If the priests on site are not destroying all evidence—and even if they are, *which* I do not believe, for the record—there should be data that Winter Bite can access." Gaer shivered then for no reason Corso could find—no breeze (beyond Windscar usual), no sudden cloud. He seemed to turn inward a little, muttered, "And it's possible. Nanomecha don't interfere with the practice of arithmancy. There are *priests*, after all. Of course there can be arithmancers with nanomecha."

"So yeah. Now you see the problem. If templars can *rot* like that—then that's the kind of secret that can't get out. I mean, the Aedis can't *let* it get out. The Confederation can't, either. The Aedis is the fucking glue that holds the Confederation together. Well. That and the fear of another surge. But if your best weapon can turn in your hand and command mutant Brood—" This had all sounded bad in Corso's head. It tasted worse coming out of his mouth. Because if the Aedis could go bad, then—then everyone was fucked.

Gaer made one of those leaky-kettle exhales that could be exasperation or deep thought or near-lethal frustration. "So you bring your suspicions to *me*, who along with *you*, is not Aedis. If some nebulous *they* moves to suppress this information—Kyrl's name, that he was a templar, never mind connections with Aedian tech—*they* may decide one contractor in Windscar is a leak easily plugged. But Five Tribes ambassador, seconded asset—I can't so easily vanish. What, Corso, am I your insurance in this conspiracy?"

"No. Maybe." There was an edge to Gaer's voice Corso hadn't expected. Not mockery, which Corso had predicted, not even impatience. But a . . . a bitterness? Like Gaer had a mouthful of vinegar and glass. "I don't think Tobin would do anything to me. *Or* that Keawe would, either. But I think no one's ever going to hear Maldon Kyrl's name again after I send my report to Keawe and Tobin. Maybe that name makes it to Seawall, maybe all the way to the Synod—but no one *else* will know. But I—it's not that I think you're insurance. I wanted your perspective, because you *aren't* Aedis and you *aren't*—" Corso jerked his chin at the courtyard, at the opposite set of ramparts, at the slagging temple and all of it. "You're SPERE."

Corso looked at Gaer when he said it—because he was in the habit of looking at people when he talked to them, it was the job, even if Gaer was almost as hard to read as one of the riev, *almost* as hard as Iari. So he saw when the color bled out of Gaer's chromatophores, soot turned to ash with tendrils of green. Like new growth after a fire, which was a *nice* thing to imagine—except Gaer flinched like someone had stuck a monofil through his guts.

That was . . . unexpected. Dread hollowed out Corso's gut. He could pretend he hadn't seen Gaer's reaction. He was damn sure he didn't want to know *why*.

And because he was a neefa, a fucking *neefa*, he asked anyway. "What's the matter? You look like—I don't know." Worry soured his tongue. "They sending you back to Seawall? The Knight-Marshals?"

"Oh, I hope not," Gaer said. He cocked his head at Corso again, more slowly. "Have you told Iari about any of this?"

"No. You think I should?"

"No. She needs to know, but let me tell her. She only needs to be angry at one of us."

CHAPTER THIRTY-ONE ═══════

I t was the day after Keawe brought *Rishi* back that Iari finally saw him, the elusive Gaer, and that was only because of the meeting. Keawe had scheduled it for midday, just after Ptah's call. Iari suspected Tobin's hand in the scheduling, because she came off nightwatch at dawn, which Keawe knew, and she'd used the morning to rest. Keawe disapproved the nightwatch posting—Iari didn't have proof of that, just suspicion, and Lieutenant L'Brek's quiet, "Heard what you did out there, from the lieutenant," and a softer, "You're wasted up here on the walls, Captain."

Iari wasn't worried. Keawe's temper would burn itself out, or Iari would move out of its orbit and return to B-town with Tobin. And there was something comforting about nightwatches. A simplicity about walking a pattern, about watching *for* patterns and breaks in the same. What her life had been like before Tobin tapped her to play templar escort to Gaer i'vakat'i Tarsik, the new Five Tribes ambassador, who delighted in live music in some of B-town's less savory haunts. Nightwatches gave her time to *think*.

They were also convenient excuse to avoid talking to Gaer. She had *intended*, the morning after her talk with Tobin, to go find him and ask about whatever Tobin had hinted at. She hadn't. She'd found other pursuits: checking on Luki and Llian, reading (rereading) Jareth's *Meditations*, and then talking about them with Char, who was also reading them, who had questions. Getting some voidspit sleep, too, around the edges of all that.

Truth, she didn't know what to say to Gaer. Sorry seemed inadequate. Sorry seemed . . . disingenuous. She had not intended, had not wanted, him to compromise his own oaths, but she couldn't say where he should have stopped. Or if he should have. That Notch was alive—that was good. And because of what Gaer had done for Notch, Luki and Llian would live, too, after the hexes in that shed burned out their nanomecha. They'd've died without Gaer. (Not directly. Iari knew Iffy had done the actual hexwork, the, the *healing*, if you could call it that. And Iari knew Iffy wasn't happy about it, that Iffy thought Gaer should've been involved. That it had been Gaer's choice not to be. But when Iari asked why—all Iffy would say was *you need to ask Gaer that*.)

So it was Iffy and Tobin both suggesting she should *talk to Gaer*, as if Gaer was incapable of climbing the walls at night and seeking *her* out. Iari knew he spent time on the ramparts looking at the Weep during the day. Char reported on Gaer's schedule with a pointed precision that Iari reckoned deliberate. *This* time, Char said, he would be in the laboratories under the Aedis. *This* time, he would be up observing the Weep. *This* time—until Iari had blurted out, *why are you telling me this?* Expecting Char to say *so that you speak with Gaer*. But Char had said—*so you know where he is, Captain. So you can choose whether or not to be there*. And then Char had added, *I provide him with comparable data*.

So it was mutual evasion. And it was, truth, on *her* to do the seeking. She'd asked too much of him.

Tell Tobin I lied. Fix all the bad arithmancy. Save everything again, Gaer, please and thanks.

And he'd done it, just as she asked, never mind what it cost him.

It wasn't fair. But she couldn't quite apologize either. *I'm sorry you saved people's lives because of what I asked.* He'd know that was neefa-shit without reading her aura.

But today there would be no avoidance. The meeting was set for *right* after Ptah's observances, squarely across midday meals, so most everyone else would be occupied. The meeting wasn't in Keawe's office, either, but in one of the largish meeting rooms where visiting important people met with resident important people, or field commanders planned strategy, or . . . or, well, the meeting required too many people for Keawe's office to handle.

Iari managed a few hours' sleep after coming off duty, a shower, a clean uniform. A half-hour's meditation in front of the hearth on a rug that did nothing to soften the flagstone floor. One of the Windscar cats had climbed into her lap, too, which had not helped her concentration, but he *had* kept her warm. So thanks to black Shadow. She left him in possession of the inadequate rug when she left. Out the door, down the corridor to the nearest stairs, the ones almost no one used, because Iari's quarters were on the far end of the hallway.

She damn near walked into Gaer on the stairs. Not coming up to her going down, but just standing, like someone had left the statue of a vakar on the landing. A statue with breath pluming out of his nostrils and through the gaps in his jaw-plates. The stairwells were never warm. But it also smelled like burnt sugar in here, and hot metal, which meant Gaer had been there a while and waiting with some agitation.

Iari stopped well shy of collision, three steps up, with him looking up at her. The long narrow window in the stairwell—thick amalgam, not glass—let through hazy grey light, enough to gleam off the polymesh in Gaer's jaw and the optic over his left eye. Enough that she could see his chromatophores were controlled, neutral. That he looked—well? Maybe thinner, but with his physique that was hard to say. Spikes and bones, standard vakari.

And Elements, what to *say*? *Hello* was inadequate. *Waiting long?* was inane. Gaer was the voidspit diplomat of the pair of them; let him find the words. Iari stood on her step and waited.

Not long. He must have been prepared.

"I hoped I'd catch you before the meeting," Gaer said, smooth as glass. "Knight-Marshal Tobin said you'd been invited."

"I imagine he insisted I was." All right, that sounded inane, too, but small talk always did. "Come on, Gaer. You want to do this *now*?"

"This?" Faintest hiss on the *s*, and the flaring of plates that would mean raised eyebrows on someone who had them. His naked eye narrowed a little. "No. Not really. But I have procrastinated too long, and if I do *not*, Char will carry us both bodily into a room and barricade the door until we speak. They have said so."

There was an image. "Not to me," Iari said. "But Char's too smart to forewarn me."

"Because you'd find a way to avoid them, or pull rank, or otherwise cheat. Yes. Whereas I am too easily found."

That *cheat* was a provocation. Iari let it slide. "What do we need to discuss, then, that can't wait until *after* this meeting?"

Gaer's chin came up. "Just how angry *are* you? At me. Right now."

She *could* say *angry for what* and make him do the work of explaining. But that was just neefa-shit tactics, and besides, "I'm not angry at you."

He cocked his head like he wasn't sure what he'd heard. "And yet."

"And yet . . . I haven't gone *looking* for you, is that it? You know where I am, too, if you've got something to say."

"I—sss. What I say depends on how angry you are."

"Well, I'm not angry."

"You sound angry."

"Chaama's unbreaking *bones*." Iari came down the steps then, hard enough to make her teeth click in the back of her jaw. "I'm not angry at *you*. I'm angry at *me*." She stopped beside him. There wasn't much space on the landing—two templars in battle-rigs would have touched if they tried to pass—and Gaer had to draw back and up to maintain his eyelock.

"Whatever for?" he began, and she held up a finger.

"Because I asked you to tell Tobin something *I* should have done. And because of that, now you've gone and fixed *Notch*. The part of me that is Notch's, *was* Notch's, captain—is grateful and glad that you did. But you admitted in front of *two Knight-Marshals* that you can hack Aedis nanomecha, and then you went off and *proved* that you could. So yeah, I'm angry, because if I'd just told Tobin in the first place what'd happened to me, you wouldn't have been in that position."

And Notch might've died. But that would not have been Gaer's fault, or anyone's.

"Oh. That's not entirely true." Gaer tilted toward her, all two meters plus of him, so that the curve of his chest spikes under his tunic and coat nearly bumped her breastplate. So that she had to choose between looking up and stepping back.

She looked up.

Heat, breath, curled out of his jaws like smoke. "What did you say? *I need you to figure out how to* fix *this. The altars, the portals, this arithmancy that keeps catching us out. That keeps* taking *us out. Find a way.* And I tried. But I needed access to the voidspit One-Eye remains, the ones from the ruins, to do that, access Keawe did not want to give me. Which—*fair.* I was SPERE. I understood. Iffy asked me first, you know. To repair Notch. I refused. But then I saw a chance, when Keawe made her demand—Notch's life in exchange for access to those remains. For a chance to figure out how to *fix this.* And I thought I'd need Notch's help to get out of the Aedis to retrieve you. I didn't expect Tobin to abscond with *Rishi* and bring me along."

The syn twitched under her skin—at Gaer's proximity, at his agitation, at hers. "You just said you *were* SPERE. Past tense. What—are you in Aedis custody? House arrest up in Windscar?"

"Sss, no. I don't think so." His gaze slid off hers, up the wall, to the window and the watery light spilling through. "I hope not. *That* would make me regret my choices. No," and he took a long breath, a slow one, like something inside him hurt. "I have asked for *asylum.* I am. Defecting. From the Five Tribes."

"You are *not.*"

He cocked an eye down at her, refusing to face her entirely. "I am. I—will. That is part of what this meeting will be about, I think. The timing of that announcement, and what we should do after."

"You mean Karaesh't doesn't know what you've done yet, with the nano? Then—don't. Don't *tell* her. Don't tell anyone."

"Notch obviously knows," Gaer said dryly. "Which means the greenest initiate will know by week's end if they don't already. There's nothing to do here *but* gossip. And fight Brood. And gossip about *that*, in which you, Char, Notch, and I feature prominently.

People say *hello* to me now in the corridors. And even if I did lie, or omit that data—Iari, Karaesh't is SPERE. She will see through any prevarication as easily as I see through that"—he gazed up at the window.

"You're *also* SPERE. Say it's protected information, that—that you can't, as the terms of your seconding. That's the voidspit *truth*."

"It is. But then she will ask, rightly—whose oaths then are paramount? Mine to SPERE, or mine to you? And I will have to answer. Or if I will not, then SPERE will arrest me on charges of treason, and *that*, I assure you, will not end well for anyone."

Mine to you. Not *my oaths to the Aedis.* Maybe it was a matter of pronouns, sure, except he'd used the singular-personal, which in Comspek could not mean the collective Aedis. She could blame syntactic mistake, except Gaer didn't *make* language errors.

"You—void and *dust*." Her voice climbed. She fought it back. Breathed it back quiet, *and* the voidspit-slagging syn with it. "You didn't swear oaths to me. I am *not* your reason for doing this. I cannot be your reason for this!"

Because if she was—if she mattered *that* much to him—then that sort of importance should go both ways, and she wasn't sure that it did. (Or that it didn't, which was more unsettling.)

Gaer continued to stare up at the voidspit window. "You are." Gentle, gentle emphasis on the *you*.

She made fists so she didn't hit him. Took herself to the other side of the step, far as she could, and put her back against the cold wall. "I don't want to be."

"I know. And now you see why I put off this conversation. Honestly, I thought Tobin would have already told you, when he asked you to come to this meeting." Then, *then* he looked at her. His jaw-plates spread, fluttered, clicked. Vakari laughter, dry and cold as the wind outside. "I think Tobin wants you in attendance because he believes neither he nor Keawe can adequately defend my interests against whatever the Aedis may ask. *You* are my advocate. So I ask you again, Iari. Just how angry are you at me?"

She closed her eyes. Held them shut through a repetition of Mishka's invocation for serenity. Clear lake, reflecting the sky, no movement except for the clouds and *voidspit* on calm right now.

She opened her eyes and looked at Gaer, who had his face locked down again, who'd stepped back and partway into the shadow under the window.

"I don't know," she said. "Read my fucking aura. Why does it matter? It's *done*. You've ruined your life." *For me*, but she choked on that.

And that sounded like Corso had, *exactly* like, when she'd chosen the Aedis instead of civilian life. (Instead of him.) She'd stared at him then a lot like Gaer stared at her now. Said the same nothing. *She'd* been angry with Corso, too angry to argue. Gaer was—Elements knew. No. Be honest. *She* knew, because she knew *him*. He wasn't surprised, he wasn't angry. He was *scared*, because she couldn't promise to defy her oaths for him, because he knew that she couldn't. Because he had nothing but faith she'd protect him.

Guilt burned the back of her throat. "You don't need me in that meeting. The Aedis won't abuse you or kill you or give you *back* or anything. They'll probably—I don't know. Make you an armorer. Make you teach arithmancy to priests. They'll protect you."

Another airless click. Dry, unamused laughter. "Except hacking Aedian nanomecha is not my only dangerous knowledge."

Gaer tapped his chest, where there was probably a pocket with a voidspit tablet with a voidspit report. "The *setatir* arithmancer Char killed, the would-be Axorchal, was a Windscar templar named Maldon Kyrl who went missing, presumed dead in the surge. Except that it seems more likely he went AWOL and started a cult, allied with a bunch of wichu terrorists, and at some point learned arithmancy and tried to bring down the Aedis—though in what order these things occurred, I don't know."

Iari stared at him. "A templar." Her gut curdled around a guilt, except this one she hadn't earned. The Aedis was sword and shield to the Confederation. The weapon against the monsters. *Not* the monster. Not even the possibility of it.

"A templar. And that is not the worst part." A faint huff of air squeezed through nostrils and jaw-plates, what passed for a vakar's sigh. "Kyrl had *active* nanomecha when Char tore his head off. And it is not . . . it is not a standard configuration. The hexes are different. The configuration is not entirely dissimilar to yours, or to what I helped Notch's to do. But it is not the same, either."

Iari uncurled one hand, spread it flat on the wall. Turned, fingers pressed bloodless, so that she was looking down the stairs, through dust motes caught in that smear of daylight. Into the shadows beyond that smear. It was a short set of stairs, narrow, one of several tributaries that led from the second-floor officers' quarters into the big corridors below. It was empty. It was quiet. Everyone was at prayers or at lunch or on duty.

"Did Jich'e'enfe do that to him? Like she tried to rot out the riev?"

"It's possible. It's possible the corruption in Kyrl's case went the other way. An excess of Brood exposure, perhaps, that turned the nano bad, and they in turn affected Kyrl. You Aedis are symbi-onts. You like to pretend that the big organism is the one in charge, but—sss. There are *reasons* the vakari prohibit implants like yours."

Iari felt for her syn, sensed it waiting, coiled around bone and nerve. It, *they*. Her nanomecha, that could channel Ptah if they wanted, and somehow not kill her. Shield, weapon—and now maybe a vulnerability, too. Her gut said that Tobin and Keawe wouldn't welcome that news, but they wouldn't blame Gaer for it, either. But . . . *but*. Someone else might. Someone might say Gaer had *made* the vulnerability, that SPERE had intended this all along. *Wichu* might say that.

Gaer did need an advocate.

She must have been quiet too long, or Gaer didn't like what her aura was doing. (What color was hollowed-out shock? She should ask.) "Iari." He tried her name out, feeling his way over the sylla-bles. "We're going to be late."

"They won't start without us." But she pushed herself off the wall. Aimed herself at the stairs. She had to pass Gaer, close enough she could feel the heat off him. The burnt sugar smell was a physical thing, stinging her nose, coating her throat.

Nervous vakar. *Stressed* vakar. She stopped, right there beside him, where he couldn't back up. Where she could see straight up into his face, into the single glittering black eye she could see. "You're all about hexes and arithmancy. But you don't dig up peo-ple's identities. Who told you Axorchal's real name?"

Knowing who Gaer would name, *knowing* it—

"Corso."

—and still feeling a flicker of anger, that Corso would have taken that information to Gaer first, and not *her*.

Because she was a templar. Because Corso wasn't sure which

way she'd jump with it. Because he trusted a *vakar* before her. No. He trusted *Gaer*.

And Gaer trusted her.

Then just to prove that point, Gaer added, just north of a whisper, "Winter Bite and Char helped collect the data from the ruins. *My* data. The, the nano and hex data. To preserve its integrity. Data that has not made it into official reports yet."

Which implied—oh, Ptah's flaming left *nut* if she knew. That the riev recognized how dangerous this kind of knowledge could be. That *they* trusted Gaer with it. That they wanted to protect him.

Riev templars trusting and protecting a failed vakar spy. Add Corso to that combination and you had quite the unlikely conspiracy.

No. You had an unlikely alliance. Which was how the Aedis had started: tenju, alwar, humans—and that first batch of nanomecha—coming together to fight a bigger threat. That threat had evolved, sure, from vakari Protectorate to Brood. And now there was something new again that no one had quite figured out, fine, but the Aedis would be there to meet it. The Aedis, and its allies.

The syn hadn't even twitched at this new revelation. Unconcerned. Sensing no threat.

Or waiting to betray her. Gaer had just raised *that* possibility.

Except it hadn't, *they* hadn't. Her nanomecha had chosen the Elements, Ptah, for their evolution, not some twisted vision of an old god. And yeah, she could guess what Gaer would say, *Nanomecha don't choose anything*—but maybe they had. The original nano, the wichu bioweapon, had been sapient. Maybe that sapience was returning. Or had returned. Maybe nanomecha could *choose* things.

Gaer might've had that thought already. And if he hadn't,

well—let him enjoy what shards of equanimity he had left, while he could, before she reduced it to powder. She'd save *that* for the meeting.

Iari gestured to the stairs. "Come on, then. If I'm your advocate, we might as well walk in together."

CHAPTER THIRTY-TWO ≡

That had gone better than Gaer had anticipated, even allowing Iari's ignorance of his defection, even allowing her (understandable, uncomfortable) distress that she was his reason. He kept a side-eye on her aura as they walked—she was conveniently on his left, same side as the optic. The distress was fading rapidly, too, into roiling blues. That, too, was better than Gaer had expected.

Barely even a hitch at the revelation Kyrl had been a templar. Perhaps that meant Tobin and Keawe wouldn't hitch, either. No outrage, no protestations of impossibility. Sensible concern for *how* it had happened, but no fear.

He would be scared for both of them, then. Because Iari's reactions would not be the Aedis's. And while she might be his advocate, she was still Aedis. Void and dust, dear dark lords, he kept putting them both in this awkward position, where she had to defend him from her own. One of these days she'd refuse.

Maybe that's what the blue in her aura meant. Resolution to throw him at the Synod's mercy. Or let him be thrown.

His heart galloped around, speeding up like it was trying to gain momentum enough to break through layers of bone-plate and spikes. He stopped looking at Iari (her aura wasn't changing much), divided his attention between trying to calm himself (not *setatir* likely) and navigating the unfamiliar halls. He hadn't been this way before in Windscar, from officers' wing to administrative offices. It was a *setatir* labyrinth of stone walls. You could *see* how far the surge had gotten, where the templars and priests had turned back the Brood. Scarred stone and new metal doors.

He was studying just one such door now—having cajoled himself into a facsimile of composure—when Iari's breath hitched. She had rounded the corner a half step ahead, on the inner wall, and so he saw the splash of startlement in her aura, and the stiff surprise in her spine.

That undid all his calm, sent his heartbeat ratcheting up again, ready to send him running. (Where? *Where* would he run?) He stopped, one foot raised, just shy of the corner. Then he clamped his plates flat and *made* himself put that foot down. *Made* himself step up beside her.

Ah.

Char and Winter Bite stood outside halfway down the hall in front of an official-looking doorway. Not like guards, stationed one on each side, but like people waiting for summons. Both of them were already looking at Iari and now him—riev senses, sss, they'd probably heard footsteps for *minutes*, probably known whose feet.

Riev faces did not, could not, move, but Winter Bite's *aura* relaxed. Char's did not. Unsettling. Gaer tried not to imagine the flickering was some kind of signal he was meant to understand, because he didn't.

Iari hadn't expected to see Char and Winter Bite, but she recovered her stride, if not all her composure (orange in her aura now, magenta). Gaer followed a little behind as she marched down the hallway. The meeting was supposed to—to Gaer's knowledge—concern *his* situation. What the riev had to do with *that*—he didn't know. They clearly didn't. And Char was worried, which in turn worried Gaer.

At least he understood now why they'd moved the meeting out of Keawe's office. The riev, if they were meant to attend, would never have fit.

Gaer realized he'd made fists and uncurled his fingers. It was too late to go dashing out into the snow and rush for the gates. It was too late, in fact, to do anything but go *forward*.

"Char!" he said (too loudly). "How are you feeling?"

Char tilted their head. Maybe their teslas flickered. (Amusement? Annoyance? Their aura could have been both or either.) "Your repairs have restored my hexwork to optimal function. The Aedis has restored me to active duty."

"Wonderful. And I hear you both got field promotions. Congratulations." Gaer snapped his focus to Winter Bite. "I see that *you* have sustained some new damage."

Winter Bite gazed down at his torso, where streaks of discoloration marred the brushed steel. "The new Brood produce different effluvia. It seems less immediately corrosive."

"Well, *that's* interesting. Are they easier or more difficult to dispatch?"

Winter Bite hummed, considering, but before he could answer the door opened.

It was one of the new doors, metal, and it slid into its socket with the faintest of whispers. Keawe's voice cracked out.

"Good. You're all here. Come in."

Aedian conference rooms looked much alike. The one in B-town, where Gaer had met Karaesh't after his seconding, had been smaller, but the design was the same. A large central table, ovoid rather than rectangular, with furniture meant to accommodate all the Confederation species set around it. There were exactly enough seats for the two Knight-Marshals (already seated, facing the door) and for him and Iari, though there was space at the table for the riev. Everyone's auras blanked as they walked through the door, turning the same oatmealish neutral as the accent stripe on the wall. A massive mosaic Aedian crest dominated one narrow-side wall. *That* was different.

Iari had already claimed her chair in the center of their side of the table, was looking up at him with a mixture of impatience and inquiry. Char and Winter Bite remained near the door, which had clipped shut and locked—audible *click,* and now the tesla above it glowed red, not unlike Axorchal's eponymous single eye.

Sss. There was a thought he wished he could unthink.

Gaer moved to the chair beside Iari, which would put him across-ish from Tobin, crossways from Keawe. Where he could see both Char and Winter Bite on his periphery. He dragged the chair out—modern, to match the door: amalgam and steel, and equipped to glide easily over the stone. It at least looked like it might accommodate his dorsal spine without shoving him off the edge of the seat. That was something. He sat and started to reach for his ventral pocket to retrieve the rolled tablet.

Iari's foot collided with his under the table. Call it a kick. Call it a message.

He set his hands back on the table.

"Captain, Corporals, Gaer," Tobin said. "Thank you for joining us."

By rights Keawe should have started the meeting. That Tobin had was, sss, that was proof of what Gaer already knew: Keawe did not give a dead neefa about ceremony. She was in charge of this

Aedis, but—ah. The templars in this room were all *Tobin's* command, Char and Winter Bite and Iari. Even he was, by some tattered technicality, until the Aedis decided what to do with him.

"Sir," said Iari. Her gaze flicked from Tobin to Keawe. She, too, had noticed the breach in protocol. "I know why I'm here, and why Gaer is—but what about Char and Winter Bite?"

Keawe shifted in her seat, the battle-rig scraping over on the chair's frame. "They're here for security. *Ours.*" A pause. An eloquent scowl at Winter Bite. "I know *he* can hear whatever we say from the voidspit courtyard, if he's so inclined. And if they're both in one place, then one can't pass notes to the other, and from there—to anyone else."

Corso. She meant *Corso.* Gaer was almost sure of that.

"Keawe." Tobin's voice was velvet over steel: patience already exhausted, which wasn't like Tobin. "This is not the reason we are here."

"We're here to talk about threats to Aedis security. I think private, *secret* communications between templars fall into that category." Keawe cocked a sour eye at Gaer. "I, we—got Corso's report."

Unless Corso had radically altered the text *Gaer* had seen, there was nothing incriminating in it. Gaer tilted his head. Mammals read wide eyes as innocence or surprise. He rounded his as far as his under-lids would allow. "Corso's report?"

"Maldon Kyrl. Seems he was a fucking AWOL templar corrupted by wichu separatists."

Corso had not included that last bit about wichu separatists. Gaer was certain of that. Keawe was betting *Gaer* knew it, that he'd say as much, and admit in so doing he'd known Char and Winter Bite could pass data from one end of the province to the other, around Aedis channels, between a contractor and an asset and *ah.* That was her game.

This was a thing Keawe *did*. Let you think you knew where she could come from, let you prepare for that assault, and then mounted a different attack altogether. Distract and exhaust and *harry* until you made a mistake.

He couldn't lie to her; she also knew that. She was . . . she was a *setatir* ass, but she was also Knight-Marshal, and he needed, if not her goodwill, at least her convinced of his honesty.

He flared his plates, drew a breath, leaned forward—caught the gleam in Keawe's eye, triumph and malice—and then Iari said:

"Don't be mad at Char and Winter Bite. *I* asked them to help Corso and Gaer coordinate research."

She was lying. Iari was *lying*. Gaer forced his plates to relax, forced his chromatophores neutral, so *he* didn't give her away.

"You did?" Keawe was staring at Iari. Tobin was too, so Gaer decided he could look, just the slightest of head turns.

Iari gazed back at Keawe, unblinking, unflinching. "I didn't see a problem with it. It's actually a help in field ops where there's a potential for Weep interference. *You* know, Knight-Marshal. That's why you took Winter Bite back out to the camp. Even if fissure activity took down comms, he'd be able to get word to Char."

The corner of Tobin's mouth flexed the tiniest bit.

Keawe shook her head. "You knew the riev could communicate privately? *Outside* of Aedis comm channels? And you didn't see fit to tell anyone else?"

Iari raised a brow. "We can *all* communicate privately. Even in the battle-rigs, we have private channels. What's official, we put in reports. In the field—Char and Winter Bite can hear us in our battle-rigs. It's not ideal that they can't talk back, but they manage. What they say to each other in private is no more *my* business as their field commander than what Notch and Dodri were talking about in dialect at lunch—I can ask, but I have to trust that they'll tell me what I need to know. Same with Char and Winter Bite, except they volunteered to use their private communications in service to the Aedis when it mattered. I think that deserves commendation, not suspicion." A breath. "Sir."

Keawe shook her head. The gleam in her eye had changed. "So *you* asked the corporals to pass private messages? Why not take the request through official channels?"

"I'm a captain in the Aedis. Char and Winter Bite are corporals in my command. And Gaer's an asset, also under my command. I *am* an official channel."

Keawe blinked. Snorted. Raked a stare from Iari to the riev and back. "So you are. All right." She turned to Gaer. "What did Corso need *your* help for? Because all he said was that you, what was it, *rendered assistance confirming identity.*"

Gaer made a move for his ventral pocket again, and the rolled tablet. This time Iari did not kick him.

"Comparative analysis of tissue samples," he said, and undid the pocket flap. "Corporal Winter Bite sent data from the site to Char; I compared it to the analyses I made on Kyrl's remains in the laboratory. Corso wanted to confirm genetic identity. But I also recovered samples of his nanomecha from the on-site remains and analyzed *those.*"

"So? Any nano he had were dead."

But Tobin had leaned forward, eyes narrow and intent. Holding his breath, Gaer noticed, as if anticipating a blow.

So Gaer looked at him and delivered it. "They were. But they were not typical Aedian specimens. They deviated in the same general pattern as Iari's, and now Notch's, and what I *assume* Luki's and Llian's will as well, if Iffy ever grants me a sample. What all of these samples demonstrate is a potential to transform their symbiont's physiology—in Iari and Notch's case, that alteration appears to be temporary, to allow tenju physiology to support the Elemental effects we've observed, before reverting. In Maldon Kyrl's case, however, the transformation appears to have been more permanent. Iari and Char both described the, ah, plasticity of his forearm. And there are traces of similar changes in his cranial tissue, when I knew where to look for them. I'm sure you've seen Iffy's report, but." He pulled the tablet out, unrolled it. "Here's mine. Shall I summarize?"

Tobin and Keawe traded a look. Then Tobin said, "Please, Gaer. Do."

They listened—Tobin, Keawe, Iari, the riev—as he talked. No interruptions. *That* was a little distressing; Gaer was accustomed to interjections, particularly from Keawe. Instead her silence grew edges, spikes, weight. Tobin listened no less intently, but with less visible rage, so Gaer focused on him.

Tobin was Iari's—whatever Tobin was, to her. Important, when that word was wholly inadequate to describe their bond. Whatever it was, it meant Gaer had to trust him, too.

It was Tobin who asked, when Gaer finished, when there had been five seconds of Keawe's glowering, towering silence: "And the badges? The hexes on the shed? You didn't mention them specifically."

"That report is still in its early stages. But I can make a few preliminary guesses." Gaer offered the vakari equivalent of an apologetic smile, the barest spreading of plates, no teeth evident. "The badges appear to be wichu-made, related in their artificing both to old records of Oversight—including testimony from the riev templars present here—and to the alterations we found in the One-Eyes. But there is variation among the sample which suggests they were a work in progress, to an end we have not quite discovered, and one that it seems was never perfected. The hexes in the byre and the shed were clearly related hexwork, though the shed's hexes incorporated some of the k'bal fog's hallucinatory effects we observed in the ruins. Neither set of hexes was *intended* to kill nanomecha, from everything I can glean from Winter Bite's data. I think that was a side effect, likely unanticipated. One that Kyrl would have noticed and capitalized on, when he discovered it."

Keawe sat back. Traded a look with Tobin. Let her breath go in a gust. "Maybe we contained it. Jich'e'enfe dies, Kyrl dies, the cult dies, we *level* those structures—and it's done."

Tobin made one of those noncommittal gestures that could mean *you're right* or *I won't argue in front of an audience*. From Keawe's frown, Gaer thought it might be the latter.

"I have a thought," said Iari. She looked at Gaer, some expression he couldn't read. "We said, when this all happened to me the first time—that my nano evolved to deal with the threat. I think that's the wrong word. I think they're reverting. They *were* a transformative bioweapon once. They still transform templars, but it's small modifications. Or it was. Now they're making bigger transformations—for me, for Notch, for Maldon Kyrl. *I* channel Ptah. Notch channels Hrok. That tells me the nano react to their templar." She glanced at Gaer. "We're symbionts, so that would make sense—they adapt to us. We adapt to them. And if *that* holds, then Maldon Kyrl wanted whatever *he* turned into."

Keawe's scowl deepened. "Or the Brood corrupted his nano and brought him along."

"They'd still have to adapt. His nano, I mean. Instead of dying outright. I think they *chose* to survive, and to some extent, they chose *how*." She looked at Tobin. "I think they're evolving sapience. Again. *My* syn's acting different. More proactive when things are dangerous. But also like it's learning to tell when things aren't a threat, and then it doesn't react."

It was like someone had opened a tesser-hex, like there was void in the room. Nothing to breathe, his lungs hollow and squeezed into fists. Somehow, somehow Gaer found enough breath to make words, to force them past a tongue gone stiff and cold. "In the ruins, when those big k'bal mecha were throwing you and Notch all over the corridor—you think your syn didn't perceive a threat?"

Keawe huffed—which made Gaer regret speaking at all, if he was giving *her* ammunition.

Iari looked at him then, not a side-eye, not a glance—a full-faced *look*, and Gaer realized this wasn't some new notion she'd conjured up in the past few minutes. No. That this was something she'd thought about, and thought through, and she hadn't said anything to him.

"Yeah," Iari said, and it took his brain a moment to track what he'd asked. "The regular syn was enough. I think the nano knew that. The syn takes a lot of energy. Templars learn when to use it. This—the Ptah smite? That takes even more. I didn't *need* to channel Ptah. I *did*, though, when the One-Eyes attacked. I didn't try for the Ptah-version that time, I just triggered the syn, and I *got* the plasma." The set to her jaw said she was sure of her story.

Well. At least he did not need to feign his horror. Gaer's jaw-plates flattened tight enough to hurt, even the unscarred side, and his nostrils sealed. That didn't make breathing easier, or speaking. That meant he had not just fixed Notch by giving his little machines some semblance of choice. No. He had given the nanomecha . . . sss. Personhood. Or he had given them the path to evolve it for themselves.

Keawe sat forward again, eyes locked on Iari. "Notch hasn't said anything about this."

Iari peeled her attention off Gaer, which felt a little like ripping open a wound. "He's experienced the effect once. He doesn't know what to look for. *I* hardly do. But he and I have talked, sir. And we've talked to Iffy." Another side-eye at Gaer. "She's trying to think of some ways we can test our theory without needing Brood or One-Eyes or something similar."

So that made someone *else* who hadn't told him everything she knew. Gaer forced his nostrils open (a vakar had to breathe, no matter the stink of betrayal), forced himself to unclench his talons. He'd left marks on the conference table. Good. Better there than on some*one*.

He realized then Tobin was watching *him*. Gaer supposed his chromatophores had done something colorful, *fine*, that made his reaction seem genuine. Let no one believe he'd colluded with Iari to keep *this* little secret.

Tobin said, "You didn't know."

"No." He was proud of how steady he sounded. How he didn't spit the word out.

Keawe looked at him now, eyebrows up. "Someone want to enlighten me? *You*"—at Gaer—"look like you just saw a ghost, assuming you people believe in them. And *you*"—at Iari—"look like you just got caught breaking curfew."

Because she should have told me, Gaer didn't say. And aloud, "Sentient nanomecha would be—a problem for the Accords, Knight-Marshal." He made himself focus on Keawe. "The Protectorate still follows the Writ. The standard Aedian nanomecha are already an abomination to them. There are proscriptions against certain types of invasive machine intelligence—"

"The Protectorate *and* the Five Tribes are crawling with mecha."

Ah. There she was. Interrupting Keawe. A known adversary, and one that settled his nerves. He cocked his head at her in the way that Corso said was unsettling. "I am not a theologian. I cannot parse out the fine points of doctrine in a way that makes sense. I am not sure it would *ever* make sense. But I *can* tell you that *sentient* nanomecha will offend not only the Protectorate, but also the Five Tribes. Both will see a potential weapon, *particularly* once word of this new mutated Brood gets out."

"Who says it's going to get out?"

Gaer blinked. "It—you can't conceal what happened with this cult."

"We can," said Keawe. "An isolated Brood incident near the Tanis fissure. You fucking *bet* we can conceal it."

"If the Brood can be mutated like we saw in the camp, *we*—" Except he wasn't a *we* anymore, was he? He wasn't Five Tribes, wasn't SPERE, even if Karaesh't didn't know it. "Your *allies* need to know. The Five Tribes. Even, sss, even the Protectorate. If that mutation spreads, you—the Aedis and the Confederation—will need vakari arithmancy to help contain it."

"Might not," said Keawe, "with the new nanomecha in our templars. And the Brood mutation might not spread at all."

Tobin held up his hand, half command, half entreaty, and Keawe sat back. Not quite smirking—she was trying, but her eyes were troubled, because whatever her bluster, she knew what came after the Accords broke down. The last time the Protectorate had fought a holy war with the Confederation, they'd torn the layers of the multiverse to its core. The Accords were a rare moment of pragmatism and cooperation, and Gaer knew—better than Keawe, *damn* sure—how fragile they were.

Tobin's face said *he* had an inkling, and he didn't want a preview acted out here and now in this conference room.

Void and dust, Iari, you should have warned me. Except what would he have said, in that stairwell, had she confessed? No, never mind, I will stay with SPERE and report all this to Karaesh't?

Gaer wanted to put his face in his hands. (No, he *wanted* to walk out of this room, find a quiet place on the ramparts, and . . . sss, not jump off. Maybe scream at the sky for a while.) He made fists instead, and set them on the table, either side of his tablet and its report.

"There are two things we need to consider," he said. "The first, we already know: that Maldon Kyrl's nanomecha survived prolonged contact with Brood, and that they mutated. That Maldon Kyrl, unlike any *other* templar I've ever encountered, was an arithmancer. Is there a connection? Probably. Add it to the list of things to study." He paused. Forced his plates wide enough he could fill his lungs, so they'd stop feeling like knots in his chest. "The second is this new strain of nanomecha. Sentient or not"—and he arrowed a look at Iari, *shut up*—"does not matter yet. That's another subject for inquiry. What *does* matter is the transformative effect. How it works. What it does. Revelation of either one of these details will remind the Five Tribes and the Protectorate of wichu bioweapons and old war crimes, and they will note that the wichu hold an advisory seat on the Confederation council, and they will begin to doubt whether the Confederation has kept to its treaties. But also: Maldon Kyrl's very existence suggests a weakness in Aedian nanomecha. Aedian *security*. The Five Tribes and the Protectorate will be *delighted* by the idea and its possibilities. The Aedis Synod and the Confederation Council, I imagine, will *not*."

Iari's stare scorched the side of his face. "You're saying . . . what, don't tell anyone? About *anything*?"

"No. Not at all." He would not look at her. No distractions. All his attention on Tobin. "Dole out the information. Leak it strategically. Slowly. Recall that we still do not know where Jich'e'enfe acquired the altars, or if we've destroyed them all—if other separatist cells have them, or where those cells and altars might be. We don't know what arithmancy she might have passed on to the other cells, or what she got *from* them. All of this could be the work of some disaffected wichu artificer on *Urse*, for all we know. Or, or Lanscot."

Tobin's chin dropped. Not quite a nod, but almost.

"Which information?" Keawe's voice was uncharacteristically soft. "Our security breach? Or the nanomecha's evolution? The fuck are you suggesting, vakar?"

"That whatever reports you make—once you make them—will draw attention. The Synod may wish to solve this new puzzle, or suppress it. The wichu may demand access to the data. They may *get* it."

"Fuck." Keawe grimaced. "Fuck, all right, but answer my second question. What do you suggest that we do?"

Now, *now* Gaer looked at Iari. "I withdraw my application for asylum, Knight-Marshals. I think it's best if I remain in service to the Five Tribes as a member of SPERE, performing those duties to which I have been assigned."

"You're a fucking *spy*—oh." A slow grin spread across Keawe's face. "But you'll be *our* spy."

Iari hissed—maybe a gasp, maybe a *shut up, Gaer.*

Gaer ignored her. "The condition is that you don't tell anyone outside this room."

Tobin's eyebrows lifted. "You're asking us to lie to our own superiors."

"Not lie," Keawe said, before Gaer could respond. She stared at Tobin until he grimaced and looked back. "You *know*—we both know—we're *here* because we don't play politics. We serve the *Aedis*, Tobin. Not the Synod. We pass this to Seawall—what do you think *Venet's* going to do?"

Knight-Marshal Venet of Seawall, oh yes. Old money from the alwar landfall, with connections all through the old Harek Empire families, which meant all through the Confederation. Gaer hadn't met him. Knew his reputation only from Karaesh't's icy contempt: vain man, spiteful, and still competent enough to be dangerous.

All of which Tobin and Keawe knew. They were all the same rank on paper. Venet's position in Seawall made him the nominal superior, though Gaer would bet Venet hadn't been to B-town, much less Windscar, since the surge.

Gaer held his breath. Risked a sidelong glance at Iari, was both disappointed and relieved all *her* attention pointed at Tobin.

Who blew out a breath. "We cannot *lie*, Keawe."

"Not saying we should."

"We have oaths."

"Yeah. We do. To the Aedis. Which *we* follow. Venet, though. Does he?"

Tobin's eyes narrowed. "Venet's oaths are Venet's business—"

"Ptah's left *nut*, Tobin!"

"—except where his failure to fulfill those oaths harms the mission of the Aedis." Tobin's eyes closed briefly. "I will agree to limit the information we pass to Seawall. For now."

Keawe nodded, apparently satisfied. Tobin looked as grim as Gaer had ever seen him.

"For now," Gaer said. "This position will not be tenable in the long term for any of us. When we can no longer maintain it, Knight-Marshals, I will revisit my application for asylum."

And from Iari, quiet and forceful and *furious*: "Gaer."

Now, *now* he looked at her. "But *until* then, I can keep feeding Karaesh't enough information to warrant extensions of my seconding. And in return I will have some access to SPERE's intelligence. I will not spy on my people for you. Or what used to be my people. But I will use what access I have to help us with all of *this*. If, at some point, Karaesh't and SPERE discover on their own that Aedian nanomecha are sentient—then so be it. And they will. But I, we, can delay that discovery. And we can in the meantime use SPERE's resources to investigate the *setatir* wichu, because I assure you, the vakari have never seen them as benign, not when they were Protectorate clients, and certainly not when they have a provisional seat on the Confederation council." Gaer gestured at his report. "If those hexes got offworld, if the other cells are using them, then SPERE will find out."

Iari pressed her lips white. "Gaer. It's dangerous."

For everyone—Tobin's career, Keawe's, Iari's. Char and Winter Bite, standing silent and offering no objection, no argument—because they trusted Iari. They trusted him, which was—extraordinary. And proof, perhaps, of miracles.

Gaer needed one more. "Of course it is, but that's hardly novel for either of us. And it will work, Iari, if you trust me. Do you?"

There was no one else in that moment: no Keawe, no Tobin, no Char or Winter Bite. Just one tenju templar.

Who let her breath go, and her anger. Gaer watched it drain out of her aura. Watched worry fill in behind, and faith. "Void and *dust*, Gaer. Of course I do."

CHAPTER THIRTY-THREE ≡≡≡

Corso saw Winter Bite come in first, when the riev crossed a beam of watery sunlight slanting through one of the tall, narrow windows. The Windscar mess was bigger than its temple (probably not, but that's how it felt): Vaulted ceiling hung with tesla-chandeliers in some archaic style that had never been native to *this* world. Long tables lined up like stripes across the floor for the regular troops, and for people who didn't care about rank and its privileges. A few smaller tables on a dais, which Corso reckoned were reserved for officers or dignitaries or whoever didn't think they should have to eat with everyone else. He'd never seen anyone use them. Keawe, when he'd spotted her here, sat with the troops. So did Mother Hesteth. Priests and templars mingled, none of the segregation he'd expected. During peak times it was packed and loud and you couldn't hear yourself think. (You could overhear quite a lot, though, if you just sat and listened.)

It was *not* peak right now, the valley between midday waves and the first surge of late afternoon. Corso knew there was training out in the courtyard, that there were priests scuttling around in the temple; he'd been here long enough to know most of Windscar's rhythms, except surge-time warfare. Best time to find a spot in here and get work done. Get a whole pot of—what was it—kahfee? Some spacer drink that Keawe drank like water. Boiled bean juice, black and bitter as regret. Corso loved it.

He had just taken a scalding mouthful when Winter Bite crossed through the sunlight. Corso swallowed and winced, both because the drink was still hot and because Winter Bite had just paused, still caught in that sunbeam like a scuffed signal mirror, like he was looking around to see who was there.

Corso set the cup down. Iffy wasn't in here, none of the usual important people were, and he knew there was some high-security meeting down the corridor with Keawe and Tobin and Gaer. Old instincts said duck, try to pass unnoticed. Except Winter Bite could probably hear his slagging heartbeat across a whole room of heartbeats, and know it was his.

Sure enough. There. Eyelock, between teslas and actual eyes. Maybe Corso imagined an extra blue flash, maybe not. Then Winter Bite turned his head, oddly fluid for someone whose skin was all metal, and looked back across the threshold, into the shadows beyond the sunbeam.

So he wasn't surprised when Iari walked in. Well. Maybe a little surprised—that it was Iari, mostly, who he knew was on nightwatch until Keawe got over her mad. Who was *supposed* to be in that meeting with Gaer, unless things had changed. Or the meeting was already over.

Or something else had gone wrong.

Iari aimed straight at him, no pretense, no casual meander. She wasn't wearing a battle-rig—wasn't cleared for one (he had friends in the armory now, too, besides Char)—but she still wore the uniform armor. Polysteel plates over ballistic-weave tunic, that stupid tabard over all of it. It wasn't a battle-rig's level of tough, but it was still formidable, and she had the axe shaft hanging off her belt, besides.

So Iari was on duty. This was an official conversation. And it was meant to be—eh, not private, exactly; Winter Bite had stayed by the door, but that wouldn't matter, not with his sensors—but private *enough*.

Corso had time to lean over and snag a second, clean cup from the service table and fill it before she got to him. She was already agitated, he could see that. Mouth in a line, which made her scar that much more obvious, eyes already narrowed, and he hadn't had time to annoy her yet.

Someone else had, though. Clearly.

He shoved the cup at her before she could speak. "Sit. Don't just blurt whatever it is at me."

She glared at the cup, glared at him. She was going to snap at him, *bet* she was, something about *no time for your neefa-shit* and then whatever crisis she'd come to announce.

Instead she blinked, and some of the tension ran out of her. She flexed her lips into a smile's wry cousin and dropped on the bench. She scooped up the cup. Eyed the steam curling out of the black.

"Tobin loves this stuff."

"So's Keawe. That mean it's a spacer thing, or a Knight-Marshal thing?"

Iari snorted. "Both." She lifted the mug to her lips, with her eyes on his face, with a calculation in them he wasn't sure that he liked.

He waited until she had a mouthful of hot liquid to ask, "So where's Gaer?" And as she started to swallow—too fast for the heat, *bet* it burned—"Because last I heard he was supposed to be in a meeting with you, among other people."

She set the mug down with less violence than he'd expected. "He's still there."

"He all right?" Though what he would do if Gaer wasn't, Corso had no idea.

Iari snorted. "Of course he is. What'd you think? Never mind. I don't care. *I* know you two have been talking—about Kyrl, mostly, though I haven't had the chance to ask Gaer for the details."

"So you're here to ask me about them?"

"No." Her mouth twitched. "Not about the details. Or about why *he* was the one you talked to first."

She wouldn't be jealous. That wasn't Iari's style. Corso shrugged, and told a truth that wasn't an answer. "Gaer knows his arithmancy."

"Gaer's a vakar." Iari took another sip, eyes gone narrow and thoughtful. Swallowed more slowly this time.

Iari wasn't a bigot, either. Corso had been. They both knew that. Heat crawled up his neck, onto his cheeks. He let it ebb before he answered. "Yeah. He is. He's also not part of *this*. And neither am I."

"This." She glanced around them. "The Aedis."

"I come to you with stories about Maldon Kyrl, failed templar apostate, turning into one of Tanis's old gods—and you tell me what?"

"He didn't turn into a god."

"Iari."

"I tell you, file a report."

"And where does that report go? Tobin? Keawe? Fucking *Seawall*? Or does it get buried?"

"So you tell Gaer, vakari arithmancer, SPERE operative, in hopes that what, he'll tell Karaesh't, and she'll pass it up *her* chain?"

This time it wasn't heat, it was ice, a fist of cold fingers wrapped round his heart. "No! You fucking know better. Or you should. About *both* of us."

She held up a hand. "I do. I'm . . ."

"Sorry?"

"Yeah. That. I'm sorry." She actually broke eye contact then, rubbed her hand over her forehead, over her eyes, before flattening it on the table. "Gaer's still in the meeting with Tobin and Keawe. Char's with him. He's fine. Fine as any of us are, anyway. I said *I* was the one who'd told you two to pass messages through Winter Bite and Char."

"Void and fucking *dust*."

"I reckoned it'd draw fire on me. It . . . didn't. Not exactly. Look. I get why you'd go to Gaer. You think you can't trust the Aedis. You think we're all." She gestured at the ceiling, the walls, the everything. "Too much *inside* to ever ask questions. And you might not be wrong about that. For *some*. For others, the Aedis is a political ladder."

"It's power, Iari. It's the fucking heart of the Confederation."

"Yeah. And it's supposed to be incorruptible. *We're* supposed to be incorruptible. I know. But that's neefa-shit. I also know *that*. Templars and priests are just *people*, Corso. That's why we've got the Catechism and the oaths and Jareth's *Meditations*."

"People shot full of nanomecha."

"Right. The other half of our incorruptible. The part no one worried about. Until now." She flipped her hand over. Studied the palm. Flexed the fingers. "That scares me."

The cold slid off his heart and settled, pooling in his guts. Not because Iari was scared—he'd seen *that* before—but because she'd admit it to him.

She wasn't here to arrest him. (He hadn't really believed that.)

And she hadn't asked him anything she didn't already know, so, "Iari. Why are you here?"

Her eyes snapped to his. "I need your help, Corso. The Aedis as a whole does—but mostly I do. Me, personally. So will you? Help?"

To do what was the obvious follow-up. You didn't agree to something without knowing the details first. Not something *this* big.

He started to pick his mug up again—take a drink, take some time, plot an answer. But that was theatre. If he said no now, Iari would walk away. She'd let him go. He'd sink back into B-town and go back to business as usual—gathering intel for cartel bosses, for the peacekeepers, for whoever would pay. And maybe the Confederation would fall to shit, maybe it wouldn't, but it would do so without him. Iari, Gaer, Char, Winter Bite—fucking *Notch*, probably, after all this—would succeed or fail without him, and he wouldn't know until the rest of the civilians did.

And if they died, well. He might not know at all.

Corso set the mug down. "Fuck yes. I'm in. Whatever it is."

Iari blinked. Then she smiled—a little one, mostly eyes, but it chased away any chill left in his guts. "Then let's go. There's a meeting happening, and you need to be in it."

ACKNOWLEDGMENTS

This book, and its predecessor, *Nightwatch on the Hinterlands*, owe a massive debt to Tan Sackett. Once upon a time, in the Before Times, when our D&D group met in person and not over Zoom, and games required braving the 405 and the 101 and finding four hours in the middle of a weekend afternoon—and were far less regular as a result—Tan ran a game set in a world that had been torn apart by magical accident. That world, and that game, were the bones and inspiration for *The Weep* series.

I think it's a bad idea, generally, to novelize a game. Games are *messy*. A novel is much more controlled. (In theory. The actual process of writing *this* novel was a thing I do not wish to repeat.) But it wasn't the events of the plot I wanted to revisit (although I did borrow a few), it was the other stuff—the emotional punch I remember from that game, that came from the politics of sentience and agency, prejudices and bigotry. And, yes, the rip from which extradimensional monsters flowed.

So I called Tan and asked her—would she mind if I did this? Borrowed the skeleton of her game, elements (and Elements) of it, reskinned some parts, reconceptualized others. And also, hey—what about shifting the whole thing into space, and trashing the magic system, and, and . . . ? She said yes, of course—you are holding this book—but she also offered to help, and so we spent no little bit of time brainstorming together.

So thank you, Tan.

Extra special thanks, too, to my amazing agent, Lisa Rodgers, who sent me back to finish the book when I pretended I already had.

Thanks to all the folks at DAW—my editor, Katie, and Josh, Stephanie, Jessica, the amazing art department, my fantastic copyeditor, and everyone else whose names I don't know but without whom this book wouldn't be here.

And thank you to Loren, always and forever, for letting me rant when I need to, and for taking care of All The Things when I'm chasing a deadline. Ya da best.